Beneath a Glass Bridge | Tali Asnin-Barel

Producer & International Distributor
eBookPro Publishing
www.ebook-pro.com

Beneath a Glass Bridge
Tali Asnin-Barel

Translation from The Hebrew: Yardenne Greenspan
Translation and linguistic editor: Michael Greenberg

Hebrew Language Copyright © 2013
Kinneret, Zmora-Bitan, Dvir–Publishing House Ltd.

Hebrew Book editor: Tamar Bialik

Contact: tal.barel12@gmail.com
ISBN 9798613354412

To my grandmother, the late Nechama Dezortsov-Asnin

1910 - 2011

*For seeing a world in a grain of sand
and Heaven in a wild flower*

BENEATH A GLASS BRIDGE

TALI ASNIN-BAREL

Acknowledgements

I'd like to express my gratitude to everyone who has contributed their expertise, each in their own area of specialty, whether in shaping the plot or in formulating accurate detail.

To my publisher in Israel, the Kinneret Zmora-Bitan Dvir publishing house, and my editor, Tamar Bialik, for the professionalism, support, and patience in the design of the final product. To Michal Schwartz, with her sharp eye and bright mind, for her helpful editorial advices, which assisted me in constructing the story from its early stages. To Dr. Amy Glassman, Dr. Nathan Mordel, Colonel (Res.) Gur Laish, and Ido Postelnik.

Thanks to Yardenne Greenspan, for professionally translating the book into English, and a special thanks to Michael Greenberg , the translation and linguistic editor, for putting so much effort into it, and helping, in a sensitive and an intelligent manner, in shaping the English version of the book.

I'd like to thank my first readers, who looked at earlier versions of this book, and the members of my book club in Atlanta, who read the book when it was only halfway finished and supported me along the way.

Finally, a special thanks to the precious, important people in my life:

My parents—Amalia of blessed memory, and Daniel.

My children—Guy, Eran, and Lihi.

And my husband, Isaac, my partner in this life journey, who has given his love, wisdom, and sensitivity to help make this dream a reality.

"A man lives not only his personal life,
as an individual, but also, consciously or unconsciously,
the life of his epoch and his contemporaries."

— **Thomas Mann,** *The Magic Mountain, 1924*

Vorarlberg - Vienna

1

I was born in darkness, on a gray winter's day, into a grim reality. Ten minutes after I came into the world, my mother bundled me up in a blue rag, dipped its corner in *schnapps* and slipped it into my mouth to quieten my meek sobs. Then she tightened the bundle to her shriveled breasts; her sunken cheeks wet with tears, her bottom teeth biting her upper lip, and in faltering steps she hurried out of the dank basement, not before dropping a few coins into the outstretched hand of the Hungarian midwife.

The stocky midwife straightened to her full height. After wiping away the blood stains, as well as any other sign of what had just transpired in the little room, she covered her hair in a crude headdress, wrapped a shawl around her shoulders, and hurried out through the creaking backdoor.

During that cold and terrible winter of 1941, Adolf Hitler tore savagely through Europe towards the realization of his dream—German reign over the largest empire in the history of the continent. Within a few short months, he had set out the principles of the "New Order" in Europe, designed to subjugate the conquered nations to the rule of the Third Reich. In this new order, suited to the National-Socialist worldview, there was only room for Aryan people, elevated to the level of "culture makers," and the Slavic people of Eastern Europe, servants of the Aryan race, who were downgraded to the role of "culture carriers." The "culture destroyers," the lowliest of races—the

Jews and the gypsies—had no room in the new order at all.

Many winters have gone by since. My mother barely survived twenty of them, through which she spoke little and cried a lot, never truly able to move past the 1940s. As she'd once whispered in my ear during a chilling, soul-reckoning moment, she had experienced three successes in her lifetime: a happy, protected childhood as the youngest daughter in a wealthy and educated Jewish-Austrian household; a short but vertiginous love for a man in the shadow of the war; and having me against all odds, managing to get me out of the fires of hell alive, and delivering me to a safe haven in a faraway land.

Having been taught as a child to nurture her inner beauty and sanctify wisdom for the sake of modesty, she did not list her breathtaking beauty as an accomplishment. However, the instinct for life that still sparked within her at the time, taught that the end justifies the means, and for her and her child to survive in this world, she must seal her heart, make frequent use of her beauty, and offer her body to anyone who might bring her even one step closer to freedom.

***

For five months, she did not give me a name.

***

My mother was born in the spring of 1918. On the first *Shabbat* of her life, her parents, Michael Steiner and Ilse-Sarah née Rosenthal, invited their four grown children, as well as Ilse's parents, to the living room of their home on the outskirts of Vienna, to take turns holding the gorgeous newborn, the youngest of their offspring.

As was the custom every week, a topic of discussion was raised in the elongated dining room, decorated with oil paintings and lined with wooden, ornamented glass cabinets laden with porcelain.

During the discussions, often on a philosophical concept and just as often on current events, sometimes tiresome and other times passionate, everyone present, whether young or old, relative or guest, was asked to offer their opinion and personal knowledge.

This week, while the household staff served the Shabbat delicacies prepared under the strict supervision of my great-grandma, the dinner guests seriously discussed the choice of the baby's name. After having encouraged everyone to take part in the conversation and to be attentive to others, as he did every week, my grandfather, Michael, eloquently took the floor. Once the different aspects of the question were laid out on the table like pieces of challah and minced to bits in the mouths of the diners, they were asked to reach a conclusion, and, if possible, a practical solution.

"A person's name," he told everyone present, "is their essence, the practical and spiritual role this person will fill in his or her life. It is a matter of utmost importance that must be considered with great care." As was his custom, he peppered his arguments with the words of the sages, this time with those of Rabbi Shlomo ben Aderet, who believed wholeheartedly that when parents are about to name their son or daughter, they are imbued with the Holy Spirit, which allows them to capture the child's true inner essence.

My grandfather's Hebrew name, Michael, originated in Scripture. Though as an adult, a disciple of science and enlightenment, he was not punctilious in fulfilling the precepts of faith, he had always taken pride in the fact that he shared the name of one of the biblical angels, who commanded the people to praise God. Among the names of angels in rabbinic literature, he had chosen the names Gabriel, Uriel, and Raphael for his three sons. Their Austrian names, used at school and when dealing with the authorities, were left at the doorstep of their home and of the synagogue they attended on the high holidays[1].

---

1   The Jewish holy days of Yom Kippur and Rosh Hashanah.

Rosa, the eldest daughter, was born on Shavuot eve. She was exactly nine years older than my mother. Her Hebrew name was Ruth, like Ruth the Moabite of the Bible, a character whom Ilse favored, and at home everyone made sure to call her by that name alone.

Though, regretfully, I did not have the pleasure of knowing *Oma* Ilse, as my mother called her whenever she lamented her orphanhood, Ruth claimed that I had been planted with the seed of her personality, and that the contours of her body were woven into mine with wondrous precision: her elongated face, her flowing lashes, her blue eyes, her straight nose, and her high cheekbones. Only our skin was different—her's swarthy, mine ivory.

As a young girl, I tended to wander in the realms of my imagination. I filled in the missing pieces of my mother's incomplete family tales with Ruth's generous and evocative stories, reviving in my mind the deceased relatives I never knew. I imagined strolling with Oma in the backyard of her Vienna home, picking raspberries, giggling at *Opa* Michael's tireless efforts at plant identification, and enjoying an in-depth analysis of the heroes of classic literature. In my imagination, we wandered together in the faraway fields of the Bible and lingered over the women Ilse adored, such as Ruth, an impoverished Moabite and widow of a Hebrew, who chose to stay with her mother-in-law after her husband's death and followed her all the way to Bethlehem, a foreign land. Ilse had been captivated by this story from her youth. Naming her eldest Ruth after the Moabite, she never ceased to discover the lofty qualities the two shared, taking every opportunity to emphasize that the girl's ability to spread love, tenderness and serenity all around her while remaining devoted to her faith, sat well with the figure of the biblical heroine.

Requested to suggest names for the newborn, the members of the family settled at ease around the table, which had been cleared of dishes, revealing the beautiful lace tablecloth. Jumping up first, Uriel suggested the name of the neighbors' daughter—Hazel—whom he had secretly loved ever since kindergarten. Gabriel chose the name of the protagonist of an old children's story he loved, Catherine. And little Raphael, his apple cheeks flushed with embarrassment, confused a few names, all of which he mispronounced. Ruth suggested naming her sister after the protagonist of the *Book of Esther*, which is read on Purim eve, so that they could both be heroines of important biblical books. Michael tried, once again, after a failed attempt with his eldest, to name his youngest daughter after his mother, Sarah, who died when he was a small child. Great-grandma Rebecca suggested calling the little one after her deceased, righteous mother, Ita, and great-grandpa Josef left the choice to the youngsters, but only requested that the Hebrew letter *yud* be included in the name. "Before it was delivered to the Hebrews, the Torah was engraved in the heavens in black fire over white fire," he quoted the words of the sages and immediately added emphasis with the words of the kabbalists, that since *yud* was physically the smallest of letters, it covered a smaller space than the light beneath it, and therefore contained greater power than any other.

Ilse spoke last. She rejected Uriel and Gabriel's suggestions, kindly postponed Raphael's ideas to another time, and refused Ruth's wishes, claiming that "this is Shavuot eve. Purim has passed." The names of the deceased Sarah and Ita were rejected offhand due to her objection to naming a child after a dead relative and with the desire to prevent insult and disappointment on the part of either her husband or her mother. She adopted her father's educated suggestion and finally proposed that beside the Austrian name Norma, the girl would be called Naomi, a name ending with *yud*, after the biblical Ruth's Hebrew mother-in-law.

"Our youngest child, just like our eldest, was born on Shavuot eve. In the Land of Israel this is the time of the wheat and barley harvest," she explained. "Such love and devotion between Ruth and Naomi, a bride and a mother-in-law, is astounding. Ruth remained devoted to Naomi in her time of need, returned with her to her hometown of Bethlehem, and together they went to harvest the fields to support themselves. The women of Bethlehem praised Ruth, claiming she was kinder to Naomi than seven sons. My eldest, Ruth, will also remain devoted to the young Naomi, doing her best to protect her from harm and imbue her with confidence and calm, serenity and peace."

Thus, said Ilse, not knowing she was speaking a prophecy.

Grandpa Michael liked the sound of the name, Ruth was flattered, and great-grandpa Josef was relieved to have his request fulfilled. Ilse thanked everyone present for accepting her proposal. Gabriel, Uriel, and Raphael were glad the discussion was over, and great-grandma Rebecca gave her blessing. Michael slapped the table happily, silently grateful for his wife's rosy cheeks and cheerful demeanor, and rang the bell to signal to Martha, the housekeeper, that it was time to serve the wine, which was reserved for special occasions, as well as dessert—slices of sweet challah coated with marmalade. Moments after the glasses were clinked and a toast was made, Ilse retired to the other room, and Baby Naomi enjoyed a hearty portion of breastmilk.

***

My mother struggled for five months before finally naming me.

Alone, under a false identity, in the frontiers of Tirol-Vorarlberg on the border of Liechtenstein, in the home of the Austrian peasant where she was employed as a cleaning-woman, working the yard and the field, chasing the peasants' chubby, snot-nosed children, carrying me around with her in a straw basket padded with a coarse woolen blanket, pulling out a thin breast to nurse me with drops of milk, sneaking bread crumbs and egg yolks into my mouth, she could not find the courage to make such a fateful decision regarding her daughter's name.

Each day she strained her muscles and ground down her bones with hard work. On weekday evenings, crushed beneath his threatening insinuations, she silently accepted the visits and revolting demands of the peasant. Although his foolish wife had no suspicions about her real identity, in his clever eyes, which knew a thing or two about the world, her bizarre, loner behavior raised several question marks as to her origins and purity of race. And at nights, burning with the fear lest her identity be exposed, curled up, shivering in her measly bed, flooded by old memories that now seemed so distant and as if borrowed from another life, she would hold me close and cry.

In this difficult reality, she was unable to detect my true, inner essence well enough to pick out a single name from the plethora of national, literary, or biblical choices, which would be so decisive, they would attest to my place in the world. "The *baby*," she called me. "The *baby* is crying." And later, "the *child*": "the *child* wants."

In June, she set out with me and the peasant in a donkey-drawn carriage toward the nearby city of Vorarlberg. This was after their nocturnal trysts were discovered by the peasant's wife, who threatened to burn down the house with the master, the baby, and the "whore" inside. The peasant decided things had become too risky, and so as not to lose the carnal pleasures he had grown accustomed to and the submissive devotion of my mother, whose beauty and fragility were the very opposite of the crass grumbling of his bitter wife, he led both of us into a shabby bedroom in the prostitution district. On the way, fearing that a lack of a name might arouse the suspicion of evil people, who would rush to spread the word in exchange for a handful of cash, he stopped by the local branch of the State Office and Federal Ministry of the Interior, "to finally settle the matter of the girl's name."

My frightened mother was forced to make an on-the-spot decision. Looking around and finding no salvation, she gazed at my blue eyes, my fair skin, and my thin hair, frantically flipping through a list of European names in her mind, names that would negate any questions regarding my identity, and chose one.

Helene.

That is what she named me. No mention of an angel or a biblical heroine, and no letter *yud*. While clinging to the peasant and holding her breath out of fright, she wrote down the name Helene on my belated birth certificate, along with the made-up Austrian family name she had adopted months earlier with the help of some officials who coveted her body. Finally, she channeled her fear, which was flowing through her veins, into a loud, clear voice, and, hoisting me in her arms before the cooing official and the terrified peasant, shouted out the blessing of a proud Austrian mother in clear, shrieking German, "May I be a loyal daughter to my homeland, to the rising and strengthening Third Reich, to the adored leader Adolf Hitler, and to the sanctified Nazi Party."

She told me this story over and over throughout my childhood, each time in a more poignant, less stylized version. Over the years, I had trouble accepting my name. I did not like its foreign sound, the way in which it had been tattooed onto my identity, and the shriek of German loyalty to the Third Reich that accompanied the non-festive occasion.

Only years later, after I had grown up, married, and had my children in state-of-the-art delivery birthing rooms, surrounded by a skilled medical team and the love of my husband, was I able to accept my name and truly understand my mother.

By then, already for decades, my name had been anglicized to Helena.

2

For close to a year, Mother and I lived under borrowed identities in a small moldy apartment in Vorarlberg, where the peasant had brought us. In the winter of 1943, my mother heard people on the street talk in an excitement mixed with terror about the Germans' surrender in the Battle of Stalingrad. By the end of the year, she had learned that the German army had been pushed back by the Russians to the Polish border, and a small island of hope emerged within the ocean of her anxiety.

I was so young at the time, my memories are blurry. But I do remember that year as being almost happy, and the only one in my life in which, despite the insufferable poverty and the dangers all around, I was blessed by an overflow of Mother's love and concern. Suffocating under question marks regarding the fate of her loved ones, Mother specialized in reducing herself to the small space she occupied, carefully choosing her words, and making do with minimal portions of air and food to make it through another day. I, her baby, was her entire world, and her one true comfort. In my presence, moved to the point of tears, she allowed herself to softly hum the songs she remembered from her childhood home, submerging both of us in her memories. To this day I can recall the tone of her voice, enveloping me with a story, with a quiet song or a hum, as well as her thin arms holding me close to her waifish frame, while her hands slipped down my hair in a tender caress. This was before her soul had been crushed, it was merely wounded. As long as the hope that her loved ones were alive and would survive the war still dwelled in her heart, as long as she dared to believe that the scratches that scarred her mind would heal, she sanctified her days and filled mine.

The peasant was our only visitor. He appeared every few days, riding on a donkey-drawn wagon. He brought in baskets with vegetables, milk, and eggs from the village; he would give me some hay to feed the donkey and occasionally even a toy or a doll he had bought me along the way to occupy me while he kept my mother busy in the bedroom. With time I learned to like him, and my mother grew to view him as our savior. She was eager to fulfil his expectations and please him, if only so that he would continue to come, functioning as a cover for our identities, delivering food, and updating her on the progression of the war.

Our neighborhood was mostly active at night, and so my mother was not required to have any contact with our neighbors, whom she made sure not to befriend, for our own safety. Each morning we both walked hand in hand to the home of Nioka the seamstress. The woman paid my mother a few pennies for some light mending and tailoring performed for the women of the city, whose financial state in this difficult time did not allow them to indulge in shopping for new clothes. I would sit beside her, quietly playing with the cheap ragdoll the peasant had bought me, dressing and undressing her in the pretty clothes Mother had made, and sailing in my imagination to faraway green meadows and to palaces in which lived the magical, beautiful, kind princesses my mother told me about at night before bed. In my mind, these landscapes took the form of the lawn we crossed on our way to our weekly market excursions, a grassy knoll dotted with green, thorny bushes of thick foliage, among which the two of us walked, as if within a maze, because Mother preferred this to walking down the open road. I pictured the palaces as the house that could be seen from afar from Nioka's window: a three-story building with a wide porch, in front of which a tree towered all the way up to the red roof.

Each day at noon, Mother sliced the dark bread the peasant brought us and served me two slices spread with margarine, sometimes adding an apple. On rare occasions, she bought a piece of meat or a potato from Nioka only for me, and, even more rarely, when Nioka was in high spirits, I enjoyed dessert: a slice of bread with jam. Mother would whisper in my ear that this used to be her favorite food as a child: sweet bread spread generously with cherry jam that Oma Ilse made herself. Then the sweet flavor turned bitter as I sensed the deep sorrow in Mother's voice.

Whenever we walked out onto the street, Mother wore wide clothing on her narrow figure she had bought for cheap back in the days when the peasant's wife sent her to the village markets. She shaded her pretty face with a simple, wide-brimmed hat, commanded her right leg to fake a limp, and blended into the grayness of the sidewalk in hopes of thwarting the attention of street vendors, peddlers, and pimps. I was so young then and didn't understand much. I remember yearning for my mother to powder her cheeks, paint her eyelids, rub red lipstick on her lips, and don low-cut dresses like the ones worn by the other women who paced our neighborhood starting in the early afternoon. They were so beautiful and glamorous in my eyes, with their strut and their bare skin, unlike my mother's dull appearance. When we were inside our small apartment, she seemed to grow taller, her cheeks reddened a bit, her limp miraculously disappeared. Then she let down her fair hair and removed the heavy village attire, slipping easily into her housedress, and although her face was so pale, I was so content to look at it, astounded by its beauty.

She was especially beautiful to me in the few times when the peasant had managed, through different excuses, to extract himself from his wife's grip in the evening. Mother would receive short notice, about an hour before his arrival. The peasant would call from one of the post offices along the way to the red phone in the hallway of Madame Butterfly's brothel, announcing his imminent arrival, and one of the madam's girls would be sent at once to our apartment, two blocks away, to deliver the news. Mother would immediately bathe, wash her hair, spray perfume on her neck, and pull out from a trunk the red sequined dress the peasant had bought her on a rare trip to Vienna. After powdering her cheeks, painting her eyelids, applying lipstick, and donning the short dress with the generous neckline, her grayness disappeared. Before my eyes, she would grow more beautiful and radiant than any of those glamorous women we saw on the street on the way back from Nioka's house. Since I was too young to recognize the faded tint of her soul behind the forced smile, the artificial gaiety, and the shiny eye shadow, and although I had to give up my nightly spot by my mother's side and sleep alone on the tattered sofa in the narrow hallway, her smile in those moments never left my mind, and there were no limits to my joy.

***

It was so hot that night. Mother undressed me and let me run around only in my underwear. When the peasant arrived, I flinched at the sharp smell of his body and the alcohol emanating from his mouth, and hid, panic-stricken, behind the sofa in the hallway.

He had not been coming as often anymore, and when he did, he frowned and raised his voice, taking his frustrations out on Mother. He was worried about the possibility of the Reich losing the war and his business going under. He was tired of his wife's increasing threats to kick him out of the house and have him live "with the whores on the street," away from his farm and his children. But nothing made him more livid than my mother's growing belly, her pale face, and her nausea, which forced him to seek pleasure with Madame Butterfly's girls and part with considerable sums of his ever-dwindling funds.

My mother was overcome with fear. As if one child to care for was not enough, now another burden was lurking, as well as a man who threatened to abandon her. But where would she go? Where? Mother was appalled when she smelled the peasant's underwear and imagined she detected the odor of Madame Butterfly's girls. When she grabbed her head in her hands in alarm and dared ask, he turned red and puffy. He screamed that she was nothing more than his slave, at his mercy, that one wife to make his life miserable with questions and demands was enough to stifle his liberty and joy. Then he slapped her hard, leaving the tracks of his thick fingers over her fair skin.

Mother cried without end. She cried in the mornings at Nioka's, between threading a needle and pulling a thread. She cried in the afternoons as she walked with me down the path to our modest apartment, her wide-brimmed hat casting a shadow over her face, her leg faking a limp. She cried in the evenings, as she tucked me in, her back trembling against my abdomen, her sobs enveloping me with terror. She cried during the dark nights when the peasant, drunk and rancid-smelling, deigned to appear. Then she would kneel down, her right hand holding onto her lower abdomen, her left-hand closing in a fist around the ends of his shirt, and her lips trembling with a plea for him to continue to desire her body. She cried for her loved ones, who had been torn away from her with inhumane cruelty, begging for one of them to arrive and put an end to the horror.

We parted in November. I was deposited at Madame Butterfly's, in the care of the young girls who had tended so well to the peasant. Mother whispered that she would be back the next day to be mine and mine alone and that the peasant would return to us as before, showering us with fruit and vegetables and eggs from the farm, so that we would never go hungry.

But Mother did not return the following day. There were

complications in her labor, and she was hospitalized for an entire week in a run-down clinic out in the country, where the peasant had taken her. Her baby, a healthy boy without a name or a clear identity was handed over to the Catholic orphanage on the other side of town.

Another tear was ripped through her flesh.

As for me, I did not stop asking where was my mother, where did she disappear to? Was she dead? If not, when would she be back? I was so worried that even the presence of those glamorous girls I was used to seeing on the street did not cheer me up. I flinched at their attempts to caress my face or run a hand through my hair, and I often turned down the candy with which they tried to buy my smile. The entire time, I awaited my mother's return with bated breath. I even kept some lollipops in my underwear to offer her upon her arrival so that she could taste a bit of sweetness and finally stop crying and start smiling again.

Madame Butterfly was the only one I listened to and whose food I accepted. When the peasant arrived at her brothel one evening, she allowed me to approach him for a moment before he disappeared into a room with one of the girls, so that I could ask him about Mother and give him a piece of candy for her, so that she would know I had not forgotten her, not even for a moment.

In late November, Mother returned, gray and skinny, coughing and short of breath. Even the toughest of Madame Butterfly's girls seemed to shed a tear as they watched me run over with open arms, while she did not even try to hug me back. I jumped onto her lap, ran my hands down her cheeks—especially the one I had seen being slapped—kissed her lips, pulled her hair, and poured all the candy I had saved for her into her hands. She barely responded, barely spoke at all. When Madame Butterfly took pity on her and agreed to the peasant's plea to host us in her abode for "a while," I grabbed the man's coattails and dragged him out to the street and into our ratty little apartment, taking the same route I used to take with Mother on our way back from Nioka's. From the trunk that served as our wardrobe, I pulled out her bright red sequined dress, so that she could dress up and become the most beautiful and glamorous of the madam's girls, and the peasant would want only her. But later, at the brothel, Mother rejected the dress with revulsion and spat in the peasant's face. When he raised his thick hand to slap her again, a wall of angry girls arose before him, and the orchestra of their yelling echoed after him as the door was slammed behind his back. Confused, scared, and filled with guilt, I hid behind the pink floral armchair, covering my ears with my hands, my eyes wide open in shock behind a film of tears.

3

August 1990
Yosemite Park, California

Dear Nurit,

Last week, I asked for a big trash can to be brought into my room. They try to quickly grant my every wish around here, and so the trash can appeared the very next day. It's just a regular metal wastebasket, about knee high, but they placed it in the center of the room, as if it were a work of art. I took a seat on the bed and looked at it. I thought about all the words that would pile up inside and all the words that would be left out. I tried to decide where they would be safer, these words. Then I became restless. The employees of the French lodge treat me with exaggerated respect. Behind my back they refer to me as "the author" and to my face it's always "Madame Helena." Every little whim is fulfilled. It's convenient, yet irksome.

Why do I even deserve this?

I tried to write Blair several times in the past few days. Each time it ended with an ink and tear-stained piece of paper crushed by my fist or ripped to shreds by the vise of my fingers, then tossed into the glorified wastebasket. I want to explain so many things, but the words aren't coming just yet.

Actually, that's not accurate. Last week, after settling down in my room. I did yoga relaxation exercises and finished reading all the books I'd bought at the San Francisco Airport. Then I began to write. You may not believe it, because we've discussed it so many times in the past, but it's really happening this time. I've started to write a new book, which is no big achievement in and of itself, except that this time it's my own story. It happened so unexpectedly that I even surprised myself.

So, with regards to this book the words are, in fact, coming, with a speed I'm not used to. Perhaps it's because they are flowing right from my heart.

I gave a lot of thought to what led me to open up and unleash the countless memories, sensations, and visions into words after keeping them bottled up for so many years. I'm not sure I have the answer, Nurit. I think I just got scared when I felt myself beginning to lose things again.

Yours,
Helena

4

August 1990
(This letter was thrown out)

Dear Blair,

I want to know how you're doing so badly, my child. It's hard to be so far away from you and so out of touch. But I understand you well, Blair. I would be angry, too, if I were you. I would pack up and leave too, and just like you I'd go all the way to the other end of the world. At least you've taken care to let us know where you are. I appreciate that greatly.

The last time you called us you were in Burma. You spoke to Dad briefly and didn't even ask to talk to me. I cried for a long time after that. Your father was embarrassed by these sudden tears. Imagine your father, the great Bridge Man, completely out of sorts!

He's having a hard-enough time as it is. One fine day you up and dropped out of college, withdrew all of your savings—your bat mitzvah money and your birthday gifts, the money you had made babysitting and in your summer jobs (I liked how you always insisted on working for a living), and bought a one-way ticket to Southeast Asia. For two nerve-racking weeks, we had no word from you. We were so worried.

I deserve this, but Dad doesn't. You hurt him Blair. You hurt him so much.

But just imagine, that wasn't even the worst of it.

The worst was that I took off next. You ran away because you were scared, and I ran away because I was ashamed. You ran away to process new information, and I ran away after unlocking the old one.

I apologize, my child, for revealing things to you so late. I was afraid of the revelation itself, because with it, I knew, the rest of the truth had to come out too.

I hope you've found a clean and safe place to sleep and that you're taking good care of yourself. I don't know your address in Burma (its name, I believe, has recently been changed to Myanmar). This letter's fate, then, is to never be sent, just like the others before it. This is precisely why I have a round waste-basket smack in the center of my room, so that I can make sure the words that were crumpled up with the paper are not going to crawl out and get away from under me.

At least with regards to my new book, the words are my loyal soldiers. They obey my orders, quickly marching in sync before my eyes, forming orderly lines across the page. I've never felt this way about any other book. Countless times, you've stood watching over my shoulder as I wrote; voicing your astonishment at the hundreds of words I crossed out while editing and proofing. "What messy writing," you muttered, pointing at the words I added in tiny handwriting above and under the lines and in the margins.... You told me I'm the most disorganized person you've ever met.

But this time, my writing is smooth and flowing, no cross-outs, as if it's not me writing. I swear, this time I feel as if the story is pouring out of the pen by its own volition. It's completely different from any other time.

You must be wondering why.

I'll try to answer that...

Because this time it's my story, spreading its long roots deep into the earth for the first time, sucking the water and minerals it needs to strengthen its grip on the dirt.

And now more than ever, you must understand that just like plants, people cannot live without water and sustenance.

That is, without roots.

5

August 1990
(This letter was thrown out)

Mike,

I wish I could stand before you right now and apologize. A simple apology, straight from the heart, for all the years I kept myself closed to you, for all the things I never told you, for all the emotions I kept hidden, the tears I held back, the smiles I faked, and even—though there weren't many—the lies.

And you let me read you like an open book... We used to talk about "everything": family, career, culture, current events, and "Mike stuff." But I never let you into my inner world.

And you never demanded anything right off the bat, never asked for anything in advance. You knew writing was my release. For years you tried, sensitively, patiently (I've always admired this about you), lovingly, to encourage me to "peel the onion" of my soul and leave the skin on the page, which—as you always said— "accepts without judgment."

You wanted to liberate me, but you had no idea of what.

Because I never told you.

There are so many things I didn't tell you, so much so that

entire chapters of my life are completely invisible to you, unless someone else told you about them. I was shutting you out of my past, just as I had been, for years, shutting myself out.

I never told you about my mother's unstable mental health, or our relationship that had eroded with time; the more my independent, opinionated, rebellious personality evolved, the more her sense of self shriveled away and her spirit became scarred. And there was Ruth, whom you knew and loved, who was often supportive and understanding, comforting and soothing, but sometimes, in her own unique way, angry, unwittingly absorbing the insult of her sister's failed motherhood.

The force of the memory chills me. Oh, Mike, how inconsiderate, stubborn, and cold-hearted I was toward my mother and how impatient and grumpy about her mental state, which made her transparent and indifferent. How ashamed and filled with regret I am now!

I chose not to tell you, Blair, Roy, or Abby about my early loves: about my dizzying, forbidden love for "the one" and about my admiration and restless yearning for "the other." I gave birth to the protagonists of all my books in worlds so far away from my own, marching their life stories down paths other than mine. Only sporadically did I dare thread slivers of truth into the beads of imagination closer to my own world, but clasping the necklace around a secondary character's neck, afraid it might draw too much attention. Many of the things I wrote were cut by my own hand in the very early stages of editing, others in the final proofreading. Over the years, I became the primary critic of my own writing, careful not to expose my own world within it, a master of disguises.

Dear Mike! I wish I were braver. I would have come to you now not only to ask for your forgiveness but to thank you, again, from the bottom of my heart, for your peace of mind and your confidence—which never drew away due to my aloofness—for opening your world to me without demanding reciprocity, for the freedom you gave me to live my own life and nurture my independence without burdening me with questions, and above all else, for your great love, which gave me an anchor, inspiration, and physical joy.

I know it hasn't been easy for you, perhaps it never was. You've never said it explicitly, and you certainly found ways of touching my heart, identifying my changing moods, and stabilizing the storms of my psyche. You are, after all, the Bridge Man… But the look in your eyes, the unintentional pressure of your hands on my arms as you stood me in front you, making me confront your penetrating gaze, and of course, your confession that dark day about that "one-time" slip…

Was it, really? "One-time"? Even if it wasn't, Mike, I might still be able to understand… I know I can be impossible sometimes, especially now…

Now, on top of everything else, what happened over the past few months has come between us, ever since we told Blair the truth, ever since I gave her the tapes. With this discovery, my secret was revealed too, and a wound was opened.

That's why I left so suddenly, just like Blair did mere weeks before me. I left you, Roy, and Abby, and came here.

Would you ever be able to forgive me?

Because, in fact, I never left to run away, but to fix things. To fill…

To fill the gaps in substance, the empty spaces in my heart, the blank pages in my story...

I hope that eventually you'll forgive and accept me, and so will Roy and Abby. Perhaps when they're older they'll understand. I can't talk to them right now. If I only hear their voices (Roy's, which has recently grown deeper, and Abby's sweet chirrup), I'll break.

I can't break now.

Because as much as I miss you, Blair, Roy, and Abby, I'm busy relieving another longing. An unsettled longing for the characters that have visited my life and are now gone, and for others whom I never had the pleasure of meeting. Once again, my flesh burns with restless desire for the beloved of my youth, with the yearning, so familiar from my childhood, to enjoy, if only once more, the embrace, the smile, and—most of all—the forgiveness of my mother.

6

In 1918, following its defeat in World War I, the Austro-Hungarian Empire fell. Ruth told me about it years later, while we sat at the small dining table in her Tel-Aviv kitchen and cracked open chestnuts. Hungary was established as an independent republic, and within its new borders, Austria—"The first Austrian republic"—was mostly a German-speaking country. Intense fights between the right and left parties were decided in the 1930s by the establishing of a fascist dictatorship, which supported the concentration of power in the hands of the government. The Social-Democratic party was outlawed, freedom of the press was revoked, and Austria became a single-party state.

"Those days," Ruth told me, "Opa Michael's forehead was carved with worry wrinkles, while Oma Ilse's hair had turned gray." She sighed. "But that was nothing… What happened in July of 1934 was a truly bad omen."

She fell silent, and I urged her on.

Her voice deepened. "Engelbert Dollfuss, the fascist Austrian chancellor, was murdered by Austrian Nazis."

I raised an eyebrow.

"They supported the annexation of Austria to Nazi Germany," she clarified. "This awoke a storm of pointed arguments in Michael and Ilse's home. They did not realize at the time it was the beginning of the end."

I remember, in one hand she held a small wooden saltshaker with three holes at its top, and, in the other, a peppershaker with only one hole. As she told me about the "tumult" at the Steiner home, she waved the shakers until salt and pepper flew onto the table. When she said, "Opinions were divided," she placed the shakers four inches apart on the table and marked a sharp border between them with a slice of her hand.

On one side stood Opa Michael and his eldest son, Gabriel.

Michael was among the assimilated Jews. His ancestors had settled in Austria as early as the thirteenth century, when the empire became one of the main centers of Ashkenazi Jewry. His entire life, he had adhered to the motto of enlightened Jews, a line from a Y.L. Gordon poem: "Be a man on the streets and a Jew at home." And convincing himself that his Judaism left no marks on his exterior appearance, he lived that way. It was no wonder, then, that, finding scant security in his venerable position as a physics professor at the University of Vienna, and holding, strong like a mule, to the opinion that the political and social state of his beloved homeland was nothing but a passing ailment, a chilling gust of wind in the Age of Enlightenment, he chose to close his eyes to the signs.

"Calm down, Ilse," he tried to ease his wife's agitated mind after she had finished blessing the Sabbath candles. "And stop mistaking the shadows of mountains for mountains. Kurt von Schuschnigg, the new chancellor, is an attorney, an educated and open-minded man of law. Look how, after his predecessor was murdered, he quickly outlawed the Nazi party. Besides, the annexation of Austria to Germany is forbidden according to the treaties of Versailles and Saint-Germain-en-Laye. The international community would never allow it. Germany is a Nazi country, but Austria is not! You'll see, my darling, the storm shall pass, and our lives will be back on track. In the meantime, nothing bad will happen. We are respected members of the community, and my position at work is secured."

With his powers of persuasion, Michael was able to alleviate the anxiety of another couple. Ruth, vivacious, independent, and opinionated, was twenty-five at the time. She divided her days between two loves: her love for Jonah Jonas, a young British Jew, charming and lanky, a third-year architecture student at the Vienna Academy of Fine Arts, and her love of the English language. In the mornings, she taught English at one of the private Christian schools in the city, and her evenings and weekends were spent with Jonah at her parents' home or in his small rented room. Ruth helped him prepare Academy projects he was required to submit on a tight schedule and in perfect German. Jonah quickly became like family and a close friend to my three uncles, especially Uriel.

In the thicket of events plaguing Austria after Dollfuss's murder, Jonah's parents began to pressure their son to return to London at once, even at the expense of completing his degree. Adding to their letters articles from British newspapers that announced a rise in the Austrian public's support of the annexation, they expressed their concern that the Austrian Nazi party was gaining strength. In the fall of 1935, they came to visit Vienna, to spend time with Jonah and meet Ruth's family, as well as to assess the danger first-hand. As they toured the city with their son, listening intently to the future architect's detailed explanations on the wonders of Viennese buildings, their eyes roamed all around in an attempt to identify ominous signs: some hint in the expressions of passersby whose language they could not speak, derisive graffiti, protests in town squares, the excessive presence of uniformed men. When they found nothing out of the ordinary, they were happily convinced by Michael's arguments, as he confidently smoothed his little chestnut beard between thumb and forefinger, that there was no reason to worry, and that without a doubt the new chancellor, who was famous for his staunch resistance to the Nazi Party, would stand steadfast with the international community against the annexation of Austria to Nazi Germany.

The young couple's wedding was announced at the end of the week, and all agreed that Jonah would complete his final year of school in Vienna as planned. The host's promise, spoken in an authoritative, self-important tone, that his "finger will constantly be on the pulse, and circumstances will continually be examined," along with the desensitization brought on by the generously poured wine, lulled the British guests into almost complete tranquility.

Gabriel, a young and gifted musician, supported his father's views. Refusing to believe that Austria, the birthplace of Haydn, Mozart, Schubert, and Strauss, would dare turn its back on its Jewish population, he, too, forced his eyes shut. As the Nazis rose to power in Germany, Gabriel took to the benches of the Stern Conservatory in Berlin as a music student, focusing on piano and conducting. A few weeks later, he was expelled due to his religion and was forced back to Austria without completing his studies. He was twenty-two at the time and twenty-three when the chancellor was murdered by Austrian Nazis. But despite the traumatic experience, Gabriel did not forsake his dream of walking down the golden path laid out by talented Jewish musicians such as George Szell, Artur Schnabel and Bruno Walter, and refused to acknowledge the danger.

He returned from Germany with his fiancée, Vera, a young German-Jewish cellist. Her parents had made sure to expedite their engagement before his departure in hopes of saving their beloved daughter from Nazi rule. Gabriel rented a small two-bedroom apartment near his parents' house and completed his studies through a series of private piano, music theory, and conducting lessons. In the summer of 1933 he married Vera, and in the winter of 1934 their son, David, was born. Gabriel was making his first steps as a visiting conductor at the Vienna Opera House, and Vera received a position as cellist in the city's philharmonic.

That year, violinist Emil Hauser went to Europe as part of the British Mandate Government delegation to provide young Jewish musicians with entry certificates to the Land of Israel with the purpose of attending a two-year program at his newly founded conservatory in Jerusalem. Many Jewish musicians from Germany and Austria, Gabriel's cohorts, accepted the lifesaving offer, but Gabriel politely declined: so content was he with his work and with Vera's integration into the prestigious orchestra, and so concentrated were they in their own world.

And thus, when it was his turn to raise his hand in the fateful family vote, deciding whether to remain in Austria or leave, he confidently lifted both his pianist's hands: one for himself, the other for Vera and David. "Austria is our homeland. It is no less ours than any other Austrian's. I am not afraid of right-wing extremists. We've got a lot to lose if we leave. We must stay here and defend our home, our property, and our jobs!"

Suddenly, Gabriel's voice broke and his face twisted in anguish. He walked over to Ilse, grabbed her shoulders, and shook her lightly.

"Besides, Mother," he said, "even if we did want to leave, where would we go? Who's to say that life would be safer elsewhere? America is so far away, and Palestine is culturally underdeveloped, and the Jewish settlement there is so small…" He put his lips to his mother's silvering hair and whispered, "Father is right. No disaster will befall us. I am staying!"

7

On the other side were Oma Ilse and Uriel.

Oma Ilse was an Austro-Hungarian native, daughter of a Jewish family from Lvov, in Galicia.

Her grandfather, Yaakov, had been a wine salesman. During his frequent business trips to Berlin and Vienna, he had been exposed to the secular lifestyle and captivated by liberal worldviews. Heartened by Emperor Franz Joseph I's sympathy toward Jews, he began following what he admiringly referred to as "imperialist culture" or "modern life." In the evenings, he liked to quote to his wife, Sheyne-Leah, from the essays of Yom-Tov Leopold Zunz, who urged Jews to step out of their bubble, become involved in general culture, and assimilate into the Christian world around them without giving up their Jewish identity. In the late 1850s, Yaakov, his wife, and their five children moved to Vienna. He announced that in the big city, the center of commercial life, he would be able to improve his earnings and firmly establish his wine business. But he had another, no less important reason for leaving Lvov: the Hasidic movement, which he abhorred, was gradually taking over the small and mid-sized Jewish communities of Galicia.

In Vienna, Yaakov worked tirelessly to spread German culture among Jews and get them involved in local and regional politics. He argued vehemently to anyone willing to listen that the Hasidim, with their odd habits and heavy clothing, with their insistence on speaking Yiddish and their tendency toward superstition, were the enemies of the enlightened rule of the "venerable emperor" who aimed to Germanize the Jewish population of Austria.

His wife thought otherwise. Sheyne-Leah's face resembled that of a bird: elongated and narrow, with a pointy nose, thin and puckered lips, and yellowish skin. She could not come to terms with her separation from Lvov and continued to feel as if she had been torn apart from her family for the rest of her life. She did not like the fluctuations of "modern life" one bit and might have even felt threatened by them. Though the number of Jews in Vienna had increased exponentially during those years—over twenty thousand of them, according to a population survey conducted at the time—she did not make any effort to get to know them. She spent most of her time feeling angry, especially at the atmosphere of assimilation. She even accused her husband of having lost touch with Jewish tradition, and argued that for him Judaism was nothing more than an heirloom to be preserved in honor of his ancestors, who had given their lives for its cause.

In 1867, when Ilse's father, Josef, was sixteen, the Jews of Austria received full equal rights. At first Josef became caught up in his father's excitement, but his spirits quickly cooled when he noted his mother's continuing fury. She was irked by her husband's foolishness and the foolishness of many other Viennese Jews, who were so naively complacent they could not see that this equality, on whose alter they sacrificed their forefathers' traditions, gave them nothing more than an imagined, temporary security. Young Josef felt closer to his mother than to anybody else, and so he listened to her muttered complaints. Torn between her and his father's conflicting worlds, Josef tried his hand at both: studying Jewish tradition on the one hand and acquiring a general Western education on the other, including literature, history and science. The deeper he went, the more completely he felt that one could not be whole without the other. As an adult, he chose a middle path in a sincere attempt to allow for co-existence in his mind between his father's favored Austro-German culture and his mother's revered traditional Jewish lifestyle. He took part in the modern historical research on Polish-Lithuanian Commonwealth Jewry and tried his hand at writing. Some of his papers were even translated into Hebrew and published in the journal *Kochavey Yitzhak.*

At any rate, after the granting of equal rights, the Viennese Jewish community quickly multiplied. Many newcomers were Galician and Hungarian Jews, and among them a girl named Rebecca, from Budapest. When Ilse, an only daughter to Josef and Rebecca, was born at the end of the nineteenth century, she was raised to keep *mitzvoth* but simultaneously encouraged to acquire a general education and develop original thought. Her father taught her to love books, and she inherited his admiration and respect for Jewish scholars.

During those frenzied days, Ilse could find no peace. The concern for the future of her family and the fate of Austrian Jews grew daily.

"You are naïve," she accused her husband, "trapped in your imbecilic beliefs and captivated by the false promises of a weak chancellor!"

Michael's attempts at appeasing her and the myriad arguments he offered to establish his standing only further kindled her rage. And yet, she could not wholeheartedly demand that they leave. How could she leave her homeland for the sake of the unknown? And what would become of her aging parents, Josef and Rebecca? Would they, at their advanced age, be able to part from their home in favor of the unfamiliar? Her mother was no longer well, and neither was her son Raphael... Thoughts jumbled in her mind and fear crowded in her heart until she could hardly recognize herself. At night, she kept having the same dream, which, in time, she shared with Ruth.

In her dream, she was sailing to an unknown destination on a rickety ship along with her elderly parents, her husband, and their five children, all hungry and dirty, wearing tattered clothing, and, having abandoned their possessions in their escape, carrying a measly handful of belongings. Of all their jewelry, they took only one item—a delicate golden chain with a wrought gold Star of David pendant, Uriel's bar mitzvah gift from his grandparents. The deck was crowded with people, all with long, gray faces, worried and hungry as they. The frozen silence all around was occasionally broken by Rebecca's hacking coughs and Raphael's moans. Now her mother was coughing blood while her father, rocking back and forth on a hard, narrow bunk, sobbed, and Michael sat on the floor at his feet, fixing her with an accusatory gaze, making her tremble even in her sleep. Then, Michael's blaming eyes grew into two saucers which sprang wings and flew away, leaving Michael mute, stunned by his sudden blindness. In the middle of the night, Rebecca died, and the gray, long-faced people forced Ilse to toss the thin, translucent body into the great, dark sea.

Drenched in cold sweat, Ilse would awake from this dream in the middle of the night. She bit her lip to hold in her whimpering so as not to disturb Michael, who, naïve and foolish in his blindness, was no longer a young man, and the heavy family burden he was carrying on his shoulders gave its mark on him.

In the morning, attempting to put order to her thoughts and soothe her worries, she would push aside the shadows of her night terrors. Quietly, gradually, and in collaboration with her father, she began converting assets into silver or gold, while declaring to Michael that if circumstances worsened and departure would become necessary, they would pack up only their most necessary items and travel to Palestine, if only temporarily, until the furor passed.

And then there was Uriel.

In the family discussions regarding the question of "staying or leaving," my mother's beloved brother adopted an independent view. He was twenty-two at the time, tall and stubborn. From his early youth, he had been a member of the *Hakoah Vienna* Jewish soccer team, which saw its most successful season in the mid-1920s, when it won the Austrian championship and defeated the British military's soccer team on a visit to Palestine.

Uriel was taken by the Zionist idea from a young age. He never defined himself as an "assimilating Jew" as his father and eldest brother Gabriel did. He was always a "proud Jew." When the pro-Nazi party gained traction in Austria, he insisted on continuing to wear the Star of David necklace he had received from his grandparents, even as his parents begged him to take it off. His pride often got him in trouble, and he would return home beaten and bleeding after being in a fight, but he never gave up.

In recent months, he had been preoccupied by the deterioration of his country. In his heart, he foresaw bad things, and he was restless. He was especially concerned for the safety of his younger sister, Naomi. She was so pretty and so pure, and he was terrified by the thought that the thugs who were occasionally seen around town would rape her and irreparably disfigure her spirit. In agreement with Michael and Ilse, he asked Naomi never to walk outside alone. Uriel joined her as much as he could wherever she went: to school, to the homes of her friends, to piano lessons or the library. In the evenings, when young men gathered in bars and beerhalls on the outskirts of town to drink themselves to intoxication, Naomi was forbidden to go outside at all.

Recently, Uriel had joined a small group of Jews his age. He often left home without telling anyone where he was headed. His parents did not pry; his siblings did not wonder. Only Naomi would cling to him, trying to glean some information: had he met a nice girl? If so, was she not Jewish? Otherwise, why would he hide her from his family? But even she, who was the closest to Uriel, could not wrangle a confession out of him. Once, he was generous enough to tell her that she was completely off track. The only ones she ever saw him whispering around with were Jonah and Ruth, and she often wondered what great secret the three of them were keeping from everybody else.

Naomi did not yet know of Uriel's plan, his intention to leave Austria, to immigrate to the Land of Israel, and build his home there. She did not know that he was considering taking his younger siblings, Raphael—as much as his frail health would allow him, as he was ill with chronic arthritis and dependent on his mother's care—and her, but only after she had graduated high school.

In two or three years.

Only then, he thought, would their parents allow her to come with him to the Land of Israel.

Just another two or three years…

8

God bless my Uncle Jonah.

As a study tool, his parents had gifted him with a special art-deco Leica camera, with which he used to take dozens of pictures of Vienna, a city he dubbed "the finest of all cities." Back in the time when families used to take pictures every other year at a photography studio, Jonah documented my family in their living room, not only on Sabbath and holiday dinners, wearing their finest garb and forced smiles, but also in spontaneous action shots, performing mundane tasks, the routine of a family life.

Looking at these pictures now, I cannot help but think of that false quiet before the storm.

I see Ruth in those pictures, already plump, her long honey-brown curls flowing down to her shoulders, her face bright, and her smile wide. If she only knew what the years would bring. There she is, photographed against the Imperial Hotel in the Innere Stadt, the Old Town of Vienna.

In another, she is sprawled across a sofa at her parents' house, cushions supporting her back and arms, the skirt of her dress spread around and under her like a lily. And there is Oma Ilse, overseeing the preparation of a meal in the kitchen of her home, which in a matter of years would be repurposed by the government; at her side her mother Rebecca and Martha, smiling awkwardly into the camera. On the next page, Opa Michael, great-grandpa Josef, Gabriel, Uriel, and Raphael are all wearing their holiday best. Michael is holding a glass of wine in one hand and a prayer book in the other and appears to be saying a blessing. At the bottom of the picture is an inscription in German lettering: *Rosh Hashanah*. Beneath that, in Hebrew: *Shabbat, 1ˢᵗ of Tishrey, 1935.*

And here's another. Oh God, it's my mother, Naomi, a young girl of about sixteen, beautiful as an angel, wearing a bright, puff-sleeved dress, her fair hair braided and rolled at the nape of her neck. She seems calmer in this picture than I have ever seen her. Ever.

These photos are more valuable to me than diamonds and gold.

***

In May 1936, Ruth and Jonah were married in a modest service in the main synagogue of Vienna's first district.

Years later, Ruth told me that the ceremony had been short, tinged with sorrow, and involved very few guests, due to a fear of crowds. The next day, the two rushed to register themselves as a married couple and get a passport for Ruth. That night, a formal, yet modest dinner was hosted at the Steiner home in celebration of their union.

God bless Uncle Jonah. The two pictures he took that night have been hanging in my home office from the day our house was built and will remain there for good.

In the first, Ruth is blushing and excited, sitting on a decorated chair, wearing a white dress with lace fringe, holding a bouquet of white wildflowers picked by Naomi in a friend's yard. Jonah is standing behind her chair, tall and striking in his dark suit, his large hands resting on her shoulders, his eyes focused on the camera, as if controlling the photo-taking and the quality of the image from a distance.

The second one is the dearest to me, because, goodness, everybody is there, in the Steiners' living room, furnished in classic

1930s European style: Ruth and Jonah in the center; to their right, Oma Ilse and Opa Michael, all four of them sitting in elegant high-backed dining chairs. To their left, are great-grandma Rebecca and great-grandpa Josef, all dressed up and sitting in plush armchairs. Behind them stand the youngsters: Gabriel and Vera in the middle, Uriel to their right, holding onto Naomi's shoulders, who is embracing little Davidi close to her heart; on their left, Raphael, his face pale, and beside him Martha, like one of the family.

And they are all together, in the same house, in the same room, for one long moment, on one passing night.

***

That summer, Jonah finished his studies and submitted his final project. In August, Ruth and Jonah packed up their personal belongings, Jonah's textbooks, some souvenirs, and photo albums. They spent their last night in Austria with Ruth's family at Café Landtmann, right next door to the grand theater.

A few years ago, I dared visit Austria for the first time in my life. I attended an impressive and moving concert at the Musikverein, where my cousin Davidi performed as a pianist with the Vienna Philharmonic Orchestra. The next day, the two of us walked over to Café Landtmann on the elegant Ringstrasse. The wide, horseshoe-shaped boulevard stretched over three miles, with the Franz Joseph pier bookending it on both ends. The Ringstrasse buildings, presenting the best of Viennese architecture, made it one of the most recognizable symbols of the city and a more than fitting backdrop for a parting from Uncle Jonah—then a young and ambitious architect—and Aunt Ruth.

Davidi and I strolled slowly, holding hands. We passed by the many picturesque cafes of Stadtpark, a public park constructed to "serve the people," and paused by the golden monument to Johann Strauss, king of waltzes. We were in no rush. I looked around and told Davidi it was easy to see why Jonah and Ruth picked such a beautiful spot for their last night there.

After a brief rest on a bench, we walked over to Schwarzenbergplatz and from there to Herbert von Karajan Center, a small, charming palace that Davidi told me with excitement had been purchased by the Austrian conductor's widow and refurbished into a center in his memory.

Café Landtmann, where we were headed, was located across the street from the town hall. Davidi told me it used to be a favorite hangout for people like Sigmund Freud, Gustav Mahler, and the operetta composer Emmerich Kálmán.

It was dark by the time we walked into the café. From a rich menu offering no fewer than forty-two flavors of coffee and an abundance of Viennese cakes, I picked a hot apple strudel and a "Maria Teresa" coffee, a mocha with orange liqueur and a dash of whipped cream on top. Davidi chose a double espresso with brandy, coffee liqueur, whipped cream, and cinnamon. I sat, contemplating the Goldener Rathausmann statue on top of City Hall.

"Look, Davidi," I said, "how stunning that statue looks at night, bathed in streetlights."

Davidi transported me to a different time. He reminded me that a few decades ago he was at this very spot with his parents, Vera, and Gabriel, with great-grandma Rebecca and great-grandpa Josef, with Oma Ilse and Opa Michael, with Jonah and Ruth, Uriel, Raphael, and my mother, Naomi.

I trembled. I told him he was just a baby then, probably passed from hand to hand, but mostly cradled in Ruth's arms, close to her heart. After all, she loved children so much. Her heart heavy, she knew she would have to part from him and all her loved ones the following day not knowing when they would see each other again, if at all.

The next day Davidi took me to the train station from which Ruth and Jonah had departed toward Trieste, Italy, through the mountainous Semmering railway, from which they continued toward their new life in London. The two of us stood on the platform where Jonah and Ruth had seen most of their family for the last time.

I recounted to him what Ruth had once told me about their moments of parting.

"First, Jonah said goodbye to Gabriel and Vera, Raphael and Naomi, Opa and Oma, and then to Uriel. Ruth watched them from a distance. 'Jonah was tall,' she told me, her eyes moist, 'the tallest and oldest of the four boys. But Uriel was the most striking—robust, proud, and upright, his black eyes always sparkling.' Four years separated Jonah and Uriel, but their similar worldview bridged the gap. Their friendship had grown over the years Jonah had spent in Vienna and become a true bond. Jonah admired Uriel's activity in the *Betar* Revisionist youth movement and his uninhibited support of Ze'ev Jabotinsky's Legion idea, which encouraged young Jewish people to devise a new image of the Jew as a man of military prowess and courage. He later became a confidant of Uriel's and learned all about his and his fellow members' dedication to the enterprise of helping Austrian Jews—mostly secular Jews of no Zionist affiliation—reach the Land of Israel. Jonah shared Uriel's belief that Nazi Germans would be invading Austria, as well as his deep contempt for the blind eye turned by Viennese Jews, including Michael and Gabriel. Ruth watched Uriel as he shook Jonah's hand excitedly and patted his back and could not help but notice the great difference between him and his brother Gabriel, between the first's bright, open eyes and the other's closed, melancholic ones.

"Then Uriel walked over to her, whispered something in her ear, turned around, and left, without looking back."

"What did he whisper?" Davidi asked.

"You won't believe it," I shivered. "He only said one brief sentence to Ruth before kissing her cheek and leaving. I don't know how he knew... It was as if his heart had predicted something to him."

I fell silent, recalling Ruth's green eyes shining with tears as she'd told me this.

Davidi took my hand. "Helena, what did he say?"

I raised my gaze to him.

"All he said was, 'Watch out for our sister, Naomi, our gem, and take care of Davidi.'"

Davidi's brow furrowed.

"It's so strange, Davidi! You and Naomi remained in Vienna with Uriel, and Ruth was the one to leave..."

"And she never asked him what he'd meant?" he marveled.

I smiled sadly and shook my head "No... because then Uriel left, and a few minutes later she got on the train with Jonah. With time, she dismissed it from her mind. Time went by. She didn't ask when she still could, when everyone was still alive. And then it was too late..."

We both fell silent, staring at the iron rails. Then I told Davidi that parting from her parents was the hardest for Ruth. I told him about how Ruth, unable to stop her tears, had collapsed in her father's arms, and how Michael had leaned over her, taking her face in his hands, his shoulders shaking.

"But then Oma Ilse took over," I continued. "She grabbed Ruth's shoulders and stood her up. 'Stand tall wherever you go,' she said, pressing her thumbs into her daughter's arms. 'You are embarking on a new path today—with everything you learned and absorbed at our home to sustain you along the way. Always be proud of your origins and faith, your family, and yourself. Your personality is strong and your spirit is firm. You are a woman of valor! Don't ever forget it and do not ever lose hope! And please, my child, please don't cry. You are breaking my heart and upsetting your father. Here, take my handkerchief, wipe your eyes, and smile at us, Ruth. Let us remember your charming smile, not your tears…'

"Ruth swallowed her tears and tried to smile. Jonah pulled out his camera and snapped a last photograph of her, standing on the platform with a blue suitcase and floral handbag, with her parents, the three of them faking smiles.

"Then Ruth, noting with worry how pale and out of breath the woman was, turned to great-grandma Rebecca. What would happen, she wondered, if harder days were to come, like great-grandpa Josef predicted—days of war—and she would never see her again? She embraced her grandmother's slight frame, caressed her wrinkled face, and thanked her for all the years she had been in her life, helping her parents run their home and raise her and her siblings. Then she kissed her grandfather's rough, bearded cheeks, and went to Naomi last. She took her hand softly and pulled her aside for some privacy."

I surprised Davidi by pulling out a small black-and-white photo that Jonah had taken that day on the platform. Ruth could be seen in it, holding her sister's hand, as Naomi's light dress clung to her thin body and her fair hair fell in soft waves over her shoulders and back, her eyes downcast.

Davidi ran his fingers through his hair, which was still thick and impressive though dominated by gray. "So that was it?" he asked. "That's how they all said goodbye, here on the platform? Just like that?"

My eyes lingered on him. "One moment, Davidi, I'm not finished. Jonah was the one to tell me the end of the story."

He fixed his eyes on me.

I tried to convey precisely how I felt when I heard the story myself. I tried to recall the exact words. "A moment before they boarded the train, with Jonah already leaning down to grab the handle of the suitcase, great-grandpa Josef clutched his hand with surprising force.

"Startled, Jonah looked up, his gaze meeting the grandfather's burning eyes. 'Where are you heading?' Josef asked thickly.

Embarrassed by the question, the answer to which was well-known to all, and astonished by the timing, moments before the arrival of the train, Jonah said, 'You know this, Grandfather, we are going to London, Great Britain...'

"Josef shook his head and closed his fingers even tighter around Jonah's arms. Suddenly, his pupils dilated, his eyes caught fire, and his lips trembled. As if he was a prophet of wrath, his words lashed out at him. 'You may be asleep,' his voice rumbled, 'and you may not be aware of just how late it is, but know this, evil dwells here, the winds of war are blowing at full force. London...a midway stop! Palestine is the last stop! There is no longer any place for Jews in Europe! They will all be killed!!!'

"I can still remember the look in Jonah's eyes," I said, "when he told me how he'd let out a gasp, drew back, and pulled his arm out of the terrorized old man's hand. Later, as he hurried onto the train that had just pulled up and dragged the heavy blue suitcase into the car, Jonah glanced at his arm, and was appalled to find three deep and bleeding scratches along its length..."

Davidi's face clouded over. That was how he always looked when a tune played through his head. I didn't ask him what he was hearing in his mind. The sounds I could hear and the shadows I could see were more than enough for me. He wrapped his arm around my shoulder and led me outside. We left that train station together, never intending to return.

9

In the Following winter, great-grandma Rebecca fell ill. Her heart weakened, and she no longer got out of bed. Under Oma Ilse's supervision, her parents' apartment down the street was sold along with the furniture, and they both moved in with their daughter. Great-grandpa Josef settled down in Gabriel's old room, and great-grandma Rebecca in Ruth's room. In May of that year, Raphael's rheumatoid arthritis worsened and was coupled with severe pneumonia.

Painfully concerned over her son's weakness, his chronic fatigue, his poor appetite, and noticeable weight loss, Oma Ilse barely left her son's bedside. She moved back and forth from her mother's room to Raphael's, feeding them, bathing them, dispensing medicine, and barely sleeping or eating herself. The ongoing care of the other family members was handed over in full to Martha, who found help in an unpredictable source—Naomi. To push aside the concern for her brother, her grandma, and even her mother, who had lost weight and grown pale, the young woman chose to occupy herself with housework. She was also worried about great-grandpa Josef. Every once in a while, he mumbled to himself through trembling lips or cried out in his sleep, and Naomi would find herself awake before dawn, shivering and drenched in cold sweat.

With a heart full of sorrow, she watched the changes that had transformed her beloved father. As of late, his back had sunken in, gray was sprinkled in his goatee and his thinning auburn hair, and his face had become wrinkled with doubt. Ilse, his own private woman of valor, had grown weak ever since the decline in Raphael and Rebecca's health. And as if that were not enough, Austrian Jews had been going through such difficult, worrisome events that even an optimist like Michael could no longer turn a blind eye to them. The halls of the university, which he loved so dearly, where he had received his degrees and taught generations of students, had become cold and estranged to him. He now thought twice before identifying himself as Jewish to a visiting professor. The recent developments in Germany made him lose sleep, most of all the Hossbach Memorandum, the summary of a meeting held by Hitler along with his senior officials and officers, in which he publicly announced his true intentions—spreading his forces eastward and occupying Czechoslovakia and Austria. Michael was especially concerned about the fact that the majority of Austrians supported a union with Germany and the legality of the Nazi Party. This union, Michael realized, could mean nothing but anti-Semitic laws and decrees against Austrian Jews, violence and degradation, mass dismissals, and deportations. The border between Germany and Austria was so sleight. A thought tortured him: did I misread the situation? Have I put my loved ones at risk?

With an aching heart, Naomi watched her father, broken and out of sorts, shutting himself up in his own world. Afraid of the cracks that were forming in her life, she curled up beside him on the sofa, just as when she was a little girl, her thin arm wrapped around his neck, her head resting on his chest, rising and falling to the rhythm of his breaths, and she felt, painfully, that his breathing was heavy.

Naomi found some meager comfort in the letters from Ruth in London, including exciting stories about the big city where "people only spoke English," the small rental 'flat' into which she and Jonah had recently moved with the generous help of his parents, Jonah's job as a construction worker, since times were tough and he had not yet been able to find work in his profession, and about her first pregnancy, which thrilled Naomi in particular.

During those ominous days, the atmosphere on the streets of Vienna was depressing, as was the stifling mood at home, which had become a makeshift hospital, where Ilse and Martha carefully followed the orders of the doctor who visited on occasion, devoting a few moments of his precious time to examining his patients. Trying to escape, Naomi sought solace in her dream world. Enveloped in her reveries, she would step out of the family house and float, light as a bird, to her sister's house in the magical city filled with spacious parks and a royal palace. There were the queen's guards, wearing tall, black fur hats, unable to take their eyes off the gorgeous girl dancing before them in a white linen dress, which shifted in the wind to the beat, wrapped around her thin body, and clung to her perky breasts at the end of each spin. For a while, loosening their upright stance and turning to watch her as she faded into the distance, the Scottish, Irish, or Welsh guards forgot about their official role, until they were called to order by the scolding whistle of their commander, and planted themselves back in their representational positions, standing as straight as tin soldiers.

Uriel was the only person with whom Naomi shared her dream. Compared with her aging father, who was losing himself in his doubts, her elderly grandfather, who sleepwalked through the house, muttering bloodcurdling premonitions, and her brother Gabriel, who seemed to be disconnected from everything around him, Uriel was a source of power, a wall of defense, a well of hope. When he walked into the house, his eyes shining mischievously, he was like a magnet. Sometimes, when Raphael felt strong enough to sit up, supported by pillows, he joined in, and the two of them listened in rapt attention to Uriel's stories. Naomi would kiss his cheeks, moistening them with her tears, and lose herself in Uriel's warm, soothing embrace.

Naomi felt additional moments of grace when little Davidi came to visit with his parents, scurried around the house, while avoiding the sick rooms, and squealed with delight. Naomi would let her worries go at once, chase after him, hum tunes into the small shells of his ears, and toss him into the air like a little ball of happiness. In her heart, she said a blessing of gratitude for the light Davidi brought with him into a home overtaken by darkness throughout most of the day, for the smile his shenanigans put on Oma Ilse, Opa Michael, and great-grandpa Josef's suffering faces, and even on Raphael's pale features, in those rare moments when his feeble energies overcame his illness.

***

A dark shadow enveloped the streets of Vienna in the winter of 1937. Austrian Jews began to show signs of nervousness at the boldness of Austrian Nazis, who were now acting almost out in the open, as a fifth column of warmongering Germany. Some Jews chose to migrate to the United States, to other European countries, even to Palestine, while many others preferred to stay in Austria and maintain their businesses and properties in a tense, desperate hope that the evil would pass. Unfortunately, they hung their hopes on the provisions of the Treaty of Versailles, which forbade the defeated Germany of World War I from uniting with Austria; they took solace in Hitler's false promises to his new ally, the Fascist Italian leader Mussolini, that he did not intend to intervene in interior Austrian affairs; and fell for the misleading and unfounded declarations of Austrian chancellor Kurt von Schuschnigg, that the majority of Austrian people objected to a union with Nazi Germany and that Hitler would not be setting foot on the outskirts of Vienna.

That is how they fell into the trap. In their naiveté, they believed in the protective power of a forced international treaty signed by hands loathed by Nazi Germany, and in their powerlessness, they put their trust in false promises and empty statements.

***

The new year was greeted at the Steiner home with a mixture of joy and sorrow. Two weeks after a telegram from London announced the birth of Gideon, Ruth and Jonah's first son, great-grandma Rebecca passed away. When the mourning family returned from the cemetery, they were met by Martha, who, crestfallen, reported a deterioration in Raphael's health. From that moment onwards, Oma Ilse and Martha never left his side.

As times were tough, nineteen-year-old Naomi was forced to carry the brunt of the household work, some for the first time. She assured herself that this new development offered many advantages. By taking on some of the household chores, she would lighten the load for Martha and her mother, who would be completely free to care for Raphael. The work would keep her busy, now that her parents and brother ordered her to leave the house as little as possible, and with her circle of friends dwindling, especially as her Christian friends began offering pathetic and infuriating excuses to avoid all contact with her. These simple tasks would also help her adapt to running a household, making her an independent and contributing member of the family, which would win her father and brother's admiration, the kind that was previously enjoyed only by Ruth. And above all, her good deeds would somewhat balance out the weakness of her character and alleviate some of the guilt and shame she felt with regards to Raphael. Recently, she had been avoiding his room. The alarm she felt at the sight of his pale face, his sickly gauntness, and his wan gaze, along with her revulsion at the smell of medicine and illness in his room, all joined together to form a dull, uncontrollable anger toward him for stealing what little attention was still paid to her by her parents and by Martha, especially now that she was more isolated and bored than ever. The scruples she felt, along with the self-criticism for her selfish attitude toward Raphael, came packaged together in a weighty bundle, making her muscles slack and her spirit depressed.

To her surprise, she found those physical tasks soothing and distracting, and was soon glad to occupy herself with stitching and needlepoint, crafts she had learned from her mother as a child but had never devoted much time to, as well as all those dull chores whose results she used to take for granted, ignoring the fact that someone had to slave over them. As she cooked, washed clothes, dusted, mopped floors, and scrubbed pots, small pockets of air made their way into her soul, little doorways into imaginary domains. Deep inside, she hoped her body would be made so worn by physical effort that she would finally enjoy a continuous night's sleep, devoid of nightmares.

10

On an especially stormy and rainy afternoon, Uriel surprised Naomi by asking her to be ready to leave the house at nine o'clock that night, right before lights out.

The events of that day—1 February 1938—were recounted by Naomi to me and to Ruth countless times in the years to come, in varying versions matching her mental state and sometimes adopting bold tones it's hard to believe the day had contained in the dire atmosphere of those dark times.

I was moved by my mother's bouts of attention toward me and by the experience of being included in her world, which I was normally shut out of. The blush that spread through her cheeks charmed me as she drew details of that long-ago story from memory. I drank up every word she said and processed them in my imagination. With time, her story became almost tangible to me, as if I had been there myself.

After all, that was the day my mother and father first met.

***

According to the popular version—or what Ruth and I called the "Mostly Version," the one my mother repeated to us the most— Naomi was ready to leave, dressed up, her hair combed, as early as seven. She had not dared leave the house after dark for months, and her pleas to join Uriel to one of his group meetings, which had become more frequent toward the approaching referendum, were pushed aside assertively with no room left for negotiation. In recent months, after more and more doors to the houses of those she considered to be her friends were closed to her, she had terribly missed the friendly meetings of her younger days. She had tired of the oppressive atmosphere that took over the street and which had recently settled into their home, disseminating the smell of sickness and death. The looks of the men on the streets of Vienna, who must have misread her ethnic origins, not only did not flatter her as they once did, but rather brought on bouts of fear and disgust. At the same time, her romantic soul yearned for a mad love to revive her mind, color her gray world, and help her survive this difficult time, whose terrible influence spread over all fronts. The thought of meeting young men and women, all Jewish, excited her, and in her heart, she blessed Uriel for finally acknowledging that she was an adult who could contribute her talents—social, at the very least—to the group effort.

She locked herself in her room at dusk and quickly tried on every dress she owned, while sadly pondering the fact that they had all been bought during happier times. Some of them were purchased years ago at the Vienna shops on excursions with Oma Ilse, when her mother was still attuned to her needs. The others were picked up during strolls with her good friend Sarah. Two years earlier, Sarah's father managed to obtain immigration certificates to Palestine, and she had left along with her parents, her aunt, and her two sisters for what she had called "the sands and swamps of that faraway land."

Naomi ran a hand over her blue taffeta dress with the puffed sleeves, felt the lace petticoat, and remembered how Sarah made her laugh the day she had bought the dress, repeatedly imitating the way the long-faced salesclerk explained through tongue clicks that the stability of the fabric allowed an impressive volume with dramatic, sculpted shapes, which is why taffeta was mostly used for eveningwear. Suddenly, she missed Sarah terribly and wondered why her friend had not written to her in so long.

She finally settled on a baby-blue knit dress with tight lace sleeves and a bell-shaped skirt, paired with a blue woolen shawl she had received two years earlier as a goodbye gift from Ruth, and a flat, white felt hat worn at an angle. When she stood, dressed and ready in her room, enjoying the fabulous image in the mirror, she was forced to push away a bothersome thought of Raphael, whom she had been avoiding for three days. She swore to herself that she would pay a visit to his room immediately after breakfast the following day.

When Martha called her for dinner, she claimed she was not hungry. She was too excited to eat a thing. Eventually, she planted herself on the chair in her room for an entire hour, waiting with a quietly pounding heart for silence to spread through the house after Raphael and great-grandpa Josef fell asleep, Martha left, and her parents retired to their bedroom. So eager was she for that old feeling, the smell of freedom and the taste of a good time, that she pushed aside any sense of danger at the prospect of going out into town so late at night, when the chances of encountering roaming gangs of thugs, whose brains were distorted with hate, was higher.

At exactly nine o'clock, Uriel knocked on her bedroom door. Naomi sat up in her chair and invited him in softly, imagining his compliments about her beauty and fine taste, as well as the marveling look he would give as he saw her in all her glory, just like in those far-gone days when she still lived like everybody else. But instead, Uriel stormed in, preoccupied and troubled, and, on his seeing his sister all made-up and dressed in her finest, his mouth opened in astonishment. How disappointed was she when he ordered her to wipe away the eye-shadow and the scent of perfume from her body, lest she draw unnecessary attention on the street. In a short time, the makeup was removed, the dress and hat tossed onto the bed with shamed frustration, replaced by a thin blouse, a sweater, and simple slacks. Only the blue shawl, Ruth's creation, remained, draped nonchalantly over her shoulders.

When she finished, Uriel wiped away her tears and pulled her into an embrace. "You're beautiful, Naomi," he said warmly. "More beautiful than any other girl I know. You don't need a fancy dress to stand out. Sometimes I worry about you precisely because of this, for, as you know, there is always someone up there, eager to pluck an exceptionally pretty flower…"

He stood her up before him. "I'll be getting you out of here very soon. That's why I decided to bring you to the meeting today. I want you to meet some of my friends and become familiar with our activity. The first chance I get, I want to send you to a safer place, and from there to Palestine."

"To Palestine?" Naomi almost choked. "Alone?!" She paled at his silence. "But Uriel! That place is nothing but sand and swamps! The sun is blinding, and the heat is unbearable. I hate sun and heat. And the Arabs take every opportunity to riot against the Jews. Besides, you know I won't go anywhere without you, Mom, and Dad. I won't even walk alone on the streets of Vienna. Where is this coming from all of a sudden?"

Uriel sighed. Naomi had often mentioned to him her dream of leaving Austria to live with Ruth and Jonah in London, where she would roam the shops, free as a bird, stroll through green parks, and, charmed, look at the royal palace. He had feared for a long time that Naomi's indulgent upbringing as the youngest child would become an issue when she had to face the injustices of life.

"Naomi," he said, his face severe, "you're a grown woman, and you must acknowledge the fact that our life in Austria is ruined. Hatred for Jews is growing by the day. It's too dangerous to walk on the streets. The Austrians are boycotting Jewish businesses and quitting their jobs with Jewish employers. Every week we hear of more Austrian employers firing Jewish workers. You must have heard of

Professor Herzog, Father's colleague, who received a notice of dismissal at his home out of the blue two weeks ago."

"But Uriel!" she tried to protest. "Father always says that Chancellor Schuschnigg doesn't hate us; that he loathes the Nazis. Soon, at the referendum, the Austrian people will voice their distaste for the annexation idea. When that happens, sanity will be regained, and we'll be safe again."

"And Mother claims Father is naïve," he answered. "The chancellor is living in a dream, Naomi, a dream we mustn't buy into. The referendum, if it even happens, will reveal the naked, ugly truth: that most Austrian people look up to Germany, yearn for a strong leader, and aspire to be an inseparable part of the Third Reich. But while this could cause a painful political defeat for Chancellor Schuschnigg, to us Jews it is a question of life and death."

He gave Naomi a moment to process his words before continuing. "Grandpa is right. We have no other place in this world but Palestine. We'll build a better country than any other with a just, equal society. We'll put in the hard work, and if need be, even pay in blood. All for the noble cause of allowing us Jews to finally live free."

Still stunned by her brother's dramatic announcement of his intention to smuggle her out of Austria, an intention that had suddenly and terrifyingly become tangible, Naomi was rooted to the spot, her gaze unfocussed. The mention of a move, not to say an escape, to that faraway land, far from her parents, her brothers, the house she grew up in, the familiar place that had become estranged, filled her with terrible fear. Within the whirlwind of her emotions, a thought flashed: that her parents were collaborating with Uriel to get rid of her so that they had more time to focus on Raphael. But, as happened often lately, each time bad thoughts like this one struck her, she was instantly overcome with shame for her selfishness toward her dear parents, helpless at the sight of their sick child, who felt agony with each inhale, barely making its way into his damaged lungs, and with each wheezing exhale.

The guilt strengthened her. She stood up and decisively spread the blue shawl over her shoulders. "Let's go," she said. "Let's not waste time. You may be right, Uriel. Perhaps the best thing is for me to leave."

The two stepped quietly out into the hallway and picked up the woolen coats that were hanging off hooks. At the sound of Naomi's umbrella tapping the floor, they held their breath for a moment, their eyes meeting. When no rustle was heard from the rooms, they rushed out into the maw of a rainy, black, starless Viennese night.

11

Uriel led Naomi, his arm around her, the two of them beneath a large, black umbrella, on a ten-minute brisk walk to a double, ironwork door at the entrance to an apartment building on Danhausergasse Street. In the light of the streetlamps and the ornamented lamps that hung over the door, Naomi immediately recognized the unique building with the rounded vaults on the façade, set with square, street-facing windows. A few years earlier, Jonah had taken a picture of her against the backdrop of this building for a project he was working on, commemorating his beloved Viennese architecture. She had walked past that building countless times since that day, never imagining that one of its apartments housed the secret meetings of what she thought of as "the Uriel Group."

Uriel and Naomi climbed briskly to the third floor, after making sure the stairwell was completely empty and that no curious neighbors, tracking the comings and goings of the building, were sticking their noses where they did not belong. Before she knew it, they paused at a wooden door that carried a sign with only a first name: Sebastian. Uriel knocked three times, whispered something Naomi did not catch, and the door opened a crack.

She needed a few seconds to grow accustomed to the dimness of the room, barely lit by two small nightlights. First, she spotted a thin girl of average height and straight shoulder-length raven-black hair. The girl walked quickly over to Uriel, grabbed his arms, and kissed him unabashedly on the lips. Then she turned toward Naomi, her smile revealing two rows of beautiful white teeth, and greeted her.

Naomi noticed three things at that moment: the girl's striking beauty, the fact that she knew her name and had expected her arrival, and the intimacy between her and Uriel. She immediately felt an uncomfortable prickle of jealousy. As if to justify her upset and disguise her unforgivably childish reaction toward her brother, she developed instant anger and insult for not having been included in the secret of his love. With time, Naomi learned that Rachel Weiss was a German from Hamburg, daughter to a Protestant mother and a Jewish father, a famous rheumatologist. In the fall of 1935, the father had decided to move his family to Austria after his civil rights were revoked upon the enforcement of the Nuremberg Laws, which legalized racism in Germany. Later in the evening, her sting of insult evolved into a true burn, when Naomi realized that Rachel was her age, and while she suffered from the younger, spoiled sister syndrome, requiring a frequent directing hand and protective arm, the energetic Rachel was one of the most active and valued members of the group. The realization flashed in her mind, that according to Jewish law, Uriel's love interest was, in fact, not Jewish. She then noted in her mind that it was due to her mixed origins that Uriel avoided sharing his relationship with her and their parents. Uriel, who, despite the dim light, could easily recognize the emotional storm that gripped his sister, by her flushed cheeks and the characteristic upright tilt of her nose, pulled lightly on her arm, signaling with his eyes that there were more pressing matters to deal with at the moment than unnecessary drama and settling scores. He briefly introduced her to ten others—eight men and two women—who were sitting around two simple wooden tables, one round, the other rectangular.

They all observed Naomi curiously. Beyond the moist film that emphasized her turmoil, her eyes suddenly glowed when she recognized one of the boys that used to play with her brother in the

Hakoah Vienna team. As a young girl, she used to go with her father and Raphael to watch Uriel's games. At the sight of him, she was flooded with distant memories of how he was consistently able, in his role as an attacking midfielder, to pass "good balls" to Uriel, who was center forward, and who would then break into the center of the field to score goals that brought lots of honor to his team and pride and joy to her, to her father, and to Raphael. She noted with pleasure that the eyes of the young men, and especially that one, Alexander Gottlieb, lingered on her face, and, in the darkness of the room, even dared to freely glide down along the curves of her body after she allowed the blue shawl to slip, as if by accident, to the floor.

One of the girls, a small figure, gentle looking with kind eyes walked over quickly, leaned down, picked up the rebellious shawl, and fixed it over Naomi's shoulders. Then she shook her hand warmly and led her to the round table. Naomi later learned that the girl's name was Leah—she offered only a first name—and that she was the life partner of the apartment owner, Sebastian—again, first name only.

Aware of the eyes that followed her every movement, Naomi took a seat self-importantly on a wooden chair offered to her at the table next to Alexander. She smiled modestly and offered her first and last name—Naomi Steiner. To her disappointment, Uriel took a seat beside Rachel at the rectangular table. She was surprised to find that the interest showed in her was, for the time being, exhausted. The members of the group moved on with the matters at hand.

Naomi's mind drifted to thoughts of Uriel and Rachel, Sebastian and Leah, and even Alexander Gottlieb, as the group around her was lost in a heated discussion of the upcoming referendum. In the fringes of her consciousness, she realized that only three of the people there, Alexander included, believed the referendum would save them, prove the Austrian people's distaste for the union, and strengthen the chancellor, who had been sending calming messages to Austrian Jews for a while.

"No people in the world would willfully merge with another, stronger people," Alexander said excitedly. "Many countries have been occupied and annexed to stronger ones over the years," he continued, "but it was a result of weakness of resistance, not acceptance or true volition." He offered an impressive array of examples, stretching all the way back to the battle of the Indians against white settlers in America, adding a list of uprisings, from the Maccabean Revolt against the Seleucid Empire in the second century B.C. to the Great Druze Revolt against the French Mandate in Syria in the 1920s.

Alexander carried on, his words mixing and merging in Naomi's mind, then forming the shapes and perceptions of horses, knights, bayonets and guns, dignified resistance, devotion, and national pride. Toward the end of his speech, he wiped his brow, gleaming with sweat, and concluded that he was therefore convinced that the Austrian people would also, ultimately, resist the union.

"That is what my father thinks too," she whispered to him once he took his seat again, trying to appear practical and attentive. In return, all she received was a slight smile and a nod of the head.

Uriel, representing the opinion of the majority, predicted the chancellor's painful defeat in the referendum. "The annexation of Austria to Germany is only a matter of time," he said gravely. "Most of the Austrian population is German-speaking. Hitler, a native Austrian, wants to see it as part of the Reich, claiming that it will enrich Germany with quarries, gold, military industry, and manpower. The annexation of Austria will advance towards the fulfillment of his vision, as he publicly defined it just a few months ago in that atrocious document, the Hossbach Memorandum—the spreading of the Third Reich over the entirety of Europe."

Now, Naomi was actually quite impressed with this counterview. Although she didn't like hearing it, she took pleasure in her brother's authoritative flow, and noted to herself that when Uriel spoke, everybody listened.

Next to speak was Rachel.

"This timing is very convenient for Hitler," she said as her hands sliced through the air. "The Italian Duce is busy with the Spanish Civil War, France is scared and torn between the Fascist Catholic right and the secular left, Chamberlain realizes that another world war would be the end of the British Empire and will avoid one at all costs, and the rest of the world is more concerned with the Japanese occupation of China..."

For the first time, Naomi could see Rachel's confidence and hear her eloquence and could not help being impressed by the power of her words. She was used to these kinds of discussions at home and had never felt any special need to participate. But this time was different. This time it was young men and women around her own age, discussing current events and debating courses of action, which only emphasized her own nullity. How could she think of winning Uriel's appreciation and support when she had nothing more to offer than a pretty face, the caprices of a romantic girl, and good grades?

The thoughts now flickered through her mind like dark figures projected against a white wall, blending into each other, changing, taking and losing form. She was so busy making unflattering comparisons between the characters around her and herself that only in retrospect was she able to reconstruct what her eyes subconsciously saw: Leah slipping like a cat to the door, opening it a crack to hear the password, stifling a cry at the sight of the man in the doorway, and embracing his neck for a long moment. Through blurred perception, she heard Rachel say that Kurt Schuschnigg had no illusions with regards to his deteriorating political status and would most likely try once more to appease the Berlin dictator.

"Look at the Austrian government. Under his rule, it is now discussing the possibility of a general pardon for Austrian Nazis, including those convicted of the murder of Chancellor Dollfuss. I've even heard talk of appointing the Nazi Arthur Seyss-Inquart as Minister of Interior and Defense in the new cabinet, and we all know he receives his orders from Hitler himself!"

Naomi refocused on the conversation, then turned her attention to Uriel, who took the stage again, reinforcing Rachel's words.

"Look how the Nazi Austrians' reign of terror has gained power throughout 1937. There's no doubt that their activity is supported and funded by Berlin. Bombings take place nearly every day in some parts of Austria, and, in the mountain provinces, frequent violent Nazi demonstrations are weakening the Austrian government's resolve and further emphasizing its helplessness..."

"And if that isn't bad enough," a voice said from the back of the room, "a reliable source told me that last week the Austrian police broke into the offices of the Committee of Seven in Vienna and found certificates initialed by Rudolf Hess, according to which Austrian Nazis were about to stage a revolt against the government as early as next spring, and, if Chancellor Schuschnigg tries to suppress it, the German military will invade Austria, presumably to prevent the spilling of German blood by fellow Germans."

Naomi could not tell what caused her to tremble more: the threatening content, which left no room for doubt, or the hypnotizing voice with the foreign accent, deep and cracked with nicotine. She turned quickly toward the speaker. The mystery man, whose name Naomi learned that evening was called Mordecai, was leaning against the wall, wearing a white shirt, its sleeves folded up to his elbows, its top unbuttoned to reveal his collarbone, a broad and muscular chest, tan and a bit hairy. Naomi held her breath at the sight of his masculine face. Uriel and the other guys rose to their feet and rushed to shake his hand as if they hadn't seen him for a long time. With yearning, Naomi watched Rachel and another girl, Trude, join the guys and hug him warmly, asking how he had been. Rachel linked her arm with his and led him to sit with her and Uriel at the rectangular table.

Naomi could not take her eyes off him. She only lowered them shyly when she thought he noticed her staring, cursing the blush that spread all too easily over her cheeks, and hoping the room was dark enough to conceal it. She was glad to find he was one of the most vocal speakers of the group, which gave her ample opportunity to watch him freely, pretending to be closely following the content of the heated discussion.

The conversation now turned to supporting the "national sport," as Ze'ev Jabotinsky, the founding father of Revisionist Zionism, called the enterprise of illegal immigration to Palestine. Ideas were thrown around the room for actions the group must take to assist in the efforts to break the quotas, determined by the British Mandate due to the pressure applied by Arabs, that limited the number of entering Jews. The group discussed different ways of leading Betar Youth members out of Austria to central and western Europe and from there to Palestine, as well as the need to battle the Jewish Agency to receive a suitable number of immigration certificates for families, elderly, and infirm people who were not members of the World Zionist Organization or of farming training programs.

Mordecai let out a hoarse cough as he depicted to his friends the image of the pioneer according to Jabotinsky: "Like a copper rod, a lump of iron in the hands of a blacksmith called Zion," and Uriel concluded the stormy argument with the famous call of the movement founder, "Jews, eliminate the Diaspora, or the Diaspora will surely eliminate you!"

***

It stopped raining at midnight. Leah boiled water, made some tea and black coffee, and placed butter and chocolate cookies on a wide china platter. The members peppered Mordecai with questions, and his answers taught Naomi that he had sailed to Palestine several months ago as a chaperone for a group of fifty-four young Betar members from Poland, Lithuania, and Latvia, who were brought there illegally by sea. Naomi was thrilled by Mordecai's descriptions of how these young men and women came to Austria disguised as students heading for summer camp, and how, as if on tour along the Mediterranean coast, they continued from there to Albania in blue and gray uniform; how in the streets of the coastal town of Durrës they lined up and marched with raised flags, led by drummers. Within a few days, Mordecai told them, the young men and women boarded the Greek ship Artemisia, which they disembarked safely at Tantura Beach, Palestine, where they were received by members of the *Irgun*[2], who supervised their distribution across the country. Mordecai stayed in Palestine for a few more weeks, until winter, to coordinate the continuation of the illegal immigration enterprise with members in the Israeli branches of the Irgun and Betar movements.

When he finished his detailed description, Naomi attempted to preserve in her memory the names of all the people Mordecai had mentioned. In her mind, they all took shape as heroic figures, and she wondered what Ilse would have said if she had known about the bold, secretive, and heroic activity of these young people, bravely participating in the success of the *Aliyah* endeavor. But by the end of the night, the names all mixed up in her mind, evaporated, and came together again as one single name: Mordecai. His image was etched in her mind as a "copper rod, a lump of iron in the hands of a blacksmith named Zion." Faraway Palestine no longer seemed like such a terrible idea.

At two in the morning, the members began to disperse, leaving in pairs into the black, starless night. Uriel kissed Rachel goodbye on

---

2   "The National Military Organization in the Land of Israel"—A Zionist paramilitary organization that operated in Mandate Palestine between 1931 and 1948.

her lips, and Leah whispered to Naomi that Rachel was subletting a room in her and Sebastian's apartment.

Only then, at Sebastian's door, did Mordecai first look at her. Naomi skipped a beat when he addressed her in his deep voice, which sounded softer to her now, introduced himself and shook her hand firmly. Aware of Sebastian, Uriel, Rachel, and Leah's glances, she turned red, smiled awkwardly, and seemed to have swallowed her tongue. Then she stepped silently with her brother down the stairs after Mordecai, never taking her eyes off his broad back, and regretted to find Trude waiting for him downstairs, near the iron door. Mordecai and Trude slipped out first, and she and Uriel followed them five minutes later.

On the way home, Naomi was so overwrought by the events of the night that she could not calm down. She was stirred up over the discovery of Uriel and Rachel's relationship, the bold activity of the group members, and the awful things that might happen to her family and the entirety of Austria's Jews if the annexation took place. But more than anything else, she was taken by Mordecai. As one who was not accustomed to excitement in great proportion, she felt a knee-buckling dizziness the whole way home and held back the sea of questions she wanted to flood Uriel with from the moment the door to their home was locked behind their backs and until sunrise.

When they arrived at home, Uriel suggested that due to the late hour they postpone their conversation, whose content he could already predict, until the following morning, and only deigned to tell his sister that the charismatic Mordecai was one of the most active and helpful members of their group, and that he was born in the city of Dubrovnik in Croatia. And no, he clarified, Mordecai and Trude were not a couple, only close friends. They were both foreigners, and as an alibi for their presence in Austria, they had both registered as students at the University of Vienna. Before he disappeared inside his room, Uriel agreed to Naomi's request to share the night's events with Raphael the next morning, "but without going into too much detail." Only when Naomi finally got into bed did she recall that she did not know Mordecai's last name.

Only his first.

12

September 1990
Yosemite Park, California

Dear Nurit,

Thank you for your beautiful letter. It's the first one I've gotten since I arrived here two weeks ago. I know that isolating myself was entirely my choice, but still, your letter… it made me very emotional.

Few people know me as well as you, Davidi, and Esther. There used to be "the other," too. Mike knows me well but in a different way. He knows me as much as I've allowed him to but doesn't know the "before."

I was so glad to hear you're doing well in your new position as the head veterinarian of the Jezreel Valley. Glad, but not surprised. You've always been determined, practical, decisive, and hardworking. The kind of person who sets goals and sticks to them. You've always worked, saved money, studied, and achieved everything yourself with your own two hands.

That's how you helped me, too. I'm the dreamer. Imagination is my bread and butter. But you helped make my dream come true with your practicality, your striving to accomplish, to fulfil, to succeed. You never let me lose my way. I learned so much from you. I often think that if I only had your determination and Esther's peacefulness, I would be a much happier person.

I think divorce agrees with you. I've always loved Danny, he's a good person, but you're right—he isn't the one for you. Everything you loved about him did not stand the test of time. Too spiritual, too gentle, too dreamy. You felt you had to carry him. After the divorce, I worried more about him than about you. You're strong and independent. You always land on your feet. But now you have a new job, and I imagine the hours are demanding. How are you making it work with the kids?

I went outside to the park for the first time today. It was hot when I got here, but now it's quite lovely outside. Before I ventured out, very early in the morning, I did some Yoga *asanas* and *pranayamas*, which helped me push aside my obsessive thoughts and my physical pain. Then I put on walking shoes, packed a bottle of water and the keys to my room, and slipped out through the back stairs. I didn't want to meet anyone. I still can't handle conversation. For now, I'm happy with written words alone.

I got into my rental car, drove to one of the best lookout points over Yosemite Valley, and succeeded in catching the last minutes of sunrise. It's one of the most breathtaking sights imaginable. I stayed a while, gazing at the valley's endless expanses. The air was fresh. From there, I continued to the little mirror lake and marveled at how that famous cliff with the half-dome (you might have seen it on your visit here) reflects in the water. I sat there with my notebook for a few hours, reading through everything I've written, then writing more and more.

It's incredible, Nurit, what this place does to me. Every little corner of it.

Then I got back in the car and drove to the main entrance. I parked the car, took the park shuttle, and went...you know where...

There.

Yours,
Helena

13

September 1990
(This letter was thrown out)

Dear Blair,

You asked so many times, and I evaded the subject. You wanted to know what drew me here, and why my eyes brightened whenever I packed a suitcase with light or heavy clothing—according to the season—books, writing supplies, and lots of paper, some already scribbled with words, some blank. And how could I be so happy to go, when it meant leaving you, Roy, Abby, and Daddy for such a long time? I asked why you called it a long time, and you said that a few weeks is very long, and that once I was away for two months. Your frustration was audible in your voice, visible in the trace of a tear on your almond-shaped, olive-toned eye.

I would turn my back on you to shove some shirts into a plastic bag or cushion the corners of my suitcase with woolen sweaters. I would take a breath and try to steady my voice so that I could answer your question. My eyes, hidden from yours, turned dark. I always gave you the same answer to the question you never ceased asking. I told you I was going there to write and, especially, to finish books most of which I'd written at my desk at home. There, in that place, I would say, I have peace and quiet, the detachment, and the inspiration I need in order to write.

You would accuse me of abandoning you for weeks at a time and complain about how you couldn't even call me, because I always removed the phone from my room so as not to be disturbed. You could only reach me for urgent matters, through the lodge's reception, which forced you to decide whether what you had to tell me truly was an emergency: was the fact that Roy's math grades plummeted since I'd left important enough? Did your failure at the auditions for the school dance group a day after you twisted your ankle justify a phone call? Or maybe only the fever Abby had that time, requiring her to go to the hospital, counted as a true "emergency?"

I would listen to your words, pummeling at my back and anguishing my heart, and wonder if defective motherhood was hereditary. Then I'd gather my courage, force my gaze to soften, so that I could turn to you and face you again. I'd spread my arms and apologize dearly for having to go again, making all kinds of promises, which lost their charm with each passing year.

And I'd repeat my worn mantra, my explanation of detachment, peace and inspiration, hoping you'd be able to understand and accept (like Daddy) or at least just accept (like Roy and Abby) and therefore forgive.

And it's true, Blair, that, in this place that you call "there," I go to disconnect, to find the quiet that I miss so badly in my regular life and the best inspiration a writer can ask for.

But all this—the detachment, the quiet, the inspiration—is only half the truth.

I'm a master of half-truths.

And at keeping the other half under wraps.

14

So, let me tell you, Blair, what this place truly means to me.

I'd like to take you back to a beautiful autumn day in 1979 to that unforgettable family trip to Yosemite. It was the first time we ever visited the enormous national park in the Sierra Nevada Mountains. Just you, Roy, Daddy, and me...

That day, I felt the taste of love at first sight. This time it wasn't love for a man or a child but a love for nature, which showed itself to me in all its glory. That day I captured with my eyes and etched into my heart the sights and sensations that have flooded my heart countless times since.

It was late October, an ideal time to see the fall foliage. Although Daddy warned us that the weather during that month could be fickle, we enjoyed a gorgeous, cloudless, comfortably warm day. Fall colors set the tops of maple and oak trees alight with a mixture of yellow, orange, and burning red. You were eight at the time, and Roy was only three, and the two of you frolicked among the trees, squealing with joy, enjoying the striking appearance of the carpet of leaves that piled up at the foot of trees and its soft crunch under the soles of your shoes. Thrilled, you ran this way and that, shouted about having found a "treasure," and began to collect leaves of bold colors and "a million shapes," while announcing that you'd gather them all in a special album as a keepsake. Roy spread his arms and circled the tree trunks, then dropped himself onto the soft foliage, burying his little face in a pile of leaves. Finally, he flipped over onto his back, spraying leaves every which way and only stopped when you informed him that he was "wasting leaves" and that rather than kicking them around he'd best help you collect them. Roy listened carefully, then ducked down, cupping the leaves in his little palms, and, gaily, ran to you. But by the time he reached you, most of the leaves had fallen between his fingers, and for every ten leaves you gathered, Roy contributed only one.

In the afternoon, an employee of the French lodge—which has become my second home since—drove us to the Mariposa Grove to the right of the park's southern entrance. A light wind blew through your pretty hair as we rode in the truck. You were so impressed by the sequoias that had been standing for hundreds and thousands of years. Roy fell asleep on my lap. He was still asleep when the driver pulled up and we stepped out of the truck. I adjusted his head on my shoulder, his golden locks tickling my face and neck. The driver riveted us with his stories of the battle over habitats: when the roots of a new tree penetrated the ground and spread out in an attempt to maintain a steady hold in the ground, after a prolonged period it caused the uprooting of nearby, older, and weaker tree and its collapse with a mighty crash.

Roy suddenly woke up in his characteristically quiet way, calmly opening a pair of eyes, blue meeting blue as his gaze fixed on the wide, cloudless patch of sky glimmering between the treetops. Rubbing my hair between his soft fingertips, as was his custom, his pupils suddenly dilated, and, as his small mouth opened in wonder, he stretched out his other arm, and the magical sight that appeared to him wrapped itself in the story of creation he'd heard at synagogue during the High Holidays.

"Mommy, are we in heaven?" he marveled.

I did not feel like a liar when I said, "Yes." From the corner of my eye I saw you examining the sky with wonder.

"Are there people we know here?" he wondered, "who really live here?"

"Yes, Roy," I said. "All sorts of people who were very dear to me and ended their lives on earth now live in heaven."

I saw you shrinking on the rock where you perched, hugging your knees between your arms, just the way I used to do when I was a little girl. Tears shone in your eyes.

"And are they near God now?" he asked.

"Yes, my child," I said.

Roy reached his soft hands upwards, as if to grasp a piece of heaven, a pinch of a better world.

15

When my mother died, I was already a young woman. I was starting my life and already orphaned of both mother and father. Her death burned within me like a flame. I felt guilty.

In the early years, I visited her grave every day. I used to stroke the gravestone we had set for her and clean the grave of dust and small clumps of dirt that had piled up, and dry leaves that had carried over with the wind. With a small cloth, I polished the silk leaves of the blue artificial flowers we placed in a vase, checking for rain, sun, or wind damage, making sure they hadn't been gnawed on by nocturnal or field animals. Each season, I would replace the flowers we had planted in a small pot, and each visit I watered them, to bring some life to the graveside. I cried there so much that at some point I ran out of tears.

That wasn't my only loss. I grew up with my losses, and with hers. At some point, I was on the way to losing myself as well. I felt that my life was pointless and without hope. Those damn losses were nearly the end of me.

Thanks to the people who loved me, I chose life. I continued to visit the grave, but, realizing it was the only way I would be able to survive, with time I came less and less. Years later, I moved to America, and the number of my visits to the grave were reduced dramatically. When I met Daddy, I chose not to tell him about my dead. For your sake, Blaire, for Daddy's, and then for Roy's and Abby's. I realized life was for the living, without grief or dark shadows.

I realized it but didn't know how to do it.

I tried to smile, to make Daddy happy, to be happy myself, but each time I fell again.

I tried to push my sorrow to a deep, distant place, but it followed me like a shadow. In the end, I escaped into a world of books, or perhaps I did so from the very beginning. That world allowed me to live a life entirely different from my own. I loved, hated, got angry. I kicked, rebelled, once even killed a man, and through an entire book, which the critiques called "brilliant," I managed to get off scot-free on a self-defense argument. Writing gave me the gift of release, the platform to exhibit emotions that remained imprisoned deep in my real life.

But to truly cut loose and write, I had to get far away. To run. But I didn't know where.

That all changed that day in the fall of '79, during our unforgettable visit to Yosemite. It was an intense, dizzying love at first sight. Such strong emotions, rising from deep inside. Sometimes a love like that is enough to explain an attraction to a place.

But there was something else, too.

It was Roy's innocent question, so pure and naïve, that clarified the picture for me. That day, far away from the place where I was born, far away from the place where I was raised, and far from the place where I had started a family of my own, I discovered Shangri-La, my own private garden of Eden.

There, more than any other place on earth, inside the enormous park at the foot of the Sierra Nevada, and especially in the Mariposa Grove among the giant trees, I felt myself communing with my mother and all my dear, gone loved-ones. There, in the endless wild and breathtaking beauty, I felt myself connecting to my shut past, far, far from the bustle of life.

With time, the park became my second home. I went every year for a month or two at a time. I wrote no few chapters for my books, hiked the Yosemite Valley, rode a bicycle, and even went horseback riding through the historical pioneer village in the southern part of the park. And every time, I also visited the sequoias in Mariposa Grove. With time, access to the thicket with private cars was forbidden, and ever since then I've been using the park's special shuttles.

I feel closer to my loved-ones there than anyplace else. That's where I told them everything. I told them about Daddy and you, about Roy and Abby. I told them about every book I wrote, the plot and the characters, and about the content of the book I didn't write through all the years when I couldn't cry.

I went there again this afternoon. I got on the park's shuttle and got off with the other visitors who were hiking to different lookout points. I walked past the tree that looked like a giant grizzly, the one you and Roy were so excited about back then, and passed through the tunnel that cut into the California Tree, just as the four of us did on that autumn day eleven years ago.

Suddenly, I felt a pinch in my heart. I looked up to the sky, which was just as blue as it had been that day. I recalled my conversation with Roy about heaven, and hoped that my mother and father, and other loved ones were happy in that world up above.

There, Blair, among the sequoias, I had a hard time.

But also the best.

16

September 1990
Yosemite Park, California

Dear Nurit,

Oh, Nurit, I just wrote to Blair…I wrote her a few unfinished letters, because I wasn't able to write what I wanted to say in one proper letter. But I eventually crumpled the papers and tossed them into that wastebasket, which stands like a work of art in the center of my room.

And what an *objet d'art* it is…at least I can let my words get trapped there, since I don't have an address for her anyway… She ran away to the end of the world.

I'm angry, angry because I'm not capable of explaining it. It sounded forced even to me, insane. How could I explain to her why every year, for so many years, I disappear for weeks at a time? And why I distance myself from home, from her, from Mike, from Roy and Abby, insisting on coming here all on my own?

Because only here can I be with my mother and with…you know who.

I wanted Blair to grow up without a feeling of loss, because who knows better than me how awful that feeling is? I wanted to spare her the pain. And it was the exact same reason that I never told her about the other loss, mine and hers.

I took away her basic right to know that she was born to other parents.

Nurit, I was so foolish, and so selfish.

Mike thought differently, of course. But I insisted on protecting her. I had that tragic passion to lock up parts of reality along with considerable aspects of my past behind a fog screen.

That's why, for so many years, I insisted on stifling my memories rather than revealing them.

Until I had to.

I made a mistake. A terrible mistake. Now I know I should have told her much sooner, and that once I did, I should not have continued to lie to her. Not to her, and certainly not to Mike.

My poor, dear Mike…how did I ruin everything?!

It's hard to talk about it. It's easier to write.

Suddenly, after she left and Mike shut himself off, I knew what I needed to do. I knew that to save anything of what I'd spoiled, I had to build anew. I knew I couldn't run anymore, that I mustn't continue to furnish my world with stories about other people. That I had to open up, to peel off the protective skin.

So now I'm here, writing. And now it's my story.

Because to explain myself, I must first go back and start at the very beginning.

Or even a little before.

Yours,
Helena

17

On a rainy winter morning in February of 1945, having heard the rumor that my mother and I were staying at the brothel, Nioka made a surprise visit to Madame Butterfly's. Beforehand, shocked to her god-fearing core, Nioka put on a heavy woolen coat, large enough to hide her body, covered her face with a green kerchief, leaving only her eyes exposed, and after taking a few deep breaths, gathered her courage together and briskly marched inside to find out if the rumor was true.

At the time, embarrassment and confusion held sway over the madam's girls, and a tenseness was apparent in the men who visited the brothel due to the recent developments on the front. On 12 January 1945, the opening shot of the war's biggest Russian offensive was fired when Stalin's armed divisions took the German military headquarters in the upper Vistula, south of Warsaw, by storm. Afterward, striding toward Berlin, they captured Warsaw and Budapest and invaded Germany. On the eastern front, the *Wehrmacht* forces began to collapse one by one like a house of cards.

The men who visited the brothel—some, soldiers on leave or prolonged recovery from injury, most, residents, farmers from the villages nearby or men who were too old, disabled, or unfit for service—were now loudly voicing their fear of the unfathomable: the Reich's possible defeat. In the lobby, where the clients and the girls met, they voiced their concern regarding the future of the Reich, their families, and their businesses, workplaces, and possessions. The older ones recalled with horror the financial downfall that had followed the shameful defeat of the Central Powers in World War I, leading to unemployment in unprecedented numbers. A few of them even confessed aloud their fears of retaliation from the victorious nations.

As tensions rose, morale plummeted. Many men chose to release their frustration by getting drunk in the nearby tavern before arriving at the brothel. When a few of the girls, in their distress, joined the men in drinking themselves to oblivion, and in their intoxication forgot to charge the fee for their services, Madame Butterfly yelled at them and even slapped their cheeks lightly, as she pointed angrily at her dwindling cashbox and asked out loud if they damn well believed that it would be possible to continue the business and clothe and feed them if this kept up.

This turmoil greeted Nioka on the morning of her visit. The moment she set foot in the brothel, she witnessed one of the madam's fits of rage, directed at a few of her girls who returned from the neighboring pub that morning, their eyes red with liquor and lack of sleep, their pockets empty. For a moment, alarmed by the shouting and appalled by the notion of someone she knew seeing her visiting a loathsome place like this, Nioka thought of turning around and fleeing. But, as she hesitated, the door opened with a bang, missing her body by inches, and one of the girls stormed out in uncontrollable tears.

It was too late to back out now. Madame Butterfly, who chased the girl, paused with astonishment when she saw the seamstress standing at the doorway. She instantly softened her tone and language and sweetly invited the lady in. Nioka accepted the invitation with a nod and held her head up high as she waddled into the parlor, her buttocks swinging this way and that.

The room, still dark with shutters drawn, smelled of stale air and alcohol. When her eyes adjusted to the dim light, she saw about a dozen plain looking girls, some of them very young, huddled together, watching her, and whispering excitedly. They must have been agitated by the madam's shouting. Nioka tried to conceal the repulsion she felt at the sight of the red, pink, and floral sofas that were scattered around the room. Her seamstress's eye spotted a large rip on the side of a floral sofa, and she noted to herself that the place was decorated in a gaudy vulgarity and disgusting lack of taste. Eager to eliminate any questions regarding the purpose of her visit, she politely yet assertively turned down a strong drink offered to her by a full-figured brunette and went right to the point, wondering aloud if a young, pretty woman who used to work for her was living here with her little girl, who, if memory served, was "older than four but younger than five."

Becoming enlivened by what she perceived as a golden opportunity to unload an unnecessary burden from her conscience and her pocket, Madame Butterfly quickly answered in the affirmative, and led Nioka to her small office at the end of the hall. There she laid out the story of how my mother and I had arrived at her establishment and complained that what had been intended as a week's shelter had become a prolonged, months-long affair, and who knew when it would end. Then the madam shook her head, her face wearing a dramatic expression. Lowering her voice, she theatrically described to Nioka, with exaggerate gestures, the mother's obtuseness on the one hand and the little bastard child's wretched yearning for love on the other. Finally, forcing a sigh, she lowered her voice a little more and confessed to Nioka that although her merciful heart would not allow her to send the two out to the street, keeping them afloat had lately become a real challenge, and she would soon be forced to take some sort of action.

When she finished talking, the madam looked askance at Nioka with anticipation. Nioka didn't bat an eye, and as she rose to her feet, swaying a little, she thanked her for her honesty and asked simply to see us. Madame Butterfly, hesitating over the impression she had left and afraid that she might have scared the seamstress off, led her silently to a small room in the attic and opened the door wide.

When Nioka entered the room, she found only me inside. Mother was busy cleaning rooms on the upper floor, while I waited for her to finish. Clutching to my chest the little ragdoll the peasant had once bought me, which was wearing a dress with a short skirt and sleeves my mother had made, I had climbed onto the small dresser by the window from where I looked out onto the gray street.

I recognized Nioka immediately. There were only a few people I had become attached to in my early childhood, and Nioka, whose home I spent hours in every day, had assumed a meaningful place in my life. Thus, as she struggled to adjust to the darkness of the room and to settle her breath after climbing the steep stairs, I pounced on her so quickly that a rickety chair standing in my way wobbled in place, and I fell on the floor beside it. Nioka let out a cry, bent toward me, took me in her plump arms, and held me to her large bosom. A little later, after having seen my mother and realized that her mental state was unstable but that she was still able to perform some work, she returned to Madame Butterfly's small, dolled-up office. Fighting to pull her gaze away from the red phone on the woman's desk, Nioka made a deal: Mother and I would remain at the brothel, as Nioka had a husband at the front, three children, a small house, and her own hardships. Other than cleaning the brothel, which would now be my mother's regular job, she would spend the afternoon performing special sewing jobs for Nioka's customers. In this way, my mother would be productive during the day and earn our keep at the brothel. Moreover, surprising the madam as well as herself with her decisiveness, Nioka declared the girl should not be allowed to leave her room after dusk, when traffic in the house was heavy, lest she be exposed to the activity that took place there. Mother would also reduce her presence among the working girls, lest the men thought she was one of them. Nioka would be allowed to visit us every Tuesday afternoon.

Before she left, Nioka placed a small basket filled with bread, hardboiled eggs, and fruit in the corner of our room, whispered something in my mother's ear, stroked my hair, kissed my forehead, and said goodbye.

I was cheerful. Finally, something good and special had happened. But, after having pulled out a small jar of homemade quince preserves, Mother suddenly began to sob. She read the label in a weak voice: "For sweet Helene, to sweeten life for you a bit. Nioka."

Seeing her crying like that—my short-lived joy died down and my eyes filled with tears. Pushing my way into her arms, which had not reached out to receive me, and attempting to wipe away her tears with my tiny fingertips, I asked why she was crying.

Mother was already immersed in faraway sights and experiences from her other life, which took place long before my time, and, without her noticing, had stretched a thin, invisible line between the present and the past. The line twisted down the devious paths of time seven years back and tied a loop around the month of February 1938. Then she whispered, possibly to me and possibly to herself, that quince preserves, kept in a very similar jar, were the last jam Oma Ilse had made before everything fell apart.

18

Raphael's twenty-third birthday took place on 12 February 1938. The day before, the doctor, normally stern, reported an improvement in Raphael's health, which was enough to set Oma Ilse cheerfully on her feet the next morning, her cheeks flushed. Ilse announced to Martha that she had decided to spontaneously invite Gabriel, Vera, and Davidi for dinner to celebrate Raphael's birthday. "God-willing that this be a holiday for all of us," she wished out loud. To ensure the involved participation of great-grandpa Josef and Raphael, the dinner was set earlier, before nightfall. Sent by Ilse, Opa Michael hurried out to buy meat and other groceries. Vera and Gabriel confirmed their attendance, and Oma Ilse and Martha began preparing for dinner, recruiting Naomi to set the table according to the finest etiquette of Viennese hospitality.

During those very hours, lost in thought, Austrian Chancellor Kurt von Schuschnigg was making his way up a narrow, twisting mountain road overlooking a breathtaking view, toward the Führer's mountain dwelling in the Eagle's Nest in Obersalzberg. Ever since the spring of 1937, the chancellor's prolonged and persistent resistance to Austrian Nazis had been weakening, after his attempts to procure a British declaration guaranteeing Austria's independence had failed. In reaction, supported and funded by Berlin, the Nazis had exacerbated their reign of terror over Austria, and now he was hoping, in desperation or naiveté—a hope that would die within mere hours—that in his imminent meeting with Hitler he would be able to appease the German dictator, as he had done more than once before.

Thus, while Oma Ilse fried veal schnitzels, skillfully tossing them over in the pan, the Führer welcomed Schuschnigg on the stairs of his villa in a brown *Sturmabteilung* shirt, black slacks, and high spirits—a total contradiction to the tense mood of the Austrian leader. And while Martha mashed tart apples and potatoes into purees, the chancellor's yearning for reconciliation was crushed as the Führer accused Austria of historical treason against the notion of German nationalism and announced in a shrill voice the kind of historical role he was about to perform in the service of the German people. And when, at the end of a list of national and financial demands, the Führer presented a horrific ultimatum in writing, demanding that Schuschnigg hand over the Austrian government to the Nazis within a week, the remains of the Austrian chancellor's hopes were ground into dust. The unequivocal ultimatum, which later was given an additional grace period of three days, was accompanied by the Führer's painful reminder that Austria had no real friends, and that neither England, France, nor Fascist Italy, would raise a finger in its aid. When, in a final attempt at resistance, Schuschnigg dared suggest holding a referendum in his country, Hitler responded with a "friendly" clarification that if his Austrian counterpart turned down this "request" he could anticipate that one day the German army would simply appear in Vienna, as sudden as a spring storm.

It is no wonder, then, that while Oma Ilse worked lovingly on her quince jam—Raphael's favorite delicacy—peeling the fruits, softening them in a large pot of boiling water with sugar and lemon juice, cooking the concoction on a low flame, and stirring it diligently, fear and anxiety gradually mixed in the chancellor's heart and mind, leading him toward surrender. Thus, as Ilse removed the jam from the flame, cooling it down, and pouring it into a sterilized jar, and as she announced with a sigh to Martha and Naomi that dinner was ready, Schuschnigg had politely turned down the Führer's dinner invitation. A moment before, with a heavy heart, in the spacious study on the second floor overlooking the eternally snowy Alps, he had signed the agreement that had been forced upon him, putting an end to Austria's independence.

At six o'clock, Ilse invited her family to take their seats in the dining table's high-backed chairs, Opa Michael at the head of the table, and Raphael, borrowing great-grandpa Josef's place for one night, supported by cushions, at the other end. Still unaware of the bitter news leaving the Eagle's Nest at those very moments, my mother's family enjoyed a fine meal and final moments of relative quiet on that fateful evening, accompanied by little Davidi's clever remarks and high-pitched laughter and Vera's and Gabriel's marvelous playing on the cello and piano.

Toward the end of dinner, Opa Michael made a warm toast to his son and expressed his gratitude for his wife, the love of his life, for putting together such a successful event, proving that even in times like these one could still celebrate among family with music for the soul and schnitzels for the palate. Her cheeks flushed, Oma Ilse, thanked Michael for his kind words, grazed a kiss on Raphael's cheeks along with wishes for a happy birthday and a full recovery, and turned to the kitchen.

And so, just as, cloaked in bitter silence, Kurt von Schuschnigg and his assistant made their way down the mountains toward Salzburg that foggy winter day, Oma Ilse pulled out the semi-sweet quince jam she had cooked earlier that day, placed it before the guests, and, before Raphael's smiling eyes, smeared a generous layer over slices of sweet challah.

***

In the middle of February, under the threat of an armed German invasion, the Austrian government accepted Hitler's ultimatum, along with a general pardon for all Nazi prisoners and the appointment of Arthur Seyss-Inquart, the leader of Austrian Nazis, as Minister of Interior and head of police and security. On 20 February, encouraged by Berlin, dozens of protests and Nazi riots broke out all over Austria. The Austrian flag was taken off the pole at the Graz city square, and replaced with the German swastika. Political and financial chaos caused hysteria on the streets. The Führer responded to the chancellor's desperate declaration of a referendum to be held on 13 March by gathering the German army at the Austrian border. Schuschnigg surrendered. In an emotional message to his people, he announced that the referendum had been canceled and that to prevent a bloodbath he had decided to resign. His final request to his army was for it to retreat quietly, avoiding any conflict. Arthur Seyss-Inquart was appointed the new chancellor. On 12 March 1938, welcomed by an enormous, cheering Austrian crowd, the German army marched into Austria. The next day, the *Anschluss* Law was passed, declaring Austria's end and its annexation to Germany as an integral part of the Reich. A month later, Hitler held a referendum in Austria. Over ninety-nine percent of voters voted 'yes,' and the Anschluss was complete. Austria was absorbed by Germany without the latter firing a single shot.

19

A few decades ago, already a teenager, I was at my Aunt Ruth's apartment in Tel Aviv when she placed before me a small wooden box containing letters she had received in London from her family during the years before the war. On the lid of the box, in the bottom left-hand corner, Ruth had written in English in an ornate handwriting, "Letters from Home."

The letters, written mostly on the Steiners' official stationery, were piled in the box by ascending dates. I remember my heart thumping wildly. I wanted to read all of them at once, but, unfortunately, they were written in German, and although my ears could understand the language that had rocked me to sleep and its sounds remained inside of me, I had never learned to read or write it. I refrained from asking Ruth for help. I did not want to hurt her by forcing her to face her loved ones' past again. I waited, impatiently, for Davidi's next break from school.

He arrived home from Berlin in June.

One morning, when no one but the two of us was home, I sat him beside me on the sofa and asked him to read the letters aloud without skipping a single letter, word, or sentence. We read them with awe. From the earlier letters rose into view the events of the lives of the Steiners and Rosenthals after Ruth and Jonah had left Vienna in the summer of 1936. We marveled at Oma Ilse's writing talent and at Uriel's sobriety; ached at great-grandma Rebecca's death and the deterioration in the health of great-grandpa Josef and Raphael; and were embarrassed by Opa Michael and Gabriel's complacence but also humbled by our grandpa's suffering as he began to realize his mistake. A few of the letters were sent immediately after the German invasion of Vienna. Their stamps were printed with the Third Reich emblem, and their wording was official and brief. But the letters that were most difficult to read were the ones recounting the painful sobering that followed Austria's annexation to Nazi Germany. Those were smuggled out of the country, often finding their way to Ruth and Jonah months later.

Among these was Uriel's letter, in which he described with revulsion the fickle nature of Austrians during that time, as well as the pain that plagued him and his friends the night of the Nazi invasion, as they huddled around the radio in Sebastian's apartment and were horrified to hear that the German military had entered Salzburg and Luftwaffe planes were circling Vienna. "We weren't surprised," wrote Uriel, "but we were in pain." We knew what this meant for all of us."

In her letter, Naomi described how the following day she and Uriel went out into the streets and were carried away with the excited crowd toward the Heldenplatz, the Heroes Plaza—in which the *Anschluss* had been announced—where they witnessed the Austrians' enthusiastic welcome of Nazi Germans. "Following the orders of the new Nazi chancellor," Uriel wrote, "Austrian police officers searched the apartments in buildings overlooking the streets through which Hitler's victory march passed, lest anyone attempt to assassinate the man." Disgusted, he described how anti-Semitism, which had merely been bubbling beneath the surface until that point, now burst forth like burning lava the day after the German invasion, accompanied with shameful violence toward Jews.

"Ruth, do you remember," Naomi asked, "our neighbor, Yehuda Berger? He was Yaakov the butcher's youngest son, just a little boy when you left. Recently, as he was walking down the street, he ran into a boy his age he knew from school. The boy, wearing a *Hitlerjugend* uniform, called Yehuda a 'dirty Jewish pig' and ordered him to get off the sidewalk and walk on the road instead. Yehuda refused, even hitting the boy. The next day, five thugs cornered him on the street and beat him until he nearly died."

In a detailed, bloodcurdling depiction, Uriel reported how the day after the Anschluss was announced, the Metropole Hotel in Vienna was confiscated from its Jewish owners and converted into Gestapo headquarters with political and police authority, which immediately launched an organized pillage of Jewish homes, confiscating artwork, rugs, furniture, and other valuable possessions. "Jonah, Ruth," wrote Uriel, "you cannot imagine what is going on. Father's banker, Gustav Breuer, was detained two weeks ago and imprisoned for days until he finally signed a declaration in which he gave up all his belongings. Everyone we know is being fired from their jobs. The offices of the Vienna Jewish Community have been closed and their managers arrested, and all Jewish committee activity in Vienna and around it has been outlawed..."

Naomi described painfully how the two Berman sisters were sent out to the street, forced to kneel and use toothbrushes to scrub off anti-Semitic graffiti from the sidewalks, and how afterwards her parents instructed her to reduce her outings to the necessary minimum. In another letter, she reported how Opa Michael broke down after being forced to accompany a group of venerable guests of the university to an exhibition that concentrated on the figure of the eternal wandering Jew and blamed him for spreading substandard culture all over Europe. At the sight of the exhibits saturated in hatred, Michael felt ill and had to leave. Two weeks later, he received a letter of dismissal at his home. Thus, twenty-three years of work as a professor at the University of Vienna came to an end.

Opa Michael's letter, the only one he wrote after the Nazi invasion, was awash in guilt and regret. He apologized for being too blind to see the imminent future, for his poor judgment, and for having ignored Ilse and Uriel's pleas to extricate his family from Austria before it was too late. "Nazi rule in Austria," he wrote, "and especially in Vienna, is exceptionally cruel. Jewish children have been expelled from most schools in town, synagogues have been defiled, and whole families, sent out to the streets to beg, have been removed from their homes. Many Jews are now trying to leave Austria, and the new government is encouraging this..."

Davidi paused momentarily in his reading, as his lips formed a gloomy smile. "Look what Opa wrote here," he said. "He wrote that Jewish immigration has been transferred to the care of an S.S. officer named Adolf Eichmann..."

A tremor passed through our bodies. I whispered that Opa Michael could not have known at the time what a monster Eichmann was. Who could ever have predicted it then?

Later in the letter, Opa Michael explained how Vienna, where visas and exit permits were demanded night and day, had become an immigration center for Jews from all over Austria. He described the long lines of Jews extending in front of the municipal offices and police stations, exposed to terror, torture, and humiliation from party troops and the *Hitlerjugend*. "Those who received exit permits," he wrote, "were forced to give up a substantial part of their possessions and leave Austria destitute..."

"Then why didn't they get up and leave?" I asked, furious.

Davidi shrugged. "Opa writes here that he's doubtful there's a country that would accept a young man as sick as Raphael, and that even if he found one, he feared he and Oma wouldn't be able to fund his expensive treatment if they left Austria without their possessions." He lowered his eyes and read on from Michael's letter. "I'm having an especially difficult time with Ilse," he wrote. "Lately, she's been hoarding so much anger inside her, often even turning her back on me... Oh, Ruth, Jonah, you can't imagine how painfully sobering this is. At any rate, we must wait and try to leave Austria in an orderly fashion. The only logical option right now is Palestine. We're trying to procure certificates but encountering plenty of challenges…"

Davidi's voice grew hoarse the more he read. Every now and then he stopped to take a breath. Toward the end of the letter he suddenly fell quiet; only his eyes continued to run over the page.

I glanced at him, surprised.

"What does it say, Davidi?"

He said nothing.

"Davidi?"

He jumped to his feet. "It says that in addition to all the other difficulties, my mother was crying constantly and insisting, 'irrationally,' according to Opa Michael, on going to Germany to visit her parents whom she hadn't seen in a very long time. My father gave in to her pleas, and it was only thanks to Opa and Oma's persistence that my parents agreed to go to Berlin for a brief visit without taking me with them…"

"And that's it? Is that the end of the letter?"

"Not really…"

"Not really?"

"You want me to read it word for word?"

"Letter for letter!"

"As you wish." Davidi sat up and took a deep breath. "'Our dearest Ruth and Jonah,' Opa wrote at the bottom of the page, 'I'm ending this long and difficult letter with a special, delicate request. We are searching for a way to at least get Davidi out of here. We thought you might agree to take him in for the time being, until his parents will be able to follow in his footsteps.'

"The end of the era of innocence," Davidi sighed. He kneeled at my feet, rested his head on my knees, and let his tears flow as my fingers played with his abundant hair and gently caressed his forehead and cheeks.

***

In July 1938, initiated by American President Franklin D. Roosevelt and with the attendance of thirty-two countries and twenty-four voluntary organizations, the Évian Conference took place in France to discuss the question of forced immigration of Jews from Reich territories. The decisions of the conference offered no salvation for the Jews of Austria, since no country in the West, save for the Dominican Republic, was willing to change its immigration laws and open its gates to them.

"The whole world is crying crocodile tears for the Jews of Germany," noted Hitler, "but isn't really willing to do anything for their sake."

By the end of that month, Jewish street names all over the Reich had been changed.

At the end of September, in Munich, France and Britain gave in to Germany's demand to annex the industrialized and fortified region of Sudetenland in Czechoslovakia to the Reich. At the end of the Munich Summit, Hitler announced that he had no further territorial demands. The British Prime Minister, Arthur Neville Chamberlain, with a sigh of relief, announced, "I have returned from Germany with peace for our time," but in the German Ministry of Foreign Affairs' documents, it was emphasized that "in 1938, the Jews lost their position of power in Vienna and Prague."

20

A month after Nioka's arrangement came into effect, I sat with my mother in our little attic room at Madame Butterfly's. Detached from the world, in slow and monotonous movements, Mother was embroidering flowers onto delicate handkerchiefs and scarves entrusted to her by Nioka. While making sure to hide the black thread she had chosen in recent days under one of the sofas, I picked the colors. Although I had hardly seen any real flowers at that time in my life, I recalled the yellow chrysanthemums that were scattered along the path leading to the small apartment the peasant used to rent for us and the colorful flowers of the tapestry that hung in Nioka's little studio. I was afraid Nioka would not approve of my mother's work and that our recent arrangement would be cut short, putting an end to her precious visits each Tuesday. That is why, when Mother asked in a weak voice why I did not like her embroidery, I told her I thought black flowers were sad, frightening, and ugly.

That month, March 1945, the Third Reich was beginning its death throes. The nervous tenseness that had been the lot of the madam's girls and clients since the beginning of the year made way to true hysteria. Nobody knew what was going to happen, and bursts of rage, yelling, even physical blows, became a common sight at the brothel. Around the time when my mother finished with her embroidering in preparation for Nioka's visit the following day, we heard a loud noise on the main floor.

Mother hurried out of the room, and despite Nioka's warnings and pleas for me to stay out of trouble, I hurried in her footsteps. My mother did not seem to mind at all. At the center of the large, pink parlor, stood a man of average height, broad-shouldered and stout, his head shaved and his hairy belly peeking from under his black, sweaty shirt. He raised a hand in salute as he loudly screamed in a sharp, harsh voice, "Heil Hitler!" and "Sieg Heil!" before breaking into a revolting, drunken laugh, coughing and spitting a green substance onto the floor, as if he himself despised the idea he had just delivered. When he raised a beer bottle over his head, I ran, alarmed, to my mother, and when he hurled the bottle against the large mirror, its contents spraying at the sound of shattering glass, everyone else panicked. One of the girls, wounded by glass shards, was bleeding in her face. Another shrieked she had glass in her eye. Madame Butterfly turned pale and almost fainted, and the other girls, shrieking in horror, ran around the room.

But Mother screamed louder than anyone else.

Only as an adult did I realize what I could not understand then. Ever since that horrible night when windows were shattered all over the Reich, Mother could not bear the sound of breaking glass. A champagne flute cracking and falling to the floor was enough to make her horridly ill.

But that day, that moment, she only closed her eyes, pushed her fists against her ears, and fell to her knees, shivering, pale, and cold as ice. Moments later, when I grabbed her shoulders and tried to embrace her quivering body, she collapsed, burying my small body under hers. As my breath caught in my throat, disorienting me, my mother's senses blurred until finally she lost consciousness.

***

On 7 November 1938, the young German-born Jewish refugee Herschel Grynszpan, who was living in Paris at the time, bought a gun at a local shop called "The Sharp Blade," left a hastily written note at his uncle's home, and headed for the German Embassy. When he arrived, he shot a junior diplomat, Ernst vom Rath, critically wounding him, in protest against the expulsion of his parents, along with twelve thousand other Jews of Polish citizenship, in cattle cars from Germany to Poland, where they were refused entry by the Polish government.

"My heart bleeds," he wrote in his note to his parents, "when I hear of your tragedy and that of the twelve-thousand Jews. I must protest so that the whole world hears and recoils against anti-Semitic persecution all over Nazi Germany."

Three days later, my mother's grandfather, Josef Rosenthal, made the biggest mistake of his life. He woke up earlier than usual, got dressed, put on a jacket, wrapped a warm woolen scarf around his neck, placed his brown hat atop his head, and stepped out silently for some fresh air. Ever since his wife had died and his country had been annexed to Germany, he did his best to leave the house before sunrise, taking shelter in the darkness of the early morning hours, before the street came to life and the demons emerged from their lairs. That day, he stopped for a short visit at the apartment of Dr. Ernst Salzburg, a sick and childless old friend, who lived just a few blocks away from Michael and Ilse, for a chat about the dangers of their times and the better days they both had known, now gone forever. He must not have heard about the horrors that had taken place all over Germany the previous night, the night between November 9th and 10th and were spreading swiftly through the rest of the Reich like wildfire through a field of thorns.

At the end of his visit, Josef bid farewell to his friend and went back out into the street. Ernst dragged himself over to the window. The days were hard, the loneliness painful and fear all-encompassing. In his heart, he thanked Josef, his old friend, for not having forgotten him during these frightful times, and for making sure to visit him on occasion, even bringing along a bit of food to revive his spirits. Ernst drew open the curtain, glanced down onto the street, and his eyes went dark. Leaning against a streetlamp, Josef was only steps away from Ernst's building, and before him stood three thugs: one tall and lanky, wearing a brown Sturmabteilung shirt, the second broad-shouldered and with a shaved head, and the third, short-limbed and stocky. The tall one ordered Josef to get off the sidewalk and kneel before him in the road, and the bald one pushed him to the ground. At the sound of Josef's fall, the short one broke into loud, jarring laughter. Ernst let go of the curtain and recoiled. His body was covered with cold sweat, and his ailing legs buckled, but for the moment he kept his composure. Determined, leaning against a cane and supporting himself against furniture and doorframes, he dragged himself to the door and into the narrow stairwell, where he crawled one floor up.

Clara anxiously opened the door to the sound of his knock and peeked out through a narrow opening. "They're burning down Jewish owned shops, Dr. Salzburg," she said, her voice shaking. "Yaakov went out early today to shelf new stock and just came home in shock!"

Ernst pushed the door open with his free hand and made his way inside. "Thugs are threatening my friend Josef right outside the building," he said, panting with terror. "Where is Yaakov? He must hurry over to Ilse Steiner's house and call her husband and sons!"

Yaakov did not waste any time. Michael and Ilse were old friends of the family. Despite Clara's pleas, he grabbed his coat, which was still drenched with sweat, and disappeared down the stairs.

At that time, the Steiners, fretting over Josef's absence, were huddled together at home. Uriel came home before dawn from his group's meeting, delivering terrible news.

"They're burning down synagogues, Mother." He drew in an angry breath. "They're setting Jewish homes and shops on fire. There are rumors of men, women, and children who were shot as they fled the flames."

"What are we going to do if they reach us?" Naomi mumbled.

Ilse, her eyes alight, cried, "And where is my father? Where has he gone to?"

At that very moment, knocks were heard at the door. Ilse grabbed Naomi and pushed her back, blocking her with her own body. Uriel glanced through the keyhole and then opened the door a crack. Yaakov walked inside, pale and breathless, after having run through backyards behind the streets' buildings. Between one strained breath and the next, he delivered the news of the thugs that were attacking Grandpa Josef at that very moment. Ilse let out a shriek, and Raphael emerged from his bedroom, startled. Uriel was the first to run out. Gabriel and Michael quickly followed him, watching the figure from afar gain distance on them until it disappeared out of sight at the corner.

By the time the two of them reached the spot, there was no sign of the thugs. Grandpa Josef was hunched at the edge of the sidewalk, moaning, wide-eyed and breathing heavily, and Uriel lay at his feet, in a stupor, his head badly bruised, and his belly torn open and bleeding. Passersby, who were already taking to the street at this early hour, turned their heads and hurried away. Only Dr. Salzburg, after succeeding in dragging himself outside, approached them, as he haltingly said in a shaky voice that Uriel, as heroic as Samson, had pounced on the three thugs fearlessly, drawn them away from his grandfather, and within moments had managed to injure them in a fist fight. He had knocked the tall one to the ground and kicked him in the stomach, strangled the shaved headed until he had almost passed out, and then...then the stocky one had pulled out a knife and shoved it into Uriel's stomach. When they saw him collapse to the ground, the tall and stocky thugs had grabbed their shaved headed friend and vanished instantly.

Gabriel hurried to Uriel's side, picked him up, and with unnatural strength carried him back to their parents' apartment, a few blocks away. By the time he placed him gently down on the rug in the parlor, he was horrified to discover his brother had died in his arms. Michael arrived a few minutes later, with Grandpa Josef leaning against him. When he entered through the building's front gate to climb the stairs, he ran into Vera, who was rushing, panic-stricken, down the stairs, Davidi in her arms. With a heavy heart, he entered the apartment, and in a fraction of a second, he caught sight of Gabriel grabbing his head in his hands and Ilse and Naomi, stupefied, wailing and desperately shaking Uriel's limp arms.

When he came closer, the father was stunned by the gaping, empty eyes of his son, by the vision of his lifeless body and the deathly white of his face.

21

I was almost ten years old. I remember the hard rain that fell that autumn November day almost without pause. My teacher, Hannah, explained that this was the first rain of the season and was called *Hayoreh*. I was captivated by the sound of the Hebrew word, rolling it up and down my tongue, and committing it to memory.

That was also the day I met my first Israeli friend, Nurit. Nurit Hadari's family lived in the building next door to the one where we lived with Ruth and Jonah after migrating to Israel in the early 1950s, but until that day we had each walked home from school by ourselves, sneaking peeks, hoping the other would not notice. I was too shy to address her because of my broken Hebrew, and Nurit, a born *sabra*, had a thorny attitude about new immigrants like myself. But that day she took pity on me, as I had forgotten to take a coat and umbrella on leaving home that morning, and, to my surprise, offered me to join her under her red umbrella.

I did.

The two of us, squealing joyously whenever our boots sank into the muddy water, walked down the puddle-dotted road and finally arrived at our respective homes drenched from the waist down but head-over-heels happy. We forced ourselves to say goodbye at the entrance to her building, and I gleefully climbed up to the fourth floor of the building next door and unlocked the door with the key Ruth had tied around my neck.

A *yahrzeit* candle was burning on the tall, dark dresser in the living room. I found Ruth and Mother at the small kitchen table and asked about the candle. The answer came only after first being rebuked for having left my coat and umbrella at home that morning, and only after I changed into dry clothes.

It was the first time I had heard the full story of my uncle Uriel. Ruth told it, and she and my mother both patiently answered all my questions. When they reached the part in which tall, robust, and handsome Uriel was lying lifelessly on the floor of their parents' house, they both wept. When Mother said in a choked voice that the next day, as she joined her father to make burial arrangements, she was chilled to witness anti-Jewish invective on the walls and shattered glass in the streets, I understood for the first time why she had reacted the way she had years earlier at Madame Butterfly's, on the day the mirror was shattered.

Trying to hide a rebellious tear that had made its way down my cheek, I lowered my head and listened as Aunt Ruth summed up the outcome of that day's events.

"That horrifying night will be remembered in history books as the *Kristallnacht*, the Night of Broken Glass, due to the shards of glass scattered over the streets from the windows of synagogues and Jewish homes and businesses that were shattered." She sighed. "What was presented in world news the following day as the spontaneous rioting of Nazi thugs in reaction to the news of the assassination in Paris turned out later to have been a Gestapo plan for an organized anti-Semitic pogrom. We were living in London at the time, but there wasn't a single article about that night I didn't read: in *The Daily Telegraph*, *The Observer*, *The London Times*... I clipped and saved them all. Hundreds of Jewish-owned shops were broken into and looted by an angry mob. The beautiful synagogues of Leopoldstrasse, Tempelgasse, Große, and Schiffgasse burned like old wooden huts. Many Jews were murdered and injured, and many others were arrested according to a pre-ordained list and sent to concentration camps." Ruth fell silent, and as often happened when the Steiner sisters lost themselves in tales of the past, my mother shook herself as if reaching into the depths of her memory for some old recollection. "Our neighbor, Herbert... You remember him, Ruth? Helga's husband? He was caught and sent to Dachau after his store in the *Fleischmarkt*, the meat market, was pillaged and vandalized... And the department store, owned by Father's friend, Felix Morgenstern? The goods were tossed out the windows, and the mob loaded them onto carts and took them away..."

My aunt drew her breath in deeply before continuing. "The abuse and murder went on all night and the following day without any interruption and were only halted through an explicit order from above. You wouldn't believe, Helena, what happened a few days later." Her hands closed into fists. "A penalty of a billion marks was placed on the Jewish community for repairing the damages!"

I remember feeling a pang of sorrow in my stomach when she said this, and my face flushed with anger. I drew close to my silent mother and thanked her in my heart for letting me hold her hand.

"That horrid night our family was ruined," Ruth's voice was shaking. "Two days after Uriel was murdered, great-grandpa Josef ended his life. He swallowed an entire bottle of pills and died. Imagine what Oma Ilse must have felt, finding her father lifeless in his bed, lying on his back and wearing the blue yarmulke great-grandma Rebecca had made him... In his brief, carefully written note, he explained that he could no longer live with the humiliation and, especially, with the awful feeling that he had brought on his beloved grandson's death. He wrote that he loved us all very much and was thereby freeing our parents from worrying about him."

Mother came to life again and contributed some of her own memories to complete the picture. "Martha left us shortly thereafter," she whispered, "apologizing and tearful, her eyes puffy and her head hanging low. Her family demanded that she hurry up and leave 'that cursed place' and save herself." Mother's eyes filled with tears. "You should have seen Oma Ilse that day. Proud, with her back upright on the day of parting. 'Thank you for your rare loyalty, Martha,' she said in a cold, metallic voice. 'Go in peace, and please, spare us your tears. We each live and die by our own fate.'

***

The yahrzeit candle burned for twenty-four hours. I spent hours standing by its side, staring at the flame, forgetting all about the rain, Nurit Hadari, and her red umbrella. A single image floated in my mind's eye and never let go—that of the shattered mirror, its glass fragments scattered over the floor of Madame Butterfly's, my mother screaming, covering her ears with her hands, closing her eyes, falling to her knees, and shaking like a leaf, her face pale. Once again, I felt her weight as she fell, her senses faint, over my small body. I remembered how scared I was that she might have died when her screaming stopped, she lost consciousness, and her body froze on top of mine.

22

On a Thursday in late November, at twilight, about two weeks after Josef Rosenthal and Uriel Steiner were buried in haste side by side in Vienna's central cemetery, near the graves of other murdered Jews, a light knock was heard at the door.

Opa Michael and Oma Ilse stood beside Naomi as she approached the door on tiptoes to glance through the keyhole. She cried with surprise and opened the door halfway.

Silently, Rachel Weiss slipped in. Her pale face, which had grown wan since that meeting at Sebastian and Leah's, and her raven black hair that flowed in an unkempt fashion over her shoulders detracted nothing away from her beauty. The same rows of pearly white teeth that had remained in Naomi's memory were bared again as she tried to smile, introducing herself to her dead beloved's parents.

Ilse and Michael froze in place. They had heard of Rachel's striking beauty from Naomi. Even Uriel, in the weeks prior to his death, was willing to tell his parents a bit about her identity, hinting that they should not pry too much. But most of the ingredients had been offered, surprisingly, by Raphael. Shortly after the funeral, which Rachel did not attend, Raphael broke his prolonged silence as his deceased brother's confidant and revealed to his astounded family the great love story of Uriel and Rachel in full, from preface to epilogue. From him, they learned about the wild, stormy affair their son had carried on with the young woman for the past three years under their very noses. It began with her being engaged to another, continued with the secret activity of their organization and Rachel's confidential trips across the border and even overseas, and ended with Uriel's death during one of his lover's forced absences. At this discovery, Ilse had wrung her hands nervously and shook her head incredulously, and Michael, moved by the power of this late revelation, whispered to Naomi that it was hard to believe such a saga had been evolving secretly right in front of them.

Now Ilse and Michael stood flustered, emotionally moved, yet silent before Rachel. This was not the way they'd imagined meeting their son's lover. At this moment, they did not care to linger over her past, nor were they bothered by whether she was Jewish. They wanted to hear only about their son, about his deep and sustained love for this beautiful stranger, who had been a part of his life they were not familiar with. Rachel rolled back the stone of memory and recounted, revealed and described, apologized and embraced, reminisced and wept. Finally, her voice wavering, she told them how she had heard the difficult news of Uriel's death from afar, how, on returning to Vienna, she had hastened to the cemetery and searched for his grave. How, wrapped in Uriel's coat, which he had forgotten in her room, she had fallen over the fresh mound of dirt, as close to her beloved as she could, and spent the rest of the night there, trying to draw from her memory the feel of his body's heat for the last time, and took her leave.

***

My mother told me all this for the first time when I was twelve, in her mother tongue, and since she was the only one to convey this information to me, I cannot be certain of its accuracy. These days, as a writer with a strong grasp of the intricacies of language, I can only say this: there could have been no better narrator than my mother,

Naomi, for such a love story. The affair between Uriel and Rachel, as it was reflected in Raphael's descriptions and in the words of Rachel herself, had ignited young Naomi's imagination, sharing equal standing with the great Hollywood love stories she had watched with her friends at the Vienna movie theaters back in those long-gone happy days. When she outlined the story of their love, her voice grew sweeter, and her words were as delicate as pearls.

Her depiction was so beautiful that as an adult I put it all in writing, transforming the tale into my first novel, *Love in the Shadow of the Moon*. I made sure to insert whole monologues about Uriel and Rachel's love exactly as Naomi had told them to me in her lovely language. She would periodically bring up the story, but each time she told it as if for the first time. She felt the need to nurse me with it, and I felt the need to receive it from her from time to time, if only as an excuse to enjoy a few moments of grace in her presence. On one such occasion, she admitted to me that the visit led her to view Rachel in a different light. The woman's deep love for Uriel softened my mother, erasing the jealousy she had felt that winter evening at Sebastian and Leah's apartment, and the grief they shared even brought them closer together as if they were sisters.

To this day, whenever I flip through *Love in the Shadow of the Moon*, I longingly recall how Mother's dulled eyes would become animated, her pink lips full of movement, as she depicted the wondrous love of Uriel and Rachel, so that it, at least, would live on. And once again I can taste that yearning, still painful, for my mother's rare smile and her even rarer embrace.

***

Later that evening, Rachel asked that Vera and Gabriel be summoned to my grandparents' home. Her request was fulfilled without any questions.

"Uriel had devised a rescue plan for you," she said unequivocally. "I was involved. The conditions, however, have changed. There is another opportunity. If it weren't for that, I might have postponed my visit. It isn't easier for me than it is for you. I imagine you have many questions, but now is not the time for talk. Now we must act. This mission is my beloved's unwritten will and is therefore of utmost importance to me."

"Will?" Oma Ilse's hands began to tremble uncontrollably.

Rachel paused, swallowing. She took a step in Ilse's direction and gently took her hand. "Uriel left instructions for me and some of the other members, in case—"

"In case of what?" Ilse cried.

"In case he found himself in harm's way," Rachel lowered her voice. "I don't know why, but he always had the feeling something bad was going to happen to him, that he wouldn't survive this decade. A kind of prophecy. That's why he was always doing things, inspiring others toward action, and loving me as if any moment could be his last."

Her words remained hanging in midair without a hook to hold onto. An oppressive silence filled the room. Choosing her words carefully, Rachel continued quietly. Her gaze turned now to Vera and Gabriel.

"New circumstances have arisen with new possibilities. Different Jewish organizations in Britain have recently begun putting pressure on the British government. The demand made by the heads of the Jewish Agency and the leaders of the Jewish settlement in the Land of Israel to permit the immediate entry of tens of thousands of Jewish refugees from the Reich territories is getting increasing coverage in Britain, greatly influencing public opinion. The British Colonial Office has been consistently refusing the demand and rolling the hot potato over to the Ministries of Interior and Foreign Affairs. The British government is finding itself torn between international pressure to open the gates of Palestine to Jewish refugees, especially after the events of Kristallnacht, and its clear tendency to please the Arabs, who, of course, vehemently object to the notion. It is searching for an elegant compromise. But now it has no choice. It must take a public stand on this burning issue. From their viewpoint, opening the gates of Britain itself to these refugees is the lesser of two evils..."

Naomi shifted uncomfortably in her seat. On the one hand, she was captivated by Rachel's confident flow of words and, on the other, concerned and wondering where this speech was leading.

"But there is a problem," Rachel continued, and Naomi could swear her voice faltered. "Although Britain will most likely open its gates to Jews, it is already clear they would prefer to take in children without parents... Children are adaptable; they more easily absorb new language and customs, and most importantly—they do not pose competition to the work force during this time of financial slump..."

The air, already stifling with illness and medicine, with the dark atmosphere of mourning, with the concerns for daily survival, and with an icy fear of the hatred lurking on the streets, was now also filled with a trembling fear of the unknown.

Gabriel placed his long fingers on the back of Vera's neck as she stood, pale and still as a wax doll. "What are you telling us, Rachel?" he asked. "In God's name, what are you getting at?"

She responded right away. "I'm involved with a new organization called 'The Movement for the Care of Children from Germany,' which, as we speak, is working to allow the immigration of a large number of refugee children, including both Jews and non-Aryan Christians, from the Reich to Britain."

"But what has any of this got to do with us?" Gabriel insisted.

Suddenly they all froze at the sound of a sharp command from the corner of the room. "Silence!"

They all turned, surprised, toward Opa Michael.

Michael was planted in place, sweat glistening on his forehead, his hands in fists, but a spark of hope lighting his extinguished eyes.

"Stop putting wool over your eyes, Gabriel! We can't bury our heads in the sand any longer, holding onto our foolish belief that this evil will pass us by. This time, the evil is directed right at us. It has already taken the lives of our dear ones and might at any moment strike us mercilessly again. God help us! If there's a way to act now, perhaps at the last minute, and at least save the child, let's act and quickly!"

Oma Ilse rose to her feet, and, ignoring Gabriel's sobs, turned directly to Rachel. "Speak, my daughter."

Rachel spoke quickly. "A few days ago, the British government officially announced its readiness to provide entry permits to refugee children ages seventeen or younger and its intention to assist with their expedited bureaucratic processing, by providing them with temporary residency status. This way, these children can stay in Britain, vouched for by Jewish and other volunteer organizations for an unlimited time, during which the younger ones will receive education and the older ones, professional training. Eventually, when the evil has passed, they can return to their home countries, to their parents." She paused and moved her eyes from Ilse to the others. "I'm able to add Davidi to one of these transports," she whispered. "I promised Uriel—"

"That's impossible," Vera mumbled, her tightening embrace waking the child and causing him to bawl. "I couldn't bear it, I couldn't—"

"It would be easier in your case," Rachel continued, her eyes skipping over the parents and wandering toward Ilse and Michael, who were standing together now like a concrete wall. "You would have to come up with a considerable amount of money to cover costs, but unlike other children, who must be put up in hostels in hopes that they can later be transferred to foster homes in London or throughout England, you have Ruth and Jonah. They would have to formally request to receive the boy into their care, but this would make acquiring immigration certificates for him and adding him to one of the first transports much easier."

***

And that is how my beloved Davidi, shelter of my stormy soul, was saved from an awful fate. I have turned this rescue story over in my head many times. It would never have occurred without Uriel and Rachel—he, murdered in the streets of Vienna, and she, disappearing after the war. Its first part was told to me, as I've mentioned, by my mother, and the rest was conveyed to me by Ruth's generous descriptions, and even by Davidi himself, but only after he was old enough to process the fragmented images of his early life into one continuous film strip, "one that stuck," as he put it.

Davidi married three beautiful, talented women and parted from them five times. Three of these marriages ended in divorce. Before, after, and—truth be told—even during, he was always surrounded by intellectual women whom he found, to use his own words, "no less exciting" than his performances as a renowned pianist in the concert halls of Europe. And as skilled as he was at playing the keys of his grand piano at all hours of the day and night, accompanied by the finest orchestras of the continent, he was no less accomplished in playing the music of desire.

Davidi, refusing to have any children, stood stubbornly before the tears of the women he married and loved, and because he loved them, he released them to bear the children of other men. I was the only one to whom he confessed, during the countless hours we spent together, his fear of fatherhood and of the bond of blood, a fear planted within him the day, not yet five years old, he separated forever from his parents at their Vienna home and went out, scared and confused, into his new life.

23

"It was windy that day too, but no rain." Our eyes fixed on the treetop that swayed to the sighing of the wind, Davidi and I were reclining on the Yarkon Park lawn in Tel Aviv.

When?" I asked, sliding my finger down his arm. I was grateful to have him back in our lives, if only for a brief visit, upon completion of his second year as a music student at the Stern Conservatory in Berlin.

"Oh, Helena." Smoothing back his chestnut hair, Davidi stood up all at once and began heading west, crushing the green grass that grew wild on the banks of the river with the soles of his shoes.

Trying to catch up with my long-legged cousin, I rushed after him. From a young age, I had been familiar with his habit of arranging his thoughts while walking. He was twenty-three and tall, and I was sixteen and reached his chest. I had waited so eagerly for him to return to unfold for him all my new concerns and enjoy his unique, non-judgmental attentiveness to my wrongdoings, especially since, when his musical ears heard them, they seemed to lose their sting and become something to be played, albeit melancholily, but pleasing even to me. Davidi was the one who taught me that things and people did not need to be perfect, but what mattered was harmony within a person's soul, between their emotions and actions, their thoughts and deeds, between their surroundings and their sense of self. I had striven for this harmony my entire life, even when things were terribly hard. But from time to time, and sometimes more often than that, I desperately needed his musical ear, leaning toward me, and his unique ability to conduct the string and percussion orchestra within me to aid me in reaching the necessary balance.

But this time, on the southern bank of the stream, Davidi paid me no mind. Walking briskly, each of his steps forcing me to take two of my own, he told me about an exciting encounter he had had in Berlin with a former violinist from the Vienna Philharmonic, who had known Vera and Gabriel personally. Following that encounter, Davidi had dared travel for the first time to Austria where he searched Vienna and found his parents' apartment and, across the street, Ilse and Michael's place, as well. Later, he was surprised to find his mother's name in the Philharmonic archives and was moved to discover an article full of praise for his father at the Vienna Opera House.

I understood. Davidi had become haunted by his past. I pushed away my urgent stories for another day and allowed him to wander in the halted scenery of his childhood. When he reached his description of the day of parting and his green eyes filled with tears, I imagined them collecting into the water of the stream, flowing westward, toward the Mediterranean Sea. Sitting him down and lacing my fingers into his, I begged him not to stop.

There, on the banks of the Yarkon River, I asked him to tell me the entire story, from the very beginning.

***

"And they kept telling me how lucky I was." Davidi burst into laughter, which ended with a nervous toss of a pebble into the stream. The pebble bounced a few times across the greenish water, until it finally vanished.

I quickly collected a few more pebbles and handed them to him, hoping he would not get up again and start walking about while talking as usual. A glimmering moisture lightened the color of his eyes, which continued to weep tears of pain into the stream that led to the sea, and I was sorry that our home country of Austria did not border the Mediterranean, so it could burn with the salt of his tears.

"I had someone to claim me," he said in an emotional tone that surprised me. "Someone to raise me and give me love. I can imagine that compared to some other children I was truly lucky."

"You mean, compared to other children who died?" I asked, confused.

"And other children who survived," he said, biting his lips.

We were silent for a moment. Davidi butted the riverbank dirt with his shoes, then focused his eyes on an invisible point at the center of the stream and let fly three more pebbles, carefully following their trajectory until they disappeared into the water.

"They say children don't remember much about their early childhood, that those experiences sink into our subconscious. But you, for example, remember things from when you were very young, don't you, Helena?"

"Of course," I said.

"Well, so do I. I remember plenty," Davidi whispered back. "I remember *Mamushka*—that's what I called my mother—the warmth of her body, the long fair hair I liked to rub between my fingers and her divine cello playing. Helena, whenever I go to a concert, I look for her by the cello, tilting her head slightly to the right, her braid resting on her shoulder, her eyes closed. I don't remember my father's features as clearly. Most of what I remember comes from Jonah's photographs. Odd, but what I remember best are his fingers. Gabriel taught me to recognize notes and play the piano as early as age three. We played scales and a few simple children's tunes together. That's why I remember his fingers so well. I only used one finger to tap the keys, but he used all of them, and when he spread them, he covered ten keys between thumb and pinky. I remember trying to mimic him, and he laughed loudly, and promised me that when I grew up my fingers would be just as long as his, and then I, like him, would be able to cover more than one full octave with my palm… Do you remember, Helena, how Ruth used to look at my hands and claim again and again that I'd inherited my father's finger structure— long and straight, with only the pinky slightly crooked?"

"I remember," I nodded.

"Well, it was only toward my first year at the conservatory that I managed to stretch my fingers over ten keys for the first time. It was a special feeling, a magical one, as if my father's promise had finally been delivered."

Davidi stretched out his fingers, and for one silly moment my forefinger and middle finger walked like little legs across his hand, a distance of thirty steps.

"Your mother devoted a lot of her time to me," he continued to leaf through his memory, igniting an envy inside of me. "She was forbidden to leave the house most hours of the day. She was young and so beautiful. At the prime of her youth she was locked inside like a butterfly in a cage. Each time I visited Oma and Opa, she snatched me into her room, played dress-up with me, piqued my imagination with her descriptive stories, and sang to me in her lovely voice."

My throat went dry. I wanted to hear more and more about Naomi, the Naomi of the past, the one "before," but Davidi was immersed in a different stream of memory. I let him.

Davidi told me then for the first time about the day he separated from his parents and the days that followed. As he spoke, he continued to sullenly toss pebbles into the water, one by one. The moment they hit the water with a small splash, the water danced circles around them.

That day, he told me about Elika, the daughter of family friends, who was seven years old at the time, with whom he was partnered on the train platform.

"I remember her well. We met at my parents' home. *Mamushka* agreed to send me away only if the two of us were on the same transport. She told me Elika was a very nice little girl who would be like a sister to me until I reached my aunt and uncle's house. I also remember being told that my parents wouldn't be able to take me to the train station. It was generally still allowed at that point, in the first transports. Afterward, it was decided that the partings would take place at an earlier time in order to spare everyone the difficult scenes on the platform. But in our case, since my father was so fragile and my mother so sensitive, we said goodbye at home. It's hard to talk about, Helena... It was so awful... I didn't completely understand what was going on, and the memory has grown blurrier with time. My parents broke down and cried. Explaining that they weren't abandoning me, that it was just the circumstances, they made all sorts of promises, and asked me to always remember their love and to never forget them. They begged me not to stop playing... Anyway, while Elika's parents escorted her to the platform, I was taken there by Oma and Opa. I remember being very quiet when we said goodbye. When we got on the train, I sat close to Elika, drawing strength from her quiet. I didn't understand it at the time, but Elika was completely frozen. Her father was very attached to her, and it must have been difficult for her to see his pleading eyes through the window. She kept whispering, perhaps to me, perhaps to herself, that she wished the train would go ahead and leave already. His face was very red. She must have been scared to see him cry."

Davidi fell silent for a moment, tossing two pebbles at once. "And then," he continued, "her father asked her for one last hug and kiss just before the train was about to leave. Elika bent down through the window, kissed his cheek, and reached out her arms to hug him. When the locomotive conductor honked the horn and the people on the platform pulled away from the train, her father suddenly pulled her out through the window. I was so startled I began to cry and called out to Elika through the window of the moving train. She stood there, crying, stretching her arms toward the train that was leaving along with her luggage, while her father kept holding her. They grew smaller and smaller until they finally disappeared. That was when I finally felt like an orphan. I was all alone."

Davidi got up and started to walk again. This time he went slower, holding my hand.

"Did I tell you I was luckier than lots of other children?"

I looked at him again, saying nothing, caressing his handsome profile with my eyes.

"Well, I've given the notion of the *Kindertransport* lots of thought through the years. Only Ruth knows how preoccupied I was with it. Families that had no money or people to vouch for them in the receiving countries made every possible effort to find help. The British papers were always featuring ads by Jewish parents from Reich countries begging foster families to take in their children. One couple described their nine-year-old son as being disabled but very cheerful. Another emphasized that their thirteen-year-old daughter could be of great help around the house…"

"And you had some place to go." I tried to contribute to the conversation.

But Davidi was lost in his own world.

"And those who were able to enter their children into the list were sending them into the unknown. Even if they believed they would reunite in the future, deep inside they must have worried that this was goodbye forever. See, many of these children felt at first that their parents were trying to get rid of them, when all they wanted was to stay together. Parents of young children often pretended they were joining them in England and only told them the truth when it was time to leave. Others showered their children with promises of imminent reunion, assuring them that once danger subsided, they'd be able to return home, and that they would be happy in the new place... that kind of thing."

"Do you know what became of Elika?" I asked.

A cheerless smile spread across his face. "I do," he said. "Her parents were able to get her on another transport, to Holland, where she spent a few years before the Nazis invaded. She was sent to a concentration camp, where she died. In an irony of fate, her mother, who stayed back in Vienna, and one of her older sisters survived."

Tears choked my throat. My stomach tightened.

"All I had left on that train after Elika disappeared through the window were two suitcases, mine and Elika's. Each child on the transport was only allowed one piece of luggage. Most children took clothes, books, family pictures, a favorite toy, stuff like that. My mother packed the clown doll I liked to sleep with at night and piano sheet music for pieces by Beethoven, Mozart, Chopin, and Bach, my parents' favorite composers. My father added the *tallit* and a small *siddur,* prayer book, he'd received as a bar mitzvah gift from Opa Michael. I remember him telling me, through tears, that they would keep me safe..."

He fell silent and raised his red eyes to the sky, which had become covered with a carpet of gray clouds. "I'm not a religious person," he continued, "but the tallit and the siddur accompany me wherever I go. It's hard to believe, but the siddur looks brand new despite all the years that have passed, and the tallit is soft to the touch as if only made yesterday and still snow white..."

"And what happened to Elika's suitcase?" I wondered.

"I kept it close all through the ride. I wouldn't let go of it, thinking that Elika might eventually show up and need her things in the new, unknown place we were going to. There were Nazi guards with us in our car, and I was very worried they might take the suitcase away. Then another girl named Rosa whispered that we ought to open it and pull out some things, since the Nazis wouldn't let me get off with two suitcases anyway. I was so afraid that Elika would be left with nothing that I unzipped it a little and pulled out a few things that were small enough to pass through the narrow opening. I don't know if I was planning on keeping them for her or just wanted a souvenir from the person who was almost my travel sister."

"What did you manage to retrieve?"

"Her family photos," he said, "and a journal, which contained a list her parents must have made."

"A list of what?"

Davidi sighed. "A kind of list of behavioral instructions, like 'Be an obedient girl;' 'Say please and thank you;' 'Wash your hands before every meal;' 'Brush your teeth at least twice a day, in the morning when you wake up, and in the evening before bed;' 'Be nice and help others;' and 'When you grow up, light candles on Shabbat eve.' You see, Helena, Elika was only seven years old, and her parents, like many others, were trying in a terribly short time to convey in a brief list the values they must have been planning on imparting to her over years. I kept Elika's things as if they were my own. After the war, Ruth contacted Elika's mother and sent over the journal with the list and the pictures but made sure to keep a copy for me. I only read it after I finally learned to read German, thanks to Ruth's insistence that I preserve the language."

For a brief, amused moment, I recalled how Ruth's attempts to plant her mother tongue in her three children while still living in London died with my cousin Gideon's bold decision to erase any sign of ever belonging to the German enemy that had bombed his city from the air. I pointed out to myself how much that 'invalid' language had helped Davidi, who was smart enough not to reject it, in developing his academic and professional life in Berlin.

I asked Davidi about his meeting with Ruth and Jonah, but he chose to tell me more about Rosa, the girl from the train.

"In Elika's absence, I clung to Rosa. I wasn't even five, and she was big, ten or eleven at least. She had red hair, buck teeth, and a large, freckled face. At the end of the journey, when we finally reached England, I was completely attached to her, and she must have developed a sense of responsibility for me as well. We were housed in a kind of big camp. For some reason, due to mixed signals, Ruth and Jonah weren't waiting for me. It took them three whole weeks, which felt like a year, to come get me. In the meantime, I witnessed the humiliating process of child-picking. Foster parents came to camp once a week to pick out children from the transport, and that evening the list of chosen children was read over the speakers, and they were to leave to their new homes the very next morning. Since I was slated to go live with my aunt and uncle, I was not introduced to the foster families, but despite my young age, I remember very well how terrible the children who were left behind felt. Rosa called it "the animal market," because it reminded her of picking out a puppy at a pet store: the more beautiful children were usually chosen first, and especially those with light eyes, hair, and skin, while the less attractive one stayed in camp and had to go through the humiliating process week after week. Rosa was among the unchosen ones. When I hovered around her at the end of visitation to try and cheer her up, she pushed me away, saying that I was going to be taken home soon anyway, while she would probably be the last one there. As she spoke, her face turned even redder than her hair, and her eyes were puffy with tears." Davidi lowered his eyes. "Just imagine. When Ruth and Jonah finally arrived, and Ruth hugged me and cried, instead of being happy and relieved, I squirmed out of her arms and ran off looking for Rosa. I couldn't find her anywhere. The other children told me she was hiding because she didn't want once again to be that red cat in the pet store that no one wanted. And so, just as with Elika, I never said goodbye to Rosa. I didn't say a word during the entire ride in Ruth and Jonah's little car to the nice place they called 'home.' The whole time I thought about Rosa's freckled face, redder than her hair."

It began to rain. We quickened our steps, and Davidi rushed to the end of his story. He never saw Rosa again, and had no idea what became of her. Jonah and Ruth, although he could not remember meeting them as an infant, smelled familiar. He called them 'aunt' and 'uncle' from the first and referred to baby Gideon as his brother. For the first time in weeks, he felt safe and protected. We made our way in silence, holding hands. When we reached our street, he wrapped his arm around my shoulders, thanked me for listening, and moved me when he called me "Sis."

Years later, when my son Roy had his bar mitzvah at the Western Wall, Davidi honored him by offering him the tallit and the siddur he had received from his father Gabriel. From the distant women's sections, as Roy placed the white tallit over his shoulders, I glanced at my cousin and swallowed down my tears. I knew how emotional this moment was for Davidi, because it was too much even for me. Praying silently, I breathed in the Jerusalem mountain air and put my hands on the heads of Blair and Abby who were standing beside me.

At the end of the ceremony, when I was reunited with Mike and Roy and the other men, I searched for Davidi and went over quietly, stood on my tiptoes, and as I pulled gently on his earlobe, I whispered three words, "Thank you, brother."

24

October 1990
Yosemite Park, California

Nurit,

I've been sitting here and writing non-stop for two weeks. Sometimes I think even if I quit halfway through, my hand will keep going on its own. When I write the past, I'm entirely there. All there. Sometimes my breath comes quick; sometimes I take long, deep breaths. Sometimes I seem to stop breathing altogether, I can't say for how long. Often when I look up, I discover myself dripping with sweat, hot or cold, depending on what I'd just been writing. Yesterday, I dared glance in the mirror and was alarmed to find my eyes inflamed, but it went away a few hours later. I didn't really have an infection, it was just the fire that flared from what was being told.

I'm so engrossed and busy that my schedule is completely out of whack. I go downstairs to eat at all kinds of odd hours, but a meal is always available for me.

God bless Pierre.

You've heard about him before, Nurit, so you know Pierre is the owner of the French Lodge and has been a close friend of mine for years, but since I'd categorized him as "personal," I never really told you how we became friends, what he's like, and what he means to me.

I met Pierre on our first visit to the park twelve years ago, and ever since, we meet each other every few months, whenever I come here. He's French, fifty years old, tall and large, sensitive and caring, and incredibly attentive. He's got a huge heart, a unique worldview, and a beautiful way of speaking. In business, he attests to being only *comme ci comme ça*, which is why he's lucky to have his life partner, Marcel, who is blessed with a sense for business, and who runs the place with him, rather successfully, it seems.

Marcel is a year or two younger than Pierre. He's a short man: short of stature, short of patience, short on smiles, but a great intellectual, probably much more than Pierre. He has a rich literary and general knowledge and he gobbles up so many books that he's even read and enjoyed most of mine. I often meet Pierre and Marcel for dinner at the French Lodge's restaurant, but sometimes we go to other restaurants around the park. They always make time for me, which is delightful and flattering (by the way, they both insist on calling me "Madame Helena" and say they are honored to have "a writer like me" devote some of her "precious time" to them). The point is, we have a lovely time together, and I'm not truly solitary when I'm here.

Marcel and I talk literature, and not just any literature—fine literature. And not just any fine literature—fine French literature. We discuss the works of French authors such as Proust, Sartre, and Camus. With Pierre, I talk about much more personal matters, things I don't discuss with any other man—not Mike, not even Davidi. When this happens, Marcel's impatience is revealed once more, and he always retires from our company, either in body or in mind.

But on this visit, although I've been here for over a month, I haven't yet spent time with them. I met Pierre the day I arrived and thanked him for the wonderful suite he'd arranged for me even though I had made my reservation in the last minute while the lodge was at nearly full capacity. The suite is on the top floor of the lodge and faces southwest. Through its windows, I can see a terrific panoramic view of the Sierra Nevadas, and every evening, the magnificent spectacle of the sunset thrills me. But since checking in, I've seen Pierre and Marcel only a handful of times and have barely left my room at all.

Last weekend Pierre broke down. He had a bouquet of flowers delivered to my room along with a short letter in which he expressed his concern for my wellbeing. I briefly wrote him back, explaining that I needed time alone. He sent back a note with a quote from *Ecclesiastes*: "To everything there is a season, and a time to every purpose under the heaven" (The idea, I assume, was Marcel's...), and asked if I needed anything.

I wrote that all I asked is that no one touch the contents of the wastebasket in my room. I added that I hoped he didn't think I was 'mad,' since all the wastebasket contained was a pile of crumpled pages (which were already filling it halfway). That was my only request. He replied quickly, asking no questions, and promised to inform the maids immediately. But just in case, I attached a note to the side of the wastebasket, in which I wrote in English and in French: "Please do not touch."

Yours,
Helena

25

Naomi had one more great love story in her unraveled weave of stories. Though brief, it was no less great in her regard than the love of Rachel and Uriel, nor any less enthralling or exciting. Ruth and I were her attentive audience, and at least as far as I was concerned, I could listen to it a thousand times or more, for not only was she an extraordinary storyteller, a talent I tried to assimilate whenever a story broke through her sea of dazed confusion, but through her glittering eyes I got to know the father I had never met, and through the mirror of her memories, my mother was revealed to me as I had never known her before.

When she remembered, reconstructed, and reminisced, she seemed to ignore my presence and spared no details, even the ones that slid down beneath her blouse and underwear, setting her desire aflame. As I listened to her talking, I had trouble bridging this woman before me, her face full of despair, her soul broken, and her thoughts entangled, with the life-loving, romantic young woman that emerged from the stories, her legs wrapping sensually around the hips of her lover, her nails piercing his skin lustfully, her eyes closing with pleasure as he penetrated her over and over with growing intensity in an ongoing conquest. This love story, which was born in flames and maintained in the dun of smoke, had few yet riveting chapters, not many pages however overflowing in content, and even the spaces between its words left little room for the imagination.

***

"Uriel devised a rescue plan for you…" Rachel Weiss had told the Steiners the day she paved Davidi's path to freedom.

Now it was my mother's turn.

It was during the hot days of August 1939. Many Austrians, citizens of the Reich, were vacationing in the cool Alps. A month earlier, Gabriel had given into Vera's pleas, and the two of them had made their way to Berlin to visit her parents and sisters, despite Oma Ilse's vehement objections to their walking into the lion's den. Now after Uriel's and great-grandpa Josef's deaths, Davidi's transport, Vera and Gabriel's leaving, and Martha's desertion, only four Steiners were left behind: Michael and Ilse, Naomi, and Raphael. The four of them had recently been banished from their spacious apartment into a one-bedroom apartment on the outskirts of town and were forced to part with their home, their possessions, and their old lives. With their funds dwindling and with no source of livelihood, they were forced, to their chagrin, to adapt to a hard, sorrowful, degrading routine.

One evening in early August, Sebastian and Leah knocked on their door. Later that same night, Michael and Naomi made their way to a small attic in a building on a side street at the other end of town. Leah unlocked the door with a small key, sat the two of them on the only piece of furniture in the room—a faded two-seat sofa on which a thin woolen blanket had been thrown, apologized quietly, and disappeared out the door. A few moments that felt like an eternity later the door opened with a creak.

Tall, his back straight, in walked Mordecai. Naomi sat up. Memory from the day she first saw him warmly shaking her brother Uriel's hand, embracing him, and mussing his hair affectionately, flashed through her mind. When he introduced himself to her father in his deep, hoarse voice, to her embarrassment, she blushed and remained in place. Mordecai was thinner than she remembered, and, despite his young age, the hair on his tan chest was now sprinkled with gray. But how handsome he was in her eyes! In awe, she looked at his face, and when he smiled at her, despite his visible exhaustion, she felt weak.

This is where my mother paused in the story each time, her face flushed. As if daydreaming, she relived the memory— "Mordecai had the most beautiful smile I had ever seen. The kind that involves the large muscles around the mouth and the ones surrounding the eye sockets. And this smile, which stretched sideways at first, would suddenly, surprisingly curve mischievously to the right, pushing his right cheek a touch higher than the left, and his right eye would slant into a kind of charming wink, embellished with laugh wrinkles. Oh, God," she sighed, her beautiful eyes moist. "Men were captivated by that smile, women were enchanted…"

I remember sitting quietly in Ruth's kitchen, my arms around my knees, not daring to say a word, afraid of interrupting my mother's flow of words and breaking the spell. After all, few and far between were these moments of grace that swept us both into the world of her memories as our thoughts wrapped around the same image. I recall thinking how beautiful she looked as she dove into her past, her eyes alight, a blush of pink spreading over her cheeks, her voice steadying, her back straightening.

***

"My eyes were still fixed on Mordecai's smile," Naomi continued to draw momentary energy from the core of that memory, "and I did my best to conceal my excitement when he began to explain the purpose of our meeting."

My mother then described how she had listened, mesmerized, to his hoarse voice and foreign accent as he described the special bond he had forged with Uriel, a bond which had begun in shared values and deepened to become a strong friendship founded on affection and mutual appreciation, and how moved she was when he said that he too played a role in the rescue plan Uriel had devised for his family, even taking on a personal obligation to help in case any unexpected harm came to Uriel.

When he finished talking, he stepped over to my mother and took her hand gently. He placed his other hand on Michael's shoulder. Michael had been tight-lipped the entire time, fidgeting uncomfortably in his seat. Mordecai then suggested that as a first stage he would get Naomi out of the house and transfer her to a hiding place, after which he would try to add her as a chaperone as part of the *HeHalutz* movement enterprise for taking Jewish children to kibbutzim and villages in the Land of Israel. Although Mordecai was a member of the Betar Movement, he explained, he had a close friend, also a native of Yugoslavia, who was a member of the HeHalutz. With her help, he said, he had a better chance of procuring a certificate for Naomi.

Michael peered with a tremor at his youngest daughter, and his answer froze on his lips. Could his tender girl manage away from home, on her own, in hiding, isolated? Would she overcome the fear, survive hardships, and avoid the inevitable pitfalls on the way? Would she, a small, fearful little bird, succeed in escaping the eagle's talons?

Would she survive?

Would he ever see her again?

As Michael tortured himself, delaying his response, my mother took the decision into her own hands. A light of hope blinked in her bright eyes, and something else seemed to be planted in them. She moved closer to her father, took his face in her hands, and asked that he let her go. "I trust this man, Papa," she said, "the man who was like a brother to Uriel." With her words, she quieted his spirit and mitigated the sorrow in his face.

Once she had gathered her courage, she extended her hand to take Mordecai's and laced her fair fingers into his dark ones, creating the appearance of a piano keyboard, containing the promise that its black and white keys would play the tune of their single, marvelous music. At that moment, Mordecai experienced catharsis. His entire body trembled. He lowered his head to his chest and let out a sigh of relief. Months later, Mordecai told Naomi that her action made every part of his body quiver, sweeping him off his feet.

When they said goodbye, Mordecai shook Michael's offered hand warmly, and the two exchanged severe looks: one mixed with trepidation and supplication and the other offering a silent promise. Then Mordecai kissed my mother's hand and equipped her with his charming smile for the road. My mother's eyes filled with tears again as she revealed the memory of that smile to me, once more describing in detail the muscles around the mouth and the laugh wrinkles around the eyes, the right cheek rising slightly and the right eye slanting into a wink.

One time, she paused in her flow of words, and, going against her habit, addressed me directly.

"Know this, Helena," her gaze falling on me, her finger raised toward me, "a smile is real only if it spreads into the eyes!"

Many years later, as I faked smiles to cover the sadness dammed up within me, I pondered that real smile, so unlike the 'American' smile I had adopted as an adult, revealing two rows of white teeth, but coming to a halt under the nose.

***

In August, mere weeks before the war broke, my mother bid a hasty goodbye to her parents and her brother Raphael.

The worst thing about that day was that Oma Ilse, always so strong and robust, broke down. The last image my mother saw as she left their shabby one-bedroom apartment that served as their home was Ilse grabbing the ends of Naomi's dress and wailing, and Michael separating the one who was staying from the one who was leaving and pulling Ilse back into the apartment. Then, the sight of the door slamming behind them, as if cutting Naomi's fate off from her loved ones and shutting out a story of a life that had been and was no more.

But my mother did not turn back. Wearing nothing but a plain dress and a light coat and with her heart pounding, she walked down the dark stairwell and outside. Leah was waiting at the end of the street, and Sebastian met them at the edge of town. From there, she was taken to a hiding place in one of the forests surrounding Vienna, near the city of Baden, where she used to visit the therapeutic hot springs with her family during happier times.

"Mordecai should be here in a week or two," Sebastian informed her. "In the meantime, you can stay here. This is a friend's house, a good Christian. And please, dear, don't ask questions."

My mother did not ask a thing. She was put in a small room in the attic of Wolfgang and Gertrude, a childless couple whom she knew only by first names. She washed her fair hair and wrapped it in a bun on top of her head, as was the custom of Gentile village women, and put on a rustic dress that had been laid out for her on a small wooden bed. Following Gertrude's orders and saying some silent thanks for having learned some housekeeping chores back home, she grabbed a cloth and bucket filled with water from the well in the yard. Grateful to her hosts but remaining enveloped in silence, she worked hard each day from dawn. While in his appearance Wolfgang evoked a sense of trust with his kindly face, a mustache at the tip of his lip, and his round belly, she recoiled somewhat from Gertrude with her pursed lips and skeptical gaze, restlessly examining Naomi's pretty face and fine body.

My mother spent most of her time polishing pots, washing windows, mopping floors, brushing the heavy, dusty sofas in the living room, and sweeping dead bugs and dry leaves that had begun falling early that year from the back porch facing the small vegetable garden. As she worked, her thoughts wandered far from the forest that surrounded her toward her loved ones that remained in the hate-filled Vienna, toward Uriel, who had been murdered so young, toward Davidi, sent far away on the train to her sister in London, and toward Mordecai. The thought that she would soon see his tall, handsome figure, his swarthy skin, his piercing gaze, and his wonderful smile made every part of her body tremble and her cheeks flush. She felt as if butterflies flew up between her legs and inside her stomach. The experience was so intense that she had to pause in her work to settle her breath. Each time she walked into the house and saw the large wooden cross hanging over the fireplace, her heart pinched with sorrow and her throat tightened. In the evening, as she looked at her sweaty, calloused hands, she thought that if Martha could see her now, she would surely put her hands together in sorrow and shake her head as if she had just witnessed a tragedy. Then she would send her to take a warm bath, wrap her body in a soft towel, and massage her hands with the special lemony lotion she once brought her as a gift from a visit to her home village.

And when she entered her bed at night, Naomi would hug her pillow between her arms, belly, and knees, and mumble a quiet prayer that her Grandma Rebecca had taught her as a child, a prayer from Maimonides *Mishneh Torah*:

Blessed art Thou Lord our God, King of the universe, who causes the bonds of sleep to fall upon my eyes, who sinks one into restful slumber, and illuminates the pupil of the eye. May it be Your will,

Lord our God, to save me from evil inclination and from danger. May I not be disturbed by bad dreams or evil thoughts. Let my bed be perfect before You and may You raise me up from it to life and peace and illuminate my eyes lest I sleep a sleep of death. Blessed art Thou, God, who illuminates the whole world in His glory."

26

On the last weekend of August, Gertrude informed Naomi that she would let her finish work early that day as Mordecai was arriving, and she would even allow her to rest for a few days. Although there was no warmth in Gertrude's tone, Naomi's eyes lit up and her spirit lifted as she rushed up to her small attic room to change from her country dress to the one she had brought from home.

Mordecai arrived toward evening, and the small, gray house was filled with color. As Naomi later learned, Wolfgang was a friend of Mordecai's from the University of Vienna. When they met again, Wolfgang treated Mordecai with excessive respect, praising his scholarly achievements as well as his success with the girls who "buzzed around him like bees in a hive." Naomi listened, and said nothing, but Gertrude was behaving exactly like one of those girls. Like a busy bee, she buzzed around him, serving soup and dark bread and a hot beverage, offering him a bath and a pillow, seeming to ignore her husband, who, for his part, acted as if there was no flaw in her behavior. And while Gertrude praised Naomi's work at home and in the yard to Mordecai, as if offering a progress report, the suspicious looks she gave her behind his back attested to the fact that Naomi was a temporary and unwelcome lodger.

After dinner, when Mordecai thanked the couple for their hospitality and asked to spend a little time alone with Naomi up in the attic, Wolfgang winked knowingly at his friend, but Gertrude's gestures turned nervous. She asked Naomi sweetly to stay downstairs "for a bit longer" and help her clear the table and wash the dishes before she and Mordecai retired to their "other affairs." Naomi could swear that drops of poison sprayed from the woman's mouth as her lips parted into a crooked smile.

***

The two sat down on the narrow bed in the attic. Naomi's heart pounded wildly. Mordecai's deep voice echoed in her ears for long minutes after he explained that she had to stay in the house at least a few more weeks, until he was able to procure her a certificate from the Mandate government in Palestine, allowing her to join a group of immigrating children as chaperone.

Her face fell.

Mordecai recruited his captivating smile in an attempt to dissipate her disappointment and agitation, took her hands and put them to his lips. When he kissed them, she felt affection, compassion, and desire. She could trust his old friend Wolfgang, he said. He had helped him several times in the past. She must turn a blind eye and ignore the ignorant Gertrude's abuse. Soon, she would be able to leave the village and Austria on her way to Palestine, making Uriel's dream come true.

Naomi's eyelashes were wet with tears, but she stopped herself from asking any questions. When she looked at Mordecai's bold, black eyes, she knew that Uriel did not just happen to send him to her. She was lucky to have Mordecai, experienced, brave, charming, and attractive, to rescue her. She must put her trust in him unquestioningly. He clearly did not travel all this way to see her just for the sake of a promise made to a dead friend. There must be something else... Concern, attraction, perhaps a budding love? When the candle went out, Mordecai responded to Naomi's kisses on the tips of his fingers and the soft touch of her hands, and then gently lay her on her back, caressed her breasts, kissed her lips, and ran his hands all over her body.

Focused entirely on Naomi, Mordecai remained in the country house for three days. "Noeymi," he called her, in his foreign accent. "My Noeymi." When his lips moistened hers, his fingers sculpting her breasts, and his warm body rubbed up against hers, she felt as if dozens of butterflies, their wings painted in all colors of the rainbow, were flapping their wings, fluttering and flying freely all through her abdomen. And when the colorful butterflies entered her and flooded her with their wonderful flight, all her fears, dark thoughts, and burdensome memories seemed to have disappeared, as if there was not enough room within her to contain all of these at the same time, and her eyes filled with tears of momentary happiness.

***

I remember my mother sitting in the green armchair in Ruth's home, telling us her story like only she could, then suddenly losing touch, getting up, searching for the matchbox, and lighting another cigarette. I hated the cigarette smell but never dared protest in those moments—neither about the stench, nor the brown nicotine stains on her teeth—afraid that any comment on my part would break her flow of words. I let her speak at her own pace, sail away in her beautiful descriptions and reveal those old pictures so that I could repaint them in my imagination in detail and win another bit of information about her past.

I found her story riveting but hard to take, awkward, and a bit odd. Was this really my mother we were talking about? Could this experienced, charismatic, and captivating man have fallen for her? She was a fragile, shy, soft daughter of privilege; so fearful, inexperienced, and devoid of any street smarts...

And yet she used to be so beautiful. I recalled all those wonderful photos Jonah took of her just a few years earlier: pretty and regal as a princess, "a model from a beauty magazine," as Mordecai would whisper to her.

Perhaps he loved her unripe purity, her tenderness, her blue eyes, fair hair, and white skin... Perhaps all these were in her favor in the face of all the dark evil that was spreading throughout the world outside.

And perhaps to him it was just a little fling. A brief episode. A wartime affair.

I do not know.

I cannot know anything other than what my mother told me. But I am comforted by the knowledge that she enjoyed a small island of pleasure in the sea of horror, and although they were only three days of joy, they swelled in her memory to the level of a true love story.

At any rate, my mother painted her time at Wolfgang and Gertrude's in two colors: a sky-blue, like a cloudless morning, and a deep-sea blue, dark as the depths of the ocean. When she described to me and Ruth her brief affair with Mordecai, her blue eyes seemed to brighten, shining like gems. And when she described her life in the village in his absence, her eyes were framed with dark circles and her pupils had a gloomy blue hue.

***

They parted ways after three days. "Be patient, Neomi," Mordecai asked her, caressing and comforting, promising that he would do his best to follow her to Palestine shortly. Though he would have to return to Europe often as part of his Zionist activity, he would be re-assured to know that his girl was safe, far away, and that his promise to his best friend had been fulfilled.

"When will I see you again?" my mother asked, though she knew she should not. Without making any promises, Mordecai said that he would do his best to come back the following weekend.

"And please, Noeymi," he said, "be patient and quiet and don't ask any questions."

But Mordecai did not come the following weekend, nor the next.

***

On Friday, 1 September 1939, Germany attacked Poland and, in a blitz, grounded its planes and defeated its army. The war was threatening to wash over Europe like a tsunami.

The terrified Naomi knew: Grandpa Josef's vision of horror was coming true.

And where was Mordecai?

Naomi did not see him for months afterward. He was gone as if he had disappeared into thin air. She did her best to stifle her anxiety and hide her concern for her own fate and the fate of her loved ones and put all her time and energy into tending to the village home, silently thanking the good Wolfgang for letting her stay and asking no questions.

She asked no questions, neither about Mordecai nor about the war, neither about what was taking place on the streets of Vienna nor about the fate of the Jews. She asked no questions when men in uniform appeared in the village home and took Wolfgang along with them, never to return. She asked no questions when Gertrude's stocky brother, Heinz, arrived, hung his uniform on a hook, and, after whispering with his sister in a corner, dragged up to the attic, where he took her like a dog from the back, growling like an animal when he reached climax. She asked no questions when Heinz came back one day with other men, all in uniform like him but decorated with ranks, and ordered her to show them a good time, sometimes one-on-one, other times in groups of two or three. She asked no questions and made no protests even when Heinz gave her a fake identification card that defined her as Aryan to her rapists, blurring her origins and darkening her past into a shadow.

My mother, who still had a drive for life, closed her heart and her ears and pretended these occurrences had nothing to do with her. To save her soul and survive the time until Mordecai returned, she made a decision: she went above and beyond the call of duty between the sheets, so that the country home could not easily give up her presence and her services. At the same time, in order to alleviate the pain and the humiliation, she kept her eyes shut even while they were open, turning the tables in her mind and picturing herself as an insatiable and cruel femme fatale, using the force of her libido to trap the poor, helpless men at her feet, able to do nothing than release some dung beetles into the pit of her stomach.

When she finally got into bed at night, turning over painfully from side to side, she imagined Mordecai entering the small room of debauchery, tall, handsome, and standing straight, pulling her up to her feet and softly kissing every aching part of her abused body, wiping the tears drying on her cheeks with his fingers and brushing his lips over hers. The pain would disappear along with the fear, the bad thoughts, the burdensome memories; the dung beetles would be replaced with colorful butterflies once more, flying inside, filling her body with the delightful fluttering of their wings.

At night, when the lights all went out and darkness took over the house, as the dream evaporated and the pain returned, her lips began mumbling again that beautiful prayer, enunciating each word carefully:

Blessed art Thou, Lord our God, King of the universe, who causes the bonds of sleep to fall upon my eyes, who sinks one into restful slumber and illuminates the pupil of the eye. May it be Your will, Lord our God, to save me from evil inclination and from danger. May I not be disturbed by bad dreams or evil thoughts. Let my bed be perfect before You and may You raise me up from it to life and peace and illuminate my eyes lest I sleep a sleep of death. Blessed art Thou, God, who illuminates the whole world in His glory.

27

Six months went by before she saw Mordecai again. She dreamed about him every night during the first month, continuously praying that he would turn up in the doorway to rescue her. During the second month, her dreams subsided and nightmares invaded. She cried through the nights of the third month, and on the fourth, her prayer became a hushed, smarting cry. Her hopes died on the fifth month, and on the sixth, her tears dried.

And then he came. Came back to make her head spin, to rekindle faded sensations, to awaken her wilting taste for life.

And to plant me inside of her.

When skinnier and paler than ever, he unexpectedly knocked on the door to the village home one afternoon, Gertrude was shocked to see him there, and, awestruck, she hesitated before pulling him inside. She offered him no food or drink but only said drily that Wolfgang was no longer there, hinted that Naomi was in the attic, and asked him to leave the house right after sundown. Thus, without leaving room for any questions, she wrapped a green woolen shawl around her shoulders, covered her head with a scarf, and rushed out the door. She must have run off to warn her brother not to come over with any of his soldiers or commanders. Tonight, she thought furiously, the chicken would not be laying any golden eggs. Since she was growing tired of Naomi's presence, she had begun to plan how to deliver her to butchering, without Heinz's knowledge, of course.

That stubby man would scarcely be willing to give up the gold, not to mention the delicacies offered by that upstairs beauty, the likes of which he had never tasted before and likely never would again.

Once Gertrude disappeared from view, Mordecai climbed quickly up to the attic. When he opened the door and found Naomi sprawled across a wider bed than he had remembered, her pretty face expressionless, her eyes closed but her cheeks powdered, her eyelids painted blue, her lips painted red, her breasts exposed, he understood everything at once.

He did not ask any questions. Instead he walked over quietly, took Naomi's chin in his hand, waited for her to open her eyes and fathom his presence, and then silently kneeled before her, took her hands in his, buried his head in her lap, and begged her forgiveness.

"Many of my friends have been captured, Noeymi. I had to hide in the woods and find escape routes for them..." He shifted his tortured gaze to hers. "But I never stopped thinking about you." His deep voice trembled. "About the beauty of your body and your face, the softness of your hands, your white skin on mine... I believed Wolfgang was taking care of you. I hoped so badly that you were safe..." Then he wiped off the white powder from her cheeks with a furious hand, removed the blue eyeshadow, brushed his lips over hers, and softly kissed every part of her exhausted body, from her toes to her forehead.

For a long time, he held her limp body against his, his hand running tenderly over her face and through her hair. "Talk to me, Noeymi," he begged in a broken voice. "Tell me you're angry...tell me you understand...tell me you hate me...or love me...tell me you're afraid...tell me you're strong...anything...please, just talk to me!"

Finally, she spoke, if barely. "Take me in your arms," she said. "Make love to me."

Mordecai flinched, hesitant to remove the clothing from this body that had been desecrated, afraid of entering it, lest he cause her more pain. Only when she insisted that it was the only cure for her ailment, purifying her body and soothing her soul, did he agree to love her the way only he knew.

But the pain did not go away, the fear did not fade, and neither did the bad thoughts or the burdensome memories. A few colorful butterflies that managed to make their way inside had trouble flapping their wings among the dozens of dung beetles that had taken up all the space within her.

They did not have much time left.

In the middle of the night, they were already making their way into the woods. Mordecai carried a small pack containing a few of Naomi's things, including her forged Aryan identification card. She, wearing the plain dress she had brought from her parents' house and that same light and long coat, leaned against his shoulder, her arm wrapped around his waist.

They bid each other farewell again, this time in the field behind the train station, after he had equipped her with train tickets, a bit of money, a note carrying the name and address of a friend of his, the owner of a public house in the Tirol-Vorarlberg region on the border of Liechtenstein, and his unforgettable smile. He promised again not to rest until his vow to Uriel was kept in full and she was saved.

But Mordecai did not come.

He could not even save himself.

It was as if the earth had swallowed him alive.

***

The story grew vague and short after that, as if everything that happened above and beyond Mordecai's love no longer mattered.

Naomi lived and worked in the pub for a few weeks, during which she discovered she was pregnant. When the owner had to unexpectedly close shop and leave, he kept his obligation to his friend and managed to arrange for her to work as a servant in the home of an Austrian peasant, one of his regular customers.

There, under the false identity she had received in Baden, as she cleaned the house, tended to the yard and the field, and chased the peasant's chubby and runny-nosed children, she rubbed her slowly growing belly with tenderness and worry, suddenly overwhelmed by the thought that she knew nothing of her beloved's family, his childhood, his previous loves, or even his last name.

She only knew his first name.

***

And I?

Each time I heard my mother's story I choked with tears, but I never dared ask her that question. I knew through experience that she could not bear the sound of shattering glass, and so I did my best not to crack her fragile hall of mirrors.

And so I would sit, huddled, hugging my knees to my chest, listening intently to Naomi's stream of memories, described as only she could, wiping her tears away with my hand, while I cried tearlessly as only I could. I lived more than half my life holding onto that awful fear that I might be the bastard daughter of a faceless soldier of the Third Reich.

Once, I felt emboldened enough to ask Ruth about it. She only blushed and said that my mother had been careful with the others, but I do not think she had a real answer for me.

Only years later, years after my mother's death, did I know for certain.

It was only when Roy became a teenager that I finally knew. Because when he smiled, it involved the muscles around his mouth and the ones around his eyes. That smile, stretching to both sides at first, would then take a surprising turn, mischievously bending to the right, pushing the right cheek a little higher than the left, causing the right eye to slant into a kind of charming wink, embellished with laugh wrinkles.

28

October 1990
(This letter was thrown out)

Mike,

I went downstairs to Pierre's office today and called home. I was gripped by a strong longing for you and the children. I wanted to hear Abby's sweet voice. I miss her so much…

Since I'm not too brave, I called when I assumed you would be out. Nelly answered me. She was very excited at first, got a little confused, and started to cry. Then she pulled herself together, and as nannies do, she gave me the run-down on Roy and Abby's routine: schoolwork, grades, after-school activities, friends. Only then did she muster up the courage to tell me in a reproachful tone that Abby is having a very hard time right now as I've been away for almost two months; and this time, the girl can sense things are different.

That's why I love her, our Nelly. I love her frankness, her caring, her devotion to all of us. She's been with us for so many years, taking care of all our children.

What would I have done without her?

When Nelly passed the phone to Abby, I had to hold back tears. She exclaimed, "Mommy, Mommy!" and cried on the other side of the line and the continent, and I bit my lower lip and kept thinking I had to be strong. *Be strong! I can't break!* What kind of mother can listen to her girl crying far away, picture the tears running down her pretty face, the puckering of her trembling lips, and not do anything humanly possible to return to her as soon as possible?

Me, I guess.

I gathered the strength I wasn't sure I had to overcome the obstacles in my heart and my primordial maternal instincts, recruiting all my explanations and promises to clarify that I hadn't yet completed the task for which I'd left.

That I simply have to stay longer.

I promised her, with no basis for my promise at all, that when I finished, we would all be happier.

And that I'd be back by the end of February, right before her ninth birthday.

I asked her to put Roy on the phone, but he didn't want to talk to me.

I didn't dare ask about you.

29

October 1990
(This letter was thrown out)

Mike,

On your fiftieth birthday, before a large, respectable audience of family members, colleagues, employees, and friends, I surprised you with a gift that many guests called "one of a kind"—a book written by me, *The Eighteenth Bridge*. I'm holding a copy in my hands right now. On the opening page, I explained why I chose to dedicate it to you, my love. It might be a little ridiculous, but I just finished reading the first paragraph again out loud to myself. Let me quote it to you in a letter I'll never send:

"Mike Myers was born in New York City and grew up in the nearby suburbs. From his early childhood, bridges of all kinds captivated his imagination—wooden and steel beam bridges, arch bridges, hanging bridges, truss bridges with their diagonal, horizontal, and vertical poles, and cantilever bridges—enormous structures, born out of magical engineering tricks, curving upwards, beneath them a breathtaking landscape of valleys, lakes, and rivers. For years, Mike studied and specialized in civil engineering. With time, he gained professional prestige and a reputation as a world-renowned expert consultant on the topic of bridges and interchanges, from the careful examination of the construction site to choosing the appropriate type of bridge. As the wife of the Bridge Man, I already know: in choosing the most suitable bridge, one must take into account the type of land and the banks of the river under the bridge-to-be, the planned length of the bridge, the necessary height for allowing the passage of ships or motor vehicles, changes in water level, the types of vehicles expected to drive over the bridge, and many other financial and aesthetic elements. If I may take literary liberties, I'd dare say that Mike's professional success is a result not only of his deep understanding of the forces of tension and compression working simultaneously on the bridge, nor of his meticulous involvement in each and every detail of the planning and construction. My Bridge Man also acquired his professional prestige thanks to his personal treatment of each bridge he built, aware of how it would, over the next decades and centuries become an inseparable part of the landscape, and thanks to his ability to humanize the bridge and imagine the panorama of history it would experience during its lifetime. At the engineering and technology faculties in which he's an in-demand guest lecturer, Mike Myers charms his audience, by emphasizing how behind every bridge is the riveting life story of the person who dreamed and conceived it, who supervised its elevation above a road, river, or some other obstacle, and of the hundreds of workers who labored over its construction…"

I've always loved that quality of yours, Mike, the way you humanize the bridges. In my book, which I'd dedicated to you with great love, I wove the stories behind the construction of seventeen of your most famous and most beloved bridges in the world. I based my stories on research and interviews and tried to put myself in your shoes and address each bridge intimately, describing its birth and life story and the things it saw during its years of existence. The narrator in my book was a virtual character, who pointed out the unique quality of each bridge and then combined together all of these distinctive qualities to form the eighteenth bridge—the ultimate one—which purports to overcome obstacles, proudly symbolizing human transcendence over nature.

I loved the book I wrote for you. I felt quite emotional as I placed it in your hands, but if you could see me now, Mike, you would notice the blush on my cheeks and feel my heavy breathing. It is just that the insult of that night is still bitter in my mouth. Later that evening, after the last guest left, while I was still gripped in the euphoria of the party, I whispered in your ear with the intimacy reserved for old lovers: "You were my bridge to a new and fertile life in America, a bridge to my femininity and motherhood, a bridge to repairing experiences from my past..." I gazed at you with eyes full of good intentions, but you, rather than being happy, appreciative, and grateful, furrowed your brow, and fixed me with a look that I found all too severe.

I'll never forget what you told me that day.

"Life is not a book," you said. "I'm a man, not a bridge. If I could only build a true bridge to you, Helena, I'd be a happy person."

It took me a while, but I finally understand.

That is why I'm here. I'm writing a bridge to you, to our children, to myself.

A bridge to the past.

30

On 30 April 1945, Adolf Hitler ended his life.
In May, Germany surrendered to the allies.
The war in Europe was over.

On 6 August 1945, the United States dropped an atom bomb on Hiroshima.
On the 9th, it dropped a bomb on Nagasaki.
On 14 August, Japan surrendered.
The war in the Pacific Ocean front was over.

World War II ended.
But not for my mother, Naomi.

For four years she had feared for our lives. Every moment could have been our last. The entire time, she had had no idea what became of her family, her mother and father, Michael and Ilse, her brother Gabriel and his wife Vera, and her brother Raphael. She did not know if my father, Mordecai, was still alive. Odd news about the horrors of war reached her ears after the German surrender, news that was passed through the streets by word of mouth, turning her mad and paralyzed with anxiety. Dreams of her loved ones arriving to save her were shattered by the threatening nightmare, which was her nightly visitor, in which no one was left in her parents' apartment in a luxurious Viennese quarter: the apartment burnt, the furniture sooty, the porcelain shattered, and Opa Michael's science books, along with Oma Ilse's beloved siddur, *Pentateuch*, and fine literature, including the *Book of Ruth*, rolling, torn in the rubble and glass on the blood-stained floor. When she awoke, Naomi would torture herself with questions: were her loved ones sent to the concentration camps and from there to the death camps? Did any of them survive the gas chambers and the crematoriums?

***

Madame Butterfly seemed more prepared than anyone else for the end of war. Post-war Austria, divided between the victorious allies into four occupational areas, returned to its previous borders. The Vorarlberg region was now part of the French territories, and the madam, aware of the shock and frustration of all those soldiers returning defeated from the battlefields, did not hesitate to switch loyalties and swiftly equipped her girls with some basic French, so that they might properly serve the soldiers of France, who were now rulers of the city. Thus, as early as the summer of 1945, the parlor was filled with the rustling of French chansons, and the girls curtsied while greeting the arriving clients with *"Bonjour monsieur"* or *"Bonsoir monsieur,"* according to the time of day, attaching their names to the introductory *"je m'appelle"* and rolling *"pardon"* and *"s'il vous plait"* on their tongues, never forgetting their *"merci"* and *"au revoir,"* hoping that the monsieur had enjoyed himself and that they would see him again in the following nights.

This was refreshing for me. Those strange words, flying through the air at all hours of the day and night, offered a diverting sound. As my mother later described it to Ruth, the girls seemed to primp themselves with the language to impress the soldiers in a clumsy attempt to trap them in their nets, so they might marry them and take them far away from the brothel to a brighter future in their home country. Even my mother, in her rare moments of grace, allowed herself to be amused by those foreign words, especially when she was busy with the sewing Nioka sent her every week. She would put aside the torn dress or the slowly embroidered handkerchiefs, dance her way into our small room, and bow elegantly to imaginary men with the accompaniment of *"Merci, Monsieur"* and *"Au revoir, Monsieur,"* distract herself from burdensome worries, and make me laugh until I cried.

But most of the time she was lost in thought, weeping and sobbing for lengthy periods before wiping her tears and staring silently out the window, as if in expectation of someone's arrival. I once asked her who she was waiting for. Was it Tuesday today and Nioka was bound to arrive? But she looked at me with a gaze so sad and tired that I could not put it out of my mind for hours later.

So I learned not to ask.

***

On one pleasant autumn day, I looked out the window of our small room to the building's forested backyard. A light wind frolicked outside, pulling down leaves in gorgeous shades of red, orange, and yellow from the trees and scattering them on the ground.

That day, Madame Butterfly announced an all-encompassing cleaning operation at the brothel. At her order, the girls got down on their knees, scrubbed the floors, and scraped off old layers of dirt that had stuck to the floor tiles, seeming to imprison the footprints of hundreds of villagers and city men, soldiers and civilians, elderly and young men who had visited the madam's house during those awful years of war, unloading their frustrations and sexual needs between its walls. My mother was also recruited to the cleaning operation, and by the madam's order, was attached to a young woman named

Gertie, who had taken on an especially important task: cleaning the toilets and bathrooms all over the brothel. Enjoying the unusual bustle and the feeling of renewal, as well as the scent of soap that had begun spreading through the halls and parlors, the bathrooms and bedrooms, I trailed behind the two of them.

I wanted to tell Nioka all about that magical day on her very next visit and did my best to commit every detail to memory: the skirt of one of the girls, which rose so high as she kneeled that I saw her behind in all its glory; the bucket of water that tumbled down the stairs, causing two girls to slip; and the soap fight between two others, which started as a joke, but ended with punches and the pulling of hair.

But most of all, I wanted to tell Nioka about the wonders of Gertie, a skinny, dark-haired girl, taciturn and hardworking. Gertie dragged my mother, who was especially gray and lackluster that day, behind her, slowly pouring some vitality into her and arousing her to brief moments of grace. Under Gertie's instruction, my mother began to move obediently and work. She filled a scratched blue bucket with a small hole in it with soap and water, dipped a worn rag inside, wrung it, persistently scrubbed the toilets, sinks, and porcelain in the bathrooms, and kneeled down to whiten black wood paneling at the bottom of the wall. Afterward she stretched her back and arms to reach the tiles that bordered the ceiling and pulled down spider webs from the corners.

At the end of the day, the girls were asked to scrub their bodies, shampoo their hair, perfume their skin, and dress "in a dignified manner." That night, the madam promised them, the brothel would be closed to customers and the girls would enjoy a respite and a feast. My mother, unfortunately, was not invited to the meal, and I felt insulted for her, seeing how hard she had worked. But my dismay was forgotten when Gertie slipped away to our small attic room with a plate of food and some pieces of cake, and, with a chuckle, described to my mother the main points of the madam's speech. It turned out she had over-dramatically announced the beginning of a new era in the girls' life, "the post-war era," laying out before them a new list of rules, including some regarding clothing, manners, and speaking style, aimed at placing them higher on the social ladder, as if they were aristocracy in a royal court.

"The madam is determined to put the business back on its feet," Gertie explained. "She has an orderly log of income and expenses, and she's always writing things in it with her little, sharpened pencil… Woe to the girl who mocks the rules, loses money, or fails to pay the madam her share. She will experience the stab of the madam's tongue or the blow of her arm…"

And I, ever since that fateful dinner, used my prematurely sharp senses to avoid running into the madam and maneuvered my mother through the hallways, so that she did not find herself in harm's way, feeling on her already scraped skin the lashing of the madam's arm, the scolding of her tongue, or the stabbing of her sharpened pencil.

***

Nioka did not show up for her regular Tuesday visit that week, nor the following week or the week after that.

"Her husband returned from the war missing a leg," Gertie informed us. My mother went into a deep depression. I was sad about separating from Nioka and simultaneously felt sorry for her, since from now on she had a husband with only one leg. Stunned at the thought, I tried hopping on my right foot for some time, then on my left, unsure which of his legs was missing, and finally gave up and lay down on the floor, exhausted, legs spread and motionless, until even my mother was startled.

But the worst was still ahead of us. Due to the amputation of her husband's leg, not only did Nioka's weekly visits cease but my mother's sewing work was cut short, and the madam's patience burst. She began visiting our room more and more frequently to check if my mother was busy and task her with new cleaning assignments whenever she found her idle. She demanded that I be as silent as a log and make sure to stay away from the parlor and the hallways of the first and second floors when clients visited the place. Once, Gertie overheard a phone call in which the madam raised her voice and grumbled into the phone that now that the war was over she could no longer keep us in her house, and that it was time we left and found old acquaintances or a new place to live. When the loyal Gertie hurried over to tell Naomi what she had heard, I watched my flustered mother and I was not spared the sight of her suddenly gagging and throwing up. Alarmed, I hurried to hand her a glass of water, and Gertie washed her face and wiped off the vomit with a rag.

The next day, hasty conversations began in our room with Gertie alone and with the madam alone and with both of them together, but most of the time my mother cried and said nothing, refusing to cooperate and tell them anything about her family and her past. When the madam asked her if she had anyone in this world, she only shook her head 'no,' and I was scared when I noticed fear in her eyes and wanted badly for Nioka to come.

One evening, Gertie came into our room and closed the door behind her. Holding a jar of quince jam with a little note from Nioka attached, she caressed my head and spread some of the jam on a slice of bread for me. Then, sitting down on the edge of the bed next to Mother, she held her hand.

"I have secrets too, dear," Gertie whispered. "I used to have a family, too, and a home with trees in the yard and flowerbeds out front. Fate was cruel to me, and I have no idea which of my relatives survived the war, if any."

Her voice trembled for a moment. Gertie lowered her head and said nothing. When she finally steadied her voice and spoke again, she made sure my mother was looking into her eyes and following her closely.

"You understand, Norma, dear, I've had a very strong feeling about you for a long time now. May God forgive me if I'm wrong, but just like you, I'm…" her lips quivered, and her eyes shone. "I'm Jewish, too."

I did not fully understand the meaning of the word. I did not know why Mother started to cry again and why the sound was different than usual, or why Gertie also broke into tears, or why they hugged each other.

Most of all, I did not understand whether the fact that one of them or the other was Jewish was something good or bad.

31

Suddenly, things started to happen.

Poor Gertie could not locate her family, although she wrote many letters to old addresses that had since changed owners, even visiting her family's home in one of the towns in southern Styria to find that it had been intentionally burned down during the war and that her loved ones had been taken to the camps. In old letters Ruth found in my mother's things, which, according to her, had been written in frightfully simple and broken German, she learned that Gertie had left the brothel in the beginning of '47 with an older, infertile French officer, who took her back to his house in the south of France, where he made her life miserable. At the end of that year, the letters, in which Gertie always asked about me, stopped coming.

But Gertie had changed the course of our life. The moment my mother opened her heart and began talking, Gertie avidly collected the bits of information and began to put them together. When there seemed to be a chance that surviving relatives might be identified, she involved Nioka and worked to locate them with the same heat and passion she utilized to search for her own. Nioka, combining forces with Gertie, returned to our lives for a short while. I never knew if she had suspected our Jewishness during the war, but I would like to think that had she known, she would have treated us the same. At some point, even the madam was included, but when she, filled with motivation to end the ordeal of the Jewish mother and daughter staying in her house, intended to send a detailed letter to the Austrian embassy in London, requesting their assistance, Nioka, appalled by the thought that the ambassador's dignified assistants would read a letter bearing the address of a brothel, politely stopped her and took over. The letter was finally sent, signed by an "Austrian seamstress, simple, proud, and lucky," because her husband who had returned home from that war, although missing a leg, was, to her good fortune, alive, and her three children had a father once more. In a simple, beautiful letter, a faded copy of which was also found in my mother's box of kept objects, Nioka asked the "Honorable Ambassador" to have his people help locate the relatives of a young woman and her little beautiful daughter, who had not been as lucky as she, having lost their loved ones in the war…

Three months later, Nioka received a response.

***

On a cold day in late December, my mother stood, staring out the window, as she was wont to do after she finished her cleaning and sewing chores. Suddenly, her breath caught in her throat. I rushed over to the window, but a heavy fog covered the path leading to the brothel, and I could not see a thing. Since I also did not hear anything out of the ordinary, I had have always assumed that Mother neither saw nor heard a thing that day but rather sensed something approaching. I stood beside her for a long moment, trying to see what she might have seen and hear the sounds she heard as she moved her head around restlessly, but I dared not ask.

Ultimately, I thought I saw something through the heavy cloud that still lay on our path: a black car, slowly emerging on the road leading to the brothel. I pressed my nose against the glass. Since Mother was holding her breath again, I held mine too, conducting a secret competition with her to see who would be the first to release air. As I lost the competition almost immediately, I held my breath again and again, wondering with concern how it was possible that she had not taken a single breath that entire time.

I think Nioka was the first to step out of the car, and I called out her name excitedly, but my mother later claimed that the tall man with the navy blue top hat stepped out first and opened the door for her. Either way, when I spotted his figure, I stood stock-still, while my mother began mumbling to herself and trembling. I walked over and hugged her narrow hips, and to my relief she did not push me away, allowing me to continue and hold her close, feeling the warmth of her body.

Then a knock came at the door.

I felt her breath catching in her throat again.

***

From up close he seemed even taller. His eyes were green, his fair hair brushed back, his thin mustache carefully combed, and his suit pressed. Only the stubble on his cheeks and his tired eyes attested to the fact that he had stepped outside of his daily routine. He was so different in his style of clothing, his facial expressions, and his bodily movements from the other men who visited the brothel that, embarrassed and confused, I clung shyly to my mother and buried my face in her skirt. The impressive man stepped inside with Gertie, Nioka, and the madam, and behind them peeked the faces of a few of the girls, who had nothing to do at this early afternoon hour and were curious to have a look at the handsome, strange guest who made his way among them without even gracing them with a glance.

He stepped toward my mother. Only then did I notice that his green eyes were gleaming and his lips quivering. My mother still remained, looking down, planted in place. For a long moment they stood before each other without uttering a sound. Abashed by their tense silence, I looked at Gertie and Nioka imploringly.

One of the girls, a chatty, thick-bodied brunette, suddenly shrieked from behind, "Well? Is it her or not?"

Madame Butterfly turned an angry face around and, with a terrifying gaze, signaled to the loud girl to leave the premises at once. The second glance was directed at the other girls. Horribly disappointed, they all left the room. The moment the door slammed behind them, they crowded on the other side, taking turns peeking in through the keyhole.

The man took another step forward. "Please," he said. "Look at me, Naomi." His voice was soft, his accent foreign.

My mother raised her face, but her eyes seemed to look right through him. "I've been waiting for you for six years," she whispered. "Six long years…" Her face paled with the effort, her head spun, her legs buckled, and her body collapsed.

Jonah Jonas cried out, caught her in his arms, and held her body to his. Later, he told Ruth that only then, feeling her light weight and sensing the fragility of her body, did he break. He could not hold back his tears, sweeping after him the deeply moved Gertie and Nioka, the girls behind the closed door, even the madam, who tried in vain to wipe her face on her sleeve.

I was so startled and confused that I began bawling. Only when Nioka took me in her arms and pressed my head to her large, soft bosom, stroked my hair and cooed in my ear, did I settle down, my cries slowly turning into diminishing sobs and finally going silent.

***

The next day everyone hovered around us. Constantly comforting my mother, who simply refused to be happy, Gertie and Nioka packed our few belongings. The girls spun around me, hugging and kissing me, showering me with little gifts so that I "wouldn't forget them" and would have "something to do along the way." The madam gave Jonah the official documents with which we had arrived at her brothel, the documents carrying our fake surname and my birth certificate, bearing my date and place of birth. Jonah was eager to leave his room at the small hotel in the German-speaking town, to leave behind the gloomy streets with their atmosphere of defeat and, most of all, this brothel, which disgusted him, and get us out to London as soon as possible, to Ruth, to his children. Home.

In the afternoon, with the help of some of the other girls and the permission of the madam, Gertie arranged a small farewell party for us. The girls cooked a light dinner, which was scheduled for the late afternoon by order of the madam, so as not to disturb business during the rush hours, and Nioka came over with a cheesecake and two jars of preserves—one cherry, the other quince.

To my regret, Jonah politely turned down the invitation to attend the dinner. Had he only been there with his black camera, whose wonders I discovered afterward, snapping a few images of dear Nioka and Gertie, the girls, and even the madam; had Jonah been there, I would have had a little memento from them and my early childhood, and Jonah would have discovered that they loved us, and that, at long last, my mother was treated with some respect and tenderness.

But Jonah did not come. He arrived the next day in the same big, black car, wearing the same suit and the same navy blue top hat. Nioka had said goodbye to us the previous night. When I had burst into tears and refused to let go of her, everyone had cried. Now it was Gertie's turn. Showering her with blessings and well wishes, she held my mother to her bosom and then hugged me too, stroking my hair, and handing me a doll, which she had purchased with her scant funds. I instantly fell in love with the doll, perhaps because it opened and closed its eyes, or perhaps because of the fair hair that ran all the way down to its thighs. I naturally called the doll Gertie and it stayed with me for years. I told it all my secrets and read it my very first stories, enjoying its lack of criticism and silent approval.

That winter day, our day of departure, I floated on air. With my mother on one side of me and Jonah on the other, I walked over to that black car, one hand carrying a basket containing the jam Nioka had given us, wrapped in handkerchiefs embroidered by my mother, the other hand clutching my new doll with its blonde hair to my chest. Jonah sat in the passenger seat, next to the driver, while Mother and I slid into the backseat. For one final moment, I waved goodbye to the girls and the madam through the rear window. I tried to discern Gertie, who grew smaller and smaller, turned into a silhouette, and finally disappeared altogether. The next moment, thrilled over my first car ride, I turned my face forward toward the sights outside, which changed with dizzying speed. A frigid gust of wind hit my face when I dared open the window a crack. After a short while, the driver dropped us off at a bustling train station. Jonah bought us tickets, and a few moments later we heard the whistling of the engine, announcing the train's approach. When it arrived, it seemed enormous, endless, exciting. Overwhelmed with the expanses that spread before me and the beautiful winter landscape that seemed to cover the outside world with a massive white cape, I took a seat near a large window and spent the entire ride with my nose to the glass.

Our trip "home" to London took four days and three nights. We switched trains and stopped for the night at small roadside inns, each astonishing me in infinite ways. I was so busy with the experiences of the road that I didn't pay attention to Jonah's stories, which were mostly directed at my mother, about people I did not know with names like "Ruth," "Davidi," and "Gideon." The sights outside captivated me much more than the words of the man introduced to me as "Uncle Jonah." I had never had a real uncle who took an interest in me and so I had trouble figuring out how to behave. Since my mother did not demand that I respond to him, I adopted the same tactic I used during my years at the brothel, keeping my mouth shut even when he spoke to me, just as I did when men who ran into me at the brothel's parlor or one of its hallways addressed me. I glued my face to the window and stared outside, gobbling up the views that changed before my eyes like a film strip.

***

Only years later did I dare ask my mother if, even for one brief moment, as we stood in our room and watched the black car immersed in fog stop on the path to our door, she believed that my father Mordecai would emerge from it.

She said, "No." As far as she was concerned, she answered drily, that expectation had ended six months after the last time they had said goodbye in the field behind the train station. Six months, she emphasized, she had expected him to return.

When Mordecai did not appear, she feared he never would. And when she gave birth to me three months later, it finally dawned on her that she would never see him again, and that I, her child, was all she had left of him.

London

32

October 1990
Yosemite Park, California

Nurit,

I took a break from writing today. I had to. I went to Lake Tahoe. I drove along the foot of the Sierra Nevada range, down gorgeous Route 49, dotted with sleepy towns, and stopped for a late breakfast in Jamestown at a bar that looked as if it had been taken from an old Western. I reached the Fanny Bridge in the afternoon. I recalled my previous visit with Mike and the kids a few years ago. Mike had explained to Roy how the gates opening and closing on the side of the bridge regulate the flow of water into the Truckee River. I photographed Blair leaning against the railing and Abby, barely five years old, tossing bread crumbs down to the trout in the river.

Bridges, Nurit, always bridges...

Ever since Blair was a baby, we've spent most of our vacations in bridge-filled areas. We would drive back and forth along the bridges and walk along every bridge that was designed for pedestrians. From a very young age, she took a great interest in the age of each bridge, especially if she thought it was ancient, or at least somewhat old, and would ask Mike to tell her the human story behind its construction. When her feet reached the highest point of the bridge or its very center, she would cling to the railing, look out at the view and dream of the sights that must have been seen from it throughout the years by hardworking laborers, adventurous boys, and even lovers, walking just like her to the center of the bridge, pausing at the same special lookout point in which she was standing that very moment.

Ever since she was young, she liked to sort the bridges into color groups according to their location and appearance. The ones that stood out in their surroundings like precious gems, winning her special attention, she called "golden," "silver," or "emerald bridges." Others she classified as "red" or "green" bridges because of the color of the iron or the landscape that could be seen from the top. "Blue bridges" crossed exceptionally wide and deep rivers, and "baby blue bridges" were the ones so high they seemed to touch the sky. "Rainbow bridges" were small bridges built in areas of varied vegetation, which made them seem colorful and gay in springtime. She used to sketch the bridges in a special notebook, note their names and locations at the bottom of the page and wash them with watercolors.

But there were plenty of bridges Blair didn't like at all because of their ugly surroundings, the murky water flowing underneath them, or due to their dull appearance or rusty beams. Those bridges she referred to as "gray," and they were deemed unworthy to be drawn in her notebook—although, for fairness sake, they were listed at the end of the notebook under the title "Gray Bridges."

She and Roy invented a name for days when we visited cities featuring famous bridges: "Arched Days," due to the curving arches of many of the bridges in the world.

Arched Days. I loved that name my children invented. So literary. An "arch" contains a rise and a fall, a beginning, a peak, and an end. An entire life.

I don't think I ever told you how I surprised Mike in London in December two years ago, just before winter break. He was participating in a conference, and I felt the need to see him. You could say I missed him (and as you know, Nurit, it isn't always possible to soothe longing. It's a privilege to be able to do so.)

But I had something to tell him, too.

Something important.

Our legendary Nelly stayed home with the kids (nothing new), and I flew to London. I took a taxi from Heathrow Airport to his hotel in the center of town. It was terribly cold outside and getting dark. The display windows of the large department stores were already decorated red and green for Christmas, and thousands of colored lights hung on branches along the central streets of the city. A breathtaking sight.

I recalled the first time I'd seen the profusion of Christmas lights.

It was in London, and I was a child.

I left a note with the hotel receptionist, who cordially promised to deliver it to "Mr. Myers" as soon as she could.

Despite my exhaustion, I spent the next two hours wandering the shops down Oxford Street. A little before eight o'clock, I hailed another taxi.

I arrived at the entrance to the restaurant moments before Mike, early enough to see him walking over in the rain, shaking it off his jacket, and searching for me with his eyes. When he saw me, he smiled. I'd surprised him that way twice in the past, once in Paris, and once in Rome. In Paris, he told me he loved my spontaneity, and in Rome, he announced I was original, but this time, seeing me at the entrance to the restaurant in London, there was a question mark in his eyes.

I walked over and pulled him into a hug. As you know, Mike is not an emotional person; nevertheless, he was excited and curious to see me. We embraced for a long moment. He was surprised that I'd come to London but not surprised by the spot I'd picked. We'd eaten there together years earlier, on our honeymoon.

This time we got a corner table in an inner room and had a wonderful three-course meal. After dessert, I dropped the bomb. I said it was time we talked to Blair, that she was almost seventeen years old and has started asking all sorts of questions, as if she suspected we were hiding something. As I spoke, I felt my heart racing.

Mike's face clouded over. This issue had been a source of tension between us for very long. But at the moment he was so pleasantly surprised by my visit that he kept his anger at bay and only said that we'd put this off for too long, and that after all these years that I'd refused to tell Blair, out of some inexplicable stubbornness, he was glad I finally realized there shouldn't be secrets like that in a family and that hiding the truth was even worse than revealing it.

Then my heart pounded even more wildly.

Because I knew he suspected I had other secrets.

But I wasn't capable of telling him yet.

Thank you, Nurit, for always being there for me.

Love

Helena

P.S.

Even though I'm cut off from the news about Israel and the world here, I learned about the riots at the Temple Mount from a couple of Israeli tourists today. Muslims stoning Jewish worshipers outside the Western Wall. It's awful. Just last year we celebrated Roy's bar mitzvah there. It's disturbing, especially considering everything happening in the Persian Gulf. Please keep me updated on the situation in Israel.

33

October 1990
(This letter was thrown out)

Mike,

Let's pretend you're in London right now, for work, and I come there to surprise you again. We have dinner at the same place we ate two years ago, where we ate on our honeymoon as well.

I'd tell you I've been writing my life story and my family's tale and, in fact, I've already finished writing the first part, the one about my early childhood in Austria, before Mother and I made our way to England when the war was over, before we moved to Israel.

I would thank you for your patience over the years; the way you waited out my ebb and flow of changing moods. I'd apologize deeply for causing us to miss plenty of opportunities for happiness by being closed off to you. I'd also tell you that you're the first person I want to give my book to and that there is no one in the world whom I'd prefer to read it before you.

Then I'd ask you to leave the hotel where you were staying and move into the double room I booked for us at a hotel overlooking the London Bridge and the River Thames. There, from the window of our bedroom, I'd look out at the beautiful bridge, in its modern edition, made of concrete, with five arches (which Blair would define as a "silver" bridge) and point out memories that must have been burned into its concrete brain over centuries—Viking war ships that passed beneath it on their way to reconquer London from a British king; fires that captured its piles inflames; a tornado that made the bridge collapse at the end of the eleventh century, requiring it to be rebuilt; and the decapitated heads of traitors that were displayed on pikes at the southern gate of the bridge during the reigns of King Edward the First and Henry the Eighth.

The next day, while you were busy with work, I'd board a red double-decker bus, visit the Palace of Westminster and the House of Commons, and climb to see the view of the city from Big Ben. For dessert, I'd circle back to the golden entry gates of Buckingham Palace. Once again, I'd watch the changing of the guards, accompanied, as in the best ceremonial protocol, by trumpets and saluting swords. Then, when the soldiers of the new shift had planted themselves in place, I'd imagine a gorgeous young woman dancing before their astounded eyes, her white, chiffon dress blowing in the wind to the beat of the dance, twisting around her slim body and clinging to her perky breasts at the end of each spin. When the figure stopped her dance, my breath would catch in my throat at the sight of the beautiful face revealed to me from within my world of mirages—that of my mother, Naomi. I would see her smiling at me, hear her whispering to me, "It's so good to be with you again, Helena, to see your tears wetting your cheeks and your smile spreading to your eyes."

And you would not be beside me.

That moment I would take a taxi and instruct the driver to get me out of there. I would ask him to drive through the streets of London, and when I'd look out the window, I'd find the city still foggy and gray.

That evening, when I described my day to you, I would say that the fog today is undoubtedly different than the fog back then. Because back then, in December 1945, it wasn't just fog, but smog, a mixture of sprinkling, moist fog and bits of soot that spread from the coals, wood, and peat the people of London used to heat their homes, polluting the air.

I'd tell you that only after the Great Smog of 1952 caused complete darkness and the death of several thousand people, laws were passed, limiting the types of heating materials permitted for use, turning the London smog into just an ordinary fog.

You would wonder out loud why I was thinking of the fog at that moment.

I'd pause for a beat, and then, my voice hoarse, I'd answer that it was probably a symbolic thought, since I was busy clearing the fog around my past.

My memory travels back in time now, and before my eyes appears an image of a train on a gray platform, on a hazy, foggy, cloudy day...

34

27 December 1945. We arrived in London early in the morning to a winter fog that covered the city, and, due to its thickness, was dubbed by the British papers "pea soup."

We waited on another gray platform for the final train on our journey "home." During the last four days, I had been riveted by the sights changing outside the windows of the trains we switched every few hours, so much so that I had barely said a word. Since Mother was also prone to long silences, the train car was filled with Jonah's pleasant, accented voice, as he tried to get Mother talking or excite my imagination with descriptions of the people who would soon become my "family" and of the place that would soon become my "home."

Now I was anxious for the train to arrive. Jonah bought tickets and exchanged a few words with some men standing beside us at the station in a language I did not understand, a language that sounded very different from French, the first signs of which had invaded our home in recent months, causing Madame Butterfly to hover with ease among the rooms of the brothel with an inscrutable expression on her face. My mother sat, shrunken, holding onto our few possessions on a bench as gray as the platform. I, bored and impatient, hopped restlessly on one foot and then on the other, thinking of Nioka's handicapped husband and wondering once again which leg was more important, remaining unanswered as always.

When the train finally arrived, I was in for a simultaneously exciting and disappointing surprise. Just a few moments after the train left the station, we were swallowed into a long tunnel, as if diving into the center of the earth. Mother panicked, grabbing onto Jonah's coattails, and I cried out and held onto her knees. Jonah wrapped his long arm around Naomi's shoulders and laughed out loud. Then he gently held onto my arm, pulled me in and sat me on his lap for the first time since the beginning of the journey. Having always been warned against the intimacy of strange men, I glanced at Mother awkwardly and hopefully, and was filled with joy when she approved of the proximity between us with her eyes, allowing me to submit to his pleasant voice as he explained in accented German the wonders of the London Underground, the first underground track-based public transportation in the entire world.

"The story of the Underground begins almost a hundred years ago," he said, "which is known in England as the time of "Railway Mania." The city realized it needed an underground train to move as many people as it could as fast as possible. The first Metropolitan train began operating in January 1863. A few years later, the expansion of the track system into the suburbs led to the population of the outlying areas…"

Jonah went on and on for a long while, enjoying, for the first time, our undivided attention. I was five years old. What I could not understand, I tried to make up with the power of imagination. Gradually, my mother's panic subsided, and I, sensing her calm, relaxed too, as if touched by a magic wand. And although the gray concrete walls outside the window was extremely boring, Jonah's tender voice was pleasant to my ears, and his picturesque stories made up for my disappointment about missing the landscape outside. When Jonah finished talking, I sunk into a light, pleasant sleep.

Years later, after marrying the Bridge Man and listening intently to dozens of bridge tales—levelled or arched, gray, silver, red, or baby blue—I would remember the first engineering story I had ever heard that day on the underground on our way to London. I had not learned much about construction, but the story did teach me a riveting lesson on humanity's power over nature and its ability to impress its mark above and below ground.

When I awoke after a brief respite, Jonah told us excitedly that Ruth, probably impatient by now and eager to take us in her arms, was waiting at the nearest station, and I was filled with glee. Since I felt a little closer to Jonah after his stories of the underground train, I wanted to ask him a few questions about the wonderful Ruth, who captivated my imagination before I ever laid eyes on her. I dared hope that unlike Mother, who was sitting beside us, silent, pale, and mournful, Ruth would take an interest in my welfare, would gently stroke my hair, hold me, and maybe, if I were lucky, give me a few gifts, like Gertie and Nioka had.

Jonah, who recognized my hesitation, removed the blue top hat from his prematurely balding head and suggested with a smile that I toss in any question that came to my mind, promising that he, like a magician pulling rabbits from his hat, would gather them one at a time, offering answers I would surely love. I was taken by the idea, and in a short while we lost ourselves in a game: I was tossing heaps of questions into his hat, which he enthusiastically answered.

My high spirits, unfortunately, were short-lived. The closer we got to the station, the more I felt Mother's body stiffening, growing confused and on edge. I was so young, but my senses were sharp. I remember wondering why, even now, with so many thrills around us and so close to meeting her sister, my mother was withdrawing into herself even more, shutting her mouth tight, biting her lips until they bled, and shrinking in her seat. Why was she not more excited about the imminent reunion? And why was she killing any joy that came my way, neither smiling nor saying a word? I remember worrying that Uncle Jonah would become angry or insulted, or, God forbid, regret traveling this far to find us and bring us to our new home. Her silence burdened me. I was afraid it would never end and did my best to hold back the tears of disappointment and anger that choked my throat.

It seems I understood even then that the two of us would never be brought together by a blue magic hat.

Years later, I asked Ruth to explain Mother's tense silence that day.

"Of course, your mother was excited to see me again, Helena," she said sadly. "But in those moments, she dreaded the news."

"What news?"

Ruth's eyes darkened. "My child, it may be difficult for you to understand, but your mother grew more and more terrified the closer she came to meeting me again, because she knew, just knew, that the moment she saw me, the moment I fell crying on her neck, she would see the answer in my eyes…the answer to the question, which of our loved ones was still alive…who survived the war. You can probably understand, Helena, that this question had been bothering her all throughout the war, causing her to lose sleep and clawing at her innards. The moment she saw the black car pulling up by the path to the brothel, she was gripped by an unbearable anxiety, fearing it was carrying terrible news."

Seeing my eyes grow sadder, Ruth gently caressed my cheek. "And so, all the way to London your mother tortured herself with that awful question, and although Jonah was with her the entire time, that was the one thing she didn't dare ask…"

I, too, spent the rest of the trip wrapped in silence. We arrived at the final stop around noon on a late, cold December day. At that moment my life was about to change.

***

Had Oma Ilse been alive, she would have invited me into her kitchen, sliced two thin pieces of challah for me, smeared them generously with her homemade quince preserves, and placed a decorated plate before me. After she was sure my appetite was satiated, she probably would have opened her story with the following words: "It was in the days of the judges, a few generations before the kings' era…" In her literary language, she would have described the wondrous paradox of the Moabite woman who converted to Judaism, the woman without whom Jewish history would not have evolved to become what we know it to be today.

And I would have asked with childish naiveté, "Why?"

Ilse would have answered that, after having lost her husband, had the Moabite not insisted to remain with her mother-in-law, Naomi, had she not told her, "Your people will be my people and your God my God," and returned with her to Bethlehem to gather the stalks left in the fields by the harvesters, as did the poor Israelites in that period, she would not have met Boaz, the owner of the field, and seduced him in the granary at night.

"What does he have to do with the story?" I would have asked, intrigued.

Oma Ilse would have answered patiently. "Because after that night of love in the granary, Boaz decided to wed Ruth, and their union gave birth to the Kingdom of David…" When she noticed my imploring expression, she would probably have run her hand through my hair, smiled, and added, "Because Boaz begat Ovad, and Ovad begat Yishai, and Yishai begat David…"

Following in the footsteps of my late grandmother, from a very young age, I, too, fell in love with the drama unfolded in the *Book of Ruth* with its prose and its plot, the story of loyalty and the story of love. Just like Oma Ilse, I too was filled with admiration for the noble heroine. The lack of description of her external appearance was compensated by songs of praise for her words and her actions. Despite the distance of time and space, I identified with the pride Ilse had for her eldest daughter, after having discovered in her some of the noble qualities of the biblical Ruth.

My mother, on the other hand, did not at all remind me of the biblical Naomi, except perhaps for the heavy personal losses they both had lived through. But I could not help but feel impressed by the fact that despite the differences—our story did not involve a mother and daughter-in-law, but rather two sisters—just like the book, and just like Oma Ilse had predicted, Ruth and Naomi's lives became intertwined like the two braids of a challah.

As a young girl, I won first prize at a Purim costume contest organized by the seniors at the Herzliya Hebrew Gymnasium high school in Tel Aviv. It was a gypsy costume Mother sewed for me, with a skirt made of dozens of bits of colorful fabric, a red-laced velvet blouse that revealed my shoulders and clung to my torso like a bodice, and a green kerchief around which Mother sewed gold fringe and tiny bells. I was flattered by the accolade, especially since "the one" was on the judges' panel and had the honor of affixing the winner's pin to my blouse. But I was no less moved by the prize—an elegant edition of the *Book of Esther* and the *Book of Ruth*, a flat wooden box with a glass top, and inside it the two scrolls on a strip of parchment, stretched between two wooden cylinders hidden in the sides of the box, which could be rolled back and forth with two wooden knobs that protruded from two holes in the bottom. The scrolls received an honorary place in my dresser drawer. Whenever I felt the need for Oma Ilse's spirit and wisdom, I would carefully pull them out. First, I would read the *Book of Esther*, about the beautiful Jewish queen, who utilized her beauty and smarts to rise to greatness and save her people. Then I would turn to the *Book of Ruth*. When I tried to picture the Moabite Ruth in my mind's eye, her kind face and the contours of her body, I would see Aunt Ruth as I had first laid eyes on her that foggy winter afternoon in late December on a gray platform filled with people at the center of the British capital.

***

She stood there alone, so excited, pink roses in her hands, her eyes swiftly scanning the passersby in the hopes of detecting her dear husband and lost sister with a young, golden-haired child. She was slightly plump, big chested, rosy-cheeked, her face wide, her nose straight, her feline eyes greenish-brown, and her hair fair and wavy. She wore a light blue dress with a white collar and a felt hat.

I think I spotted her first, before anyone else, although I did not know her. When I saw her with the pink roses in her hand and the laughter in her eyes, I knew immediately that she was the one who had been promised to me by the blue magic hat. Ruth, for her part, liked to tell people for years later, how before she even spotted my uncle Jonah and my mother Naomi at the busy station, she had seen a small child with ivory skin, pretty as a gazelle, with her small hand waving hello, and knew immediately that the girl was me, Helene.

Weeping, Naomi fell into Ruth's open arms before she could even read the news in her sister's eyes. Ruth's voice was so soft and tender as she spoke into Mother's hair, the German in her mouth devoid of any foreign accent, that it took my breath away. I loved her with all my heart from the very first moment. A few minutes went by before Mother dared look her sister in the eye. She understood it all. The bad news passed between them wordlessly. Embracing and sobbing, the two sisters walked out of the station. Uncle Jonah and I followed them silently, Jonah carrying our belongings in one hand, his other hand holding onto my small palm, which was moist with excitement. Ruth and Jonah's black, two-door Ford Anglia was waiting in the parking lot. Its bumper reminded me of a face, its headlights a pair of dark eyes. Our luggage was stored in front, and Ruth, Mother and I slipped onto the backseat, me in the middle. Despite Mother's tears of longing and pain, and despite all the questions that would remain unanswered, I decided not to allow her sadness to halt my happiness and gave myself over to Ruth's soft, caressing hand and sunny warmth, which radiated onto me, making my heart leap with sublime joy, the likes of which I had never known.

Evening had descended: outside it had already grown dark. A heavy fog and poor visibility slowed my uncle's driving. But I did not see the haze all around. I was hypnotized by the holiday lights that twinkled along the streets, decorating the city for the first Christmas season after the war.

Twenty minutes later, we pulled up beside a wide stone building with several entrances and shops on the ground floor. Jonah parked the Ford by the gray sidewalk, and we stepped out of the car. Ruth wrapped her coat around me, and we all hurried inside through the right-hand entrance and climbed three floors up, passing several doors on each floor.

Then we walked into the place Jonah called "home," and I was dumbfounded.

It was not a large apartment, but, compared to our small room in Vorarlberg and our attic at the brothel, it seemed immense. Moreover, it was marvelously tidy, with floral sofas placed over a warm wool rug, landscape paintings on the walls, a dining table with eight high-backed chairs, and a small kitchen that spread cooking aromas, which immediately tantalized my empty stomach. A small heater in the corner of the room emanated a lovely warmth that spread through my limbs, soothing my shivering from the cold. I was so moved by everything around me, so unfocused on everything that was said, that I did not even notice when Ruth took my hand and led me gently to a room at the end of the hall. I was preoccupied by the sight of open rooms along the hallway, the photographs of strangers covering the walls, and the softness of the rug beneath my feet, that I did not expect what I was about to see a moment later.

I had seen creatures of that kind before but never close enough to truly take in. They had often walked down the street below my window in Austria, had mixed with the crowds in the stations we had stopped in throughout the past few days, and were sometimes mentioned in the anecdotes shared by Nioka, Gertie, and even my mother.

Now there were several of them in this room. Two were lying on the rug on their stomachs, another was seated by a small desk. I stared at them, astounded. They had high-pitched voices and small bodies, and they were more or less my height.

They were—children.

35

They were playing war games. The oldest among the three, wearing brown pants and a long-sleeved dark green shirt, was lying on his belly, his knees bent at a right angle, and his calves dangling at the sides. He was handling small brown and olive-colored vehicles, which moved back and then raced forward swiftly, accompanied by cheers of glee. His shoulders were broad, his hair brown and wavy, his face somewhat wide, his nose straight, and his ears stuck out. As he looked up and his brown eyes turned toward me, his gaze was kind and warm. Then he smiled a handsome smile, revealing white teeth.

The other one playing was wearing shorts and a striped blue and green, short-sleeved shirt, despite the cold weather. His hair was fair, almost white, falling stick-like down his forehead and cut straight above his brow line; his body as thin as a matchstick, his face narrow and elongated; he had a small upturned nose, and his eyes were blue. He was holding onto small, gray-winged planes. After flying them at low altitude while lying on his belly, he suddenly stood and paced the room, flying the planes over his head as he droned intently. He circled around the room several times, and then brought the planes down toward the brown-olive vehicles the boy with the brown pants and green shirt was holding in his hands. This complex maneuver was accompanied by sounds of explosion escaping from his lips and was answered by sounds of shooting from the ground vehicles, made by the boy with the green shirt. The flight of the gray-winged planes ended with them landing safely on the rug. The boy in the striped shirt now dropped the two planes from his hands and picked out two others, repeating the same route and the same sounds, ignoring my presence altogether.

The third, who appeared to be the youngest, was sitting on a chair, leaning over the small desk with his back to us, preoccupied with something. All I saw was his brown shirt and light-colored pants, and the fact that his feet did not reach the floor.

Ruth walked into the room with me. I noticed that while she spoke to me in German, she addressed the children in the other language. My senses sharpened. Ruth kneeled down on her knees and hugged my shoulders.

"Meet your cousins, Helene," she said. "This is Gideon." She pointed to the older child in the green shirt, who not only looked up at me, but quickly set the vehicles aside, rose to his feet, came closer, and shook my hand with a smile.

"And this is Jonathan," she continued, pointing to the thinner boy with the blue and green striped shirt. After his mother called his name once more, Jonathan, obviously uninterested, finally got up, the planes still in his hands, and turned to me. Before I could figure out what was going on, a small blue plane was flown at me, still held in the boy's hand, pausing an inch from my eye. My pupils focused on the plane, then dilated to take in his eyes.

They were the most beautiful eyes I had seen in my life, blue like the sky, narrow like half-moons. And they had that spark, that teasing, ridiculing spark that immediately set me on fire.

Later, I often dwelt on when it happened. When did I fall in love with my cousin so deeply, a love that would grow to fill my days, ignite my imagination, cause me such strong emotions, and at the same time dictate my steps, trouble my soul, and make me lose so much sleep. Anyone who does not believe that a love like that can flare up as early as age five, at least in a premature, unripe form, is either narrow-minded or short on faith.

Because I know exactly when it happened to me.

It happened then, the first moment I saw him.

***

Ruth scolded Jonathan in that language I did not understand and, tightening her embrace around me, pushed him back lightly. Then she called the third child, and only when he turned around did I find, to my surprise, that he was a girl.

Ruth introduced me to Esther.

When my mother was born, as Ruth told me years later, her mother rejected Ruth's suggestion to name her little sister after the heroine of the *Book of Esther*. "The Hebrew month of *Adar* is over," she had argued, "and the book is no longer being read at synagogue." When Ruth had a daughter after two sons, she named her Esther—even though she was born in the Hebrew month of *Tevet*—simply because she loved the name.

Esther was slightly shorter than I, skinny and redheaded like Opa Michael. Her face was as wide as Gideon's and freckled, her hair short and wavy, and she too, had a small pug nose. Her brown, slightly sunken eyes were covered by long, black lashes, and her lips were as red as Jonathan's. Esther was not pretty. There was nothing in her to conjure that good-looking Jewish princess whose name she bore. But her lack of beauty was compensated by her self-confidence, her sweet temper, her kindness of heart, and her powerful personality.

In any case, Esther wanted to be a boy. She and I did not have much in common.

Now she waited for her mother to finish introducing her, curtsied, which caused Jonathan to giggle, and hurried back to the chair at the desk. Ruth sighed, apologized to me for the children not speaking any German, and turned around.

Only then did I see another child in the room.

He was leaning against the wall, staring at me. He looked older than Gideon. Tall and slim, with long legs, a narrow face, and green eyes. His hands were shoved in his pockets, his chestnut hair was slicked back.

Ruth introduced me to Davidi.

She extended her hand and asked him to come closer. Davidi walked over, leaned down a bit, and his gaze dove into mine. He said something in German, something like, "We've been waiting for you, welcome." I must have looked scared, because he did not leave my side from that moment on, holding my hand and speaking to me softly in the only language I knew. There was warmth in his eyes, warmth in the touch of his hands, and warmth in the music of his voice, which made me feel safe around him, protected from the others. The moment Ruth left the room, I clung to him, becoming his shadow.

Esther came closer and spoke quickly. Of course, I could not understand a word she said.

Davidi giggled. "She's telling you," he translated, "that I'm twelve years old, Gideon is eight, Jonathan is seven, and she's five."

I said nothing, lowering my head.

"Now she's asking how old you are."

Still silent, I pointed at her briefly before lowering my finger.

Davidi understood right away, without me having to explain. This would be happening to us a lot throughout our lives. "She's five too," he said, pointing at me, satisfying Esther's curiosity.

The sounds of war grew louder in the room. Gideon charged forward with three tanks and threatened to invade Jonathan's base. Jonathan did not try to keep the peace. In an instant, he raised two jet planes with blue bows up into the air, circling them around the room to the sounds of his whistles and shouts, as he leapt from the floor to the chair, then to the sofa, and had the airplanes execute back-flips dangerously through the air. Frantic, I took shelter behind Davidi's back. Esther chuckled and began to follow her brother around, hopping on one foot, then the other, a bit like I had done when I tried to mimic Nioka's husband, and Jonathan paused flying his planes and whistling, rolled on the floor, and held onto his stomach, bursting with laughter. Blushing all the way up to my earlobes, I quickly realized I had made an embarrassing mistake. Gideon reproached his brother and sister from his position on the rug, and Davidi saved a bit of my trampled honor when he grabbed hold of Jonathan, raised him into the air, and placed him on top of the chair, forcing him to confront his angry gaze.

At that moment, the door opened, and Jonah walked inside. Esther and Jonathan jumped on top of him with cheers of joy, and Gideon and Davidi shook his hand warmly. To my regret, Davidi, delaying his interrupted lesson until a later time, made do with a withering stare sent to Jonathan behind his father's back.

Jonah addressed the children in English, asking them to line up in front of the door. The war games were abandoned on the woolen rug. When Ruth and Naomi walked inside, all four children fell silent and fixed their eyes on my mother. I looked at her, too. I remember feeling ashamed of her gaunt frame and paleness, her unkempt hair, and her faded dress. If I only could have, I would have pulled out the red sequined dress from our brown suitcase, brushed her long hair back, the way she sometimes allowed me to do at the Madam's, and tied it with a bow at the nape of her neck. I did not want her looking so faded, gloomy, and with no light in her eyes. I wanted her to be beautiful and radiant like Ruth, to stand upright like Ruth, be happy, with a smile on her lips and love in her eyes.

Above all else, I did not like seeing the children look at her like that.

I was embarrassed.

Mother stood there, limp-limbed, still under the impression of the harsh news, and offered the children a glum smile and a dull gaze. But when Ruth introduced her to Davidi, something in her changed. A light appeared in her eyes and her indifference was gone. She approached Davidi in small, hesitant steps, lifted her bony hand, and touched his cheek, his lips, and his hair. Her eyes filled with tears.

"Davidi," she whispered. "My little boy..." Suddenly, she put her lips to his forehead, closed her eyes, and began to softly hum a lullaby. The humming gradually became a song as her voice grew louder. I could sense the other children's unease, but I felt proud. My mother sang so beautifully, and her voice was so soft and comforting. Now, I was ashamed of my own embarrassment toward her and felt responsible for her behavior, confused and perplexed.

More than anything else, I was surprised by Davidi's reaction. He grabbed Mother's emaciated face, kissed her colorless cheeks, and ran his long fingers through her hair. "Nimi..." he whispered. "I remember you... and that lullaby you used to sing..." Moisture brightened the green of his eyes.

I loved him for that.

Mother trembled, Ruth cried, and the children were more embarrassed than before. All except for Davidi, who remained by my mother's side, holding her hand. I walked closer, and he let me take his other hand. He had a pleasant body odor and his clothes smelled clean.

Jonah was the first to break the spell. "Let's eat," he said. "Naomi and Helene must be very hungry after our long journey."

The food Ruth cooked was the tastiest I had ever had—Jewish-Viennese delicacies: hot goulash soup, cooked beef in thick sauce, sauerkraut, potato dumplings, and in the tradition of Oma—thin slices of bread with sweet cherry preserves for dessert, which brought tears of longing to my mother's eyes and mine. Mother longed for

Oma Ilse, and I longed for Nioka's embrace.

After dinner, Ruth led me to the bathroom, where she removed my old clothes, put me in the tub, scrubbed my body with lilac soap, and washed my hair. Finally, she dried my body and dressed me in a small white long-sleeve nightgown she had prepared for me in advance. After putting me to bed on a sleeper sofa in the room that used to belong to Jonathan and Esther and was now repurposed for me and my mother, Jonah walked inside, a picture book in his hand, and took a seat at the edge of the sofa. The book was *Winnie-the-Pooh*. I had never had a book read to me before, and I was transfixed by the plot, the characters, and especially the illustrations.

While I was enjoying a bedtime story, Ruth bathed my mother and tried to cheer her up. She scrubbed her skin with the lavender-colored soap, washed her, dried and brushed her long hair, and dressed her in a warm nightgown.

Shortly before the two of them entered the room where I, riveted by Pooh and his pals, was sitting with Jonah, he pulled out his blue hat again and, with a smile, proposed that I toss in any questions that came to mind.

I asked and asked without stop. About Jonathan and Esther, Davidi and Gideon, Ruth and Jonah, and for every question he had an answer. He even said, "Yes," when I asked if he would be willing to be my father, too.

I think he might have cried a little.

But I also remember one question he did not answer. I asked if Ruth could be my mother, too. He only cried a bit more and fell silent, embarrassed.

36

November 1990
(This letter was thrown out)

Blair,

My mother was mentally ill. Sometimes, I was ashamed of her. Of her empty stare, her crying spells, her odd behavior. The first time I felt that way was when we left the brothel where we had hidden during the war and arrived at Ruth and Jonah's home in London. Suddenly I saw a father, a mother, and children. A family. As long as we had lived in that shoebox of an attic at the brothel, I had had no idea. My mother was the most important person I ever had.

But then I got out of there, and I saw things. I saw the world.

Mother never succeeded in adjusting to the post-war world. She couldn't truly get past the 1940s. A part of her had died back then. I didn't like it. I wanted to devour life, to move forward, to live… I despised her melancholy, the fragility of her soul. It scared me. I was afraid of sinking along with her.

I just didn't understand…

I tried, at times. I truly did. I sought out her intimacy, yearned for the heat of her body. I listened, riveted, to stories of the past she'd unfolded to me in blessed moments of alertness, truly impressed by her magical storytelling ability.

But most of the time I didn't understand. I was hard on her, indifferent to her needs and impatient. I was selfish.

I'm ashamed of it today. I've been lamenting my behavior for years.

Ruth once told me that I was lucky to have had a mother. So many children lost their mothers during the war. You only get one mother, she said. Mothers should be cared for with love and devotion.

Oh, Blair, if you only knew what I'd be willing to give just to go back, what I'd be willing to do to enjoy her hug and her smile, and, most of all, her forgiveness…

Now that I'm so busy thinking and reminiscing, I feel bad about you, too.

You were born to another mother, another father. Different parents. I legally adopted you and gave you all my love. But at the same time, I also treated you as if you had come from me. I kept the identity of your biological parents secret for so many years.

I was afraid that if I revealed this one secret, I'd have to reveal others.

Your father objected. We had many conflicts on the topic, if only you knew how many. But I was more determined. When we told you, only recently, that you were adopted, you took it hard but claimed to have suspected it for years. You realized we'd been married for a shorter time than you'd thought, and that the rest of the family had collaborated with us in hiding the truth.

I didn't use to see it that way. I wanted to protect you and give you the sense of security that I never had had as a child. I wanted to spare you the sense of loss. It was twisted, of course. I had no right. I should have known: you're not me. Unlike me, you don't talk much, but when you say something, it is like a ring landing around the neck of a bottle on the first toss. You like order, as straight as an arrow. Unlike me, you can't lie. I could have learned so much from you and your mother. She was like you…

After the painful discovery you pulled away, mostly from me. It hurt, but I understood. You can't imagine how hard it was for me to gather myself together and give you the package your mother entrusted me with.

She'd given it to me almost eighteen years ago, and I hadn't touched it since. It remained packed exactly as your mother had left it, with the wrapping paper she'd chosen, reddish-brown like the earth, tied in twine with two bows.

You took the package from me, your mother's gift, and opened it in your room, alone.

Less than a month later you packed your things and left. You went far away.

I get it. I would probably have responded the same way, or worse.

Your mother was a wonderful woman. She loved you and your father more than anything in the world. You got her exotic beauty, her dark skin, flowing black hair, and almond-shaped, olive-toned eyes.

Someday, after we both come home, I'll sit down and tell you all about her.

But not only about her.

About him, too.

37

I grew up on stories of the blitz. Years after the war ended, we could still see signs of the destruction German bombers caused to the cities of England between September 1940 and May 1941. It seemed that every Brit had some terrifying or heroic story to share about that time.

I realized very early in my life that in the same years I was born and survived the hardships of war with my mother in Austria, our family was suffering in London from sirens in the middle of the night and the nightmare of bombs, as they ran to the public shelter across the street and glanced fearfully at the sky, only to find, to their relief, that Hitler's bombers were no longer alone. Like hundreds of thousands of others, Jonah and Ruth watched the aerial battles that took place thousands of meters over their heads between Luftwaffe planes and the planes of the Royal Air Force, praying that no one had been hurt in a building that had been hit by a bomb and was now on fire and that the plane that had been downed, black smoke wafting from its tail, was not one of "theirs." Along with their prime minister, Sir Winston Churchill, they were proud of the robustness of the British spirit, able to stand up to the Nazi aggressor. Like many of their neighbors and friends, they chose to send their children away from the bombed city to smaller, safer towns.

Ruth once told me that when the war broke, she vehemently refused to leave her home and Jonah and take her young children and Davidi, who had only arrived a few months earlier, to the countryside. Even in June 1940, after Germany occupied France, and hundreds of thousands of British schoolchildren, the disabled and elderly, pregnant and breastfeeding women were evacuated from London to remote villages according to a government contingency plan prepared before the war, Ruth pushed aside any thoughts of leaving. Instead, she voluntarily helped in creating fortifications by filling hundreds of large sacks with sand and stacking them around the public shelter across the street.

But then September arrived, and the city was pummeled. Fire was burning on the streets, devouring houses. Jonah volunteered to the Engineering Corps and Ruth remained alone, frightened and at a loss. First, she moved with the children to Jonah's parents' home at the edge of town, only to find that the public shelter in central London was preferable to the space under the staircase in her in-laws' living room or compared to what they called a "shelter," which was nothing more than a hole hastily dug in their backyard and later strengthened with provisional walls. Then she returned with her children to their apartment on a day of especially heavy bombings and, helpless and anxious for their welfare, settled into the shelter across the street. Finally, she gave in to reason, and like many before her, submitted a rush request for rehousing for her, Gideon, Davidi, little Jonathan, and baby Esther, who was only a few weeks old, sheltered by her arms and fed by her milk.

The day of parting arrived. Jonah drove Davidi, Ruth, and their children to the train station, which was crowded with women, the elderly, and other children, possessions in their hands, rectangular brown boxes containing gas masks hanging loosely from their shoulders, and I.D. badges hanging around their necks. He said goodbye to them on the gray platform with great difficulty, mustering up all his strength in order to explain to the fallen little faces that they were going to be happy out in the country, with open spaces to run around in, instead of the unbearable overcrowding of the shelter, and fresh air instead of the smell of smoke. He promised again that they would be able to sleep soundly rather than wake up in the middle of the night to the sounds of sirens and have to run out into the cold to a shelter. The three boys stood there, with their arms around each other, alongside dozens of other children: boys in shorts, black shoes, knee-high socks, long-sleeved shirts, woolen sweaters, and dark jackets; and girls in dresses and overcoats, holding onto favorite dolls. Davidi's and Gideon's gas mask boxes were slung across their shoulders, and in their hands, they held lunch boxes containing some modest provisions that Ruth had packed to tide them over until they reached their host family or shelter.

Ruth repeated her description of Jonathan's crying, which mingled with baby Esther's wails of hunger and alarm; and, from a distance of time and place, their crying broke my heart. She recalled that Davidi promised Jonah to "be strong" and to take care of her and the younger children away from home—his emotional promise caused my heart to ache. And when she portrayed his green eyes, clear of tears but so sad, I became sad too.

When Jonah turned to leave, after he kissed and hugged, made promises, gave instructions, made sure his wife and the children had gotten on the train, and turned toward his Ford Anglia, Ruth sat up and took a deep breath. She had once promised her mother, Ilse Steiner née Rosenthal, that she would not break, no matter what. In her imagination, she joined her husband on the ride back to their apartment building, which was now almost empty of children and adults who could had left. Their apartment was suddenly so vacant and cold, and she wanted to lie down in their bed, close her eyes, and wait for the nightmare to end. But Esther's crying brought her back to reality, and once again she recalled her mother nudging her to stand straight and whispering to her, "You are a warrior, Ruth. Your personality is strong, and your spirit is steadfast." Then, praying that the sirens would not go off exactly at that moment, she straightened her back, picked up her baby from the pram, leaned back in her seat on the train, pulled out a breast, and thanked God for blessing her with an abundance of milk, and that despite everything else that was happening, baby Esther was gaining weight beautifully.

***

I sometimes felt as if I had been there too. My childhood in Austria seemed dull and utterly unheroic when compared to what my cousins had been through, and my heart was filled with a bizarre mixture of compassion, awe, and envy.

In the first weeks after my arrival, before I could even speak a word of their language, I used to sit in the children's room, fascinated by Gideon and Jonathan's war games. These reached an apex of loud excitement with aerial battles, in which were involved chairs, beds, pillows, and everything in between, as well as Esther, who stood on a chair and announced each plane that had been shot down and repeated the promised victory of the British Spitfires and Hurricanes over the German Messerschmitts, despite their clear numerical inferiority.

When I knew a bit more English, I was entranced and appalled by the descriptions of the awful blitz, whose signs of destruction were still visible all over London. I drank up every word and believed every tale, even when Gideon and Jonathan gave their over-dramatic descriptions, although they had been very young at the time and it's doubtful they remembered.

And then there was Davidi, who depicted the sights as they had remained frozen in his memory. From his point of view, the RAF and enemy planes looked like small insects clashing in midair. Only when he heard the whistle of a nearing bomb, when one of the houses caught fire, or when black smoke rose from a downed plane, did the insects take on the appearance of vessels of war. Once, a German pilot parachuted down near his hit plane, and, to the sound of Ruth's protests, Davidi rushed out to watch the unusual attraction, cheering along with his friends when the enemy pilot was detained and led, wounded, bound, and docile, to the police car.

I remember how I used to listen, captivated, to Davidi's stories about the life they used to have out in the country. But most of all I remember his painful descriptions of the day when he was forced to leave Jonah and, for the second time in his life, be sent to "a safe place away from danger." I only truly understood the threads of sorrow interspersed among the words years later, the day we strolled on the banks of the Yarkon River together, when Davidi told me for the first time about the day he had separated forever from his parents.

***

One afternoon, when the two of us were home alone, Davidi asked me if I wanted to hear something that reminded him of Gabriel.

"Gabriel?" I asked.

"Gabriel was my father," he explained. "And your uncle."

I thought then how nice it would have been to have another kind, loving uncle, like Jonah, who would allow me to ask questions and provide answers to them all, pat my head and make me meals. Wanting to get to know this Gabriel a little better, I nodded gladly.

Davidi led me down the stairs to the first floor of the building and knocked on one of the doors. An old, wrinkled lady opened the door. She was delighted to see Davidi and invited him inside as if he were the most venerable of visitors. Then she stared at me and asked him in her hoarse, deep voice who this beautiful child was. Davidi spoke my name proudly; I will never forget that. Then he walked confidently into the living room, like someone who knew the place well, and pointed to a large, brown piece of furniture, the likes of which I had never seen before. It had keys, some black, mostly white. I was in awe when Davidi announced that beyond the thing's beauty, it also produced sounds.

He sat me down in a small chair and said simply, "Helene, meet my friend, the piano, and meet Mrs. Rothenberg, my music teacher."

I smiled politely at Mrs. Rothenberg, stood up and curtsied. I had never seen anyone as old or wrinkled before. Davidi took a seat at the piano, and Mrs. Rothenberg stood behind him, her hand on his shoulder.

"What would you like to play?" she asked in heavily accented English.

Davidi flipped through the music books on the nearby shelf and chose a piece by Beethoven, who he explained was an important, deaf composer, and one of his parents' favorites.

"*Appassionata*. Piano Sonata No. 23 in F Minor," the teacher announced, raising her crooked finger into the air.

Davidi started to play, and a shiver passed through me. His playing was—how can I describe it? It was divine. The keys of the piano seemed to devote themselves to his confident playing and the touch of his beautiful, long fingers. Davidi smiled as he played, his eyes closed. I did not make a peep. The shriveled Mrs. Rothenberg pursed her mouth with concentration, and her entire body trembled. Davidi finished playing, but I did not want to leave. I asked him to keep going, and he did, on and on, just for me. Chills crept up and down my spine, and Mrs. Rothenberg's body continued to tremble as Davidi's fingers fluttered confidently over the black and white keys.

When it grew dark outside Ruth arrived. She apologized to Mrs. Rothenberg and led us back to our apartment. The old teacher's voice accompanied us as we climbed up the stairs, saying—perhaps to us, perhaps to herself—that she had never had a student as talented as Davidi, and that he reminded her of her only son when he was a young boy. Her son had also had a promising gift, but fate was not kind to him, for he was killed while serving in the Polish military during World War I.

When we arrived at my aunt and uncle's apartment on the third floor, the sounds of the piano mixed in my mind with the sounds of war coming from the children's room, and I ran inside to tell them that I had just heard God's music. But instead, a toy plane, which had been flown toward the door and hit my head, had Jonah, Ruth, and me rushing to the emergency room to treat the deep gash that would not stop bleeding.

I spent that weekend in bed, letting my stitches heal. Jonathan was grounded as punishment for his recklessness, and since his father had also confiscated his fleet of planes, he shut himself in the children's room. On the rare occasions when he emerged, he made no effort to disguise his anger, which was directed at me and made me miserable.

If there was any comfort to be had, other than from the divine music that continued to play in my mind, it was in the relative quiet I enjoyed, if only for a short time, from the ruckus of planes and the whistling of bombs that were always coming from the children's room. For a spell, no sounds of war were heard in the house.

38

I was fluent after only four months of broken English. About that time my name was anglicized to *Helena*. The children called me by my new name, but Mother, Ruth, and even Davidi, every now and then slipped back to my old German one.

Moved by her admiration for the Queen of England, my mother tried to speak English, too. But unlike Ruth's flowing, musical English, Mother's English was gripped by a heavy German accent, and lacking many words; and, in any case, she often preferred to slide back to her mother tongue, especially when she was in pain, and I could swear that when she cried, she did it in German.

The little girl I used to be did not like that.

The little girl I used to be loved Ruth. She saw Ruth as being so different than her mother, even after eliminating the element of mental illness. Like the Moabite heroine, Ruth had a pleasant personality, a warm heart, and wisdom. Wherever she went, she quickly won people over. Even as a girl back in London, I was always proud to walk beside her. Ruth seemed to float above the sidewalk, her fair hair flowing down her shoulders in soft waves, her cheeks flushed, and a hint of laughter in her feline green eyes, while the anguish she kept, the pain of loss, was buried deep inside her.

Everything that Ruth requested, I tried to fulfill, even when she asked me to be more patient with my mother. Except for one thing. Gideon's persistent refusal, to Ruth's great dismay, to speak the language of the enemy that had destroyed his city from the air, imbued his younger siblings with courage, and quickly became the refusal of Jonathan, Esther, and me. Thus, even though my mother usually spoke to me in her mother tongue, I refused to answer in German. The Jonas' enemies were my enemies, their friends were my friends, and our language was one.

***

When my mother and I arrived in London at the end of 1945, the city was in the midst of an extensive renovation. Everywhere you looked were giant bulldozers, pumps, and tractors, beside cement mixers and equipment for paving roads. Cranes worked all hours of the day. The British government subsidized the construction of rental apartments, and hundreds of thousands of new buildings were slated to be built all over England in the six years following the war, alongside dozens of new factories, many of them in less-fortunate areas. Jonah acquired plenty of construction experience during this period, after having successfully supervised the reconstruction of a large factory in east London that had been bombed during the war.

One morning, he took me to see a construction site where he was working. He answered my dozens of questions patiently and at noon drove me through the city and told me stories of the destruction and resurrection of buildings, factories, train stations, and airports. His stories taught me about the resilient spirit of the English, which had not been broken during the terrible days of the blitz. "Ask the British what was our finest hour," he told me, "and they will all tell you it was during the war." When he said this, he pursed his lips with appreciation and nodded. I was moved by his words and kept asking more and more.

That evening, when we returned home together, Jonah marveled to Ruth about how he had spent the entire day roaming through

London, giving lengthy and detailed descriptions of that awful war to an exceptionally intelligent little girl, not even six years old.

The girl I used to be loved London.

I loved everything about it. The old city with its Roman and Saxon remnants, its medieval, gothic buildings, its long streets, and the underground stations that in wartime were used as bomb shelters and nocturnal bedrooms for tens of thousands of people whose homes were ruined. I loved the monuments, the parks, and the old buses. I loved the school where I studied in the same classroom with Esther, even though it was strict. I loved Miss Berkeley, my stern, redheaded teacher, even though she slapped our wrists with a ruler. I loved the weather, even though it often rained. More than anything else, I loved Ruth's habit of hosting her friends for five o'clock tea, in which they chatted, exchanged gossip, and had cake. In her generosity, Ruth allowed me to participate in one such get-together, as long as I sat quietly beside my mother, which I preferred immensely to the noisy crowding of my cousins and the guests' children in the children's room, especially because I wanted to listen to the women's moving stories, which aroused my imagination and illuminated the war in a different light.

One of them narrated that on the first night of the blitz, she had been out at a large dance hall in Hammersmith, in west London, with her new husband, when suddenly sirens were heard outside, harbingers of the approach of enemy planes. "The conductor announced that the orchestra would continue to play as long as people remained in the hall," she said. "And imagine, out of the 1,500 people who were there, only half a dozen left!" Another woman described the lunchtime piano concerts given during the long months when London was bombed from the air. "After all," she emphasized, "the German Luftwaffe planes mostly dropped their bombs at night." A third pointed out that British cinema received unusual recognition during that dramatic time for its artistic expression, since the films made at the time succeeded, with a creative realism, in conveying the sense of separateness, sacrifice, and loss, which were an inherent part of war.

Aunt Ruth contributed to the conversation by praising BBC Radio, which, despite its conservatism, gained popularity among the British public over the six years of war, thanks to its reliable reports and its broadcast of Churchill's fiery speeches to the nation, and thanks, as well, to the voice of the singer Vera Lynn, "the forces' sweetheart." At her guest's request, Ruth turned on the gramophone, and Lynn's voice enveloped me with melancholy as she sang "There'll Always be an England." But when she sang "We'll Meet Again," and Lynn promised her beloved, away in battle, "Don't know where, don't know when…but I know we'll meet again some sunny day," tears appeared in my mother's tired eyes, and all the other women looked at her with wonder and compassion. Once Ruth explained that all traces of my father, her love, had vanished during the war, their compassion multiplied.

After a second cup of tea and another slice of Ruth's plum cake, the guests moved on to discussing the frequent changes England had gone through in the post-war era under the rule of the Labor Party, led by Clement Attlee. I understood very little of this conversation, but I remember well the longing in the women's voices for the previous prime minister, war hero Sir Winston Churchill, who had surprisingly been defeated by Attlee and the Labor Party in the general election that took place at the war's end.

A tall, big-boned woman recalled how Churchill had said in one of his speeches that "success is not final failure, is not fatal: it is the courage to continue that counts." The other women nodded to signify they remembered it well. Another woman, who had not parted with her purple hat the entire afternoon, pointed out that Churchill would be better off not criticizing Attlee's legitimate election, for he himself liked to repeat that "Democracy is the worst form of government, except for all the others," and her words brought forth a series of loud arguments spoken over teacups. Then a third woman, angel-faced, leaned forward, and in a conspiratorial tone whispered that their venerable leader, who was known for his affection for whiskey, had also once said something sarcastic to a political rival who accused him of being "disgustingly drunk." "Well, my dear," he said, "you are ugly, and what's more, you are disgustingly ugly. But tomorrow I shall be sober, and you will still be disgustingly ugly!" This quote and the wave of laughter that followed redirected the conversation into a flow of gossip and bad-mouthing, which were offered in a pleasant tone and proper English, but which, to me, were almost as lethal as the blitz.

At this point I grew tired with the idle chatter and moved to the children's room. I walked in carefully so as not to get hit by another plane, and I found a pile of children on a small rug, moving small jeeps and tanks along imaginary roads, shouting, cheering, and making war sounds. I remember being surprised. The children I met at school were mostly obedient and quiet, attentive to their teachers and full of awe. But here they were unbridled, bouncing from one side of the room to the other, roaring with laughter. I could not help but notice that while Gideon was trying to keep the ruckus at bay, Jonathan was the bold leader of the group.

It was a fine autumn day. At Jonathan's request, our mothers allowed us to go down to the nearby playground. In Davidi's absence, Ruth conditioned Esther's and my attendance upon Gideon's supervision.

We slid down the banisters, nine cheerful children, and burst out into the streets with merry cries. But rather than head to the playground, Jonathan pulled us in the opposite direction. Even responsible Gideon, excited and in high spirits, did not stop him. Jonathan led us to a building at the end of the street, which had collapsed during the war and had not yet been rebuilt. I remember the spark of mischief in his eyes and his teasing look as if inciting us to do wrong.

We all knew we were not allowed inside. Large signs warned of danger. But the ropes blocking the entrance to the building were not impassable.

We crept inside, Jonathan in the lead. I had never felt so free. We stood, in awe, before the ruins. Broken-down walls and sticky plaster piled up on top of shattered furniture, old radio parts, towels that had turned into rags, bits of toys. Jonathan was the first to step inside. When he leaned down to pick up a radio that was lying on its side, Gideon shouted at him to stop.

"Don't touch anything, Jonathan!" he ordered. "We shouldn't be here! We've got to get out immediately!"

But Jonathan raised the broken radio in his hand, as if he had not heard a word.

One of the girls cried that it was dangerous, grabbed her sister's hand, and dragged her out into the street. Esther panicked and began to run toward Jonathan. Gideon's shout, that she must stop, still echoed through the room when Esther bumped into a loose board and fell onto a broken chair. The chair flipped over, and we all saw it, right behind her: a large, gray, rusty piece of metal that made a creaking sound. Something inside began to tick.

Gideon ordered us to run out to the street. My heart was racing. I saw the other children fleeing in terror, Gideon dashing to Esther, and Jonathan dropping the broken radio. I heard the radio shattering and Gideon calling my name, but I was paralyzed in place. Each second felt like an eternity. I watched Gideon raise Esther in his arms and stride toward me, but before I could even figure out what was going on, Jonathan landed at my side, took my hand, and forcefully pulled me outside. The four of us ran out into the street, distancing ourselves from the shattered building, Gideon holding Esther's hand, Jonathan holding mine. Then an explosion propelled us all forward, and within moments the tenants of all the buildings on the block ran out and a scary number of police cars showed up, followed by experts and sappers, investigators and journalists, who would report about a live bomb found in a residential London neighborhood by a group of children that was most likely dropped by a German plane during the war but had never exploded. Now, due to impact, its activation mechanism had been set in motion. It was also said that this was no rare occurrence in this post-war era, and that a considerable number of live bombs had been uncovered recently all over London, which had been massively bombed from the air during the blitz.

And us? Other than a scare, a few bruises, and a bleeding scratch down Esther's knee, we had all come out unscathed. Ruth's guests, so relieved to find us alive and well, showered us with kisses, hugs, and tears. My mother was there too, with Ruth and the other women, but she was completely frozen. Only later, at night, did the tears and shivers and uncontrollable sobs emerge. She ended up in the hospital for a week.

I felt terrible. I felt awful. I felt guilty.

When Ruth and Jonah unleashed their wrath on Gideon and Jonathan and punished them dearly, I felt even worse. I was also a bit angry at them. Gideon and Jonathan were courageous in my eyes, in Esther's eyes, and in the eyes of all the children in the neighborhood. They had saved my life and Esther's, and overnight they became my heroes.

In the evening, when the sun set and the air grew cold, I tried to pull away from my Mother's weeping and my uncle's anger and sought out Davidi to soothe me.

Dear Ruth, who perceived my agitation and took pity on me, allowed me to go down with Davidi to Mrs. Rothenberg's apartment. The old lady was excited to see us and hugged me as if I were a survivor of the Titanic. That day, in her house, I enjoyed a full hour of relaxation and musical grace, with Davidi playing a Mozart piano sonata and a Chopin Nocturne especially for me.

39

November 1990
Yosemite Park, California

Dear Davidi,

I was so touched to receive your letter today, but also a little surprised. You've never written me here. In general, you haven't written to me in the past decade. During the times we didn't see each other, we spoke on the phone. I thought letters were a thing of the past for most people. I thought I was the last of a dying breed.

And then I get a letter from you, from Berlin, written on lightly perfumed stationery (a trick you must have learned from your Italian lover, who liked to spritz perfume on everything), filled with your familiar handwriting, deviating over and under rows, as if you were writing music; your words, the notes.

I assume you weren't just missing me. I'm guessing you heard about what happened at our home, about how I left, about how Blair left. How did you find out, Davidi? Did you call our place and speak to Nelly? Or was it Mike? If it was Mike you spoke to, please describe what he sounded like when you talked about me... I apologize for the unusual request, but I must know. Mike is normally a calm guy, in full control. But this time was there a note of anger in his voice? Acceptance? Longing? It would mean so much to me to know, because right now, for the first time in my life, when it comes to Mike's thoughts and feelings for me, I'm totally in the dark.

You asked about Blair. I wish I knew more. She left in the summer, went all the way to Myanmar. She might be someplace else by this point. My entire relationship with her now comes down to the letters I write her but never send, partly because I don't know her address. Recently, I've begun to worry that she might decide to go to Israel at what seems to be an inopportune time. It looks like war is brewing over there.

You know why she left, Davidi. You know exactly what happened. You were aware of all my misgivings. I know I hadn't acted wisely, hiding too much and waiting too long, not being more open with Blair and Mike over the years. Mike accused me of lying to him. When he said it, his handsome face turned red with anger, and his eyes narrowed.

I never felt as if I were lying, but perhaps Mike is right. I would like for you, the one person who knows me better than anyone else in the world, to tell me what you really think about all this. Your opinion, as you know, means a lot to me, even though you sometimes think I don't take your advice seriously.

Don't worry about me. I came here because I decided to put my life on paper. All these years I asked you, Gideon, Irit, Esther, and, at the time, Ruth not to discuss my life too much with the children or even with Mike. The geographic distance helped. Against your will, I made you complicit in the fog I'd covered over my past. I've always been somewhat self-centered, but you know there was nothing malicious about it.

You also know why I chose to come here, of all places. You even joined me on one of my visits. I was writing the final chapters of my book *Not Just a Grain of Sand*, and you wanted to rest up after a very busy concert season and to relax after your separation from your second wife, which you'd defined as "final."

I mostly arrive here alone. I need quiet and detachment to write. But that time, when you suddenly showed, was very special and left me with a magical memory. We walked together down the foggy path. As always, I had trouble keeping pace with you. I was especially moved when you joined me at the Mariposa Grove, because ever since that first autumn, I've always visited those sequoias on my own.

Mike wasn't too happy about the idea of both of us staying at the lodge together, even though we had separate rooms. It seemed odd to him, although we'd met in private many times before, sometimes in Israel, other times in Europe. But eventually he came around. Mike has so much respect for you. He knows how dear you are to me, and understands that, after all, you're only my cousin.

Dear Davidi, write to me again from time to time. I'm always missing you. Tell me if there is any new and exciting woman in your life. Things are always interesting with you, and I'm curious to hear all about it.

Yours, with love,
Helena

40

One evening, in early November 1947, Ruth and Jonah had us all convene in the living room and announced that they had decided to immigrate to *Eretz Israel*— the Land of Israel. Stunned and silent, we stood there. The only sound was Jonah's enthusiastic voice. "Villages are being established, sometimes overnight," he said, his eyes glittering. "Young men and women are joining the *Palmach*.[3] Just imagine young Jewish people holding weapons, rebelling against British rule and against everyone attempting to thwart the Jewish people's renewed right to its land... The image of the Israeli sabra is gradually forming, and the Hebrew language is heard on every street..."

When he became choked with emotion, Ruth took over. "The small Jewish settlement in the country is fighting to absorb the remainder of European Jews. The lucky ones receive certificates, but these are being handed out sparingly. With no other option, most of the immigrants arrive at the shores of Palestine on illegal ships to be absorbed in the middle of the night by the boys of the *Palyam*,[4] right under the noses of the British government officials attempting to hunt them down..."

---

3   The elite fighting force of the Haganah, the underground army of the Jewish community during the period of the British Mandate for Palestine.

4   The sea force of the Palmach.

I glanced sideways. Gideon and Jonathan were fascinated. Mother stood still, and Davidi looked down at the floor.

The presentation came to its climax when Ruth stood up and waved a stack of papers in the air.

"Do you know what these are?" she asked, her eyes laughing, "right here in my hands?" Without waiting for an answer, she called out, "These are very important documents!" His eyes shining with joy, Jonah picked up a surprised Davidi in his arms. "We're one of the lucky ones!" he cheered. "We have certificates for each of us, bearing the seal of Her Majesty's government. All in all, eight beautiful, perfectly legal certificates… Could there be anything better?"

It would be years before I learned that while the certificates bearing the names of the five members of the Jonas family were special immigration licenses, granted to Jonah due to his profession, which was "vital" to the Mandate government, the certificates provided to my mother, Davidi, and myself, were acquired by Jonah for a hefty sum. He purchased them for a thousand pounds each, with the help of his parents and loans he had taken from the Zionist Organization.

But at that moment, we knew nothing about these things. Baffled by the news, we all stared silently at those very important documents.

The first to react was Gideon, who asked a long series of questions. Davidi kept silent, and Mother began to weep again. I was moved and confused, but this time my mother's tears did not moisten my eyes, as they were such a common occurrence by this point that I did not even linger over them. From the corner of my eye, I could see Jonathan's half-moon eyes twinkling with mischief as he hopped excitedly in the air, dragging Esther along with him. For a moment, I felt compelled to do the same, for I was prepared to do anything to please him.

But something stopped me.

Something stronger than myself.

The world of the imagination.

I fixed my eyes on a small oil painting of Jerusalem hanging in the dining room and began to sketch the landscapes of the country in my mind, as they appeared in the evocative stories Ruth liked to tell Esther and me at bedtime. In her stories, the Land of Israel was the land of milk and honey; its mountains dripping nectar and its hills milk; honey pouring down the carpets of its fields. When we wondered, "What does milk signify?" she explained that some attribute it to the juices of fruit and others to animal milk. And when we asked, "What do you mean by 'honey'?" she said that while some attribute it to the honey of figs or dates, others believe it signifies the honey of forests or bees.

After he patiently answered all of Gideon's questions, Jonah concluded agitatedly that, one step at a time, a new country was forming, and that soon enough the British government would fold up its flags, return its soldiers to their own land, and an independent Jewish state would rise in the land of our ancestors.

***

Blair once asked me, when she was only ten years old, what my favorite subject was at school.

"History," I answered.

She asked, "Why history?"

I remember shifting my cup of tea along the table, pondering the enormous influence of history on the private lives of humans—the way history can fling them about from one place to another like weightless grains of sand, and the way the great fluctuations of events in the world control the small lives of each individual. In those moments, I also considered how some centuries were peaceful, others agitated, and the era and place a man is born into is only a matter of luck. History does not end only with past events, but it abounds and accumulates in the events of the present. To our eyes, these become part of it only when leaders speak, generals win or lose, markets respond, and historians summarize everything into words, recording it all in the books.

But Blair was only ten years old, and I did not want to burden her with such weighty matters. Instead, I only quoted something that Ruth told me when I was around the same age.

"Because," I said, "that's where everything begins."

***

Jonah was right. Not a month went by from his dramatic announcement, which swept us all away in a turmoil of emotion and preparation, and he was gathering us in the living room once more.

"Do you know what day it is?" he asked.

"Tuesday," Gideon, Jonathan, and Esther said in unison, and, recalling something he had heard in the synagogue, something to do with the seven days of creation, Gideon added, "Twice as good."

Jonah burst out laughing, picked his eldest son in his arms, raised him into the air before our marveling eyes, and cried out, "That's right! And not only twice as good, children, but ten times as good!"

The memories of that abnormally good day now form one long, happy continuum in my mind. Ruth standing, teary-eyed, at her husband's side, announcing to us that in a short while we would all gather around the radio and listen to what was about to take place many miles away from us—the United Nations General Assembly in Lake Success, New York. Jonah telling us, his voice shaking, that in just a little while, the nations of the world would make a crucial historic decision, irrevocably changing the fate of the Jewish people. My mother whispered a question—what would become of us if the nations of the world disappointed us again, as they always had? Jonah wrapped his arms around her and asked us all in a booming voice to always remember this day, 29 November 1947, as the day in which good news came from the West, spreading its wings and reaching all the people of Israel, wherever they may be.

I do not know what gave him the confidence that a majority vote would be achieved and the decision would, indeed, be made. But I remember how I gazed, charmed, at my uncle Jonah, whose name meant "dove" in Hebrew, comparing him in my mind to another dove, one from Ruth's biblical stories, that landed from the heavens with an olive branch in its beak, signaling that the flood was over.

A knock came at the door, and in came Jonah's parents, followed by two of Ruth's friends, along with their husbands and children, and Mrs. Rothenberg, who had made the effort to climb the stairs to our apartment to alleviate her tense anticipation and share the greatness of the moment with us. The black radio was turned on, and we all surrounded it in euphoric high spirits. Ruth was prepared with a pencil and a piece of paper to list the countries that were in support and the ones in opposition. All through the assembly, we held our breaths along with the hundreds of other Jews who were in Lake Success, and the thousands crowding the streets of New York, and our prayers intertwined with that of the hundreds of thousands of Jews in the Land of Israel and the world over, who must have also been sitting around their radios with bated breaths and anxious hearts.

One by one, the different states' ambassadors voiced their positions with a single word: "Yes", "No", or "Abstain." Then came the yearned-for message, delivered in the dry voice of the President of the UN General Assembly, announcing their recommendation on a partition of Mandatory Palestine into independent Arab and Jewish States. The excitement at the Jonas home was tremendous. Everyone cheered, clapped, hugged, and shed tears of happiness.

Immediately upon receiving news that the leadership of the Jewish population in the Land of Israel had accepted the partition plan, the Jews of the world rejoiced. Those in Israel stepped out into the streets to dance all over Palestine. Strangers were kissing each other tearfully, climbing on British tanks without any protest, hanging from the sides of trucks, banging the roofs of cars, and roaring together over and over: "A Jewish state!!! Free immigration!!!"

At the bottom of the Arch of Titus in Rome, the symbol of the destruction of the second temple, the Jews of the city said the *Shehecheyanu* blessing, thanking God for this special gift, and in Lake Success, tens of thousands of Jews inside and outside the hall spoke a prayer for life and danced the *Hora* on the sidewalks, their glee washing over the streets. Everyone indulged in the elation and waved the flags of the state that had yet to be established—their backgrounds white, two blue stripes running across it, and a Star of David floating between the stripe of sea and the streak of sky.

41

But our immigration plans were about to be postponed by at least two years.

***

It was a winter afternoon in 1948, shortly after the New Year celebrations ended. Esther and I watched Jonah as he paced the bedroom like a caged lion. I had never seen him as restless as he was that day. A short while earlier, Ruth had spoken to him with a beseeching voice, but when he turned his back on her, she had buried her face in her hands. Then she had walked into our small room, her eyes red, and helped Mother prepare for her doctor's appointment.

I knew this was no regular doctor, the kind that checked your ears, throat, or stomach. Jonathan called him a "mind doctor" and I wondered how his stethoscope could reach so deep. I decided I would ask Jonah about it afterward.

I waited for Ruth and Naomi to go out, leaving Jonah, Esther, and me behind. Then I lightly knocked on my uncle's open bedroom door and found him busy with paperwork that was scattered all over his desk in the corner of the room, between the bed and Ruth's trunk of starched linen.

To my surprise, Jonah asked me meekly to leave and close the door behind me.

As I retreated, embarrassed and disappointed, I tried to spot his blue top hat on the hook, the bed, or the linen trunk—Jonah always kept the hat in his bedroom—but found it nowhere. When I stood with Esther on the other side of the closed door, and we both put our ears to it in a failed attempt to eavesdrop on Jonah's whispered phone calls, I asked her softly if she happened to see her father's top hat. Esther shrugged and said she hadn't.

When we heard Jonah's footsteps on the other side of the door, we flew away like two startled birds, rushing to take cover behind the credenza. Jonah stepped out towards the chest-of-drawers in the entry hall. He stood up with his back to us, fished out a manila envelope from a drawer and pulled small and large papers out of it. He perused them for several minutes, then returned them to the envelope. Frozen in place for a moment with his fists leaning on the bureau top, his balding head lowered. Esther and I were shocked to see his shoulders shaking. When he let out a quiet sob, our breaths caught in our throats. I saw the terrified look in Esther's eyes and squeezed her hand in mine, although I was equally scared. When he left the room, we rushed out of our hiding place and stood, at a loss, by the dining table. A few moments later, Jonah returned. He seemed relieved to see us.

"Where have you been, girls?" Then, without waiting for an answer, he asked for our permission to leave us alone at home for "no longer than thirty minutes."

Esther shook her head no, but I grabbed her hand, and nodded in agreement. "Yes, Daddy-Uncle." That is what I called him.

The moment he left the apartment, we approached the drawer. We knew we were forbidden to look inside. I told Esther we should not, we must not, but she whispered that if Jonathan were here, he would have done so a long time ago.

I needed no further persuasion.

With shaking hands, I removed the papers from the manila

envelope and spread them on the floor before me. After a quick re-view, I informed Esther that these were those "very important docu-ments" that Jonah and Ruth had discussed two months ago. When I saw her imploring expression, I explained impatiently that they were the immigration documents from the Mandate government.

"Oh, the certificates," she said, and I was surprised she remem-bered the word.

I quickly shoved the papers back into the envelope and returned it to the drawer. Esther and I were still very confused. She asked me why her father was so sad, and I shrugged and said these certificates were a very good thing, and that grownups can sometimes be a little irrational.

Suddenly, I spotted his blue hat. It was on the floor, at the foot of the heater, a bit crumpled on its right side. I quickly picked it up and felt its sides. Tears choked my throat. I tried to smooth out the crumpled part, but to no avail. Eventually, I placed it gently on the linen trunk in Jonah and Ruth's bedroom.

I suggested we play a letter game that I always won, but we had trouble focusing. Esther was suddenly afraid about having been left alone, so I suggested we go play with Gideon and Jonathan's planes, which might give us some courage.

She said that if her brothers found out we touched their planes, they would be awfully angry at us.

I said that if Jonathan were here, he would definitely touch them.

We played with the planes for a long time until Jonah got back. When he stepped inside the apartment, we ran over and clung to him with relief. He looked a little guilty for having left us alone for so long.

I took advantage of his guilt, rushed into the bedroom, and picked up the blue hat. When I returned to the hallway, I handed it to him.

I think Jonah was glad to have his hat back. He held it tender-ly, rubbing its edges, and tried to push out the crumpled part and smooth the sides.

I stood there, my eyes fixed on his.

He needed no more than a moment to understand.

He suggested we sit down in the living room. We walked past the chest of drawers into which Esther and I had shoved the manila envelope with those important documents not much earlier and sat down on the sofa—Jonah in the center; Esther and I on either side of him. Jonah placed the blue magic hat on his lap, upside down.

To my first, worried question, what happened to his hat, he answered with stammered, conflicting versions, his head bowed. He said the hat had fallen, that something had been accidentally placed on top of it, that he was not sure what happened. Finally, he admitted that he himself damaged his hat in a moment of uncalled-for anger.

I had never seen him stammer like that before.

I asked him why he had been angry, and in general, why everyone had been so nervous and upset lately.

"Adults can be ridiculous sometimes," he said, and I shot Esther a victorious glance. But when Esther began to ask something about "those papers," my expression became enraged. Jonah put his arms around our shoulders, and, after organizing his thoughts for a moment, he addressed me.

"Your mother isn't feeling well, Helena," he said, selecting his words carefully. "It seems our plans to immigrate to Palestine are going to have to be postponed. I hope not for too long."

There was pain in his voice. Esther sighed with disappointment.

I felt ashamed of my mother again. Why was she being so difficult?

With my face turned toward the open mouth of the hat, my eyes fixed on its crumpled side, I asked my Daddy-Uncle why my mother did not want to go to the Land of Israel. I just could not understand why she did not want to go to that Promised Land, whose mountains dripped with nectar and its hills with milk; where honey ran down the carpets of fields.

My uncle did something very unlike him—he evaded the question. Instead of answering, his lips stretched into a crooked smile. Then he turned the hat over and left the room without another word.

***

My mother first heard about the war in Palestine from a childhood friend of Jonah's. The man had served as a soldier in the British military's Jewish Brigade during World War II and had migrated to Palestine immediately afterwards with his young wife, settling down near the Tel Aviv beach.

During a drunken, dizzy moment on his visit to our home in London in 1947, the former officer ridiculed the British Kingdom's arrogant attitude: not only did it abstain from voting on the United Nations' Partition Plan, but now it was heaping difficulties upon the small Jewish population just before its soldiers left the country and, all the while, swiftly losing colonial settlements and its power as an empire. The friend went on and on, describing the war that was taking place between the Arab of Palestine, assisted by the Arab Liberation Army, and between the Jewish defense forces, right under the noses and to the great fury of the British soldiers. Influenced by his intoxication, he spared no details, and Mother, although she appeared not to be listening, internalized the horrors of war.

My mother was afraid of it. She was afraid of the thunder of bombs and rockets; of the damage they caused. She was afraid of snipers shooting at the Jewish neighborhoods of mixed cities, afraid of attacks on isolated Jewish settlements and of ambushes on the armored convoys that carried equipment, food, and ammunition to those settlements.

The more Jonah tried to convince her that there, in the Land of Israel, we would all be better off—now that the establishment of a free Jewish state was imminent, now that our enemies would not be able to break our powerful spirit and destroy us —the more she closed herself off, petrified.

And the more he tried to convince Ruth that he, being an architect, would be able to take an active part in building the new country, and the more he begged her to continue supporting his Zionist dream as she had in the past, ready for any necessary compromise, the more she found herself torn between her love and support for her dreaming husband and her Moabite loyalty to her mentally scarred sister.

***

Tensions at home grew as the end of the British Mandate drew near. It was slated to end on 14 May 1948. Jonah praised the initiative taken by the Jewish forces during the month of March and the commencement of taking on the form and activities of a permanent military. He applauded their success in occupying dozens of Arab villages, in addition to Jaffa, Tiberias, and Haifa, and—most importantly—in forging a path to besieged Jerusalem. Ruth, out of concern for Naomi and the children, pointed to the worrying shortage of Jewish fighters and weapons, the harshness with which the British soldiers treated the illegal Jewish immigration, and the Hadassah medical convoy massacre on the way to Mount Scopus. She emphasized the falling of the Gush Etzion region in the hands of the Arab Legion, and—most importantly—the fact that the road to Jerusalem was blocked once again.

The open suitcases that Jonah, hoping Ruth would fill them with their possession, had placed in the center of the guestroom , remained empty. The important documents remained stuffed in that manila envelope in the drawer. During the day, a tense silence stifled the air in the apartment, and each evening Ruth's tears seemed to seep out from behind the closed bedroom door, and we heard her quiet plea to Jonah to be patient and wait just a little while longer, just a little more, until the sounds of war in Palestine died out.

We, the children, listened to Ruth's crying and begging through the walls. Jonah's smothered fury also trickled out through the cracks.

She said that if the leaders of the Jewish population announced the establishment of a Jewish state in the Land of Israel, the armies of neighboring Arab countries, joining the war, might attack them. "And then," she asked, "what chance would the small Jewish population have? We can't risk the children."

Jonah said that although the road was long and filled with obstacles, we belonged there, and must take part in this crucial, just fight for the existence of a Jewish state.

"But Naomi," Ruth pleaded, "Naomi won't be able to take it…"

"The national cause comes before the individual," his voice thundered. "We've waited long enough! We cannot possibly wait any longer!"

"Shh," she whispered, "they'll hear you," and we nodded our heads on the other side of the wall.

"The children are old enough to understand… And Naomi's smart enough to get it…"

"She won't be able to take it, Jonah." Ruth's voice grew louder. "As long as the fighting continues there, Naomi will wilt like a flower without water. I won't let that happen!"

"Ruth…" Now it was his turn to beg.

"I'm sorry, Jonah." She sounded determined. "I promised my mother."

You could cut the tension with a knife.

We, the children, each dealt with the stressful atmosphere at home in his or her own way. Davidi spent long hours in Mrs. Rothenberg's apartment, leaving his frustrations at the piano and awakening beloved sonatas into new life at the magical touch of his long fingers. Gideon and Jonathan raised airplanes into the air, with their voices imitating the sounds of war and the whistling of bombs. But this time the planes they were envisioning were Egyptian Spitfires and Dakotas fighting against the *Haganah's* light aerial fleet, a battle which had not yet taken place but would occur very soon. Esther drew dozens of pictures, mostly of airplanes, and for the first time received familial recognition for her artistic talent. Meanwhile, I sat in a corner of the kitchen, writing words that connected to form sentences, filling pages, and eventually whole notebooks of impressions.

But in the evenings, we all gathered in the children's room and listened with alert silence to the conversations, pleas, and tears that trickled through the walls of Jonah and Ruth's bedroom.

But we were not alone.

From her spot in our little bedroom, also listening in—and trembling—was my mother Naomi.

42

Friday afternoon, 14 May 1948. The British mandate in Palestine was about to end the next day. Naomi asked to stay alone at home while we all went to the house of family friends to gather in their living room for quite a special occasion. Jonah's childhood friend, who lately started to work at one of the British Mandate post offices in Tel-Aviv, had called him that morning and informed him about the news: in the late afternoon, David Ben-Gurion, head of the Jewish community in British Mandate Palestine, was slated to announce the establishment of a Jewish state in the Land of Israel. He and his wife were going to be there, at Rothschild Boulevard in front of the Dizengoff House Museum, where the declaration was about to take place. They wanted to experience the historical moment firsthand. All of us had been convinced by Jonah that the historical declaration would be broadcast on the BBC radio station, just like the UN Partition Resolution that was transmitted several months earlier.

Through a window, Mother watched us walking away. She withdrew old stationery, its heading bearing the Steiner family seal, from the desk drawer in our room, and smoothed its pages with shaking hands. Then she fished out a blue pen from her purse and began to write. When finished, she carefully folded the page, slipped it into an envelope, and spritzed a few drops of the perfume Ruth had given her for her thirtieth birthday. After placing the envelope carefully under a pillow and smoothing the blanket with her hand, she went out and walked to a pharmacy, which she left, clutching a white paper bag to her chest.

When Mother returned home, she ran into Mrs. Rothenberg, who later reported that Naomi had looked perfectly calm, asked about Davidi's progress with the piano and even voiced her wish that I, too, would learn how to play one day. From there, she continued to our apartment on the third floor and walked inside without locking the door behind her.

At the same time, at our friends' house, excitement mingled with anxiety as the time of the declaration drew near. Jonah called all of us to gather near the radio, which was tuned to the BBC station. At that moment, Jonathan beseeched Ruth and Jonah to let him run back home, three blocks away, and get something very important he had forgotten.

His father was angry. "What can be important enough that it might cause you to miss this once-in-a-lifetime historical declaration?"

"An airplane," the boy's eyes glowed, "a Jewish Haganah airplane…"

Jonah stood up. "Unthinkable!" I saw Jonathan's eyes watering and Ruth biting her lip.

Jonathan grabbed the ends of his mother's dress. "The airplane," he pleaded, "I need it…"

Ruth shot Jonah a look and whispered into Jonathan's ear. "Go, Jonathan. But come back quickly." Then she called after him as he ran off, "And bring Naomi back with you. Maybe she's changed her mind."

But Naomi had not changed her mind. While the declaration was about to be read, she went to the bathroom, opened the white bag with trembling hands, pulled out two Wilkinson Sword razors, and tested them with the tip of her finger.

At our friends' home, long-stemmed glasses were filled with red wine. The excitement continued to grow even when everybody in the room understood that the declaration, which was being broad-casted live on the *Voice of Israel* station, wouldn't be transmitted by the BBC.

"This is the day of the declaration!" Jonah called out, excitingly embracing Davidi and Gideon.

"But who knows what will happen tomorrow," whispered Ruth, worried.

Jonathan was already halfway home.

At four o'clock exactly, standing on a makeshift stage, Ben-Gurion hit a golden gavel onto a desk. Naomi rolled up the sleeves of her blouse and ran her thumb over the blue veins running diagonally down her wrist.

Jonathan was close enough to see the building.

The crowd at Dizengoff House, breaking into a spontaneous ren-dition of "*Hatikvah*,"[5] rose to its feet.

Tears pooled in my despairing mother's eyes.

Jonathan strode up the stairs to the third floor.

Silence fell in the Dizengoff House Museum as Ben-Gurion read the Israeli Declaration of Independence in a formal, yet excited tone:

"The Land of Israel was the birthplace of the Jewish people. Here their spiritual, religious and political identity was shaped... After being forcibly exiled from their land, the people kept faith with it throughout their Dispersion and never ceased to pray and hope for their return... In the year 1897, at the summons of the spiri-tual father of the Jewish State, Theodor Herzl, the First Zionist Congress convened and proclaimed the right of the Jewish people to national rebirth in its own country... This right was recognized

---

5   The national anthem of the Zionist Movement and, later, of the State of Israel.

in the Balfour Declaration of the 2nd November, 1917, and re-af-
firmed in the Mandate of the League of Nations..."

By the time he emphasized the participation of the Jewish community alongside the allied forces in World War II, my mother had made the first slit in the veins of her right wrist and watched the trickle of blood that flowed out.

Jonathan reached the apartment and pushed in the unlocked door, walked into his bedroom and located the small plane into which he had etched the word "Israel" in English. For a moment, he paused and recalled his mother's request to bring Naomi back with him.

At that very moment, as Ben-Gurion announced the establishment of a Jewish state in the Land of Israel, Jonathan heard a dull thump from the bathroom. He ran over, the plane in his hand, and was shocked to find my mother's limp body on the floor, lying in a pool of blood.

Everything around him seemed to freeze.

This was Mother's first suicide attempt; the first of two. Later, after Jonathan was showered with praise for the resourcefulness he had shown when he wrapped towels around her bleeding wrists and hurried to call for help; after he had received Ruth and Jonah's hugs and my silent thanks; after Mother was rushed to the emergency room, followed by a long stay at a mental hospital, Jonathan found his airplane on the bathroom floor, awash in blood.

***

At midnight on 14 May 1948, the British Mandate in the Land of Israel ended.

The British flag was removed from the flagpole at the Haifa Port, and the first orders for new Israeli rule were posted. Within just a few

Beneath a Glass Bridge

hours, the armies of Egypt, Syria, Jordan, and Iraq invaded Israeli territory, armed with artillery, and, at first light, Egyptian Spitfires bombed the Tel Aviv airport.

Our plans of immigration were postponed by many months, until after the war.

Just like Moses, we could see the Promised Land but could not enter it.

***

My mother stayed at a mental clinic for a long time. Ruth took devoted care of her, but I was barely allowed to see her at all. I only visited the hospital with Ruth once, just she and I. I held her hand tightly. I had no idea what Mother would look like and how she would respond to me. I was terribly worried. But the place was prettier than I had expected. It had large lawns and big, beautiful flowers, and it calmed me down some. Mother was sitting outside in an upholstered chair, her gaze planted on an invisible spot in the distance. She looked pale and yet so pretty, even in her white hospital gown. Her fair hair was in a bun on top of her head, her long lashes shaded her dazed eyes, and her hands rested in her lap like an inanimate object.

In the beginning, she only sat there, motionless, staring at the view. Then her eyes moved to us. Suddenly, she began to talk. In a chillingly cold way, her eyes dead, she described her suicide attempt in detail. Then, out of the blue, she began to reveal in full her love story with my father, Mordecai.

It was the first time I had heard her tell the story, in all its glory, including the precise description of his smile that melted her heart. Her eyes glowed preciously, her lips filled with movement, and she even let me hold her hand, which was so thin, fragile, and cold.

But the worst was when she turned to face us and begged us to tell her if we had seen him.

"Seen who?" Ruth asked.

"Mordecai," she said.

Ruth answered meekly that we had not, and Naomi shook her head sadly and said he could be anywhere, but who knows, he might show up one day. After all, he appeared to have vanished into thin air during the war.

To this day, I still remember this image of my mother, wearing a nightgown and sitting in her chair in front of large lawns and pretty flowers in the yard of a mental hospital on the outskirts of London. She was pale and pretty, her cold hands motionless in her lap, her eyes fixed on the distance, and her thoughts garbled, but her memories clear and sharp, painted with the colors of her imagination.

43

November 1990
(This letter was thrown out)

Blair,

Dad and I had our honeymoon seventeen years ago in London. We went together to see some of the pretty bridges arching over the River Thames—London Bridge, Tower Bridge, Westminster Bridge… We walked around from morning till night, having a ball. We were fairly young.

On the last day of our trip, I gathered courage and took Dad on a walking tour of my childhood neighborhood. I showed him the building where we used to live and where Jonah parked his Ford Anglia. Then, my heart racing, we climbed up to the third floor. We paused at the door to our old apartment. Dad wanted to knock on the door. He said we should tell whomever lived there that it used to be my home years ago. But I didn't let him. I was quite flustered. I told him that the people who lived there wouldn't like it if strangers knocked on their door without warning, and that at any rate I didn't want to see it on the inside. The apartment would look completely different to me, I said, with these new people's furniture and things, and it might ruin my memories.

As we walked downstairs, we passed by Mrs. Rothenberg's old

apartment. She'd passed away years ago. To my surprise, I heard piano music from behind the door and felt weak all over. I took hold of the railing, and Dad grabbed me. He had no idea what was going on. I asked him to wait with me outside that door for a little longer. We sat down on the stairs and I closed my eyes. The memories were mine and I wanted to experience them on my own. I knew he was watching me, worried, confused, but I continued to sit there, my eyelids glued shut, silently listening to the sounds emerging from behind the closed door.

A pleasant memory ran through my mind: Davidi, as handsome as a prince, sitting in front of the black piano, his eyes closed and his long fingers confidently dancing over the keys, while Mrs. Rothenberg, her body quivering with emotion, stood behind him and moved her fingers to the beat of his playing.

The next memory, of the airplane Jonathan flew at me hitting me in the forehead, shook my entire frame. I felt Dad's arm tightening around me. My hand reached instinctively to feel the faded scar on my forehead. But it wasn't the pain of the injury that had shaken me. It was the memory of Jonathan as a little boy that forced the tears. When I opened my eyes, I saw your father looking at me with a piercing gaze. I was afraid he could read my mind. I shook. Then I stood up and asked to leave. When we went out into the street I said nothing, and he, as always, asked nothing. I led him to the spot where that building used to be, the building where my cousins and I accidentally awakened the activation mechanism of an old bomb. I'd discovered that in the 1950s a new apartment building had been built on the ruins of the old one. We continued to the old grocery store on the corner, Ruth's favorite bookstore, the neighborhood synagogue, where we celebrated Davidi's bar mitzvah, and the school we attended. Toward the end of the tour, I led Dad to a nearby building, where our friends used to live—the ones in whose home we had gathered in hope to listen together to the declaration of a Jewish state on the radio.

But I didn't tell him that in the very moments we'd sat there listening, only three blocks away, my mother wallowed in blood in a failed attempt to end her life; an attempt after which we remained in London for many more months.

I think about it now: about my shut eyes blocking Dad from my memories, about his wondering eyes, his pursed lips, my secrets and half-truths.

That, Blair, is what has always come between me and your father.

You might ask how we'd survived until now.

Honestly, I have to confess I'm not proud of it. We "kept it together" for eighteen years, because as I raised walls between us, your father built bridges.

But now I'm here. I'm here to tear down the wall and build a bridge, hoping I can make it as wide and as stable as can be.

Tel-Aviv

44

In the summer of 1950, we sailed from the Romanian coastal town of Constanța to the port of Haifa on board the ship Transylvania.

As the ship approached the shore, the excitement rose. When the sun appeared over the horizon, its rays skipping on the water, we saw the city of Haifa in the distance. The hundreds of passengers, most of them Europeans like us, crowded on the deck. Children cheered and pointed to the strip of beach stretching the length of the city, which sprawled over the slope and foot of a mountain. When the ship dropped its anchor in the waters of the port, the excitement reached its climax. We, the children, squealing and in awe, circled Jonah, who, holding his Leica camera, snapped images of the porters running around on the dock and the Carmel Mountain rising above.

In the pictures we look ecstatic and excited. I'm leaning against the railing, Davidi hugs me from behind. Gideon is standing next to Esther, who is pointing to something in the distance, and Jonathan is orbiting in circles, his arms stretched out like the wings of a small plane. Only Ruth and Mother are standing apart, Ruth shading her eyes with one hand and holding Naomi's hand with the other, as if to calm her against the surrounding chaos.

Then Esther, pulling at her father's coat, asked to see the sights of the new country through the camera lens. Jonah gladly obliged, ducked down to match her height, and together they clicked the button. Roaming to and fro with the heavy camera clutched in her hands, Esther continued to take more pictures by herself and caught an image of her father grabbing incredulously at his head, his mustache smiling along with his lips, his eyes in tears. She also documented other sights from the landscape in front of us, as well as the images of other passengers, all atwitter, their backs to their past and their eyes on their new world.

When we reached the shore, the excitement was tempered by a great bustle. Their possessions by their sides, families, couples, all lined up along the deck and closely followed the shouted conversations between the sailors and the port workers. We were all eager to leave behind the rocking of the ship, which had made most of us nauseous half the time, and step on solid ground. Some of us were lucky enough to have someone waiting to welcome them to the new country, but both those fortunate ones and those who did not yet know anyone, waved hello to the people on the dock. Their enthusiastic calls were carried on the wind in a mélange of languages and landed softly on the sun-warmed dock.

"This is it," Jonah said with a hoarse voice. "We've reached the promised land!"

"This is where Uriel wanted us to be," my mother whispered. "This is where Mordecai had been…"

Muscular, burly men in khaki shorts and white sleeveless undershirts now helped women, older children, and the elderly down the metal chain staircase descending to shore. Esther and I were passed from one to the next in their strong arms, until we stood firmly on the dock. Only then did I realize how hot it was. Jonathan was the first to remove his long-sleeved shirt and wrap it around his head like one of the dockworkers who climbed up onto the ship. When he called to him in English, "I'm Israeli too," the man answered in English with a heavy Greek accent, "And I'm also a new immigrant! from Saloniki," and around us everyone laughed.

Young women and a few children, wearing khaki pants and blue shirts, approached us. The women offered us cold water, and the children lined up in two rows and sang a welcoming Hebrew song. I watched, mesmerized by the lights that began to flicker on top of the Carmel Mountain and by the trees that filled its slopes. Everything looked like a dream, especially in light of Jonah and Ruth's beaming faces. For one brief moment, I even caught my mother smiling.

When we returned to the dock, Esther pulled on my shirt. I let my gaze follow her pointing finger and saw a short, swarthy man searching for a lighter for the cigarette butt in his mouth. The man dragged a small girl after him, her dress faded, a dark braid on her back, tears glinting in the corners of her black eyes. The man tried to tell something to the Jewish Agency representative, who had greeted us earlier, in an indecipherable language, then shrugged, threw his hands up in the air, and walked away, the little girl dawdling behind him. A while later, I saw him on the dock with the rest of his family—a raven-haired woman with a baby in her arms and a kerchief on her head, an older, wrinkled couple, and a few other children running around, including that skinny girl with the long braid. Esther asked her father for the camera again. She approached the family silently, and without asking permission, lifted the heavy camera and clicked the button. The raven-haired woman looked over awkwardly, adjusting her kerchief, the elderly couple shook their heads in confusion, and the children gathered together, eyeing Esther curiously. Only when the father walked over, raising his hand toward them, did they scatter, and Esther covered the lens with her hand, a small smile hovering on her lips. She nodded at the woman with the baby in gratitude, and continued to commemorate the sights of that long, marvelous day for hours on end, her small hands working the camera skillfully, and her eyes seeking out appropriate subjects, mostly new immigrants huddled in small groups, sitting atop their luggage, their backs to the mountain, their faces to the sea.

Months later, when the pictures were printed in black-and-white and spread over the dining table like a fan, Ruth and Jonah would be astonished by the quality and angles of the shots, as well as by the sensitivity with which Esther, only nine-and-a-half years old, documented the atmosphere of that special day. Years later, the pictures would be exhibited in photo-journalist Esther Jonas's first photography show as part of Israel's twenty-fifth anniversary celebration. In the center, among many images of the immigrants from the 1950s, who arrived via ships and planes in the *On the Wings of Eagles* and the *Magic Carpet* immigration operations, one blown-up image of a little girl, around the photographer's age at the time, would stand out. Her eyes looking shyly into the camera, her narrow face framed by dark hair arranged in a long, heavy braid dangling over her shoulder, her faded, tattered clothes taking nothing away from the beauty of her smooth, olive skin.

***

We spent that first night—a long, hot, sticky night—in a transit camp near Haifa, in a large sleeping hall, with only makeshift partitions separating one family from the next. Since we were scheduled to move to a small, pre-arranged apartment the very next day, I could not have imagined that most of the immigrants that arrived in Israel in the state's early years lived in these horribly crowded camps for weeks and even months in that difficult atmosphere and horrid neglect.

For us, it was a liberating and wondrous experience. Jonathan led us in running barefoot through the hall before lights out, our arms spread sideways, hopping over suitcases and belongings, improvised bunkbeds, and slumbering babies while humming like airplanes. Finally, we were brashly hushed by some of the adults, who were exhausted from the swaying of the waves and the heavy heat of this new country, and sent back to our bunks to drown our excitement in sleep.

***

Our first disappointment occurred when we arrived at the tiny apartment Jonah had rented for us in advance in Jaffa. None of us liked our first Israeli apartment. Neither its location—on the fourth, top floor of an ugly, elongated building on a curving, constantly dusty street—nor the awfully narrow stairwell, which Ruth and Naomi had trouble navigating, and most of all the smell of burnt meat wafting up from the eatery on the ground floor.

It was a two-bedroom apartment with a small kitchenette, a toilet, and a shower. At the center of the larger room Jonah stretched a heavy curtain that served as a partition. On one side, he placed a narrow bed from the Jewish Agency for Mother, along with a dresser, and on the other side was a small wooden closet for him and Ruth and two beds pushed together to create a double bed. In the smaller room, three mattresses were arranged side by side for the five children. Jonathan and Gideon shared one, Esther and I shared another, and only Davidi enjoyed a mattress to himself. Our consolation was the small, open balcony off the large bedroom, from which we could look down to the street.

Life was not easy. For several months Jonah struggled to find work, and new worry lines furrowed his forehead and the corners of his eyes. Ruth took initiative and, equipped with her language teaching certificate, applied for jobs at schools and kindergartens around Tel Aviv, Holon, and Bat Yam. We were all ordered to learn Hebrew at an *Ulpan*—all except for my mother, who often spent hours home alone. The children we met dressed, spoke, and behaved very differently from us, and the streets were filled with a cacophony of languages.

It was as if our former life had taken place in an entirely different era.

Jonah assured us that in a matter of months he would find a job and we would move into a larger, prettier apartment in Tel Aviv, at which point his parents would ship over our furniture from England. The others were patient, but I was full of complaints. A small, black, persistent demon had begun to nest inside of me. At the time, I didn't realize that we were part of an enormous wave of immigrants that had flooded into the country in its early years. I knew nothing of the ingathering of exiles or the fiery melting pot of this new state, nor about how lucky we were compared to many other immigrants.

Whenever I grumbled that the bedroom was too crowded, that the naked walls made me sad, or that I couldn't find a corner in which to sit and write down my impressions, a grimace appeared on Ruth's beautiful face.

***

Two months passed since our arrival. Ruth got a job as a teaching assistant on behalf of the Jewish Agency in a kindergarten at the Beit Lid transit camp.[6] Grateful for her good fortune and her ability to help care for the family, she made the tiring journey to the camp each day, returning home wiped out from exhaustion. In the evenings she would tell us about the hardships of the camp dwellers. "Those poor people," she said, "live in tents in which there is no electricity or running water, where they are exposed to rain and wind in winter and to heat and wild animals in summer. What was supposed to be a temporary solution is taking far more time than expected." She insisted that we children should also be exposed to such sights, so that we could learn to appreciate what we had and make do with

---

6   One of the refugee absorption camps (*ma'abarot*) which had been founded in the 1950s to provide accommodation for the large influx of Jewish refugees and new Jewish immigrants arriving to the newly independent State of Israel.

our share. She took Davidi there first, then Gideon and Jonathan but did not push Esther or me to join her.

For my part, I showed no interest in the transit camps until the day Esther asked Ruth to join, and, equipped with her father's camera, boarded the bus to Beit Lid with her. That day, Esther wandered about the tents in which the immigrants lived and used her small, already experienced fingers to snap shots of women in dresses made of coarse fabric, scarfs wrapped around their heads and tied under their chins, and of children in ragged clothes, smeared with mud.

Jonah printed the photos at Rudy's well-known photography shop on Allenby Street in Tel Aviv. When they were ready, he brought them home and spread them on the dining table. The one I remember most vividly is of a group of children, around Jonathan's age, with unkempt hair, catapulting stones at stray cats. Esther said that photos could not convey the feeling of revulsion she felt at the piles of rancid garbage scattered all over the camp or the stench of sewage flowing among the tents. Jonathan examined the pictures closely, hugged Esther's shoulders, and voiced his admiration. My throat filled with instant, burning jealousy. I went over to Ruth and whispered in her ear that I wanted to go, too.

A few weeks later Ruth announced that she had been switched to another camp, called *Machaneh Yisrael*, where she would be a daycare teacher. She told me I could join her there the very next day and made a festive promise that I would return with many impressions with which to fill my diary.

The next day, tense and eager, I armed myself with a hat, a canteen, and my notebook, which I carried with me everywhere. When we finally arrived, after a long bus ride, a stench that Ruth seemed impervious to filled my nose. As we approached the camp, my ears caught the loud buzzing of garbage flies, crowded over piles of trash, as well as the yowling of cats in the distance. The sights that were revealed to me were similar to the ones reflected in Esther's photographs, with one significant difference. The Beit Lid tents were replaced with old military structures with long, gaping cracks in their walls. I realized this used to be a military camp. A heavyset woman took Ruth and me on a tour of the camp. We went into one of the rooms. It contained a few iron beds with straw mattresses, a cracked wooden table, and two wooden chairs. The room, lit by an oil lamp, was dim even at this morning hour. The woman pointed to one of the corners. "That's the kitchen," she said. The "kitchen" was a pile of plates, knives, and forks surrounding a lit primus stove. When Ruth asked if they had a fridge, the woman laughed, shaking her head. It was so hot and stifling that I had trouble breathing. The sight of the shacks, the buzzing of flies, the yowling of cats, the stench of the sewer—these all weighed heavily on me. But more than anything else I could not bear the sight of small children walking aimlessly in those dirt roads. When I saw a little girl in rags and bare feet, carrying a doll in a torn dress that reminded me of my Gertie, I asked Ruth to leave at once.

Nevertheless, I had to wait for another hour until Ruth finished touring the place. Then, she spoke with an agency representative, who met us in a makeshift office, and filled out pages bearing the Jewish Agency's watermark with her personal details. Impatient and dripping with sweat, I sat in that small room. Before me, I saw the image of the children playing in the mud and the girl with the ragged doll in her hand and felt pity and discomfort.

After Ruth finished, she took my hand and we walked together back to the bus stop. The stop consisted of a gray, dull, concrete shelter with narrow windows letting in only a few rays of sun. We waited twenty minutes for the bus. On our way home, Ruth let me curl up in my seat and lose myself in thought. I didn't say a word.

When we finally got home, I was glad to find Jonah in the kitchen. I walked over on tiptoes and pulled on his arm. An hour later the two of us were sitting on a stone bench near Eliyahu's kiosk in a nearby neighborhood, and I unloaded dozens of questions about the camps and the people who lived in them. Jonah answered all my questions patiently as I licked a cone of Whitman's chocolate-vanilla ice cream while wistfully pondering that girl with the doll that looked so much like my Gertie, who had probably never enjoyed such delicious, velvety ice cream in her life.

Ever since that day, I did my best to complain less: about the noise, the close quarters, and my aunt and uncle's thrift regarding expensive food and clothing. Whenever I was bored, I opened my bedroom window, which faced the backyard, glanced out over the railing, and counted cats. When I wanted to write, I hunched down on my mattress, opened the notebook across my knees and filled the gray lines with my pencil. When I felt too stifled and crowded in the apartment and needed some air, I slid down the stairs, alone, and walked the streets aimlessly, lost in thought, killing time.

45

In the winter of 1951, with the help of a dedicated clerk in the special Jewish Agency department for the absorption of academic immigrants, Jonah was offered a job in the Tel Aviv City Engineer's office. Shortly thereafter, Ruth found work as an English teacher in the Ironi Daled High School, which was housed in a Tel Aviv building not far from the Yarkon River. In March, they bought a rather spacious four-bedroom key-money apartment. It was on Ben-Yehuda Street, which was already one of the important commercial streets of Tel Aviv. The place had two large balconies, one of them to be enclosed later to serve as a bedroom for my mother.

To Ruth and Naomi, the street was a source of pleasure and satisfaction. As early as the 1930s, it had become a center for German immigrants who arrived during the *Fifth Aliyah*, and most of its buildings, built in the international style, had elongated balconies and sprayed plaster in brown, green, and red on the exterior walls. On the mornings when my mother didn't have an appointment with her psychiatrist and Ruth wasn't teaching, they went down to the street, Ruth's fleshy arm in Mother's pale, matchstick one, both carrying baskets. Between a visit to the grocery store and a visit to the greengrocer's, they would glance at store windows and Ruth would chat in their mother tongue with the haberdasher, the grocer, the peddler, and with other people who lived on our street and were also strolling down the sidewalk. Sometimes, while Jonah worked and we were at school, the two of them grabbed a corner table at Ginati-Yam or Herlinger Café. Mother would order a cup of coffee and already draw a cigarette and a green lighter from her purse, and Ruth would order a glass of tea with a slice of lemon. By the time the lemon slice sank to the bottom of the cup, the cigarette was already lit in my mother's hand and held between two long, trembling, red-nailed fingers.

On rarer occasions, they went out in the evening with Jonah. After Ruth got dressed, she would help Naomi pick out a dress and a hat, apply light makeup to her face, and gather her long, fair hair into a bun on top of her head. Then the three of them would go on a "night-out for grown-ups." They liked to go to a café on Dizengoff Street where people danced, or to friends' houses, and sometimes even to the cinema, to watch an English-speaking film, like *The Black Knight*—which Jonah picked—at Migdalor cinema—or that movie at Moghrabi Theatre that my mother loved so much, with Burt Lancaster and Barbara Stanwyck, which I believe was called *Sorry, Wrong Number*.

We, the children, began going to school during that period. Davidi was a high school student at the Herzliya Hebrew Gymnasium, and Gideon, Jonathan, Esther, and I attended the Tel Nordau Elementary School. Esther and I had classes during first shift, from morning to the early afternoon, in the older of the two buildings, while Gideon and Jonathan attended the second shift, from afternoon to eve.

Davidi and I were the first to catch on to the language. Gideon and Jonathan took a bit longer, but within a manner of months we all spoke to each other mostly in Hebrew. Esther was the only one who had trouble getting the hang of it, and since she was slow to learn Hebrew, she fell behind in grammar, literature, and Bible studies. Every evening Ruth sat her down as she labored over dinner and narrated in her pictorial language biblical tales. Davidi devoted thirty minutes a day to her, and together they did her Hebrew and grammar homework. Jonah spent evenings working with Esther on her math exercises. The little black demon would awaken in me from time to time, and, feigning empathy, I'd ask Esther, how she could have failed to understand the teacher's explanations, which were so clear? Then I would arrogantly suggest that we do our homework together and would finish the work so quickly that my cousin would be left behind, even more frustrated and confused than before. Since she didn't complain about it to me or report my behavior to Ruth or Jonah, my conscience awoke, and I would immediately attempt to compensate my kind-hearted cousin with a game of hide-and-seek, a jumping contest, even hopscotch—a game in which she usually won. Thus, I killed two birds with one stone: clearing my conscience while alleviating her disappointment.

***

One afternoon, as I returned home from a stroll along Bialik Street, where I passed by the home of the famous poet, after whom the street was named, and sprayed some water on my face from the fountain in the square, I saw in the distance a large truck parked by our building. Sweaty porters pulled out tables and chairs. Our furniture had arrived from England! I ran back to the building and skipped up the stairs. The glass-fronted display cabinets were standing in the foyer, assembled and dusty, as if awaiting to take their place in our home and be enriched with pretty objects. A thin fabric separating them from each other, Ruth's oil paintings and watercolors leaned against the kitchen wall, and only the front one—a Jerusalem landscape— was exposed for all to see. There were also the beds and dressers we had left behind in London, Jonah's desk and our living room sofa, with the high back, the round armrests, and the delicate floral upholstery. Among the furniture were stacked ten boxes of books, including Jonah's professional tomes, Ruth's German and English grammar books, an oversized atlas, a bilingual dictionary, and dozens of novels. There was that chest of drawers which had contained "those important documents," and I wondered whether they were still there, in the top drawer. There were also a new set of pots, a gift from Jonah's parents, who had overseen the shipping from London, a large iron skillet, a set of Rosenthal porcelain dinnerware, boxes of toys, Davidi's sheet music, Gideon and Jonathan's airplane collection, and some suitcases containing jackets and winter clothes.

Toward the end of the freight operation, the porters pushed one last large piece of furniture into the crowded room, wrapped in so many blankets that it had lost its shape. The blankets were not removed, despite Esther's pleas, until evening, when Davidi finished his music class and walked inside. The apartment was overflowing now with furniture and boxes strewn chaotically all over the hallway, kitchen, and living room.

When Davidi finally arrived and the blankets were removed, our marveling eyes feasted upon Mrs. Rothenberg's Steinway piano, on all its old-time glory, power, and beautiful keys. Davidi stood before it, still and moved. A moment later he was already lifting the lid and gently running his long fingers over the keys, as if caressing them in love. Jonathan, who stood beside him, found a small note written in German inside the lid, which contained a goodbye message from Mrs. Rothenberg to Davidi, along with a letter from Jonah's parents. In the letter, they wrote that a few weeks before her death, the piano teacher had contacted them and asked to bequeath her beloved piano, which had been with her for most of her life, to her "dearest, most talented student," who reminded her of her only son—who had also been such a promising talent, killed in World War I.

Just as the note was read aloud, Gideon found that a small cardboard package wrapped in paper had been attached to one of the piano's legs. Davidi peeled the paper from the box and pulled out Mrs. Rothenberg's old mechanical metronome. Impressed to find the spring still intact, he placed it carefully on the seat beside him and turned it on. Then, tears running down his cheeks and ours, he pulled over another chair and sat down at the piano, as he spread his beautiful fingers like a fan, steadied them on the keys, and played, especially for us, in the midst of this disarray, Beethoven's "Moonlight Sonata"—one of his parents' favorite pieces.

46

One Friday eve, after the candles had been lit, the blessings spoken, and we all sat down around the table, I noticed that Jonathan was playing with his silverware and ignoring his food. Jonah frowned at him. At the time, Gideon and Jonathan spent most of their time playing out on the street and in the improvised soccer fields they constructed with their friends on the beaches of Tel Aviv. But while Gidi—as his friends had taken to calling him—managed his time well and made sure not to neglect his schoolwork, Jonathan was undisciplined.

After Jonah finished his soup portion, he ordered Jonathan to eat. His eyes on his plate, Jonathan shrugged.

Ruth placed her hand on Jonah's. "Jonah, please, calm down."

He ignored her, his eyes still fixed on Jonathan. Esther and I sat up straight in our chairs. Jonah asked Jonathan to say what he'd done, and when the boy wouldn't, his father turned to Gidi.

"Tell us, Gideon."

Stunned, Gidi looked at his father. "You want me to tell it?"

"Yes!"

"Why me?!"

Jonah insisted, and Gidi was forced to report his brother's behavior at school in recent weeks. It turned out that Jonathan had been neglecting his homework, talking back to his teachers, hiding notes the school sent to his parents, and—heaven help us—even forging their signatures. Jonah and Ruth had found out about all this that morning in a note delivered by Gidi, in which the school principal depicted their son's misbehavior in detail.

I understood why Uncle Jonah was angry, but to me Jonathan was a hero. His shenanigans and rebellious nature lit a fire inside of me. I shifted in my seat and looked askance at him, trying to catch his gaze. When our eyes met for a moment, I shot him a quick smile. Eventually, Jonathan was sent to his room without eating a thing.

Ruth tried to lighten the heavy atmosphere by launching into a monologue about the German-speaking Ben-Yehuda Street, the gossip of the women at Abraham's grocery, and the odd, recent exchanges she and Naomi carried out with the loud fruit and vegetable vendors at the Carmel Market. When the silence around the table lingered, she tried a new tack. She informed us of a sewing class taking place in an apartment near the Bezalel Market. "Naomi," she said, "wants to enroll. She's already rather skilled in sewing, but if she learns more and gets even better, who knows, she might find work in the future at Lola Bar's studio."

Naomi blushed and wordlessly shook her head, as if baffled at the sound of the word "wants" in proximity to her name. We asked who Lola Bar was, and Ruth explained she was an *haute couture* seamstress, who from her studio on Hayarkon Street, dictated the styles of the wealthy women of Tel Aviv. Esther and, especially I, flooded Ruth with questions: what kind of dresses does she design? What kind of women wear her clothes? And where do all these wealthy women live? Suddenly, Jonah awakened from his reveries and stood up. He walked over to Jonathan's room and knocked on the door, which opened to swallow him inside, like Jonah the Prophet in the belly of the whale.

None of us could hear the details of the conversation that took place behind the door, an argument that stormed like the sea rocking the prophet's boat, then gradually subsided. None of us knew at the time that a significant improvement in the boy's behavior would take place as early as the following days. But when Jonah left Jonathan's room, we could all see that he'd calmed down from his fury, the storm had abided, and the evening took on the Sabbath aura as if by magic. And so, although it was already late, we all gathered in the living room, sitting around Jonah, Jonathan among us. Jonah watched with pleasure as his son voraciously polished off the soup Ruth placed in front of him, and in a conciliatory spirit, sat back in his chair, moving his gaze over us and asked if we wanted to hear the story of how the city of Tel Aviv rose "from the sands."

We were glad to see him pacified and nodded enthusiastically.

Jonah pushed his chair back and laced his fingers behind his head. "Well," he began. "It all started with an idea, which was formulated into a plan, which took shape, just like the story of the entire state. About 120 Jaffa Jews gathered one hot summer evening in 1906 at a local club to listen to the proposal of their friend, Akiva Aryeh Weiss, to build a new, modern Jewish town—a real city, with running water, sewage pipes, and electricity; with European-style gardens, spacious neighborhoods, wide streets, and long avenues."

We all listened intently. Jonah's stories were always so engaging.

"In its first incarnation, the city was called *Ahuzat Bayit*," he continued. "It began as a modern suburb of Jaffa, which was crowded and mostly populated by Arabs. In the pamphlet Weiss spread among the Jaffa Jews that summer, he outlined his vision: a modern, independent, Jewish city, which would, with time, become the Israeli New York City, the main gateway into the country..." Jonah fell silent for a moment, his gaze darting between us. Then he raised his voice: "You see, children, every deed begins with a vision!"

I looked at him. At his prematurely balding head, his thick eyebrows, the grooves on the sides of his mouth, and the glow in his eyes whenever he spoke about Zionism.

Jonah's story wore on, until Esther pulled on his sleeve. "And the name?" she asked. "When was the city's name changed to Tel Aviv?"

Jonah turned to Ruth imploringly, as if afraid to lose the children's attention and the magical moment would be over.

"I think it was in the end of 1909," Ruth said, wrinkling her forehead. "Hilde told Naomi and me about it. You know Hilde, she's the older neighbor downstairs, who seems to know everything there is to know about the history of the city, the country, and every person in the neighborhood..."

"They were thinking of calling it *Neve Yaffo*," my mother chimed in in clear Hebrew, startling us. "Or Aviva, or *Sha'anana*, or *Ivriya*... they even thought of naming it Herzliya, after Herzl, the state visionary..."

We all turned to face her. Mother hardly ever spoke in public, not even in our intimate circle, barely even to herself. But now she continued.

"Eventually, the name Tel Aviv was elected, inspired by Nahum Sokolow's translation of Herzl's book *Altneuland—Old-New Land.*"

When she suddenly fell silent and detached herself again, Ruth took over. Her voice soft, she raised her hand to take her sister's. "And just think how interesting this word combination is, wrapping together the old and the new—*Tel* means an ancient ruin, while *Aviv* means spring, the season of blossoming and rebirth..."

47

I recall Hilde, our downstairs neighbor, who had welcomed us warmly and assisted us in taking our first steps in the city, even though she herself had only arrived in the mid-1940s. She came to Palestine with an ill husband and an unmarried sister, a number tattooed on her arm, and no children. She spoke fluent German and broken Hebrew for the rest of her life but learned to read Hebrew, so she could "peruse the papers." And I owe her so much.

A year earlier, one fine day, her husband, Felix, had disappeared. After the police and an army of volunteers spent two intense days searching for him, he was found, lifeless, on the beach in Jaffa. No one knew how he'd gotten there, but Hilde said he'd been getting very confused of late and experiencing bouts of memory loss. He must have gone out, she hypothesized out loud, and then forgotten how to get back. So he wandered, hungry, thirsty, tired, and confused, letting his feet carry him where they might until finally he arrived at the beach and collapsed on the sand, lost consciousness, and died.

Felix made a living selling ice. Every morning he would buy a few blocks from a factory in Jaffa, load them onto the back of his pickup truck, inside a large, insulated box lined with tin, and drive around the neighborhood. Sometimes Hilde joined him, boldly ringing a big bell and calling out, "Ice! Ice!" through the open window. After Felix's tragic death, the grieving but practical Hilde sold the truck and sought other sources of income. Soon she had begun to work as a washerwoman. Two days a week she would go up to the laundry room on the roof of our building, carrying piles of sheets, duvet covers, pillow covers, and clothes, delivered to her by women who were not fond of doing laundry and had the means to pay someone else to do the job. I liked joining Hilde on the roof in the afternoon, especially on sunny days. I'd help her carry up a primus and a large aluminum pail with two small handles. We would set the primus under a tripod, Hilde would light it, and once it began making noise, Hilde would place the pail, filled with water and melted soap, on the tripod, shove in the laundry, and stir it with a wooden stick. While her hands were busy, her ears were all mine, and I was grateful for her listening, and told her trifles about my social life and my teachers. Hilde had small, alert eyes, a husky voice, a kind heart, and a wide mouth, as well as a love of people. Sometimes I even consulted with her about boys. I had the impression that she knew everything and was able to solve any problem. Sometimes, when the burner holes inside the primus got clogged with soot, Hilde would unblock them with a long needle, while murmuring German curses, and I would hide my smile behind a piece of fabric. After the laundry boiled, she would pull the items out of the pail with wooden tongs and move them to another pail, which she also filled with soap melted in faucet water, then scrub the stains vigorously against a wavy tin sheet. As she scrubbed, she told me an anecdote, usually inspired by something she'd read in the paper, and which always opened with the words, "Listen, Helena, this is a real-life story…" She always added a lesson at the end and finished with a deep sigh, the kind that rises straight from the chest, and my eyes would wander to the blue number on her arm. Once she had polished off stains and stories, Hilde would run the laundry several times through clean water, and then ask me to throw a small, fabric-wrapped roll of "laundry blue" into the final rinse. The roll turned the water in the pail deep blue, and magically turned the whites, after they dried on a line she stretched across the roof, to bright white. Sometimes, if I had nothing else to do, I even helped Hilde take the dry laundry down from the roof to her apartment, where she ironed and folded it, made piles, and attached small labels, on which she wrote down the names of her venerable customers but with spelling mistakes. I would gently suggest corrections. I loved Hilde. I didn't want anyone to see her errors.

***

One afternoon, a knock came at the door. Hilde swept in, in a blue house robe, brown slippers, and rollers in her hair.

"How are you doing, Mrs. Ruth?" she called out while approaching Naomi. "I have something to show you," she said, pulling on my mother's sleeve and presenting her with an ad she'd cut out of the *Maariv* newspaper.

Surprised, Naomi picked up the clipping. "Hilde, this is in Hebrew," she mumbled. "I can't read it, I don't understand…"

"Then, I'll read it for you!" she said. "Listen to what I've brought you here. There's a recommendation in the paper by this lady, Shoshana Malachi, for mothers with small children…"

Ruth came nearer and glanced at the paper. "Yes, Hilde, but what does that have to do with us?"

"A lot!" Hilde thundered. "We have a seamstress among us! And these are difficult austerity times… There's a recession, budgeting, stamps for buying clothes and shoes, fuel, newspapers, even milk and eggs! What's come of this country?! And the stamps a woman gets are barely enough for one skirt and one cotton dress, one undershirt, a short woolen jacket, a pair of underwear, and a pair of socks! She barely has anything left for shoes… Today I went out on Ben-Yehuda Street, and what did I see? A long line outside the cobbler's shop on the corner. He told me that ever since the government announced the budgeting, and as long as soles and heels are not part of the stamp system, people have been flocking to him with shoes to be fixed."

"Hilde," Ruth cut her off gently. "What did you read? And what does this have to do with Naomi? Are you suggesting she start making women's clothes? Where would she get the fabric? That's also expensive and part of the budget."

"Not women's clothing." Hilde's wide smile revealed three crowns. "Bibs for babies…"

"Bibs?" Ruth marveled. Mother raised her brows.

"Yes, exactly! This Mrs. Shoshana writes here that babies are constantly getting their clothes dirty, and that's why bibs come in handy. In summer, they can be used as a piece of clothing, a dress, and in the winter, they can protect woolen clothes, which cost a lot of points. Bibs can be made out of old clothes, but they require a strong, light, comfortable fabric to allow the little ones to move easily…"

Naomi, practical all of a sudden, fixed her eyes on Hilde and asked for some clarifications. Hilde pointed at a pair of small sketches in the ad. "You see, Naomi, this nice lady is suggesting two types of bibs: the first is a smooth kimono, buttoned in the back. Paired with a shirt, it can be worn as a pinafore by little girls; the other is bell-shaped, one piece of fabric, no stitches."

And so, my mother began to sew again. Hilde procured an old Singer sewing machine and collected her friends' old clothes, and Ruth rummaged for simple, strong fabrics sold for decent prices at Delfinger and Zacks Silk. Later, a shipment of quality British fabrics was sent by Jonah's parents. Mother sat in our Ben-Yehuda apartment and, with silent concentration, sewed bibs according to the ad's recommendation, with some improvements and in an array of colors. She added more fabric around the neck to the bell-shaped bib, creating a wide fold through which a decorative ribbon could be threaded. She created triangles on both sides as arm openings. She made a row of buttons for the kimono bibs and added a few bits of fabric to form long sleeves, attaching a few pairs of under-wear made of the same fabric. The bibs were sold for a good price at Anna's Clothing Store down the street. Naomi, Ruth, Hilde, and I were proud to see many toddlers using her bibs all year long, all over the city.

Thank you, Hilde. Thank you for giving my mother something to do and some peace of mind, thank you for helping her fingers and lips start moving again. In those moments of grace, when Mother felt relatively at ease, cutting fabric according to a paper pattern, push-ing the fabric into the machine, pressing the pedal to create precise work, she also sewed together the threads of her thoughts, telling me the old love stories, painting them in the colors of the bibs.

When she dove into her past, the abysses of her memory, her eyes shone, her voice grew steady, and red spread through her cheeks, turning her pale skin pink. I would shut my mouth and lean in, my doll Gertie on my lap, my arms hugging my knees.

And I watched her.

And she was so beautiful to me.

48

In a matter of months, the other children and I blended into the bustle of the vibrant city. Davidi joined a musical group in his school led by Hadassah Sherman, an alumna and teacher at the Herzliya Hebrew Gymnasium, who had received her college education in Germany during the same years when Vera and Gabriel studied there. He spent most of his free time at music lessons at the Shulamit Conservatory, often stopping on his way home for a quick visit to the Music Library located at the Tachkemoni School on Lilienblum Street. He liked to glance at the sheet music collection of the music teacher Rebecca Chertok-Hoz and listen again to some of the impressive record collection donated to the library by the Quakers in the United States.

Gidi and Jonathan joined the Tel Aviv Scouts, the Dizengoff Troop. The Jonas boys swiftly gained reputations as courageous, especially once the heroic tale of how they had saved me and Esther from "certain death by an old bomb in a blitzed house" in London became known. Unfortunately, Esther and I were still too young to join the movement. We watched yearningly as the boys put on their khaki uniforms and ties, and headed out, filled with enthusiasm, to another meeting or another activity, while we slowly expanded our circles of friends, which did not overlap.

I was especially worried about Jonah. Ruth often told us, in sorrow, that Jonah had come to Israel twenty years too late, and that she was sorry he had not taken part in the beautiful architecture of the 1920s and '30s, when the British already ruled the land and the city grew to form a true metropolis. He was hired by the municipality as a junior planner of workers' housing in the city's periphery, south of Jaffa and north of the Yarkon River. Thus, he abandoned his dream of leaving an architectural mark on the homes of Tel Aviv. The need to feed eight souls took precedence over everything else. Ruth said that the workers' housing was painfully plain to him, and that he had no outlet for his talents. "He can only admire the work of others," she sighed.

But Jonah naturally took in an inclusive, broad picture. From a bird's eye view he took everything under his wing. "I'm just a small cog in a great, big machine," he often told us, "willingly acceding to the needs of the day and the dictates of the time. If the city needs to spread into the periphery to provide housing for its laborers who cannot afford to live in the north or center of the city, I'm honored to be the man building it for them."

I remember the long hours Jonah spent at the offices of the city's construction department during the time of austerity, back in the early 1950s, when contractors were given iron quotas and suffered an extreme shortage of construction materials. Jonah fought against the black market and the excessive rights demanded by contractors building on expensive land uptown. On the hottest days, he wore a three-piece suit, a hat, and tie, and went to speak to municipal clerks and the city's philanthropists, trying to convince them to provide the town with a unified look by designing similar facades for buildings erected on a single street or around a square. Even in the simplest of buildings, he tried to offer some planned beauty.

I remember him telling us in detail, feigning excitement, about iron railings, reinforced concrete, edifices built on pillars, bay windows, roof shelters, window glazing, pergolas at the entrance to stairwells, folding shutters, different shapes of fences, cement and mosaics and fountains. But I also remember tiny tears in his eyes as he spoke about Arieh Sharon, a disciple of the Bauhaus in Germany, and Ze'ev Rechter, a follower of Le Corbusier in Paris, who along with Tel Aviv architect Dov Karmi and others, started the Tel Aviv Architect Group in the early 1930s, a group to which he had not had the luck to be accepted. "They met daily at Sharon's office on Pinsker Street or at the nearby Ginati-Yam Café," he said with a melancholy smile, as if sharing a secret. "With time, they accepted more architects to their organization, took positions at the Tel Aviv Architects and Engineers Committee, and gradually managed to establish the foundation of collectivist construction in the International Style, contributing to Tel Aviv's growing reputation as a vivacious Mediterranean city."

I looked at the dull light in his eyes when he spoke, and, from a distance, my eyes caressed his bald head and handsome face. As I imagined Rechter, Sharon and Karmi sitting at a café, making plans for the city's design, I vowed to follow Jonah's motto, "Every deed begins with a vision."

49

November 1990
Yosemite Park, California

Dear Davidi,

Thank you for your quick reply. I know how busy you are this time of year. I was glad to hear about the success of your last concert and especially that you played Chopin's Piano Concerto. Chopin is a romantic. I have a special sympathy for him. His melodies, with those long, lingering lines, always touch my heart.

I gather Nelly was the one who told you I'd left for here. Then you spoke to Roy and Mike, and even called Nurit. I'm not surprised to hear that Roy sounded angry to you, or that Nelly sounded worried. It saddened me to hear that Mike was restrained in his conversation with you. You assumed it was because of pain, and I tend to agree. Your musical ear catches nuances, stops, breaths. I don't think you're wrong.

You said that Nurit sounded understanding and supportive. Dear Nurit... I think you and Nurit, and, maybe, Esther know me better than anyone else in the world, even better than Mike... He hasn't known me as long, and he's missing a lot of information. I ache for him and I miss him so much. I'm especially sad for Roy and Abby, but I'm trying to push away thoughts about them and my longing for them, so I don't break. I hope things get better when I return, and that one day they'll find it in their hearts to understand and forgive me. Sometimes you just have to do things the unorthodox way. Most people don't allow themselves to do that, but I, as you know, am not "most people."

I'm writing about our Tel Aviv years, reminiscing and writing, writing and yearning. I'm drowning in memories, sensations, thoughts, and you play an important role in all of them.

I understand you don't have a lover right now. No matter, that's temporary. Sometimes I think it's a shame you never wanted to have children. It caused you painful separations and all sorts of deprivations. And yet, children aren't easy. There are very high expectations you can't always meet. And anyway, being a parent might be the hardest mission in the world. I didn't always see it that way. I used to be that kid with the high, unmet expectations.

I'm sad now. I think about the pain I'm causing the people I love, and it makes my heart ache. Besides, it's been raining all night and all morning. There are many enormous cedar trees and deciduous black oaks around here, and I can see them, fully naked, outside my window. They shoot out naked branches, which multiply into thinner and thinner ones. Only a few mustard-brown leaves have miraculously held onto the trees, and a carpet of rotting leaves covers the ground beneath them. It's depressing. I'm also depressed because last night Pierre and Marcel informed me that tensions are heating up in the Middle East and the Persian Gulf. The United Nations gave Saddam Hussein an ultimatum. If he doesn't retreat from Kuwait until a specific date, his country will be attacked. The threats that snake has been making toward Israel are scary. The Israeli government decided to equip the entire population with gas masks in case they're attacked with unconventional warfare. Just imagine, Davidi... will it never end???

The rain that was incessantly knocking on the window in my room stopped a few moments ago, leaving a trail of drops dripping slowly down the pane. I followed the trajectory of three of them, which at some point merged to create one large drop, gleaming in the sun that had suddenly emerged from between the clouds.

I like it that the sun suddenly came out.

I think I'll go back to writing now... excuse me, darling.

Yours, with love and longing,
Helena

50

"'So, the land had peace for forty years,'" I said. "Can you imagine, Nurit? Forty years of peace in this country?"

"*Judges* 3:11," Nurit answered right away. We were walking home from high school after Bible class. "It was a regular cycle," Nurit concluded. "The Israelites sin by abandoning God and worshiping foreign deities, God punishes them by enslaving them to a foreign, enemy king, the Israelites cry for help, God sends a temporary leader to save his people from their enemy, and the land has peace for years."

With Nurit Hadari I could talk about everything. Any topic was relevant, discussed, parsed out and worked over. Nurit appreciated my love of history, Bible, and literature, and encouraged my passion for writing, and I admired the unbearable easiness with which she excelled in biology, math, and physics, and her impressive erudition when it came to the animal kingdom and human anatomy.

I didn't always need words with Nurit. Any whim was allowed; any emotion expressible.

Nurit was the only person from whom I kept no secrets.

But that day, my thoughts twisted around the passage "So the land had peace for forty years." Forty years without any wars.

"Jonah thinks there will be no more big wars here," I reported to Nurit. "He thinks the ceasefire agreement of 1949 will hold, but Ruth isn't as optimistic…" My voice died out.

Nurit shrugged and said glumly that her father was not optimistic either. "He's very concerned," she said, "about the *Fedayeen* infiltrating Israeli territory."

I paused by the old oak planted between our two buildings and looked at her. "Do you think there's going to be a war?" A chill ran through my bones. Nurit understood immediately. Dalia, her mother, had lost her younger brother in the 1948 War, during the battle of Kibbutz Mishmar HaEmek. On the recent Memorial Day, she had taken both of us to a hill overlooking the kibbutz, and showed us the basalt stone memorial erected there, set with a marble plaque with the names of her younger brother and the other soldiers who were killed in that battle.

Nurit didn't ask a thing. She just wrapped her thin arm around my waist, leaned her head on my shoulder, and said everything was going to be all right.

***

Gidi had enlisted two months earlier, in the beginning of October 1955. That fine morning, he packed a bag, left us with a hug, a kiss, and a pat on the back, and went on his new way as a soldier in the 890th paratroop Battalion. While Davidi, who had enlisted almost three years before him, was a musician in the IDF band, Gidi was a combat soldier. Shortly thereafter he began a regime of strenuous exercise, hand-to-hand battle training, fieldcraft, long marches carrying heavy equipment, and survival, parachuting, camouflage, and weapons training, as well as fighting in an open field.

Ever since he became a paratrooper, concern for his wellbeing became a permanent resident at our home, especially after we heard about his unit's participation in reprisal operations. When, only two months after his enlistment, he took part in the "Alley Zait" operation—a raid of Syrian posts in response to Syrian harassment of

Israeli fishermen at the Sea of Galilee, our concern for him doubled, and our anxiety about his welfare and the welfare of his companions increased.

Aware of her sister's nervousness when it came to uniforms, Ruth tried to hide Gidi's uniform, equipment, and rifle whenever he was home on leave. She shoved the red beret with the infantry symbol to the back of the closet and stored the rifle on Hilde's balcony. Making sure they were roomy enough to contain his wide feet and had no holes, lest gravel made its way inside, she polished his red boots out in the yard. She scrubbed his green uniform by hand only in the small hours of the night, in a sink out of sight of Naomi, while praying that God take care of him and that he got home safely.

But we were not the only ones worrying. Irit, Gidi's classmate and high school sweetheart, worried along with us. For every letter he wrote us—which Ruth opened excitedly, always in the kitchen, all of us standing in a circle around her—Irit received three. He wrote us brief notes in the respites between training and operations but filled whole pages to her during his nightly guard duties. When I once dared grumble about the unequal division of his precious time between us and Irit, Ruth placed a hand on her heart and said this was how things go between lovers, and that there was no point in searching for logic. The main thing, she said, was that Irit was so nice and shared the news she received in each letter, even reading us the lines she marked as permitted for sharing. Wordless, my mother wrote something in the air with her fingers, perhaps an answering letter to Gidi, and Esther embraced Ruth gently, as always, making do with little, both accepting and reconciled, and reminding us how good it was for us to hear from him at all.

51

Ever since I was a young girl, I took on a double life, the one lived in reality and the other lived in imagination. Sometimes I even allowed myself, in a controlled manner, to mix the two. Ruth was impressed by the precision of my discernment and would sigh and say that if Oma Ilse had been alive, the two of us would have been very close. "Like you," she said, "she had a rich spiritual world, a passion for books, a developed imagination, ennobling the people she knew with the qualities of biblical figures…but her feet were also planted firmly on the ground," she added, and I wondered if she was implying unlike me.

From a young age, I would categorize things, people mostly. I would label them with images from the world of animals and objects. I would suddenly say to Nurit, "That boy, what's the first image that comes to mind when you look at him, animal, plant, or still life?" And Nurit, who, beyond her logical, mathematical world, also knew how to rise with me to my airy level, was fully in the game. She would call one a poodle, the other a wolf, another a donkey, and we would both crack up. Once, on our way home from school, I asked her to take the game more seriously, and she asked for an example.

"Here you go," I said. "Jonah, my uncle, is a dove, just like his Hebrew name. He sees the big picture from a bird's eye view, moderate in his opinions, a dove of peace. Even his love for Ruth is like a dove's."

Nodding, Nurit smiled generously.

"Gidi is a rock," I thought out loud and was struck with longing. "He's steady and reliable, robust and emanates confidence. You can load any task on his broad shoulders and know he'll perform it in the best possible manner."

"Is that what rocks do?" Nurit wondered, for a moment returning to her world of logic. I explained that the comparison didn't have to be perfect; a general image was enough. I added that one person could have more than one image attached to them.

"Gidi is also a lion," I said after further thought. "Because besides his physical strength (he wasn't large but muscular, and no one at school was ever able to beat him at arm wrestling or at tug-of-war), he's also strong on the inside, a leader, the kind people follow.

"Do you know," I continued, "the year before he enlisted, he would wake up early every morning to swim in the sea before school? Even when it rained, the tide was high, and it was cold."

"Brrr…" Nurit shivered, hugging her shoulders. "I just got chills." I concluded that Gidi was cut from a unique cloth. "But I'm so worried about him," I said, my voice breaking. "It's hard for me to have him out of the house. And soon Davidi will be leaving for Europe, and then Jonathan will enlist…"

Before we separated and Nurit went home to the building neighboring mine, "*the twins,*" as we called them, we took a seat on the bench on the sidewalk exactly midway between the two at the foot of an old oak tree. Nurit sighed. "Your cousins are something special, Helena. All the girls in class are jealous of you and Esther."

Then she asked what kind of image I had for Davidi. Two weeks earlier she confessed to me that he was "in her dreams." I once proposed that term as part of our secret code, to be used instead of saying outright that we were in love with someone.

First, I made her swear to keep these images just between us, so that no one else found out about them. She, of course, agreed. "What are you worried about?" she asked.

I thought about Davidi and was filled with warmth. Every evening, I waited for him to return from his base so that I could find my place between his arms, unload my burdens to him, and settle my soul. Davidi was close to the end of his military service and eager to make his dream of going to Europe come true, especially now that he was accepted at the Stern Conservatory in Berlin, and I dreaded the moment he would leave. But I knew: Davidi didn't belong here, in Israel, and he did not have any desire to belong. "Europe," as Ruth always said, "suited him better."

I told Nurit that Davidi was a wild horse, and she widened her eyes at me. "Davidi is enveloped in magic," I explained. "He has an otherworldly, more expansive air about him. He loves open spaces and freedom, is afraid of human commitments, and he's beautiful, tall, long-limbed, just like a purebred Arabian horse. His thick, chestnut hair, which used to reach his shoulders before he joined the army, is like a horse's mane, and he has a mark of nobility on his forehead." I recalled our strolls along the Yarkon River and how I always had trouble keeping up with him. "This cousin of mine," I said, my voice suddenly shaking, "with those slender legs, he is a long-distance runner, sometimes carrying me on his back as he gallops, and then all the background noise dulling my soul fades away, and all I can hear is the whistling of the wind."

Nurit stared at me. "That was beautiful," she said. "You sound like a writer..."

A wave of warmth washed over me. That was the first time anyone had ever said something like that to me. "But Nurit," I said, "this description of Davidi is real, all true."

***

There was that day when I shocked Ruth and Jonah by asking them to show up alone to the first parent-teacher conference at the Gymnasia Herzliya High School. Since Ruth didn't fathom my intentions and said that from her experience with the boys, students were not obligated to attend, I was more explicit.

"I know that," I said. "I meant I'd like you to come without Mother."

That day Ruth cried so much that I almost thought it was hereditary. She cried just like Mother. Only much later did I realize that Ruth was able to accept many things but not Naomi's damaged motherhood. While Ruth served as a backup mother for me, a kind of fortified maternal wall to bolster my mother's weaker one, she never willingly took on the role.

"You," she once told me, "were lucky. You have a mother..." Perhaps unlike Davidi, Naomi, and herself, who had lost their mothers at war. "A mother should be exalted," she murmured. "She is someone you never give up on..." Then her eyes filled with tears, and I could practically see the longing in them.

My mother, I knew, had fallen into a deep depression. Recently, especially since Gidi was enlisted, she flinched at any noise or physical touch, suffered insomnia, lack of appetite, and fits of crying, and was tortured by a sense of emptiness, guilt, and abysmal despair.

Ruth took care of all her needs. She carried Mother in her warm, large arms, bathing her body, beautifying her face, powdering her cheeks, painting her eyelids and nails, combing and pinning her hair. She took her to the general practitioner, the dentist, and the gynecologist, as well as a series of psychiatrists, especially those who specialized in caring for people who had gotten out of the hellfire alive. But she was not content with psychiatrists and antidepressants and sought out her own ways of bringing her sister back to life.

I believe Ruth utilized cognitive and behavioral therapy methods before they were even invented. She spent hours talking to her sister, attempting to join forces with her to attack her depressive thoughts and illuminate reality in a happier light. She encouraged her to take that sewing class near the Bezalel Market and emphasized to us the importance of "successful experiences," and "positive reinforcement" for the improvement of Naomi's mood and self-perception. She brought Naomi along to each women's meeting, even if she just sat there, silent, staring at an invisible spot on the wall all night long, her hands lying limply in her lap. Almost every afternoon the two of them went out on a walk along Ben-Yehuda, Allenby, or Dizengoff streets, sometimes sitting at a nice café, or outside under the sky, on a sidewalk paved with interlocking paving stones, their faces toward the street. In the evenings, Jonah sometimes joined them at the Mograbi Theater, built in the Art Deco style at the end of the 1920s with vertical windows and sand lime brick facades, on the corner of Allenby and Ben-Yehuda. The films, chosen carefully by Ruth, who made sure they did not contain any violence, tragedy, or war scenes, caused a dramatic change in my mother. For the two hours she spent watching them, her muscles loosened and her breathing quieted, and the plot on the screen as if got under her skin, clearing the cobwebs from her faded soul.

And sometimes, for a spell, my mother would reenter her old skin, becoming more of a person and function. So it was whenever she sewed baby bibs from old fabrics or when she attended sewing lessons. This was also the case whenever she reminisced about the distant past, before things fell apart. Her eyes were sparkling then and her cheeks flushed; her words were directed right at me, her gaze on mine, no blinking, no lowering of the eyes.

Ruth told me that she'd made a promise to care for Naomi her entire life. She didn't only make this promise to Oma Ilse but also to Uriel, the day she said goodbye to him at the train station. And she swore it to herself thousands of times: that if any of her loved ones survived and she had a chance to reunite with them after the war, she would gladly give her life for them.

"And I was so incredibly happy," she would tell me, "the day we received a letter from Austria informing us that you were both alive. I was overcome with joy. I had trouble breathing. My life became enriched in an instant the day I saw your mother again, held by Jonah's arm on that busy train platform in London, almost a decade after I last saw her on the platform in Vienna…so thin and pale, but alive… And suddenly I saw you beside them, a girl with ivory skin, beautiful as a doe, and you waved hello to me. How did you even recognize me? And I fell in love with you right away…"

I listened and felt ashamed. How could I dare find fault with my mother? Wasn't her tangible defect, the result of all she had undergone, enough?

But the truth was, I wanted my mother to be like Esther's mother—feminine, maternal, and beautiful, turning heads, bringing light to the eyes of people around her, making all the high school students want to only study English with her…

I wanted her to be Ruth.

I didn't like walking down the street with Mother, standing beside her at school, her pale skin drawing baffled looks from my friends and compassionate looks from my teachers. She didn't even have a number on her arm to demonstrate where her madness had come from. And those baffled and compassionate looks that stared at her then shifted toward me…

But I loved my mother so much. Truly loved her. The moments when she opened up to me, her mouth filled with stories of her past, enriched my life. I want to believe I wasn't ashamed of her then, and that, just like Ruth and Davidi, I loved her unconditionally.

But did I?

Or perhaps I loved her less than I thought, only secretly, when we were alone?

These thoughts tortured my soul and twisted my mind. Despite her empathy and sensitivity towards me, Ruth neither understood nor accepted my behavior. As far as she was concerned, I transgressed the fifth commandment, and the reproach in her eyes whenever I doubted my mother's motherliness undermined my confidence.

"You shouldn't feel ashamed of your mother," she said. "Mothers should be revered..." You never give up on your mother..."

Then I would run to Davidi, climb on his back to gallop against the wind and whisper my distress to him. As soon as I began speaking to him, the percussion and string orchestra inside my body would slow down, telling me a different story.

Davidi would tell me that things and people do not need to be perfect. That what ultimately mattered was to have harmony within a person's soul, between his emotions and deeds, between his ways of thinking and behavioral patterns. He would also tell me that I must devote my entire life to striving for this harmony.

Then I would hug my wild horse, run my hand through his thick hair, kiss his forehead, his chin, and his cheeks, and even flutter a quick kiss on his lips.

52

Nurit shook me. "And what about Jonathan and Esther?" she asked.

"What about them?"

"What images do you have for them?

I said nothing, trying to focus my thoughts on Esther. We were cousins, born the same year. We'd grown up together from age five. Esther was an average student who had a hard time at school. Education experts did not know how to diagnose dyslexia at the time. I excelled in most subjects all through my student years and did especially well in literature, history, Bible, and grammar. She worked hard to overcome her hardships, to get better, to succeed. It came easily to me. Esther was skinny and flat-chested, not tall, her small nose covered in freckles; her honey-colored eyes were a bit sunken and shaded by long, black lashes; her wavy chestnut hair was always cut short. I was already taller than most of the girls in my class, long-legged and narrow-hipped. A local artist, a new immigrant from Hungary, once asked Ruth for permission to paint my portrait. "Something about her high cheekbones, her carefully etched lips, her light blue eyes makes her so special," he told my aunt in a heavy accent, "an unripe woman." My fair hair flowed in soft waves to my bra line, and at age fourteen I was already blessed with round breasts perking defiantly through my tight blouse.

Esther, who was very active in the Tel-Aviv Scouts, aspired to become a group leader like her brothers and always enjoyed the appreciation of Davidi, Gidi, and Jonathan, as if she were one of the guys. I remember Gidi's compliments regarding her gumption and kindness and the proud looks Jonathan gave her. What I wouldn't give for a look like that. Davidi liked to say that Esther was like an old-time pioneer. "Had she been born fifty years earlier," he said, "she would probably have been one of those strong, Jewish women who plowed the land, conquered the earth, bore arms, and helped build the country." And I wondered how he saw me. He also said that Esther naturally enjoyed the harmony between her emotions and deeds, her thoughts and actions, a harmony that for me was such a distant, coveted wish. "You," he said, making my cheeks turn red, "should learn from her."

And indeed, Esther had an awareness of her own worth, the kind I yearned to have too; she was always comfortable with her choices, and I never was. She had a rare emotional calm about her, while my emotions were always tumultuous. There was an exceptional kindness in her that made me strike her with my black demon from time to time, so that afterwards I'd torture myself for my behavior, especially because she never held a grudge and always cared for me.

That's wasn't all. I loved the city, the busy, crowded streets. Esther loved nature and the inanimate world: the overnight camping trips she took with her two brothers and, afterward, only with Jonathan, with a pack on her back and a camera strapped around her neck. Always with her camera. Together, they toured the Galilee Mountains and the Negev Desert, the valleys and the coastline plain, and the forests of the Carmel. They covered the whole country, along its breadth and length.

I once joined them on a trip to the Judean Desert, just because I wanted to sleep under the open sky besides Jonathan. Wearing a backpack, I walked beside them and, along with them, marveled at the landscape. A hole opened in my right shoe and small bits of gravel made their way inside, my clothes were covered in dust, and

Jonathan, afraid I might become dehydrated, gave me his canteen after I had emptied mine.

"A long hike like this doesn't suit you," he said.

I protested. "That's not true! I'm having a great time! I'm so happy I went on this trip with you! The desert is gorgeous, with its mountains, cliffs and valleys, its few streams that have cut into the earth to form enormous canyons, and especially its virginal, primeval landscape…"

"All right," he said dryly. "You can write down your impressions later, I'm sure you'll produce some gems. But in the meantime, in reality, you don't seem to be having a lot of fun."

I fell silent. Esther softened the dry brush that had started to fire up in my throat when she exclaimed that I was a terrific addition to their trip, and how glad she was I joined. "There's nothing like experiencing this stunning view firsthand," she said, adding that no picture she took could ever convey the deep sensations the desert conjured.

Although I was thankful to her for saving some of my trampled honor, which now matched my generally dusty, crumpled appearance and my rumbling stomach, the truth was Jonathan was right. Most of the time I felt bored with the yellow landscape, my legs grew tired from walking its endless stretches. I was too hot during the day and terribly cold at night, and the silence was just too formidable. But most of all, I felt I didn't belong there, to that special bond between Jonathan and Esther, their wondrous understanding, the peace she inspired in him, like the peace of the desert.

***

"I don't know," I said, confused. "I can't think of any simile for Esther. Can you, Nurit?"

My expression was so serious that we both started to laugh on that bench between the Twins.

"I guess," Nurit said once we calmed down, "there is no animal, vegetable, or mineral, that can describe Esther."

But then it hit me, and I said, "Yes, there is."

Nurit seemed surprised.

I told her Esther was a lighthouse. Like a lighthouse, she was planted deep in the ground, but she also had a stature that allowed her to see into the distance and from above, to take in the big picture. I also said that Esther never lost her way, always peaceful and content with herself, even when things all around were chaotic. That she had a rare ability to spread light all around her and help me navigate my way out from my turmoil as if I were a boat lost at sea. Speaking about Esther, I was filled with warmth. I knew that even if I didn't spend as much time with her as I did with Nurit, even if I didn't share all my secrets with her, I'd always be able to turn to her at a time of need, and she would help me find my way anywhere and take on any obstacle. Our relationship was not only that of blood, it was a deep, special, and unusual connection; and her love for me was unconditional, pure, and unadulterated like a sister's.

Nurit, who always liked and admired Esther, although they were not friends, considered this and nodded in agreement. "You nailed it," she said, smiling. "So, what have we got so far? A dove, a rock, a lion, a horse, and a lighthouse."

I smiled back. "Only one left," she said, and I turned serious.

Nurit knew that Jonathan had been in my dreams for quite a while. "Sometimes," I had told her, "I think he's been in my dreams since I was a little girl. It's as if he was born there, in my dreams..." I often asked her, concerned, "But how can I feel this way about a cousin? It's almost incestuous!"

"But it isn't," she said. "A cousin is not like a brother, even though you did grow up together. And now you aren't even sharing an apartment anymore."

I nodded and said it was lucky we were not.

***

At first, when Ruth and Jonah announced that Mother and I would be moving, my spirits fell. It was after that unfortunate parent-teacher conference at school, the one I asked that my mother not attend. Jonah and Ruth discussed this with her, and together they decided that it was time to separate, or as Ruth put it, "to separate just a bit." The apartment she and Jonah rented for us was in the same building, on the second floor, right across the hall from Hilde's. Jonah thought this would make Naomi more independent, and Ruth thought that an apartment shared by just the two of us might bring us closer together. Hilde promised to keep an eye on us, and Mother stammered, saying it was a fine idea.

But I felt exiled from the upstairs apartment, sent away so that the Jonases had more room, and I clammed shut, mourned, pulled away, withdrew into myself. For two whole months I did not go upstairs. I did not know at the time that Ruth, out of ancient female intuition, added another reason for this move when she whispered to Jonah that the hormones around the house were getting out of hand, "those of Helena and Jonathan…" These were things only she could see, but Jonah understood them right away.

"In that case," he said, "it's good that we're separating them a bit, and better now, before it's too late."

Only after a few weeks did I begin to see the advantages—the peace and quiet I had in the new apartment with my silent mother, the intimacy that formed between us, thin as a thread and invisible, on the nights when I stayed in and we were together just the two of us. Suddenly she became a bit of a homemaker and, spinning more and more family tales, she opened another window into her past, and occasionally accepting my request to tell me once again the great love stories between Uriel and Rachel and Naomi and Mordecai.

Once, when the two of us were sitting close together on the sofa, I inched carefully and snuggled up to her, and, in a moment of unusual alertness, she reminisced about another similar moment, years ago.

"You were sitting next to me in the brothel," she whispered. "You were only four years old, and you told me something I'll never forget." I waited, moved, for the rest of the sentence, which did not come. I decided not to push. The next day I adopted the exact same position at her side and, astounded by the translucency of her skin, her thinness, placed my hand on her arm, and she suddenly continued where she had left off.

"You were cuddling next to me," she said, "your tiny hands embracing me, and you said—I remember your sweet, little voice so well—'I'm never cold when I'm next to Mama's heart.'"

I remember my heart beating wildly and how I tried to get the most out of that special, brilliant, rare moment, after so many years, when we touched again the edges of that thread, the emotion of love. Both of us cried for one long, passing moment, and I wrapped my arms around her, and she put hers around mine, not letting go, and I could feel the soft beating of her heart against my ear.

And I felt warm.

Two months later, after gaining some inner harmony, as the black demon shriveled a bit, I agreed to return to the upstairs apartment for a Sabbath dinner around the family dining table. I mostly agreed to go thanks to Esther, who had come downstairs to knock on my bedroom door. When I opened it, she took me in her arms, and said with moist eyes, "Enough of this." She asked that I come because she, Ruth, Jonah, and her brothers all missed me. Surprised and flattered, I liked to feel wanted and came upstairs.

***

"Besides," said Nurit, "nothing ever happened between you and Jonathan."

I looked at her silently, recalling Jonathan's searching eyes as I walked into their apartment that day. In recent months. we'd done our best to avoid each other in the school's hallways, the soccer field, and the courtyard. When our paths did accidentally cross, I turned my back on him at once. With time, I developed sharp senses that helped me pass around his whereabouts; but once, when I saw him in the distance, my eyes clung to him. Jonathan was so handsome. His thin, muscular body, his wide shoulders, his tan skin and blonde hair, bleached by the sun, and of course, his blue half-moon eyes. Even from a distance, I could guess his skin was glistening with sweat after a run. He stood there, surrounded by boys and girls drawn to him like butterflies to nectar, and I could swear that one sophomore girl was standing especially close...

On my way home with Nurit, I whispered to her that I was in trouble, that my feelings for Jonathan were growing stronger. I added that he wasn't just in my dreams anymore, but taking over my nights, until there was no room left for anything else. That day, I made Nurit swear that from that point on, whenever we spoke about him, she would not mention his name. "When you talk about him, please call him 'the one,'" I requested, "only 'the one,'" so that if anyone happened to hear, they wouldn't be able to connect the dots.

I remember that when we walked into their apartment that evening, Davidi, Gidi, and Esther showered me with love, Ruth hugged Mother, and Jonah was delighted. Only Jonathan stood apart, a spark of ridicule passing through his eyes and piercing my heart. I was tense the entire night. I thought that if I had a black demon inside of me, his was much worse. When we said goodbye at the end of the night, everyone hugged me, even him, but only I felt his iron fingers poking me in the ribs, and how he lingered his hands on my hips for a moment, his breath surrounding my face.

Another memory came to me. Three years earlier, a few days before my thirteenth birthday, Jonathan walked into my room, tucking his khaki shirt into his trousers, and mocked me for still holding onto my doll, Gertie. "It's time you got rid of it," he said.

I smoldered at the insult. In a fit of rage, I grabbed Gertie by the hair and threw her out the window to the yard. Jonathan stood before me, smirking, then turned around and left. A moment later I heard the front door opening and his footsteps fading down the stairs. Agitated, I watched him through the window as he walked off to his Scouts meet.

Once he had disappeared from view, I strode three stories down with a racing heart, only to discover that someone had already taken Gertie away, and I would never again be able to clutch her to my chest. I tried to hold back the tears of sorrow that choked my throat.

I learned an important lesson that day. I went upstairs and stood before my reflection in the mirror and swore out loud that I would never, ever give up a part of my personality for another person again.

But that night, and every night afterward, Gertie was not by my side.

And Jonathan never mentioned her again.

***

Now, when Nurit asked me what animal I saw when I thought about him, the words swirled about, smoothed out and sharpened inside of me. My heart pounded as I muttered, "A predator." I saw her mouth opening, and dark spots flickered before my eyes and formed animal skin. I called out, "A cheetah!"

Nurit thought this over, perhaps, in her imagination, feeling the cat's claws against her skin, and shuddered again, saying she felt cold.

I offered her, and myself, some information I had no idea where I'd learned—perhaps I'd dreamed it, too—that the cheetah was the fastest land mammal in nature. "Its body is slender," I explained, "its spine flexible, and its legs muscular, especially the hind legs, which provide the most speed when it lunges…"

The next day, sitting by the same old oak tree, on the same bench, I supplemented this information through a little research I'd conducted that day at the school library. Nurit was all ears. "The cheetah is significantly faster than its prey," I said, "It starts by following the prey from an elevated position, then advances in a light trot, which turns into a sprint when the prey senses its presence and tries to escape. Once it knocks its prey down with the strike of a paw, it clutches its neck in its mouth, and with a single, swift bite, strangles it to death."

"Oh," Nurit said, shivering.

"Besides," I raised my voice a bit, "the male cheetah is not as picky as, say, the lion, nor does it put in much effort when it comes to courtship—"

"Helena!" Nurit was shocked by my boldness.

I jumped to my feet. "And at the end of intercourse, it lets out a loud roar…"

53

In July 1956, Egypt nationalized the Suez Canal and closed the Straits of Tiran to Israeli sea vessels. In response, Britain and France, in coordination with Israel, planned Operation Musketeer for the capture of the canal.

That summer, we said goodbye to Davidi. Hastening to fulfil his dreams in Europe, he left me downcast and melancholy, after I realized that I would no longer be able to listen to his wonderful music every evening or run my fingers through his hair or whisper my deepest emotions into his attentive ear.

"I'll come visit in the winter," he promised, putting his lips to my forehead. Then he gently raised my chin and fixed his warm eyes on mine. He asked me to take care of myself. He also asked me to be kind to my mother and love her unconditionally. I looked at him and felt the distress that had been weighing down on me evaporating under his loving gaze. I fluttered my long lashes to dry my tears and tried to steady my eyes on his. He wiped my tears away with the tip of his fingers.

Then he hugged Ruth, Naomi, and Esther, and shook the men's hands. He asked Gidi to take care of himself as well, not only of the country; he asked Ruth to look after Naomi and Jonah, whose heart had weakened of late; he asked Jonathan to keep an eye out for Esther and me—it was like leaving a cat in charge of the cream, how could he not see that?—and all of us to take care of Mrs. Rothenberg's

Steinway piano, making sure Ruth didn't forget to call the Russian piano tuner from Pinsker Street over at least twice a year.

***

Two months after Davidi left, on 29 October, the war broke when Israeli paratroopers, fighters of the 890th Battalion of the 202nd Brigade, landed deep in the Sinai Peninsula, only a few dozen miles from the Suez Canal.

"Gidi's one of them," Irit whispered, and we didn't ask her how she knew.

I asked Nurit to meet me urgently near the old oak tree. "Everyone is terribly nervous at home," I reported. "Jonah is withdrawn, and Ruth is so worried about him. His heart is weakening, and he needs peace and quiet, rest, and relaxation. Esther, as usual, says little and takes pictures constantly, I'm not sure of what. We barely see Jonathan at all, and Davidi is so far away…" I paused for a moment, lowering my gaze. "But the worst is my mother."

"What happened, Helena?" Nurit asked, alert.

"She's in a terrible state." My voice broke. "The tension is killing her and it's getting harder and harder to make her calm down. She keeps mumbling 'War,' 'war again,' asking about Gidi and Uriel, if anyone's seen Mordecai, or Gabriel, and what about Raphael, he's so sick and needs medicine…"

"Who's to say for sure that Gidi was one of the paratroopers that landed in Sinai?" Nurit offered. "How can Irit even know?"

"Ruth," I answered, "claims that a woman knows where her lover is even from afar."

"Nonsense!" voiced Nurit, recruiting a long line of logic. "It's a simple yes or no question, not a matter of intuition!"

But at that moment the rest of the 202nd Brigade forces crossed the Egyptian border, occupied Quntila and advanced westward in a vehicle operation to join the parachuted force, and we no longer dealt with hunches and guesses. Gidi could have been with the 890th Battalion or with one of the other battalions of the 202nd Brigade, but, either way, it was clear as the day rising over the Sahara Desert— Gidi was there.

***

The next day, France and Britain posed an ultimatum for Egypt and Israel to evacuate their forces at least ten land miles on either side of the canal.

"Jonah," I informed Nurit, "says Israel is acting in complete synchronization with the British and French forces, who controlled the Suez Canal through a joint company, until Abdel Nasser nationalized it."

"Of course," she said. "This entire coordinated operation was born to take over the canal again."

In a matter of days, the Israeli army, assisted by the British and French air forces, occupied northern Sinai. Pressured by the United States and the Soviet Union, the leaders of the new world, they would evacuate the peninsula and the Gaza Strip within a matter of months.

***

"Stupid war!" I wailed to Nurit when she told me that Avner Rachamim, the neighbors' son, was killed on the battle of Mitla Pass. Nurit showed me the November issue of *Davar L'yeladim,* the children's newspaper, featuring a front-page photo of Israeli paratroopers raising the Israeli flag on Mount Sinai.

That moment, Ruth and Naomi appeared, walking home from the green grocer's and carrying baskets of fruit and vegetables. They walked hand in hand, and I couldn't say which of them was leaning on the other—Ruth, who looked so tired and pale, or silent Naomi, so faded from her anxieties that she became almost translucent.

"The atmosphere on the street is so tense," Ruth whispered. "The grocer knows someone who left for Sinai and still hasn't contacted his wife, and the one with the limp, who's been working with him since summer, said that five of his high school friends are in the battles and that one of them, he'd heard, has lost the sight in one of his eyes and had his face burnt..."

Ruth didn't mention Gidi, and Nurit and I said nothing. We quickly took the baskets from their hands and supported them up the stairs. When we reached the third floor, Esther greeted us with a telegram from Davidi in Berlin, wanting to know how we were managing during these hard times, and ending with a question: "Have you heard from Gidi yet?"

The next day during morning formation, the high school principal announced painfully that last night he received some dire news: one of the high school graduates, Ephraim Kaplan, was killed in the battle of Sharm El Sheikh. "Our brave boys are still in Sinai," he added, "and we have yet to receive the names of all those who were wounded, or killed, God forbid..." For a moment, his voice died down and the silence enabled his statement to seep in. Then he cleared his throat, gathered his voice again, and said, "Let us say a prayer for the safety of our sons, may they speedily return to be among us."

Ephraim Kaplan. The name echoed through my mind. In Gidi's year, enlisted a month before him as a paratrooper... With my heart about to burst, I made my way through the formation, my eyes searching for Jonathan. Esther, it turned out, had done the same. At some point, I took her hand in mine as we crossed the lines of students. We finally found Jonathan, his face grave, standing apart from his friends, talking to the gym teacher. Esther rushed to his side.

"Jonathan, did something happen?" she asked anxiously.

He wrapped his arm around her shoulders. "No," he said. "Nothing yet."

"Don't say that!" Esther sobbed; her face crumpled, a tear ran down her cheek.

Jonathan bit his lip.

Close enough to touch him, I restrained myself not to squeeze my way under his arm, the way Esther had done with such natural ease, not sure how he would react if I did. Jonathan turned to face me. He'd been home very rarely during the war, and when he was there, he spent most of his time discussing the battles in the south with Jonah. Now his eyes were red and full of stress. He stared at me for a moment, then offered his hand. I came closer and he gathered me under his arm. My heart pounded from the proximity and the gesture. I hoped he couldn't sense it and tried to stifle my tears.

Suddenly, as if from nowhere, Irit appeared before us, her face beaming. The three of us, as well as the gym teacher, all looked at her with eyes full of hope.

"I think it's all right!" she said.

"What's all right?" asked Jonathan.

She tried to smile, her eyes shining. "I think Gidi's on his way home," she said, "I think he made it out all right."

"Irit, this is serious," said Esther. "How do you know? Did you get some message from him? Did someone tell you he was coming home?"

"Not really," said Irit. "But I have a feeling inside that he's on his way. I always get this feeling whenever he comes home, even if he doesn't let me know, and I'm never wrong. I've been feeling it for the past thirty minutes, so strong…"

I saw Jonathan grimace and wondered how Nurit would have reacted, but at that moment Esther and I were ready to hang onto anything, even just a hunch.

That evening, Gidi did come home from the battlefield, healthy and tired, dusty, and in one piece.

***

Once, in ninth grade, we were asked to write an essay on the meaning of happiness. When Esther told Ruth and Naomi that I'd won
first place in the municipal high school essay competition, after my
essay, which had won in the high school, was sent to represent the
Gymnasia in the municipal competition, they were filled with pride.

In the preliminary research I'd conducted at the Sha'ar Zion
Library, poring eagerly over books, most of which had not yet been
translated into Hebrew, I collected words of wisdom written by nov-
elists, poets, and thinkers about the sublimity of happiness. I was
moved by the definitions of the philosopher Aristotle, the theologian
Jacques-Bénigne Bossuet, and the playwright George Bernard Shaw.
I was amused by the definition of Françoise Sagan, and especially
liked those of Mahatma Gandhi and Dale Carnegie. Eventually,
overwhelmed with different definitions, I realized that if I asked
twenty different people what made them happy, and they would begin a rapid inner journey in attempting a definition, I would likely
receive twenty different answers. I smiled when I remembered Nurit
saying decisively that philosophy was not math and not for her and
decided to define what happiness meant for me. Since much greater
and wiser people had already addressed the colossal notion of "life-
long happiness" or "constant happiness," I decided to stick to a small
bit of this thing called "happiness," a very particular, very temporary
variety of it, which one might experience without lifting a finger.

"Happiness," I wrote, "is the sublime sensation experienced
by those who win back something very dear to them, which they
thought they might have lost forever." Then as an example, I depicted
in poetic, evocative language the happiness that filled our home like
sunlight the day Gidi returned, alive and well, from the war.

***

Before the school year was over, British and French forces were forced to retreat from Sinai. This signaled to the entire world that the military campaign was a much greater matter than a battle for control over some canal in the African continent and that a new balance of power had been born in the arena.

The Israeli prime minister, David Ben Gurion, one David among many Goliaths, insisted that the evacuation of Israeli armed forces from the Gaza Strip and Sinai Peninsula take place only after receiving an international guarantee of open straits and open sailing rights for Israeli vessels in the Suez Canal. While preserving Israeli rights under International law, he bravely announced that any future shutting of the Straits of Tiran to Israeli ships would be reason enough for another war, which would, indeed, break out in a little over a decade.

54

One afternoon, before the canal was nationalized and the war broke out, my mother and I were home alone.

The sound of weak knocking from her room awoke me from a daydream about "the one," and I went over right away, quietly pushed the door open, and watched her unnoticed from the side.

In this early afternoon hour, only a few rays of sunshine, speckled with a million little dust motes, filtered in through the shutters, and Mother was standing in the spot where the light gathered on the floor, her clothes in a pile around her, trying them on one by one—a purple skirt with a white cardigan knit by Ruth, then a cotton dress.

When she noticed me, she smiled shyly and froze in place. I suddenly yearned for her and came closer, taking her hand softly and picking up a blue sweater from the floor, saying it suited her eyes. Then I found a matching blue skirt and asked, "Where to?"

"To take a walk," she said.

"On Ben-Yehuda Street?"

"No, on Dizengoff."

I picked up a wide-brimmed hat that Mother had sewed for Ruth out of old slips and handkerchiefs and placed it on her head. Out of nowhere, I was struck by a memory of a different hat from my childhood, a simple, wide hat. I shuddered. I removed the hat from her head and said, "This doesn't work with the outfit, Mama." I reached into the pile and fished out an English silk scarf that still looked new, wrapped it softly around Mother's thin, pristine swan neck, and fluttered a kiss on her cheek. I watched her as she began twirling through the room, her eyes closed, her skirt hovering around her. Then I came closer, took her hands, and began to dance with her in the middle of the room, between the table and the sofa. She opened her pretty eyes and smiled at me.

But the war ruined everything. It brushed aside small islands of contentment and daydreams, replacing them with Mother's old nightmares. From the way she muttered in her sleep, I realized she was plagued by those painful, long-gone visions, her feverish imagination once again searching for loved ones who were no longer alive and for her beloved who was swallowed by the grim maw of another war. Mother fell apart again and was admitted into a mental health clinic for many weeks. Offering her love and devotion, Ruth visited her regularly several times a week.

Almost sixteen years old, I was left alone in the apartment, one floor beneath Jonah, Ruth, and Esther.

And Jonathan.

When the war ended and Gidi returned to the army, the little black demon emerged from its lair and lay in silent wait for the right time to attack.

***

The streets of Tel Aviv returned to normal with surprising speed. Only two weeks had gone by since the war in Sinai ended, and I was already attending concerts at Beit Ha'am, on the corner of Shalom Aleichem and Ben-Yehuda Streets, and on a Friday afternoon I strolled with Nurit down Dizengoff Street and shared a piece of plum cake at Café Roval.

"Nurit, I want to get a job," I told her. I explained tearfully that

Jonah had been fired from his job at the municipality. "Some contractor was making his life miserable," I explained, "and after Jonah refused some of his exaggerated demands, he turned on him and used his contacts at the municipality to get him fired."

But Nurit must have heard about the wall that had collapsed south of Jaffa in a public housing building, which Jonah had been responsible for, burying beneath it an Arab laborer, who miraculously got out injured but alive. She didn't say a thing. I fell silent too, glum, only daring to wordlessly wonder whether my good uncle Jonah, knowledgeable, master of stories, bearer of answers, might not be as talented as we thought. But I didn't dare say this to a soul, certainly not to Ruth, who was taking on longer and longer hours at school, and even giving private English lessons to the children of a wealthy family that lived down the street.

"I don't know what's going to happen," I told Nurit. "Things at home are rough. Jonah won't accept help from his mother in London, especially now that his father's health is deteriorating."

"Let's find a job together," Nurit suggested. "I want to pay my own way too. Perhaps we can apply for a job cleaning cages at the zoo?"

I grimaced in revulsion. "Me? Clean animal cages?" When I saw her eyes lit up, I added, "That suits you, Nurit, you'll probably become a vet one day. But me? That isn't for me at all!"

"All right," she conceded. "Then let's hear from you. What do you want to do?"

"The truth?" I asked.

"What else?"

"I want to write," I said quietly.

"To write?"

"And make a living doing it…"

Nurit smiled. "There's no doubt in my mind, Helena, that you'll make it". Do you have a plan?"

"A plan?" I marveled. "A plan for what? I don't even have any stories yet..."

"You'll have stories!" she said decisively. Nurit always had faith in me, even when I barely had any in myself. She claimed that my writing talent was a God-given gift. "But it's very important to have a plan first..."

This is the kind of person Nurit was. To her, anything was possible, as long as there was a will and the proper plan for execution. But I...what did I have besides Ruth and Nurit's support? I had the essay that had won me the city award, the respect of my teachers, who saw some spark in me, and dozens of pages hidden in my drawer, containing my musings, the beginnings of essays, rhyming poems, and first drafts...

But I also had the dream that formed slowly, late at night, after the lights went out, the dream I had yet to share with anyone... I said nothing for a long moment. Then I quickly arranged my thoughts, gathered my courage, and revealed my aspirations to Nurit, presenting it as a plan. For, in the end, this was only Nurit, with whom any notion was permitted, especially if it had a smidgen of practicality.

"Yes," I said, a ruddiness spreading over my cheeks. "I want to sell my stories to magazines. As a start, I thought about the children's weekly journal *Our Land*. I could publish a serial there. Then, when I become better known, I'll contact *Haaretz*. Did you know they used to publish at least two stories by S.Y. Agnon every year? And that his story *A Guest for the Night* was serialized over dozens of issues before it was printed as a book?"

No, Nurit had not known, but she loved the idea. "Terrific," she said matter-of-factly. "Tomorrow we have two places to go, just you and I." She wouldn't say where, not even when I begged.

The next day after school, Nurit led me to the bus stop on Rothschild Boulevard, and I called out to Esther to tell my mother and Ruth I'd be late coming home. We took a bus to Dizengoff Street, got off on the corner of Keren Kayemet Boulevard, and walked briskly to the Ibn Gabirol Zoo, near the Hadassah Park. We passed quickly by the deer and gazelles, the zebras and the antelopes, the Syrian brown bear and the black bear. We glanced from a distance at the seabirds, flamingo, and turtle pond, and, flustered, paused by the barred cages with the black Bengal tiger and the Siberian tiger, and adjacent to it, the round, corner cage of the lion and the lioness.

We found Johnny in a different corner of the zoo, where the baboons, langurs, squirrel monkeys, and lemurs lived. Johnny was the zookeeper, who had become famous among Tel Aviv children due to his habit of walking with the leopards, tigers and lions as if they were pets, and for entering fearlessly into their cages for nothing more than a hug. He and his wife lived in a small house within the zoo, where they took care of predator cubs, feeding them by bottle. Johnny loved animals; and children like Nurit, who loved animals, loved Johnny, too.

By the time we left, thirty minutes later, after we had fed peanuts to a small baboon, Nurit had a job. I was impressed with the confidence with which she spoke to Johnny and the manner with which she presented her love of animals. I admired her readiness to show up at the zoo at any time of day and reach her hands into smelly cages to wipe away urine and collect feces.

But Nurit didn't leave me much time to ponder her achievement. "Now it's your turn!" she announced, pulling me back to Dizengoff Street. We went to *Pizza*, a snack bar north of Dizengoff Circle, which, despite its name, was not yet serving pizza but rather Italian ice cream in colorful plastic cups with half-clear plastic spoons. Licking ice cream, we sat on folding metal chairs, and Nurit showed me a piece of paper ripped from her notebook, bearing the names of several cafés. "These are the places frequented by writers and poets. We're going to choose one and go there today, and who knows, you might catch the eye and ear of some important writer, who can give you some starter tips. Or maybe you'll just find some inspiration." I turned red and tried to object, but Nurit said this was a beautiful day, unseasonably warm for late November, and that we ought to take advantage before the weather turned rainy and cold.

Nurit pointed to the first name on the list: Café Kasit in the center of Dizengoff Street. "It's the center of Tel Aviv bohemia," she said. "My aunt's neighbor, who's an actress at the Cameri Theatre, goes there daily. She told me that it's Nathan Alterman's favorite spot, but that Avraham Shlonsky, Haim Guri, and Uri Zvi Greenberg also go there frequently, and even Alexander Penn..."[7] She winked at me. I'd once seen a black-and-white photo of Penn and said he was handsome. I shifted uncomfortably in my seat, but my eyes were already glowing like the Northern Star.

Further down the list, Nurit also included Café Sheleg HaLebanon and HaMedura. I decided to start at Sheleg HaLebanon, both because I wasn't prepared to just show up at a place like Kasit out of the blue, meeting all the who's who of Tel Aviv at once, and because I liked the sound of the name. Something about the word *sheleg*—Hebrew for *snow*—reminded me of my European homeland and sounded pristine, like a fresh start.

We headed toward Allenby Street, hand in hand. My heart pounded, threatening to burst right out of my chest, and Nurit soothed me with her determination and warm touch. Suddenly, she paused, turning to face me. "Last night," she said, "I went to visit my aunt and met that actress from the Cameri at her apartment. I told her about my plans for today and about you. She asked me to tell you something." Her eyes turned serious. "She said that the art world may not be as easy to enter as to find work cleaning cages, but that the clique of Tel Aviv writers and thinkers is just like the zoo: both

---

7   Famous 20th-century Israeli poets and Intellectuals. Penn was famous also for his Bohemian lifestyle.

are a kind of urban jungle, and in a jungle, she said, you have to know the rules and learn how to fit in. But the most important thing is to project determination and strength, Helena. People can smell it. Just like animals."

55

December 1990
Yosemite Park, California

Dear Nurit,

I miss so many things. I miss the people who have passed through my life, especially those who are dead. I miss the days of my childhood and youth, my loved ones who are gone, and the Tel Aviv of long ago. I miss the many hours you and I spent together, our endless conversations under the old oak tree... And I miss your loving advice, and most of all, your courage. I wish I had a tenth of your courage.

Remember the day we went to get you a job at the zoo? The day you dragged me to Sheleg HaLebanon to meet "the literati"?

That's when I saw "the other" for the first time.

You never liked him. Maybe because you never really knew him.

Sheleg HaLebanon is long gone. So are the Hadassah Park and the old Tel Aviv Zoo. But in my memory, they are still so vivid! The animals in their cages, the strong smells of the zoo, the flavor of the Italian ice at Pizza, the aroma of the cake, you standing boldly in front of Johnny, explaining what you wanted, and I, mesmerized by "the other" and his striking appearance.

That's where our lives took off, yours in a predictable route (other than the divorce, which was a total shock), and mine much less so.

This year is almost over, a new decade about to begin. Everything is going by so quickly. The hotels and lodges around here are all gearing up for Christmas, decorating mainly in red and green, but also in yellow, blue, and white. There are much more upscale hotels than the French Lodge, but to me the Lodge is the best. It's like a second home, and the prices are reasonable. Last night, Pierre and Marcel invited me to join them at an old, elegant restaurant at the center of the park. We made an early toast for the new year, but my mind was elsewhere. I was thinking about Mike and the kids, about Blair. I was thinking about the imminent war in the Persian Gulf, Saddam Hussein's scathing threats, and the panicked preparation in Israel. I was here in body, but my thoughts were in Atlanta and Tel Aviv. I wondered what would happen if a missile landed on the Gan Ha'ir shopping center, which was built on the ruins of the zoo, and I felt so sad.

I hope this dark mood lifts soon.

Write to me, Nurit, if you have the strength and desire to do so with everything that's going on.

Love and miss you,
Helena

56

Nurit and I walked quickly down Allenby Street on our way to Sheleg HaLebanon. It was late afternoon; the sun hid behind a cluster of clouds; the sky grew dark and the air, colder. We walked inside and took a seat at a corner table, facing the interior of the café, so that we could see the other patrons. Nurit was wide-eyed and alert, and I was petrified until I realized there were no poets, writers, actors, or playwrights on the premises, only regular people like Nurit and me. I was filled with a mixture of relief and disappointment.

I drank up the juicy details Nurit had heard from that Cameri actress, according to which Sheleg HaLebanon was the first café in Tel Aviv that had served as a meeting place for the literati; that Abraham Shlonsky, Avraham Halfi, Nathan Alterman, and Leah Goldberg were some of the regulars; and that this was where Alexander Penn whispered his love to Hannah Robina, the first lady of Hebrew theater.

"That actress told me," Nurit said, "that the greatest dramas in Tel Aviv take place not on theatre stages but at the city's cafes, just like in Paris and Vienna. Many of the writers and poets make these cafes their regular working places, like open ateliers and second homes. You can see them sitting there, writing and sketching, carrying on literary arguments and poetical brawls, learning about newly published books or plays-in-progress."

Intoxicated by all this new and unexpected knowledge, I opened my eyes wide.

"But personal rivalries also become mixed up in all this," Nurit continued to surprise me. "You should have seen the actress's eyes sparkle when she told me about it. You can even learn about the animosity between literary camps by looking at the patrons of the different cafes. The territories of the different literary groups are well-defined, and whenever a new generation of writers rebels against the old, they move tables, or worse—switch cafés—and the muses depart the abandoned ones..."

I sat there, listening to her intently, stirring my tea, crumbling my piece of apple cake with my fork, and turning over the stories Nurit told me about the bohemian world of Tel Aviv, about its artists and urges, their creations and passions. An urban jungle.

***

Only as we were about to leave and Nurit lingered for a moment at the dessert glass display did I notice him.

Something about his appearance, his body language, his manner of speaking, riveted me even back then. He was significantly older than me, wrinkles furrowed his brow, his dark hair was turning gray around the temples. He crushed a thick cigar in a round ashtray until it went out completely and jotted something with pencil on paper. His gray eyes were fixed on the woman sitting across from him at a square table with a checkered cloth. The woman seemed attentive to everything he said and occasionally broke into short, nervous laughter. His low voice radiated an odd heat as he spoke English with a foreign accent, an accent that was familiar to me from home.

He paused for breath without taking his eyes off her. I could practically feel the wheels in his brain turning and the nerves tingling in her body. Had I dared, I would have taken a seat at a nearby table and followed their interaction more closely. Nurit pulled on my arm, and I signaled to her to give me another moment, that I wasn't finished yet; I remained standing against the counter. I detected the confusion on Nurit's face when she shifted her eyes to the couple.

Suddenly, the woman's face turned yellow with anger, and when the man tried to place a hand on her arm, she shook him off, and stood up rapidly, scraping her chair against the floor. She gripped her black purse with her long, manicured fingers, and stormed out.

"That was no literary debate," I murmured.

Nurit stifled a giggle.

I looked, curious and stunned, at the man. His face was completely still, save for his lips, which puckered a bit. Without looking around, he pulled a thick, brown cigar from his coat pocket, lopped one tip and then the other, warmed it over the flame of a match, and only after making sure it was fully lit, placed it between his lips, sucked, and released smoke rings into the air.

Nurit tugged gently on my arm. "What are you doing, Helena?" she whispered, "standing there, staring at that guy? Have you gone mad? What's going on with you? This looks so weird!"

"I don't know," I mumbled awkwardly. "That man really is strange… Did you see with what indifference he lit that cigar after the woman ran out on him?"

"Of course I did. He's not only strange, he's a stranger, and even if he is a journalist or some famous writer, you definitely should meet someone local, someone who's been in this country for at least twenty years."

"Yes," I nodded. "You're right, Nurit, as always. But how would I approach a guy like that? Why would he agree to discuss my dream with me as if he's got nothing better to do?!" I looked at her. "Maybe I should clean animal cages with you after all?"

Nurit laughed and hugged me. "Come on," she said. "Don't be silly. You'll publish your stories in magazines. One of them could be called 'My Friend Nurit, the Lion Lady.'"

I laughed. We left the café hand in hand, headed home.

The stranger's expressionless face, however, didn't leave my mind. Even Nurit admitted later that he'd left a mysterious impression on her.

But at the time, we had no idea what a powerful influence that stranger would have on my life.

57

I said goodbye to Nurit by the old oak tree and went inside our building. I paused at the mailbox. My mother and I received very little mail, but occasionally we were surprised to find a delightful letter from Davidi, and I was eagerly awaiting winter break, when he would come visit.

The mailbox was empty. Perhaps the mailman is late today, I thought, and just then I heard a bicycle approaching behind me. Expecting to see Rachamim, our friendly Yemenite mailman, on his old bike, his threadbare brown bag overflowing with telegrams and stamped letters slung across his torso, I turned around quickly.

But it was not Rachamim. It was Jonathan. And not just any Jonathan, but Jonathan in a wet undershirt and wet hair, his skin shiny with sweat, his pungent smell titillating my nose. He must have come back from a soccer game at one of the sandy seaside lots where he and his friends would set stones in the corners and along the goal lines and declare them soccer fields, and play in undershirts, khaki shorts, and their everyday shoes, since only a few of them could afford proper sneakers.

"Hello, Helena," he said, fixing his gaze on me.

"Hello, Jonathan." I tried to give my voice a light tone, but a heat wave rose from my belly through my neck and up to my scalp, staining my cheeks with an embarrassing ruddiness.

"Why did you jump like that?" he teased me.

"Me? Jump?"

"It was like you were expecting to see someone else and saw me instead..." He could be so irritating sometimes.

"Oh, actually, I thought you were Rachamim, the mailman, you sound the same, pedaling on your bikes..."

"Are you going to enter the school's costume competition?" he changed subjects.

"Costumes?" I asked, surprised. "Purim is in another three months!" And since when, I wondered, did this guy care about things like that?

"Yes, but after the war ended, the school board decided to include some cheerful things in the students' agenda, and so it pushed the preparations forward." He chuckled and mimicked Miss Carmela, the senior year coordinator. "And guess who's on the judging panel?"

I grimaced. "Who else but Jonathan." Why did they always reveal my discomfort? I thought, irritated: my voice and that terrible blush in my cheeks.

"None else!" he announced without modesty. "Well, actually, me and four others." His eyebrows rose, rounding over his indifferent gaze. "Two girls from my class, the gym teacher, and—"

"Miss Carmela," I completed his sentence. I was no fool.

"Very good!" He smiled slyly. Why couldn't he ever just smile warmly, a normal smile, a pleasant one?

"So now that you know all this, you'd better find yourself a suitable costume, Helena. You've got potential to be the belle of the ball!" He winked at me as he locked the front tire of his bike to the iron railing, then ran inside the building. As he took the stairs three at a time, he called down that he was late for a Scouts meet and that he still had to shower before he left. His voice echoed through the stairwell.

I stayed thus behind, with that offhanded statement about being the belle of the ball, which I would turn over again and again with Nurit and by myself for many days to come.

***

The next day, right after school, I headed over to Sheleg HaLebanon again, this time alone. I sat down a bit sheepishly at a small table with a checkered tablecloth and ordered a cup of tea and a piece of cheesecake.

But the strange man did not show up.

I kept going, first every day, then every other day, then every three days. When the café employees grew used to my regular visits, I dared to cut back on my expenses, which threatened to empty my wallet already depleted of pocket money, and skipped the cake, making do with a cup of tea and the latest issue of *Haaretz*, which I swiped from Jonah's desk, focusing mainly on the literary supplement. I'd sit, sip, and read, my eyes occasionally wandering to the door in hopes that he might appear again.

One afternoon, I had a surprise. About fifteen minutes after taking my regular seat at Sheleg HaLebanon, the poetess Leah Goldberg walked in, erect and elegant in a brown suit. She arrived alone, enveloped in the rings of smoke that emanated from the cigarette in her hand. Goldberg, I knew, had begun her literary career writing for children and youth newspapers. Just a week earlier I'd read in *Haaretz* that she'd left Tel Aviv and was living with her mother, Tzila, in the Rehavia neighborhood of Jerusalem and was working as a lecturer in general literature at the Hebrew University.

And now here she was, in the same café as I, the one she used to visit so frequently.

I was so excited I forgot why I was there. I snuck glances at this woman in her mid-forties, her short hair clinging in waves to her head, revealing a high forehead over a pair of dark, melancholy eyes. I wanted to ask if she truly loved children. I wanted to tell her that in the goodbye letter I wrote to my cousin Davidi before he left for school in Europe, I quoted a few lines from her poem *Pine*, which seemed so apt for his world, torn between two continents:

Perhaps only migrating birds know –
Suspended between earth and sky –
The heartache of two homelands.

With you I was transplanted twice,
With you, pine trees, I grew –
Roots in two disparate landscapes.[8]

But most of all, I wanted to discuss one poem from her collection *What Do the Deer Do?* which moved me even though it was intended for small children. The poem was called *Magic Hat*, and it was about a little girl who dreamed of a magic feathered hat that did anything she wanted.

I wanted to tell her I also had a magic hat like that at my uncle's home, a blue hat which, for me, had been truly magical for many years, providing answers for dozens of quandaries, helping me arrange conflicting thoughts and somewhat calm my soul.

But instead of going to the poetess, I stayed planted in place, staring at her, wondering what, leaning over a table, she was writing at that very moment, a piece of paper spread before her, a pen in her hand. I noticed the silence that fell over the café from the moment she walked in, as if no one dared interrupt her creative mind and her scribbling hand. It was as if she were surrounded by a halo of respect and an aura of love.

I stayed there two hours, by that same empty cup of tea, watching her tenderly and daydreaming. I finally left ten minutes after the poet got up; she wrote coffee and cake on her tab, and walked quietly into the early night darkness.

---

8   From *Pine* by Leah Goldberg.

58

December 1990
Yosemite Park, California

Dear Davidi,

I'm scared. Nurit wrote me that Blair arrived in Tel Aviv two days ago. The atmosphere in the region is heating up, and now, of all times, she chooses to go there.

But that's Blair. She has no fear. She has gumption.

Nurit still hasn't met with her. Blair called her out of the blue and announced she'd landed in the city. She said she was staying at a friend's house, but Nurit thinks she'll move into Gidi and Irit's soon. At least I'll have an address, at last, and be able to truly write to her. Nurit will find out everything. She'll also ask Gidi to make sure Blair has a gas mask as soon as possible. Who knows how all this will end?

I've had no contact with Mike since I left. It's been almost five months.

It's terrible, Davidi. Especially since I feel so guilty.

When I first met Mike, I was a little jealous of him. This was before the Yom Kippur War. I was envious of his big family, which, unlike ours, had emigrated from Europe in time. Over the years I became very attached to Mike's parents and siblings and, most of all, to his grandmother Sonia.

I wish you'd have met her, Davidi. She was a character. Short, but still a woman of exceptional stature. Something about her made people admire her right away. Mike's grandfather, Favel, had trained as a doctor in his hometown of Orenburg, in the southern Ural Mountains, but it was the shrewd, energetic Grandma Sonia that pushed him to start a private clinic in the foyer of their small New York apartment. Afterward, she encouraged him to also start a business importing medical equipment to hospitals, and, in this way, he began to accumulate a fortune. In addition to raising their six children, Sonia found the time for feverish public activity. As a young woman, she was active in one of the *Landsmannschaft* organizations that provided financial and social support to Jewish immigrants from Russia, and later became involved in the Independent Order of B'nai B'rith. There was an enormous picture on the wall of her living room, painted by a Judaica artist, with the symbol of the order: a seven-branch menorah, each branch symbolizing a noble ideal—light, justice, peace, benevolence, brotherly love, harmony, and truth.

In their family, Grandma Sonia was affectionately referred to as the "founder of the Myers dynasty." Her descendants are now scattered all over the continent, but of all her many grandchildren, Mike was the closest to her. That must be why she left him the picture of the menorah when she died. To this day, the picture bestows certain splendor to the western wall of our living room.

I loved spending time with that old lady with the clever eyes, perhaps as compensation for Oma Ilse, whom I'd never known. The details of the conversations I'd had with her over the years were treasured in my memory as precious stones, and the words of wisdom she'd produced from her life experience often made their way into my books.

Mike's sister once told me that Grandma Sonia often said that Mike couldn't marry just anyone. Whomever he married had to be "very special," compatible with someone as distinctive as Mike. I've always been very proud to be that "special someone." But these days I'm not even sure I deserve the title.

Why me? Who am I to have received such an honor?

And now, Davidi, I don't know what's going to happen anymore.

Will Mike ever forgive me? Will he take me back?

Yours, loving (and worrying) as ever,
Helena

59

January 1991
Yosemite Park, California

Dear Davidi,

This morning the receptionist gave me a manila envelope containing a letter from you. I went immediately up to my room, curious and concerned. It took me a few minutes to open it.

You spoke to Mike on the phone about me... I felt very emotional about it at first, thinking it might have been misguided. But then I realized you did it out of concern for me after receiving my last letter. The truth is, I'm very grateful to you. The letter taught me a lot. For example, that Mike won the bid to build a large bridge over the Connecticut River. I was so glad to hear it. I know how hard he worked on that bid. Another engineering company that oversaw the project had to quit mid-way under court order due to severe engineering flaws found in the structure. Many companies competed, and Mike won.

This is nothing new. It's happened many times before.

What is new is Mike opening up to you. It's very unusual for him to open up like that to someone, especially you... On the one hand, he said it was good for him to have something to occupy his time and "run away to," but with the same breath he admitted he was so worried about so many things—thoughts about the two of us and Blair, fear of the missiles that might be launched at Israel—that he couldn't really focus on the project. He also said he was sending other engineers from his office and only showing up on the site itself occasionally, when there are problems to solve. That frightens me, Davidi. It's very unlike Mike. His people must be working at an insane pace day and night and need the presence of their "captain."

I hate to think of the children feeling neglected. Especially Roy, who's in the very emotional, rebellious phase of adolescence. I left, and their father is having trouble coping.

Mike also said that our love can't make up for everything, and that now that the truth and the lies have been revealed, Blair left, and I ran away (is that really what he called it? "Running away?"), he feels abandoned. When you asked what he meant to do about me, he said he didn't know yet.

I'm not surprised, just so sad. What did I expect? What is he supposed to do that he hasn't done yet? And why should he realize I'm here to fix things, in order to try and truly return?

As far as he's concerned, I kept a secret and "ran away" once I was found out.

Mike, my poor love.

Thank you for being honest with me, Davidi, for not taking pity on me and revealing to me the content of your conversation with Mike word for word. That only encourages me to hurry up and complete my mission here as soon as possible. I must finish writing my story or else nothing can work.

Just a little bit longer. I'm taking a big breath for one last push.

Yours,
Loving, Helena

60

One mid-January afternoon, Ruth surprised me by placing a small, wrapped package in my hand. I moved my eyes from her to the package, and she said, "Open it, Helena. Naomi and I bought it together. Naomi picked it out."

I quickly removed the wrapping paper. Inside, carefully folded, was shiny red velvet cloth soft to the touch. I looked at her, surprised. "It's so pretty," I whispered. "It's for me? What for?"

"Well," she said, "the high school costume contest is in exactly two months. I spent two hours at the fabric shop with Naomi yesterday. She was a little restless. She checked every piece of fabric at the shop, even asked the salesclerk to spread out some of them, so that she could get a better look and feel the texture. You should have seen how serious and professional she was."

She told me how my mother suddenly discovered a bolt of red cloth on one of the top shelves, how the salesclerk called her husband, who climbed up on a ladder and pulled it down, and how my mother's eyes lit up at the sight of the cloth spread out in front of her while her fingers ran softly over the velvet.

Two days earlier, I had told Mother about the costume contest that was to take place in mid-March. "I'd like to make the costume myself," I told her, "a pretty, dignified costume." When I could tell I had her attention, I continued to express my wishes to her. "I really want to win first place." For some reason, I added that Jonathan was one of the judges, and that this was not necessarily a good thing for me. When she asked why not, I blushed and said nothing, and she seemed to swallow her tongue. I came closer and took her arm. I ran my finger over the thin veins protruding from her pale skin, and told her that, only if she could, I would love for her to help me with the sewing, but only if she wanted to and it wasn't too much trouble… My mother's eyes lit up. She placed a trembling hand on my arm and ran the other one through my hair. Then she seemed to think up a rhyme, and said, "A pretty costume, with a skirt that twirls, for my little girl."

My body shook.

And then, two days later, the fabric.

Ruth and I went one floor down to my mother's and my apartment, the fabric clutched under my arm. When Naomi opened the door, there were tears in my eyes. Mother was beaming.

"Helena!" she cried, reaching for the fabric, touching it again. "I have a wonderful idea for your costume! Can you guess what it is?"

I shook my head no, surprised. How would I know? At that moment, Hilde's voice came from inside the apartment, greeting me. Judging by the heavy smell in the room and the sight of the empty cup and the overflowing ashtray, I knew she and Mother had been having coffee and smoking cigarettes before we came in.

Back then, I still hated the smell of ashes and smoke.

My mother announced that we would use this fabric to make a bodice for a gypsy costume.

"A gypsy?" I marveled. "Me? With my dirty blond hair and fair skin?" I burst out laughing, sweeping Ruth and Hilde after me. Only Mother remained serious.

"Yes, a gypsy…" her voice trembled. We fell silent at once.

Hilde lit another cigarette and broke the silence with her loud voice. "So, Naomi, how are you planning on designing this costume?"

My mother stared at the piece of velvet in her hand and said she would sew a bodice with small hooks and black laces in front and make a dress from bits of colorful fabric and ribbons. She disappeared for a moment to the bathroom balcony and returned with a large paper bag full of fabric.

Hilde asked about a costume for Esther. Ruth shook her head and said Esther was not interested and that she had already volunteered to document the event. "She's happier that way," she said, "behind the camera."

I was buzzing with excitement, my eyes moving gratefully from Mother, to Ruth, to Hilde, then pausing on the red velvet. I reached out to feel its sensuous softness.

The next day, as we walked home from school together, I told Nurit about what The One had said to me, and about the gypsy costume my mother had dreamed up, and about how we were going to make it together, something we had never done before.

Nurit was happy for me. When I offered to have my mother make a costume for her too, she politely declined. We did not have to worry about her, she said. She had a tiger costume that Johnny's wife found in an old clothing trunk. Then my wise friend added that she would have said no anyway. "Because it's important that this experience be only yours and your mother's. Just the two of you."

I was sixteen years old. Hormones raged in every bit of my body. Boys from school wooed me, leaving notes in my pencil box, and one even left a letter in an unstamped envelope in our mailbox.

Flattered by the attention, I began to put more thought into my outfits, taking care of my hair and my nails. I also shortened my skirts a bit, hemming them just below the knee. I liked talking to boys in the sports fields, especially when I could sense Jonathan's gaze from afar. I gave those boys my best smiles, which were actually directed at him. When one evening a boy rode over on his bike to pick me up for a concert at Beit Ha'am, I let him wait downstairs for fifteen minutes. I wasn't too excited about inviting him inside to meet my mother anyway and was hoping that Jonathan would pass by and see a handsome boy waiting for me outside.

I was upset by Jonathan's frown as he noticed that I had left one additional button in my blouse undone and that I was wearing red lipstick. Then I did not yet know whether to read this as an expression of desire or disgust, and all this time, I was gnawed by the fear that he preferred tom-boys, athletic and short-haired, like Esther.

Sometimes I walked down Allenby and Dizengoff, between clothing stores such as *Ivanir, Ilka, Bat Adam*, and *Seventeen*, the new store for young women. I would look longingly at the skirts and dresses, most of them beyond my means, worn by faceless mannequins. I would pass by the hair salons that had begun to pop up in our petit bourgeois city, and peak in at the ladies getting their hair washed and afterward sitting beneath enormous dryer hoods, where their hair rose like a babka with delicate airiness.

These hair salons were typical female territory at the time, serving both as a hairdresser's and a place to exchange gossip in the tradition of the five o'clock tea I remembered from London, except without the cake.

Ruth and Naomi used to frequent one of the hair salons on Allenby Street every other Thursday. After Ruth had her hair washed and dried in one of those enormous dryer hats, she always stuck to a style coiffed carefully with rollers and spray—her hair flowing down to her shoulders in sculpted waves that resembled round cornices. Naomi chose the demure and noble 'banana' hairdo, her hair rolled and pinned to her head with the help of many bobby pins.

Girls' haircuts came into existence somewhere outside the hair salon. Nurit usually wore her curly, rebellious hair tied with a ribbon "to remove some of its formidable volume." Esther's hair was always cut short, against fashion and norm. And I often wore my long honey-toned hair with natural blond highlights in a high ponytail, or sometimes in two braids, and even more rarely, down over my shoulders.

But I never knew which of these styles, if any, was Jonathan's favorite.

61

In the meantime, I continued to go to Sheleg HaLebanon, hoping that the stranger would show up again. I began bringing my textbooks, as well as my notebook of impressions, hoping I'd get inspired like all those writers, poets, and playwrights in that Cameri actress's stories.

Occasionally, a famous person walked in. The voices in the café were lowered for a moment, and a mixture of quiet and awe hovered over the tables. Assuming the person was some important artist, I tried to commit every feature of his face to memory, so that I could later recognize his picture in a magazine gossip column.

One afternoon, when the café was almost empty, just as I had finished my Bible homework and cracked open my math notebook, he walked in.

By himself.

My heart began to pound. I forced myself to look away, recalling Nurit's warning not to stare at him, not to look strange.

In honor of this special occasion, I ordered another cup of tea and a slice of plum cake, so that I could pick at it and prolong my stay without arousing any suspicion.

"I hope no one joins him at his table," I wished silently. "I hope he stays by himself."

The man chose a corner table, removed his jacket, and dropped it on one of the chairs. I noticed he'd grown a small beard in the weeks that had gone by since I had first seen him. Then he walked over to the waitress behind the counter, ordered a cup of coffee and a piece of cheesecake, and immediately returned to his table, as he pulled a black leather-bound notepad and a small, sharpened pencil from his shirt pocket. I followed his expressions and the motion of his writing hand, and instinctively began wracking my brain to find the animal that would best describe him, so that I could share my thoughts with Nurit later.

His nose was aquiline; his face, pockmarked, his brows bushy, and his hair dark and full. A thick plume of hair peeked out of his shirt, whose top buttons were undone. When the waitress emerged from behind the counter with his coffee and cake and placed them in front of him, he mumbled a thank you but didn't look up at her. The girl muttered something back and made herself scarce. "He is anything but sensitive," I wrote down in my notebook. Having no idea if and when I would see him again, I debated whether to approach him, all the while tossing about all the animals of the field and the forest through my mind without finding a single match. When he suddenly stood up, my breath caught in my throat. I was afraid he would leave, and I would lose him again. But I quickly calmed down when I realized that he only retired momentarily to the place where, as Ruth would say demurely, "even the king walks by himself."

He lingered in the men's room for a while, and I quickly cleared my mind, stood up, ordered another cup of tea and another plum cake, and moved to a table closer to his, along with my books and notebooks, while I ignored the waitress's glares. When he returned, zipping his pants as he walked, he shot me a cold, gray look. In response, I lowered my eyes to my cake, scraped my fork against the plate, and fidgeted uncomfortably. His eyes, I sensed, were on me. He must have been wondering why I switched places, choosing to sit so close to him in a nearly empty café.

Only after he sat back down, his chair scraping against the floor tiles, did I dare look up at his steely eyes, which were now shamelessly scanning my face and body. Suddenly, I felt as if an eagle with an impressive wingspan was gliding over me, and I wondered why I was always attracted to predators and birds of prey.

The man did not take his eyes off me. His fingers reached into his jacket pocket and pulled out a cigar.

"I hope you don't mind cigar smoke," he said in smoky Hebrew, and I lied when I shook my head. He lopped the tip of it, warmed its dome over a match until it was fully lit, and then put the cigar between his lips. I followed his every move and the sound he made as he sucked on the cigar. We said nothing for several minutes. He looked at me, amused. He must not have had anything more interesting to do at the time than stare at a young woman sitting across from him, bare high school notebooks in front of her, a black pencil clamped between her fingers. Luckily, a dash of Nurit's gumption must have infected me, because I stared right back at him, my look shameless and direct.

When his cigar was halfway gone, he offered a coarse hand—I never could figure out how a writer's hands had grown as rough as a laborer's—and introduced himself.

When he said his name—Wilhelm (Will) Adler—I shivered.

"Adler", I knew, was German for "eagle." Had I not just deemed him, in my fantasy world, a bird of prey? Later, as I rummaged through zoology books at the public library, I would learn that the eagle is a large, formidable member of the falcon species, its wings long and its flight speedy, its beak sharp, strong, and bent at its end, and its eyebrows shading its eyes, affording it an aggressive appearance.

I stared silently at the man's aquiline nose and his gray steel eyes.

"Helena," I said, clearing my throat. "Helena Steiner." Mother had taught me that one should always offer their full name when making an introduction.

His amused look was gone; his steel pupils widened.

"Are you from Germany?" he asked, and it seemed that his eyes lit up with interest.

"No, Austria," I said. I apologized, explaining that I rarely spoke German, although I could understand it, and felt much more confident in English, having lived in London after the war. I recalled the conversation this man before me had a few weeks earlier in fluent English with that elegant short-haired woman, and thought it might be easier for him, despite his foreign accent, to chat with me in English.

Will liked the British English that "rolled down my tongue." He thought it was "ten times prettier" than his American one, which he claimed to have used more than any other language for the past quarter-century.

He had a special talent for languages—newspapers he read in English but nonfiction, fiction, and poetry mostly in his mother tongue, German. For Hebrew, he had a special affinity that was an enigma to me: his ability to read, speak, and understand a language he had never formally studied, was wondrous. In time, he would teach me how to play with its words and command its semantic fields better than anyone else, and gift me with the ability to fill the empty spaces between lines with hinted meaning.

But despite his love of Hebrew, he never agreed to use it as his primary speaking language.

"The throat, the roof of the mouth, the tongue, the teeth, and the lips are our instrument of expression," he once told me. "The parts of the body in which the sounds we make are cut." In his case, he complained, English was infected with a German accent and German was dipped in English, but when he spoke Hebrew both accents mixed together, which was why he avoided speaking it in public. "But in your case, Helena, all five instruments of expression work together in unison, and each language remains perfectly pure."

Since the day we met, in early 1957, Will cherished my ability to separate English and Hebrew and use both as mother tongues, devoid of any foreign accent.

We spoke to each other in English from the day we met.

62

When Will and I met, he was twice my age.

He was born in Berlin in 1925, the son of a Jewish screenwriter named Ernst Adler and a converted theatre actress who died during childbirth. In the 1930s, after Jews were forbidden from working in the German film industry, his father was one of hundreds of actors, directors, producers, writers, cinematographers, and composers who migrated from Germany to Los Angeles. A handful of them would become influential in the American film industry, in a wide range of genres, gifting the world with such classics as *Fury, Sunset Boulevard,* and *The Killers,* and transforming the role of the musical score forever.

Years later, people would say that the Third Reich's greatest loss was Hollywood's greatest gain.

But most of the immigrant artists who arrived in the city full of hopes and dreams, and among them Ernst Adler, failed where only few succeeded.

Ernst's career as a screenwriter began to blossom in the 1920s, when German film gave birth to expressionist cinema, delivering such masterpieces as *The Cabinet of Dr. Caligari* and *Metropolis.* The dark genre perfectly matched the gloomy, melancholic soul of Will's talented, pessimistic father. Most of his screenplays received a warm welcome in the flourishing industry, and even after the genre died down, a single year after Will was born and his mother died, Ernst continued to create dark stories that reflected his mood.

Only two months after the Nazis rose to power, he packed up a few of his belongings, books, and works, took his eight-year-old boy, and left Germany for America, the land of endless possibilities, only to discover that luck wasn't waiting for him there. His difficulties in adjusting to the new lifestyle and English language held him back. While other directors of his generation, such as Fritz Lang, succeeded in introducing to American cinema expressionist horror films and crime melodramas featuring borderline lunatic criminal characters and sets with distorted perspectives, the studios turned down every one of Will's German scripts without a second glance. Hurt and frustrated, his young son like a lodestone on his shoulders. Ernst sought alternative sources of income.

Will could not tell whether his father went through more jobs or more women. One day he was a tour guide to the homes of Beverly Hills' rich and famous; the other, he was a stagehand. One day he was a taxi driver, a used book salesman the next.

He had trouble understanding what drew in the many women who visited their indigent apartment in a shabby building in West L.A. There were white women who had come from Central and Eastern Europe, Hispanic and Asian immigrants, and local African-Americans, whom his father found especially mysterious and thrilling. Will liked to listen behind his father's locked bedroom door, trying to guess the women's origin and profession by their diction and the way they rolled the English language in their mouths. He especially enjoyed the moments when, in the heat of lovemaking, they let out cries in their mother tongues, in one moment of abandon giving away the secret he was looking for. He would later claim that he had acquired his love of languages during those evenings he spent eavesdropping on the nuances of accent and lingo heard between rustling sheets.

Will's stories reminded me of my own early childhood, the sounds

Mother made in her bed whenever the peasant farmer came to visit and the sounds emanating from behind closed doors in Madame Butterfly's brothel. I thought about us—two children of different generations, growing far away from each other, listening in on the odd sounds of the adult world, using their sparse resources to try and interpret it.

Will said his father had taught him the love of reading and writing during the little time they spent together. They both had memberships to the public library and read a lot. Once, the library announced a special clearance sale, hundreds of books offered for close to nothing. Ernst emptied the small savings jar that he kept in the pantry along with jars of pickles and cans of beans and walked hand-in-hand with his son over to the library. When Will asked anxiously how they would be able to afford food the following day, the father waved the question away. His eyes were illuminated by an inner light as, darting his gaze over the words, he flipped through the books. Eventually he stuffed the two tattered suitcases he had brought from Germany with books of all kinds, which he later stacked beside his bed and Will's. The next day, Will's stomach was empty, but the rush he felt at the sight of the books dulled his hunger, if only for a short while.

One evening, Ernst asked his son to take a seat beside him in bed.

"Do you know who Aristotle was, Wilhelm?"

"No," said Will.

Ernst shook his head with disappointment. "How about Descartes?"

Will shrugged.

Ernst threw his arms up in the air. "And Einstein? You must have heard of him!"

Will bit his lips.

In the next few minutes, he learned that the first, a philosopher from the fourth century B.C., was a student of Plato. The second was a seventeenth century philosopher, a pioneer of the modern era. The last was a famous Jewish physicist of the twentieth century.

Will made a quick calculation, figuring that about twenty centuries separated Aristotle from Descartes, and another three-hundred year separated Descartes from Einstein, and wondered what connection his father had made between the three.

The answer became clear during a brief, poignant lecture, only a few minutes long. Aristotle had taught his father the importance of wonder, Descartes had introduced him to the significance of consciousness, and from Einstein he had borrowed the glory of imagination. The latter was the part Will remembered best of all because when his father spoke of Einstein, he embraced Will heartily and his body trembled with excitement.

"Einstein said that imagination is more important than knowledge," his father explained, raising his arms up in the air and spreading them like a fan. "For knowledge is limited, whereas imagination embraces the entire world."

And thus, sitting in their tiny, spare, book-filled apartment, his father offered his worldview in a nutshell: wonder, consciousness, imagination. "These three elements," he said, "are the foundation of humankind's superiority and creative capability, a proof that feeding your mind is more important than nourishing your body."

When Ernst finished talking, he wiped his nose on his shirtsleeve and his gaze grew gloomy once more. And that was the exact moment when Will's hunger became intolerable.

Hunger followed him around for most of his childhood. When he was fourteen years old he found work as an assistant in a small shoemaking workshop and as an errand boy. At age fifteen he went to work with his old man, who was scraping by as a used books salesman in West Hollywood. At nights, he went out to search for his father in the neighborhood bars, where he usually found him, drunk, and then led him faltering back home, his arm around his waist. At age sixteen he dropped out of school and divided his time between the bookstore and caring for his dad, who had contracted a lung disease. At eighteen, he buried his father and remained alone in the world.

But he only told me all this a long time later.

On the day we met, at Sheleg HaLebanon, Will told me almost nothing about himself. He mostly asked about me, his steel eyes magnetizing my gaze.

I told him I had celebrated my sixteenth birthday in January, that I was going to dress up as a gypsy for Purim, and the costume was made especially for me by my mother.

That kind of thing.

I also told him I dreamed of becoming a writer, and that I had already written a few essays, as well as the opening lines for several stories and poems.

My heart pounded, and my cheeks flushed the whole time, and Will never took his eyes off me.

And then he smiled, and there was something so soothing and warm about his smile, softening the steel of his gaze, the threat of his bushy eyebrows.

I recalled Naomi's description of Mordecai's smile, and searched his face for the curve of the lip, the narrowing of the right eye, the laugh wrinkles.

But they were not there in the face of this man sitting across from me, who looked older than thirty-two.

63

In 1956, Purim was celebrated in late February. By age sixteen, I was reading the newspapers regularly, learning all about the assassination of Rudolf Israel Kastner, a member of the Budapest Aid and Rescue Committee during World War II, and about the Israeli retreat from the Sinai Peninsula following the Suez Crisis.

I thought about the traditional Tel Aviv Purim Parade and wondered what special performances would be featured this year. The previous year had included a giant doll float, a marching band, and hundreds of costumed children. I recalled a cardboard car in the parade with two round windows in front, rising over a wide, toothy smile. Two mannequins made of clay, Papier-mâché, wire, and fiber were placed atop the car: one of the Israeli Prime Minister, David Ben-Gurion and the other of the Egyptian president, Gamal Abdel Nasser. Both leaders held hands. At the bottom of the car was a large sign, reading: "Vision of the End-of-Days."

On Purim eve, the seniors threw their costume party in the gymnasium, with the help of teachers, class coordinators, and all the upperclassmen.

Turning the process into an over-extended ceremony, my mother helped me into my costume. I did my best to remain patient after she had worked so hard for me. First, she pulled the skirt made of dozens of colorful scraps of fabric up my legs and fastening a wide, black belt around my hips. Then she helped me into the red velvet bodice and took her time hooking twenty hooks into small loops across my chest and tying black laces over them, the ends dangling over my abdomen. Once she had finished carefully putting the costume together, she painted my nails red, applied blue powder to my eyes, brushed my hair, tied a thick headband around it, and slipped heavy hoop earrings into my ears. Her effort was apparent in the small wrinkles around her eyes and the beads of sweat on her forehead.

When she was finished, she stepped back and looked me over. Her lips bent into a smile.

I stared at her smile, surprised, not by its crookedness, but by its mere presence. I tried to recall the last time I had seen her smiling.

Then she came closer and ran her hands down my stomach, my waist, and my hips, smoothing the clothes over my body with an expression of great concentration, ironing out wrinkles only she could see.

I looked at her hands. Her nails were trimmed, her hands rough, hardworking, reminiscent of Hilde's. I wondered how they had gotten so rough. I asked her, surprised and embarrassed, "Mommy, what are you doing?"

For a moment, she gaped at me and then pressed her fingers down on my shoulders. "Today you are Esmeralda!" she answered and asked me to keep my back straight and hold my head up high. "Point your nose up," she ordered me.

I took a deep breath and closed my eyes. The image of Esmeralda, Victor Hugo's gorgeous gypsy, rose in my mind.

Mother continued to smooth the bodice and skirt against my body.

My eyes stayed closed.

A pleasant warmth spread through me. I liked her touch; the monotonous ironing motions imbued me with calm and confidence. It was as if she was applying the gypsy costume into my skin, making it a part of me.

I embraced Mother's thin frame and kissed her lips, which spread into another smile.

When I said, "Good-bye," and walked downstairs to meet Nurit to go with her to the Purim celebration, I straightened my back and held my head up.

For one day, I was Esmeralda. I didn't even feel the chilly air outside.

All I could feel were Mother's smoothing-caressing hands on my body.

And I felt cozy and warm.

***

The night of the party, Israeli songs were played on a record player that one of the boys had brought from home, and the girls started a big hora circle. Light refreshments were served alongside carbonated water mixed with apricot and apple-flavored syrups.

I danced with my friends all night. I spun around in circles, letting my skirt made of tens of colorful pieces of cloth wrap around my body and the tiny bells Mother had sewed to its fringe tinkle delicately.

The height of the evening was the costume contest. When I was called to walk across the stage before the judges, I stood up straight so that my breasts were thrust forward, blatantly swayed my hips, and placed my hands on my waist. I felt as if Mother's warm hand was against my back, helping me stand straight. I saw Esmeralda before me. I stretched my fingers to emphasize my red nail polish. Esther's camera flashed. Later, she and Nurit told me that all the boys held their breath when I walked past them, unable to take their eyes off my breasts and buttocks.

At the end of the night I won first place in a 4:1 vote. The one opposing vote was Jonathan's. When he volunteered to affix the winner's pin to my bodice, he shocked me by whispering in my ear that he would have preferred it if I had preserved my explosive sexuality for his eyes only, in private. As he said this, he fixed his gaze on mine and his fingers pressed lightly against my breast, shooting crimson arrows into my cheeks.

Then Miss Carmela approached me, festive and formal, and handed me a package wrapped in paper. Later that night, having found her waiting up for me by the window, I placed the package in my tearful mother's hands.

"We won first place, Mother," I said, and she peeled off the paper with a trembling hand and carefully pulled out a flat wooden box with a glass top. Inside, on a scroll, were the *Book of Esther* and the *Book of Ruth*, which could be scrolled up and down with two elaborate wooden knobs.

64

"His name is Wilhelm Adler," I told her on the bench under the old oak tree.

"Whose name?" Nurit wondered.

"The strange man from Sheleg HaLebanon," I explained, unfolding our no less strange meeting to her in detail.

"Oh," she said, smiling and nodding. "You naughty girl. You kept going there without me?"

I smiled. The recent weeks had been the most exciting in my life. My romantic soul hovered between Jonathan Jonas and Wilhelm Adler, and an odd anticipation coursed through my entire body.

"Is he at least a poet, a film director, or some important journalist?" Nurit asked.

I laughed and offered everything I knew about him at that point. "He's a Jewish-American writer and journalist," I said, "thirty-two years old. He visits Israel a lot, mostly Tel Aviv and Jerusalem. He writes a column about Israel for some Jewish-American paper in L.A."

"So, he isn't one of our local artists!" Nurit was disappointed.

"No, he isn't," I said, a little upset. "So, what? You have no idea what an interesting man he is! I've never met anyone as fascinating as him."

Nurit stared at me silently.

"Why are you looking at me like that?"

"That spark in your eyes when you talk about him… it's strange!"

"No, Nurit, it isn't. Try to understand, his world view is so unique… He's unlike anybody else I know! Smart and experienced."

"Well, all right, Helena, that's too much for a girl like me." Nurit's brow furrowed. "But I hope there hasn't been any physical contact between you two. Don't forget, he's sixteen years older than you!"

I recalled one of Nurit's zoo stories, about intercourse between a male and female baboon, and blushed deeply, not because of the mere idea of intercourse, but because of its absence. I had met Will several times already, and he had never laid a hand or even a finger on me. He seemed to take greater interest in my mind and soul than in my face and body. I said nothing.

"What did you say his name was?" Nurit suddenly asked.

"Will. Wilhelm Adler." I stood up. "But Nurit, we must find him an appropriate nickname."

"All right," she said. "Any suggestions?"

My heart began to pound. "We'll call him… We'll call him…"

Nurit's face was a question mark.

"Simple, Nurit," I said. "We'll call him 'the other.'"

**

Two days later I met "the other" at our regular table at Sheleg HaLebanon and handed him two first chapters from a story I was working on. He read the first page and set it aside.

"Helena," he said, "I'm going back to California tomorrow."

My heart was racing, but I said nothing.

He placed a small package in front of me.

I looked at him imploringly. "What's this?" I whispered. "A good-bye gift? We barely know each other…"

But "the other" just smiled and promised he would be back. A sense of relief spread through me. He said a sixteenth birthday was a big deal in America, a day one does not forget, and since he had missed my big day by only a couple of months, he wanted to give me a meaningful gift.

A gentle shake revealed the contents of the wrapped gift.

"A book?" I asked, smiling shyly.

He gave me a warm smile. The look in his gray eyes sent an uncontrollable tremor through my back. "You're a very special girl, Helena," he said. "You're pretty, emotional, passionate, and creative. There's fire in your bones, but your view of the world is still virginal…not yet sharpened."

No one had ever said anything like that to me before. My heart beat loudly and I felt a bizarre weakness in all my limbs.

"You're right, it's a book," he continued. "Because you, just like me, love books. But this book is especially for you. It was originally written in Italian and has only recently been published in a Hebrew translation."

He asked me to take a look. Excited, I peeled off the wrapping paper and pulled out a book by Laura Orvieto, *Storie Della Storia Del Mondo*, in a worn-out brown cover.

My eyes lit up.

Will enthusiastically told me in brief what I would read later that night: in the book Orvieto unfolded stories from Greek mythology in dialogue form between an Italian mother and her two curious children, Leo and Lia. "The mother tells her children about the building of the walls of Troy with the aid of Apollo and Poseidon, the abduction of Helen, the wife of Menelaus, king of Sparta, by Prince Paris, son of the king of Troy, and the great war that followed."

I listened intently.

On the inside cover, he had written a dedication: "To beautiful Helena, with friendship and admiration, Will."

We parted with a handshake. My palm was damp with excitement. Then he reached over and ran the tip of his finger over my lips with a laugh.

The entire time a lit cigar was perched in the corner of his mouth.

I was only sixteen years old. Emotional, romantic, rebellious. The stories of Greek mythology touched my heart in thousands of ways, and the book received a place of honor in the green bookcase beside my bed. On one page, the mother tells her son, Leo, that a woman who feels unloved can never be happy. In those days I felt courted and loved, enveloped in an aura of light.

From that day on, "the other" always called me "beautiful Helena" at every meeting and in every letter. Whenever he said this, my mind was flooded by the tale of that ingenious warring trick, centered around a wooden horse containing warriors in its belly, and the story of the princess considered the most beautiful woman in the world, whose face launched a thousand ships and led to a terrible bloodbath.

65

The spring of 1957 was especially rainy. The rain, accompanied by thunderstorms, was heavier than average all through April, May, and June.

The weekend the rain relented, Ruth, Jonah, and Naomi went to a sanatorium in Safed, and Esther joined a photographer friend on a trip to Ein Gedi and the Dead Sea.

I had different plans altogether.

Jonathan was about to enlist that summer to a pilot training course, and at school, the seniors were already rehearsing for graduation. In a short while, he would leave our home, and nothing yet had happened between us. Now I waited patiently for everybody to leave the apartment and, afterward, baked him his favorite cheesecake. I knew that on Thursday afternoon he played soccer on the beach with his friends and returned home at sunset.

And in spring, I knew, the sun sets late.

Around six o'clock I went up to Jonah and Ruth's apartment and let myself in. I placed the cake on the kitchen counter and ran my fingers down my blue floral dress. The pattern accentuated my narrow waist, and the straps, tied with a loop in back, revealed my tan shoulders. I paced the apartment, and when I heard footsteps approaching from the stairwell, I rushed to Jonathan's bedroom and stood, quivering, behind his bed.

Jonathan walked in like a cheetah, and, before noticing me,

removed his sweaty shirt, balled it, and dropped it on a stool. The sight of his naked chest and the ripe smell of his sweat flooded my senses. The muscles of his arms and chest stood out beneath his taut skin, which sparkled with sweat. His calves were big when compared to his skinny legs, which were more muscular than I had remembered, and covered with light fuzz.

I stood still in the corner, my breath held and my back against the wall. I prayed that he could not hear the beating of my heart, which sounded like a drum to me, and bit my lip until I felt the flavor of a drop of blood trickling from it.

Suddenly, my senses grew fuzzy. If I could only blend into the wall, settle into a landscape hanging on a nail, or evaporate, disappear, become invisible, being, not being… I had little time to think. I felt the half-moons fixing on my eyes. I heard the cheetah footsteps approaching. His grip on my arms steadied me. His expression was grave, and when he spoke, his breath stung my face.

I remember he asked what I was doing there, in his bedroom, and that I was unable to answer. I remember a flash of pain in his eyes. Then he asked if everyone was gone, and when I nodded, he pushed me against the wall, his lips parted mine with force, and his tongue made its way between my teeth, found mine, dancing with it in a convoluted dance. Then he removed my dress and examined my body. His fingers sculpted my white skin, cradled my breasts, and gently tugged on my nipples. His other hand slipped between my thighs and began to massage my crotch with surprising tenderness. Next, I felt him penetrating me, his warm skin against mine. My clouded senses dulled all pain, and when his gorgeous body began to move in complete harmony with mine, my excitement reached its apex. I don't know how I knew what to do. Maybe memories of my early childhood in the brothel had been preserved in a blue, inner capsule, which had suddenly broken open, letting its contents trickle out and move my entire body. Suddenly, the beautiful, colorful butterflies from Mother's stories fluttered through my abdomen, flooding me in the wonderful flapping of their wings. When my body began to shake uncontrollably and my throat produced strange, unfamiliar sounds, I realized I had reached heights I had never experienced before. Tears of happiness filled my eyes, dampened my flushed cheeks, and slid below, mixing with the sweat that covered my skin.

Jonathan and I spent the next hour on his bed and on the cool floor of his room, lost in a passionate frenzy.

I stunned Jonathan. I stunned myself, too.

That day, I was physically closer to my childhood love than any day that came before.

That day, I lost my virginity.

***

The next morning, Jonathan waited for me by the school gate and asked me to meet him that afternoon at Independence Park, at the top of the ridge overlooking the sea. He explained exactly next to which tree and by which bench. When school was out, I evaded Esther and Nurit's imploring eyes and hurried outside.

I remember the sea was silent and blue, the air perfectly still. I remember Jonathan speaking with freezing quiet, apologizing for what happened and what he had done to me. He said he should have stopped it. We should not have done it, should not do it now, and must never do it again. I shook wordlessly. When he finished speaking, I had a lump in my throat and was out of breath.

And the sea was silent and blue, the air perfectly still.

***

Two weeks later, Davidi came for a brief visit from Berlin. Emotional and upset, I asked him to go for a walk, just the two of us, along the

Yarkon River. The wind ruffled the treetops, but there was no rain, and it was not cold. Davidi was twenty-three years old and tall, and I, at sixteen, reached his chest. I had waited so eagerly for him to return so that I might share my fresh turmoil with him, at least the parts I was willing to share, enjoying his unique, non-judgmental attentiveness to all my endeavors. But this time Davidi did not attend to me. As he walked swiftly along the southern bank of the river, each step of his requiring me to take two, he told me for the first time about the day he parted from his parents, and the days that followed. And I understood. Davidi was haunted by his past. I put off my burning issues until a later time and let him graze for a while among the images of his childhood.

In the evening, alone in my room, I sat on my bed, pulled a block of paper from my drawer, and wrote a story. A fictional story about forbidden love. I sent the story to the *Haaretz* literary supplement, and, as if my life was a fairytale, I received an answer within three weeks. My first story was published in one of the May issues. As soon as it was printed, I bought ten copies of the issue. I gave one to Nurit when we met at our regular spot on the bench. I hugged her and thanked her for always believing in me and for encouraging me to plan and be practical. I gave the second copy to Ruth and Jonah, along with a dedication on the front page: "Every deed begins with a vision." I gave the third to my emotional mother with a special inscription, and the fourth to Hilde. I sent two issues by mail: one to Davidi, along with a letter, and one to "the other," with a thank you note and a picture of a flower. I kept the other four issues as a keepsake.

I quickly received an answer from "the other." It was brief and affectionate, promising me that this was "only the beginning." I also got lots of support from friends, teachers, neighbors, and family acquaintances. The high school principal summoned me formally to his office, where he served me a letter of appreciation that moved my mother, Hilde, Ruth, and Jonah to tears. Davidi and Gidi sent hugs from afar, Esther celebrated, and my soul was overjoyed.

But I saw question marks in Jonathan's half-moon eyes.

And they hurt me terribly.

66

January 1991
Yosemite Park, California

My Blair,

I was so happy when Nurit gave me your address in Israel. So excited that I dropped everything and went out to the park. I walked outside all day before finally returning to my room at the lodge to write you. So many thoughts were running through my mind. So many things I wanted to tell you but had no address.

First thing's first: the situation. In two weeks, the ultimatum the UN gave Saddam will expire. If a war breaks in the Persian Gulf, experts estimate that missiles will be launched at Tel Aviv. God knows what made you go to Israel now, of all times, Blair. Of course, my worry level has skyrocketed in the past week, especially after I heard you'd volunteered to participate in orange-picking around Kfar Saba, but I know asking you to leave Israel and come home right now won't work.

Certainly not now.

I was very touched to hear you were staying at our family's apartment on Ben-Yehuda Street. Nurit wrote to me that the previous tenants had broken their lease and left Tel Aviv earlier than expected due to the chance of war. I understand them. They're Dutch. What do they have to do with any of this mess? At any rate, with them gone, the apartment was free for you. Nurit told me that Gidi and Irit arranged for a second-hand fridge, and that the rest of the place was already furnished.

That apartment means a lot to me. So many memories of my childhood and youth are stored in it, in every corner of it. In the beginning, we got it for key money, an outdated method that I hope (but am not sure) has since disappeared. Only years later were Ruth and Jonah able to purchase it privately. In the floor below are two apartments. The one on the right is the apartment my mother and I lived in for several years, and the one on the left belonged to our dear neighbor, Hilde.

My mother, your grandmother, Jonah, Ruth, and Hilde are long gone, but the memories remain. So many that you could fill whole sacks with them. I haven't been to the apartment since Ruth passed away. I avoided going there on my visits to Israel, although it remained in the family and belonged to all of us. I couldn't bear to touch the memories, and it was rented out most of the time, anyway. However, I did walk by a few times and looked at the building from the outside. Ben-Yehuda Street hasn't changed much in the past thirty years. On the one hand, that's delightful, but, on the other, painful because this keeps the memory alive and throbbing.

Take a look at the old oak tree between our building and the adjacent one. It looks as if it's two-hundred years old. There's a bench under it. Ask Nurit about it. We spent half of our teen years in its shade. You have no idea how badly I want to sit there with you now on the bench beneath the old oak tree of my childhood. Perhaps that's where I would be able to begin to explain things. It would certainly be quicker than writing a book. But I've never known the quick, straight paths. Only the long, twisting ones.

You must remember the poem *The Road Not Taken* by Robert Frost. You studied it at school. Of two roads diverging in the woods, a traveler must choose one. He chooses the one that looked prettier, less trodden and trampled on. At first, he is quite pleased with his choice, but with time he is plagued by an inevitable sense of loss—the road not taken, whose nature he would never know.

Frost wasn't necessarily right. The sense of a missed opportunity is not inevitable. It can be prevented. I'm making this long way back into the past, to that fateful point of divergence. This time, I hope, I'll be able to take the quick, straight path: no lies and no omissions.

I hope this will be my way to Roy and Abby's hearts but mostly to yours and your father's...

Will you want to walk down this new path with me, my child, when I get there?

You and I have so much catching up to do. Of course, we can't do it all in a letter. I hope to finish writing this book by the end of February. I promised Abby I'd be home in time for her ninth birthday.

Please, dear, take care of yourself over there. These are mad times. Listen to the orders of the Home Front Command. Prepare a sealed room in the apartment. I think the best room for the job is the one that used to belong to my cousin, Jonathan. It's an interior room with only one window. Irit once told me that the furniture in that room has remained untouched—the desk, the chair, the closet, the bed...

Please prepare some water bottles and snacks in the room, just in case. And get a television in there, so that you can watch the news, or, at the very least, a radio, and a phone too, if you can. In light of everything that's going on there, you don't have the privilege of shutting off the world like I do here at the park. And please, Blair, promise me if things get really bad, you'll consider going back to Atlanta. You don't have to be a hero.

With love and much worry,
Mom

67

Hard days followed. In early summer my mother sank into a deep depression, her mind mixing people from her past and present. She refused to eat, fell silent and sporadically shook herself awake and burst into tears. Once again, she was admitted into a mental hospital until further notice. During that time, Jonah had his first heart attack. Since he had had trouble finding work, he had burdened himself with concerns about his family's livelihood. Even when he slept at night, his heart had stayed awake. One morning, he had collapsed on the sidewalk on Ben-Yehuda Street, nauseous, out of breath, and covered in cold sweat. He was admitted to the hospital for a week, and upon his release was ordered to stay home and rest. Ruth scrambled between school, her husband, and her sister, never knowing any peace. And if all this was not enough, to my deep regret, Jonathan began seeing Alona, a junior at Ironi Daled High School and a leader in a youth movement, *HaNoar HaOved*. She was skinny and tall, her hair in a long braid, her smile wide, and her laughter loud. Alona was accepted with unbearable lightness into the Jonas household, captivating Ruth and Jonah's hearts while mine broke. I burned with anger, insult, and jealousy. More than once I was struck by the sensation that I was being punished by God, and my reckless, irresponsible behavior had caused this to happen.

But the more I cried into my pillow at night, the more I was fired up with emotion, the better my writing became. My early stories were all published in the *Haaretz* literary supplement and enjoyed the critics' acclaim. Some even compared me to the young French writer Françoise Sagan, who was only a few years older than I, and whose first novel, *Bonjour Tristesse*, was published when she was only eighteen and was a smash hit.

One morning, Rahamim the mailman delivered a letter from Will. It was a short letter, in which he congratulated me for my publications and praised my writing, but in the same breath warned me that arrogance was the greatest enemy of success. My style, he said, reminded him of another young writer named Adele Wiseman, a Canadian-born Jew who lived in England, and whose debut novel *The Sacrifice* had been critically acclaimed in America. He admitted he had not yet read Sagan's first novel.

The question he asked in the postscript to the letter pained me. "And who, my beautiful Helena, is the young man who was the inspiration for your story? You must be harboring an unresolved, unrequited, painful love, which adds sensitivity and honesty to your writing. Do not fight the pain, Helena. Let it inspire you and improve your work.

Yours forever, Will."

I tore the letter up in anger. Will was so far, seas and continents away. How dare he? Would my emotions always be so plainly apparent to him? And what did he even know about my pain? Did he know I was willing to forego all my persistent suitors and toss all my stories into the trash, along with the flattering criticism, for just one more display of love with the one who broke my heart?!

I was a whirlwind of emotions and so self-involved that I had nothing to give anybody else. I saw Ruth tearing up when she returned from a visit to my mother at the hospital, but I did not ask any questions or offer to visit her myself. I saw Esther helping out, caring for her father, cleaning the apartment, preparing food, pulling off Ruth's shoes when she came home tired, and serving her a bowl of soup and some chicken, or a cup of tea and a piece of cake, depending on the time, but I never offered any help. I became rebellious and angry, and rude, too. The black demon was awakened again. Why did I not try to be a little more helpful? Understanding, taking part, being more like Esther—being good…

And then came that terrible night when Ruth and Jonah summoned me for a conversation. Jonah explained in a weary voice that there wasn't any choice, but with the cost-cutting forced upon all of us, they must stop renting the apartment on the second floor, and my mother and I must come back to live in their apartment with them. Ruth added that there was no need for another apartment now anyway with Davidi in Europe, Gidi in the military, and Jonathan about to enlist.

Jonathan… was it possible nobody knew? Did Ruth not sense it? Did Esther not guess?

I was filled with anger at the entire world, which was actually treating me quite well then. Determined, I stood before Jonah and Ruth and announced coldly that I was an adult, who had reached independence, and that I had long ago decided to quit school, move out, and go out into the world, earn my keep, and rent my own apartment. "Just last week," I said, "I answered an ad posted by an international literary printing house urgently seeking experienced Hebrew and English typists, and I was accepted, even though I've never used a typewriter!"

"And another ad," I said, goading them on, "was offering an apartment for rent. A one-bedroom apartment on Zeitlin Street, on the third floor, not too expensive…" I muttered between my teeth that I would be able to pay all of my expenses with the money earned as a typist and from the publication of my stories and summed up my monologue of selfishness with sharp words: "I'm telling you, I don't need anyone in this world!"

When Ruth and Jonah, shocked, tried to protest and persuade me otherwise, I hurt them even more. I yelled, tearful, that I had no parents anyway, was free as a bird, and that by choosing to leave I was honoring my dead father's lively spirit and liberating myself from the burden of my living mother's trapped soul.

This memory is painful even now, so many years later. I remember Ruth's eyes turning red, Jonah's tormented face growing pale, and Esther suddenly emerging from her bedroom, grabbing my hand and pulling me down the stairs. I remember walking together for three whole hours down Ben-Yehuda, Allenby, King George, and Dizengoff Streets, and from there crossing a few side roads to reach Frishman Street, which we traversed all the way to the Herbert Samuel dock by the sea.

68

I have been thinking a lot about Esther today.

Esther never had any children, only photographs. In the past twenty years she has officially been living in London but is always traveling with her camera to all sorts of far-flung, exotic locales, working as a freelancer for prestigious nature journals with her life partner, a talented Dutch nature photographer named Johan. Every winter they go south to Africa, visiting a different desert country, or sometimes to Australia or New Zealand, only returning to London in spring.

"The other" once told me his life was made up of small achievements and large, missed opportunities.

I am not summarizing my life just yet, but I already know that my chilly treatment of my cousin is one of my greatest regrets.

Esther was always by my side and on my side, loving me whole-heartedly, unconditionally, undemandingly. But I closed my world to her and had only opened my heart an inch.

But not that night.

During those hours we spent hitting the pavements of Tel Aviv, I opened up to Esther as I never had before. She walked beside me, listening silently, and I bled it all out, no commas or periods.

I told her. Everything.

I told her, upset, about my love for my mother and the revulsion I felt toward her, about my odd attraction to "the other" and my limitless love for Jonathan, who had deflowered me a month earlier and ended our relationship the very next day. She only nodded, saying nothing, but I could feel her hand squeezing my arm. I do not know what images passed before her eyes, and which she chose to freeze on the thin, flexible celluloid strip of her commemorating and documenting mind. I only know she was angry.

But not at me.

At Jonathan.

***

Twelve years earlier, four young children had made a pact in their home in a tall apartment building in Northwest London. This was after a brief letter, arriving through the British Ministry of Foreign Affairs, signed by a "simple and proud Austrian seamstress," informed Ruth that her young sister had survived the war, and that she had given birth to a little girl in the middle of the chaos.

Jonah and Ruth gathered the four children in the dining room and shared the exciting news. Jonah then told the children he was about to go to western Austria where this woman was living to find out if she was, indeed, their aunt. "And if she is," he said, "I'll be bringing both of them here, Naomi and her young daughter, Helene, who is supposed to be the same age as Esther."

He also explained that this meant things would become a little more difficult financially, that they would have to crowd together, eight of them in the apartment, and that the children ought to be understanding, opening their hearts to their young cousin, who must have been through a lot during the war, and most likely did not have a father.

When he finished, his eyes moistened. "Sometimes in life, dreams come true," he said. "And soon enough we will know if this is the case for us…"

Little Esther fixed a pair of big eyes on her crying mother and wondered if dreams coming true always entailed so many tears.

Shortly thereafter, when Ruth and Jonah hurried out to make arrangements for his trip, the four children convened in their room. Davidi asked everyone to promise that, no matter what, they would accept this new girl, who would soon be entering their lives and sharing their apartment, as one of their own, and that they must help her and keep her safe. Gidi agreed immediately and said that, to leave no room for doubt, they would have to make a true pact.

And so they stood, four children ranging in age from five to twelve, close together, grave and silent, linked hands, and took an oath.

That day, as I walked through the city with Esther, opening my heart to her, I knew nothing of this. Nor did I know that engraved on Esther's memory was a faded image from the day I had arrived at their home—a small child with a tattered dress and a simple doll clutched to her chest, her fair hair in two braids, her pretty face sad, her eyes torn open with wonder. At that moment, she had wanted to hug me and promised she would always love me and be my sister and friend, but, feeling embarrassed, she didn't know how to do so.

And now she was angry.

But not at me, at Jonathan.

For breaking that pact.

***

Esther and I returned home late that evening, hand in hand. We found Ruth in the kitchen, her eyes red, and Jonah looking pale, both distraught with worry. Esther stood beside me as I apologized and admitted in a trembling voice that I was deeply sorry for the things I had said and for causing them so much pain. Through a choked throat, I told them I loved them with all my heart, and that I did not know why they were so good to me while I was being so bad. "As soon as possible," I promised, "I will be packing our things and moving up here." I also told them I missed my mother and was planning on visiting her at the hospital the following day.

That never happened. I did not visit Mother in the seven weeks she was gone. But that evening, my words earned me Ruth and Jonah's hug, which had truly begun years earlier, never slackening. Esther suggested I spend the night in her room and told me she was so proud of me and would always be by my side, no matter what. "And don't worry, Helena," promised the girl who always kept her promises. Then, mixing English with Hebrew, she made an oath, "Now and forever *et hasod shelach ekach amadi el hakever,* I'll take your secret with me to the grave."

69

January 1991
Yosemite Park, California

Dear Davidi,

Good news! I contacted Blair! I was finally able to send her a letter. The mere fact that she gave Nurit her address was a sign she was ready.

Blair is a bright, wonderful girl, but still just a girl. At first, I thought the months she'd spent in Southeast Asia would afford her some peace and common sense, but I'm not so sure anymore. There was definitely little to no common sense in her decision to go to Tel Aviv now. At any rate, she's there, volunteering, keeping busy.

In light of the goings on in the Persian Gulf and of my great concern for Blair, Nurit, Gidi, Irit, and the boys (both in the military) and for the country at large, I broke my iron rule and asked the lodge employees to return the television to my room. I'm very nervous about everything that's going on and want to keep updated. Like many other people, I've been hoping for the triumph of the international pressure on Saddam Hussein to retreat from Kuwait and from his lunatic declarations of war. But in the meantime, not only has he refused to back down, he's also been declaring that the coming war will be "the mother of all wars."

Believe it or not, Blair is staying in our childhood apartment. I was so moved when Nurit told me. I myself have not been there since Ruth died. It contains too many memories, and up to now I haven't been able to. Writing this book is bringing me face to face with all these memories.

I know that if you were here with me, things would be easier.

That's the kind of effect you have on me.

Dealing with memories is so difficult for me that my breathing gets heavy and my throat is suffocating. Then I stop writing, pack a small bag, and run out to the park.

There, along the paths and within the scenery, I relax.

That's the kind of effect this park has on me.

I wonder sometimes, Davidi, if certain memories are mine alone, even if the events themselves occurred right under others' noses. If I only dared, I would ask you a few questions, namely, if you know things about me that I never told you. I might ask you some time. But right now, I haven't the courage.

I miss you, Mike, Blair, Roy, and Abby. I miss everybody.

But I must stay here for now.

For just a little while longer.

Yours,
With so much love,
Helena

70

In the fall of 1957, Jonathan enlisted into a pilots' training course. In high school, he had continued his fascination with airplanes by joining an aeronautics extra-curricular class where he had flown balsa wood planes on the beach. At sixteen, he had left the Scouts to join the aerial pre-IDF *Gadna* program and attended a glider summer camp at Kibbutz Givat Brenner.

Now that he had successfully passed the rigorous selection process and was accepted as a novice pilot, we had a small family dinner to celebrate the occasion.

We all circled him. Jonah's eyes twinkled with pride, while Ruth's were filled with worry. Irit and Hilde served drinks and refreshments; Esther bounced around the guests with her camera as usual; and Gidi patted his brother's back warmly and announced that he was finally about to live his childhood dream. And there was that Alona girl, who stood beside him the whole time with a smile so wide I thought her face would crack. To my regret, she looked terrific with her lithe body and her flowing hair, which she wore down for a change.

In honor of the event, I wore a blue knee-length skirt and a matching cerulean short-sleeved shirt. I did my best to act naturally, chatting and smiling amiably. I did everything I could to ignore the painful presence of Jonathan's doting girlfriend and avoid the gaze of his beautiful half-moon eyes.

Esther asked us to go into the living room to take a few pictures. She had us stand close together and pose; a pose that demonstrated the formality of the moment but could not conceal Mother's stiff stance and scattered gaze or the turmoil reflected in my eyes and my body's stress. Then Esther suggested that Jonathan have his picture taken with each of us separately. She winked at me when nobody looked, and I smiled awkwardly back. In her wisdom, she made sure there was a photo of him and me together, just the two of us alone.

When it was my turn, I enlisted the acting talent I never had to take my place beside him, standing proudly, smiling like any loving cousin. But my breath caught in my throat when his rough fingers pinched my waist, and I felt his breath on the back of my neck. When his chest was flush with my back, I felt his heartbeat against at my skin.

In the picture, Jonathan is not smiling, his eyes burning with some bizarre, indecipherable force. My face is gloomy, my smile imbecilic and artificial, and even though the photo is in black and white, I can tell that my cheeks were awfully red.

To my relief, a short while later Alona announced that she had to leave to attend an important youth movement meeting. She said goodbye to Jonathan with a loud kiss after they had made plans to meet at her home later that night.

I gathered my courage and turned to Jonathan. I asked him softly to go downstairs with me for a few minutes. I hoped for some privacy. Jonathan did not turn me down. He put on his gym shoes, thanked everybody, and said he was going out for a run, to burn some energy. I mumbled that I was popping over to see Nurit.

When we were on the street we began to walk silently. I led him to Independence Park on a hill overlooking the sea. Later, it would become the site of a hotel, but it was then still empty, open, and beautiful, its green lawns flanked by thick bushes.

Now I was the one to ask him to sit down on the bench. I

commented on the pleasant weather and the cool breeze that seemed to announce the coming of fall. I pulled a small, wrapped box from my bag and offered it to him. I saw a flicker of surprise in his eyes. He seemed to be as nervous as I was. Jonathan quickly unwrapped the box, opened it, and pulled out a small, golden Star of David pendant hanging from a thin gold chain. He cleared his throat and closed his eyes. To alleviate the awkward silence, I mumbled that I had bought it at the Menorah jewelry store on the corner of Allenby and Ben-Yehuda, using the money I had earned publishing my stories. When I thought I saw the muscles of his face loosening a bit, his eyes softening, I dared slide over and sit closer to him.

"I hope my Star of David protects you, Jonathan," I whispered in his ear. "You are very dear to me."

He smiled at me, handsome and sad, and his half-moon eyes moistened.

I let out a whistling sigh of relief from the depths of my bosom. When Jonathan asked me to put the necklace around his neck, my hands quivered, and my fingers dampened.

"The necklace is very pretty," he said. "But not as pretty as you, Helena."

He drew me in for a long hug and promised to wear it whenever he could.

My heart trembled, my voice was lost.

The sea was blue and raging.

The wind blew, and the air danced.

Then he stood up, walked me home wordlessly, and turned toward Alona's house.

***

The pilots' training course was divided into six stages, lasting many months. The students of the late 1950s already underwent a methodical, institutionalized training, each with a personal tracking file. Throughout the course, their instructors were required to get under their pupils' skins, examining their skills without any emotion or prejudice. The suitability model considered personality and behavior, learning abilities, and operational talents in flying and controlling an airplane, along with qualities such as bravery, responsibility, and performance under pressure. The results of these calculations were checked every few weeks.

In the personal file of J. Jonas, the flying-school sociologist, an active participant in the weekly assessment meetings, raised a question mark regarding the young pupil's level of responsibility. In a note, he said that special attention ought to be paid to this young man. There was no doubt about his flying skills, but he exhibited a measure of arrogance and over-confidence that might lead him to take unnecessary risks in the air.

This query was only raised once during the course. Despite it, Jonathan was one of the lucky men who completed the course successfully, its conclusion marked by an impressive ceremony on the Tel Nof base, in which each pupil received his winged pin.

Jonathan was stationed at the Ramat David air base as a Vautour fighter pilot in the Northern Knights Squadron. During his service, General Ezer Weizman was appointed as the sixth Commander in Chief of the Israeli Air Force. Weizman's arrogance, his motto ("the best to the air force"), his declared goal of constructing a winning force, and, no less so, the 'wild west' tales whispered about him, all captivated Jonathan's heart.

Jonathan became a pilot in the Israeli Defense Forces.

To him, there could be no greater honor.

71

January 1991

(This letter was thrown out)

Mike,

Yet another letter I don't have the guts to send to you. Last night I called home from Pierre's office. My heart was pounding, but you weren't home. Nelly picked up, and I heard anger in her voice. It was strange, she'd never allowed herself to talk to me like that before. After all, she's only the children's nanny, my employee. When I get back, I'll have to put her in her place.

But that's not important. The important thing right now is Blair. The girl is in Tel Aviv, exactly a week before the UN's ultimatum to Iraq expires. Where is her common sense? Why would she do that? She doesn't have to be there!

I know nothing either of us tells her will make any difference. Blair will stay there, in the heart of Tel Aviv, even if the city gets bombarded by dozens of missiles. She's angry with us, she's rebellious, still stubborn and frivolous as a teenager, and fearless. Oddly, I think she finds this whole scenario romantic, adventurous, and incredibly appealing.

I can't handle the differences between here and there. The tension in the Middle East and the Persian Gulf versus the stoic peace and quiet of Yosemite. This is a different world. I'm in a different world now.

Davidi tells me you won the tender to construct the bridge over the Connecticut River. If we had spoken, I would have told you how happy I am for you. I remember how hard you worked for it. You had told me the original company in charge of the project had made many engineering errors and that the bridge is dangerous. Now these errors need to be fixed, and I know first-hand that no one is better at fixing things than you.

You are my private Bridge Man, Mike. I love you so much.

I hope you know that.

I might not have told you often enough.

72

Fixing and repairing… Jonah used to say that the housing laws imposed by the Israeli government in the early years of the state were responsible for the prevalence of ugly buildings in many parts of Tel Aviv. Despite his weak health, in the summer of 1959, he started a small business as a renovations contractor and provided customers with reasonably priced proposals for repairs, renovations, and maintenance of neglected stairwells and poorly preserved facades. He told us with a half-smile that wrung Ruth's heart that he would never let go of his modest vision to sprinkle some architectural beauty over the charmless concrete edifices.

Ruth and Naomi made it their mission to help care for our family. My mother was fairly calm at the time, and she returned to her old Singer sewing machine and took on light mending for neighbors from Ben-Yehuda Street and acquaintances of Hilde and Ruth. Ruth, for her part, extended her working hours at Ironi Daled High School and took on an increasing number of private English lessons in the afternoon.

Davidi completed his studies at the Stern Conservatory that summer on a discord when his affair with the wife of his conducting professor was revealed. This unpleasant affair was somewhat compensated for by his certificate of excellence and the attractive job offers that came his way. In a short while, he signed a contract with the Berlin Philharmonic, conducted by Herbert von Karajan,

whose questionable past as a member of the Nazi party was correct-
ed, Davidi claimed, by his marriage in 1942 to Anita Gütermann, a
woman of clearly Jewish origins.

Those days, the military invaded all of our lives. Gidi bound his life
to the army and to Irit, the first as a career officer in the Paratroopers
division; the second, by getting engaged. Jonathan, Esther, Nurit and
I all performed mandatory service, and Hilde made sure to wash our
uniforms away from Naomi's eyes.

And so it was that whenever we all came home on leave, we would
stop by Hilde's apartment first. When she was not home, we would
use the key she hid especially for us under a blue vase, filled with
twigs covered in green foliage, by her door. First, we would remove
our uniforms and drop them into a large basket in Hilde's bathroom,
then we would change into civilian clothing and go upstairs. The
uniforms would be returned to us within a day or two, clean, fragrant, and perfectly ironed.

I served as a clerk in the Communications Corps' quartermas-
ter's store, a dull role I could not fathom how I'd ended up in. Back
then we did not ask questions. Nurit and Esther had a much more
interesting service: Nurit was a clerk at the head medical officer's
headquarters in Tel HaShomer, and Esther was a photographer for
the military magazine *Bamahaneh*.

Going against my nature, I did not protest my fate as a clerk, although I was bored to death most of the time. I arrogantly ignored
the clumsy wooing of the soldiers who served with me as well as the
disturbing attention of the base commander, whom everyone knew
was married, although he tried to hide it. All I cared about was getting home, meeting Nurit and Esther and a few old friends, making
sure my mother was well, that Ruth was taking care of things, and
that Jonah's mood was all right. With each leave I also hoped to find
a letter from Davidi on the green bookcase in my room, or—even
rarer—a letter from Will.

And I always hoped for, from the tips of my toes to the roots of my hair, for Jonathan to come home that weekend too, that I might run into him on the street in his handsome uniform, which accentuated his elongated muscles and lithe body, and see the pilot wings embroidered on his shirt, with the blue Star of David at their center.

***

One Tuesday in late autumn, I went home on afternoon leave. Mother was home alone. Her eyes lit up when she saw me. I took a seat beside her on the living-room sofa.

"Where are Ruth and Jonah?" I asked.

"At work," she answered laconically.

I asked her how she spent all these hours home alone. She pointed at a small pile of mended clothes carefully folded on a bureau next to the sofa, and said, "I sew." Then she added, "I also think thoughts."

I looked at her astonished. "What do you think about, Mother?"

"About your father," she said, her eyes blurring with tears.

I said nothing. I spent the following hour sitting quietly, my arms wrapped around my knees, and listening to my mother tell, for the hundredth time, the story of Naomi and Mordecai. A whirlwind of sensations and unanswered questions were released in me again: what did Mordecai see in my faded mother? Did he even exist? Was he really my father? What kind of father would he be if he had survived?

As always, I felt a strong, totally irrational urge to be there, if only for a moment, in the room with them, so that I could see him and receive first-hand proof that this story had a foothold in reality. As always, when I listened to her speak of him and saw the passion in her eyes and the blush in her cheeks, I cried inwardly, feeling compassion for them both, for my mother with her shriveled spirit and my father who had died so young.

I felt sorry for myself, too. For having been born to a mentally unstable mother and without a father.

That was the last time she told me about him. But I did not know that back then.

How could I have known?

Then she said, out of the blue, "It's not good."

I asked meekly what she was referring to.

She said, "Jonathan."

My breath caught. What did she mean?

She said Jonathan was taking too many risks, just as Mordecai had done. "Mordecai," she said, "also went all sorts of places and did things, putting his life at risk, and now he is no longer here…"

My skin was covered in a cold sweat.

She looked straight into my eyes. "Do you really think that I don't see his uniform when Hilde returns it, clean and ironed?"

I said nothing.

"Don't tell Ruth. I don't want her to know I know…"

I excused myself to go use the bathroom. As I turned to leave, she spoke to my back: "I just thought perhaps you could speak to him; talk some sense into him."

I turned back as if bitten by a snake. "What do you want me to tell him, Mother?"

"Tell him to be careful…" she whispered, seeming to shut herself off from my yelling. Her eyes were wet.

I turned my back on her again, the image of her crestfallen face following me as did the sound of her broken voice, informing me that I had received a letter that day.

I hurried to my bedroom.

There, on the green bookcase, was a long, sealed envelope, signed by "the other."

***

Will Adler was busy covering California's higher education master plan, which was led by the president of the University of California, Clark Kerr. His letter was composed in proper Hebrew. He never used a typewriter, always writing by hand. That way, he once told me, he felt closer to the text: the small additions in the margins, the cross-outs, and the varying degrees of pen pressure expressed his changing mood. "A typewritten letter," he said, "is much less personal."

Sixteen years separated me from Will. Almost an entire generation. He was a journalist who spent most of his time in California, and I was a 19-year-old Israeli soldier. Our lives took place on two different planets. I had no idea whom he spent his time with on the other side of the ocean, what his life looked like in that remote state of California, or even what California itself looked like. I imagined it as a magical, fascinating place with a 'different' aroma. Will told me it resembled Israel somewhat in terms of climate and appearance. A land with a desert and a sea.

I yearned for this place without knowing it.

Nurit said I felt that way about California only because of my feelings for Will. She couldn't understand what I saw in the man with the piercing steel eyes, the bushy eyebrows, and the aquiline nose. "Besides," she said, scrunching her nose, "He's thirty-five! So old! What do you have to do with him? He should marry someone, maybe a California Jew, and you, Helena, need to find someone your own age, three years older at most, not a cousin or such an old man!"

But to me, Will was not old at all. He was manly, tall, experienced, and striking. He had charisma, a hankering for life, and extensive knowledge on any topic. He had lived on three continents, was fluent in three languages, read hundreds of books, wrote dozens of stories, and had published numerous newspaper articles. He had firm legs and long arms, which ended in large hands with wide, rough fingers stained with ink. His face was long and lined, as if he had spent years working under the scorching sun, and the sideburns of his black, thick hair had turned gray years ago, when his father had died.

To me, Will was a masculine, attractive man. To me, he was something special.

Something else.

In his letter, Will asked how I was doing and requested a picture of me in uniform. "You must be the prettiest soldier in the IDF," he wrote, and I felt moved and even managed to crack a smile despite my dark mood. There had always been sparks between us, I knew, even if they had to shoot their way across an ocean. When we did meet, he never laid a finger on me but did not take his eyes off me, either.

He always called me "beautiful Helena," and I wondered if he saw me as a real woman or just some literary heroine.

At the end of the letter, he announced that he was about to come to Israel to cover the latest developments in Israel's relationship with the UN and the Vatican. In early January 1960, I knew, the head of the Lutheran Church in Germany sent a letter of apology to the Israeli prime minister in light of new expressions of anti-Semitism in his country. The Vatican issued a public defamation of anti-Semitism and racism. Two days later, Israel demanded that the UN work to root out both phenomena.

Will had a personal interest in the matter.

73

He arrived in the middle of January 1960, about a week before an enormous rally was slated to take place in Tel Aviv, protesting the cooperation between Israel and Germany in light of the rising wave of anti-Semitism in Europe. We met at Sheleg HaLebanon. He complimented me on my appearance and took a long, piercing look at my body in uniform. Then he suggested that I join him covering the rally on 23 January. I was moved by his invitation but did my best to preserve a serious, dignified expression as was fitting for a mature woman and the situation. I accepted his invitation with restraint.

In those days, as I knew, Israel and Germany did not have an official diplomatic relationship. The two countries' interrelation, revolved around commerce and the Reparations Agreement signed on September 1952. The day before the rally, Will procured an entry pass for me into the *Haaretz* archive. "It would be worth your while," he said, "to read a few of the pieces published around the time the reparations agreement was signed and in the following years, as well. I would like to hear your opinion."

I spent hours in the archive that day, perusing yellowing newspapers gathered in enormous, heavy binders by ascending dates. My eyes grazed quickly over the headlines and sought out every piece of information published on the topic in the past decade.

I was just a little girl when the reparations agreement with West Germany was signed. I had only been living in Israel for two years at the time. All I wanted was to resemble the *sabra: prickly pear*, children, born and raised in Israel. I was unaware of the sharp polemic that had gripped the Israeli public and Knesset around the charged topic of reparations for victims of the Holocaust. All I knew was that Germany paid my mother a monthly stipend to fund her medical expenses.

But the many articles I read taught me plenty. I was upset. "The other" asked me to form an opinion, and I wanted to show him I was up to the challenge. I read the opinions of those who supported the agreement as well as those of its critics. Picturing the blurry images of Oma Ilse and Opa Michael, Gabriel, Vera, Uriel, and Raphael, whom I had never known, I took a deep look at personal stories. My memory contained a frozen image of my father's enchanting smile, described to me in detail and from multiple angles so many times. I thought about my poor mother, physically and mentally hurt. This was not the way her life had been meant to unfold.

I tried to form an opinion. I was young, rebellious, and emotional. I was filled with rage against all generations of Germans.

And this rage had only one outlet.

Will waited for me by the newsroom building at six o'clock, as scheduled. I was flushed and upset. I had never before confronted my family's past as part of such a powerful, overarching phenomenon. I held the pages, covered with small, crowded handwriting in my hand. I had often pressed the pen, emphasizing distractedly whole sentences as an expression of my turmoil. When I reread the pages at night, I could barely recognize my own handwriting.

"So, what do you think?" Will asked me right away.

I answered decisively that I stood wholeheartedly with the opposers of the agreement. I quoted Menachem Begin, head of the *Herut* right-wing party, who had said that "Accepting such an agreement is tantamount to forgiving the Nazis for their crimes," and that "putting a material price on the suffering of victims is an eternally shameful act."

"That is my opinion," I said, unintentionally raising my voice. "And tomorrow at the rally I'll join the people protesting the cooperation with Germany."

Will listened carefully. He apologized for having to cancel our dinner due to an important meeting that had suddenly come up with a reporter from *The Jerusalem Post*, drove me home, and said he would pick me up the following day, an hour before the rally began. Only later did he confess that he could sense my distress at that moment and wanted to give me more time to process.

That night, in bed, although I was exhausted, I read fervently through everything I had written that day at the *Haaretz* archive. As I read, a thought flashed through me: I did not know what Will's opinion was.

I found out the following day.

The rally was tempestuous. Posters were raised in protest of the collaboration between Israel and Germany. More than once, I found myself shouting along with the crowd, an unusual thing for me to do.

When the rally was over, Will took me to Café Tamar on the corner of Shenkin and Ahad Ha'am Streets. It was my first visit there. The café was built around a large tree trunk. The treetop rose over the café, shading it. The place contained simple chairs, Formica tables with plastic legs, and a cash register from the days of the Palmach. The food was tasty and homemade, and I especially enjoyed the poppy seed cake served in a small plate. Will's voice was hoarse that day. He gave me his position in a low voice. He said he certainly understood my stance and that many people, some of whom he knew and respected, obviously shared it. But he thought differently.

I was disappointed. I had hoped he would support my opinion, that our positions would be alike. He explained that our feelings about what the Germans had done to the Jewish people, intense as they may be, cannot take precedence over common sense. Sometimes, one must be pragmatic. He quoted Prime Minister David Ben-Gurion, who said that Germany today was not Nazi Germany, but "a different Germany." "Fact is," he said, "that, upon the end of the war, Germany became accepted among the nations." He sunk his gaze into mine. "Besides," he added, "the reparations help Israel handle the dire problem of a shortage of foreign currency, an obstacle that cannot be overlooked. Israel is a young state with existential survival challenges…"

When he finished talking, I burst into tears, hiding my face in my hands. The café-goers looked at us questioningly, and the owner, whose name I only later learned was Sarah, came over and asked with concern if I needed any help. Will signaled to her that everything was all right. Perhaps they knew each other. Then he opened his arms and held me close. We sat like that, close together, for several minutes, until my crying died down, reduced to broken, stifled sobs.

It was the first time Will ever touched me. I was upset and stunned. I still could not define what I saw in him—whether a lover or a father figure. When he held me in his arms, my entire body shook, but I slowly relaxed, a pleasant warmth spreading through my limbs.

But then he informed me that he had to leave for California the very next day.

The very next day arrived and Will left. He went back to America, leaving me confused, disoriented, and sad.

***

In the winter of 1980, as I visited Israel for the launch of one of my books in Hebrew translation, I went to Café Tamar. I was glad to find it still in business and full of patrons. The design had not changed much since I had visited with "the other" twenty years earlier—the plain Formica tables, the plastic chairs, the tin spoons, the cash register, and the sign out front with a simple, pretty picture of a palm tree.

Sarah, the owner, was still there. She swayed between the tables, wearing a blue button-down dress, a blue sweater, and blue earrings. Even her graying hair was slightly blue. I was moved. Images from the day of the rally ran through my mind. I recalled Will putting his arm around me. I wanted to ask her if she remembered that once, a long time ago, a handsome man sat here with a young woman who wept out loud.

But instead I just smiled when she approached me and ordered a cup of coffee and a piece of poppy-seed cake to see whether the taste had remained the same.

74

Jonathan came home from the military in early February. We had not seen him for an entire month. I ran into him in Hilde's apartment when I came downstairs to bring her a challah that Ruth had baked for Saturday. Jonathan removed his uniform and put on sweatpants and a long-sleeved shirt. I told him that Esther and Gidi were also supposed to come home that day, and that Ruth had a *Tu BiShvat* meal planned for all of us. When he was dressed, we said goodbye to Hilde and went upstairs. Jonathan stopped me on the way up, held my arm gently, slipped his hand under his shirt collar, and pulled out the Star of David necklace I had bought him.

"You're wearing it!" I cried, surprised, offering him my best smile.

Suddenly, he took my other arm too and pulled me close. I felt as if my heart had jumped out of my striped shirt. At any moment, one of the doors could open. Jonathan's beloved face was right against my eyes, his breath on my face. His lips fluttered a kiss on mine and then bit them, and for a moment I could see the inner struggle in his eyes.

I only said, "Jonathan..." or perhaps I dreamed it and in fact said nothing.

Jonathan pulled away from me, closed his fingers into fists, and shut his eyes tightly. Then he lowered his head and shook it. "Come on, Helena," he said, "let's go inside, I'm starving."

That evening, Gidi and Irit, Hilde and her sister all arrived, and there were ten of us, without Davidi. We all wore white in honor of the holiday. I wore a simple white dress that flattered my figure and revealed my legs. I wore flat, white cloth shoes and the pearl necklace Ruth received as an engagement gift from Oma Ilse and Opa Michael. Jonathan wore a white button-down shirt, the Star of David chain around his neck.

Ruth and Naomi arranged three bowls of different sizes on the table. In one they placed oranges, nuts, and almonds; in another, apples, dates, and olives; in a third, figs, carobs, and raisins. Jonah said a blessing on the wine and then the blessings of *HaMotzi Lechem*, *Borei Minei Mezonot*, and *Borei Pri Ha'etz*.

A lively conversation evolved around the table. Due to Mother's sensitivity, we avoided subjects like the military or politics. Jonah told us about a renovation he was running on an old apartment building on Hayarkon Street. The plaster on its balconies, which protruded from the building, had loosened and fallen off due to its proximity to the sea. This kind of renovation, he said, would prevent the rusting of the steel beams surrounding the balconies and improve the appearance of the entire building.

Hilde contributed a description of her efforts to enforce her authority over a new, partly automatic washing machine she had recently purchased. This kind of machine was a rare vision in those days. It included two containers, one that washed the clothes, and another that spun the clothes to extract the moisture.

Irit updated us on Gidi's friends and classmates. Some of them had begun studying at the university after their honorable discharge, others were forced to find a job first. Two of them, she said, had already married—one couple lived in Jerusalem near the Hebrew University, the other near the Technion in Haifa—and when she spoke of this, she and Gidi exchanged looks.

The festive atmosphere grew a bit gloomy when Ruth told us how a few days ago her heart ached when she walked down Herzl Street, where the old building of the Herzliya Hebrew High School had stood until recently. We had all attended the school in its previous location and all had fine memories of it. Although we knew that Herzl Street had long since become a busy, commercial street and that the old high school building had grown old and decrepit with years—its plaster flaking, its floor cracking, and its ceilings leaking in winter—we had trouble accepting the city's decision to demolish it. Jonah said it was "an eternal tragedy," architecturally speaking. The building, which had been situated on a small hill at the end of Herzl Street, was built in the eclectic style of the early twentieth century and brought together Middle Eastern and European influences. Recently, he said, an article in *Haaretz* claimed that within a year or less, construction would start on a commercial skyscraper of American dimensions on the ruins of the old school. It would be the tallest building in Israel and perhaps in the entire Middle East. Ruth said it was also "a loss for generations" educationally speaking, since the building's elevated position at the edge of Tel Aviv's main street established the school's status as an educational institution of utmost importance in the minds of the city's dwellers. She cried as she spoke about it and Mother got carried away after her.

A few moments later, after the topic of the "loss for generations" was fully exhausted, my mother stood up and retired to her bedroom. Then Hilde and her sister left, and the young ones cleared the table and washed the dishes.

Jonathan and I exchanged occasional looks. Whenever I passed by him and our arms touched, I felt weak in the knees. I think Esther must have noticed, and perhaps Irit, who was always perceptive, did too.

But just then a knock came at the door and Alona appeared. Jonathan went to greet her and walk her inside. Alona, taller than ever in funny high heels, did not leave his side from that moment on. She looked at her pilot with admiration, smiled on hearing every word, and never ceased to rub his arm, which was adorned with a watch she had bought him in honor of their two-year anniversary, if one ignored three breaks along the way, the longest of which lasted six months.

I could not stand her presence for obvious reasons and was glad to find that Jonathan was no longer as passionate about his long-legged girlfriend. His body language told his story for him, as did his eyes, which I could feel all over my body, even when he did not face me.

Jonah, Gidi, and Jonathan started to talk about the military. Ruth made sure Naomi was asleep, and Irit signaled to Esther, Alona, and me to follow her into the kitchen. There, as we made coffee and tea and sliced pieces from the cheesecake Irit had baked for the holiday, she told us we must give the men some time alone. I loved Irit and greatly respected her. I tried to ignore the possibly reproachful questioning looks she turned my way. Now I had no doubt that she had noticed the turbulent emotions between Jonathan and me. When I walked from the kitchen to the living room holding a tray of cups, a jar of black coffee, teabags, a sugar dish, and a small pitcher of milk, my ear caught a tone of plea in Jonah's voice when he told Jonathan, "Be careful!"

The memory of Mother's words flashed through my mind. My hands trembled beneath the tray; Ruth's china cups rattled and clattered, threatening to crash to the floor. Gidi hurried over and took the tray from me. "Are you all right, Helena?" he asked. I said I was and thanked Alona, who rushed to the kitchen to get me a glass of water. Later in the evening, we all discovered the following alarming report: during a high school graduates' visit to the Ramat David Airbase, Jonathan and another young pilot decided to pull a prank. At the end of a training session, before the marveling eyes of the high schoolers, and while committing a severe disciplinary violation, they performed an aerial maneuver called a "barrel roll," in which their airplane made a complete rotation on both its longitudinal and lateral axes, while forming a large spiral of frozen vapor trails on the horizon. In an inquiry following the incident, Jonathan and his friend were accused of an incredibly severe misdemeanor, including the breach of many safety rules. The two of them received a warning and were forbidden from flying for three months—a term that would end in four weeks. Jonathan's personal file was stained with the details of his misdemeanor and his punishment, and now included the opinion of the military sociologist, who warned against Jonathan's arrogance, which could lead to disaster.

That night, Jonathan stayed in. When everyone left or went to bed, I waited for him as he stepped out of the shower and went into the kitchen for a glass of water. I could have asked him about Alona, or anything else, but his eyes were red with fatigue.

I only said, "Please, Jonathan, be careful... Take care of yourself... Don't fool around."

He turned his tired eyes to face me, smiled cockily and asked, "Be careful? For you?"

We heard footsteps approaching, and, grateful for the dim light in the room that hid the crimson arrows that shot onto my cheeks, I only managed to nod.

Then I said, or perhaps my eyes said it for me, "Yes, Jonathan, for my sake... Do it for me."

75

17 January 1991
Yosemite Park, California

Dear Nurit,

That's it. I think I'm losing my mind.

I'm here, a storm raging inside of my body, spewing out and swirling, and finally unfolding on the page. All around me, there's a stoic peacefulness, which seems to only be available in a place like Yosemite, with the magnificent views of the Sierra Nevada, the waterfalls, the streams, and the enormous trees.

And far away, the Gulf War is breaking in full force.

True, the chronicle of events could have been foretold—the failed diplomatic efforts, the forming of a coalition of thirty-four countries, the UN's ultimatum to Iraq, the concentration of land forces and American fighter jets on Saudi land; battleships and aircraft carriers in the gulf; bombastic, belligerent declarations, and the arrival of the ultimatum date, 17 January ... Winds of war... again...

And despite it all...

The moment Pierre knocked on my door this morning, almost bursting inside to tell me that the allies' aerial attack on Iraq had begun (he's an emotional guy, prone to dramatics) all the blood left my face. I couldn't believe this was really happening. The Iraqi government's warning from before the invasion that if Iraq was attacked by the American-led coalition countries, it would attack Israel flickered through my mind.

A few minutes later, Pierre, Marcel, and I gathered together in Pierre's office to watch the CNN coverage of what had received the evocative, somewhat romantic name "Desert Storm." Less than twelve hours had gone by since the beginning of the operation, and Iraq's national radio was already broadcasting Saddam Hussein, who announced in his despicable voice that the great battle had begun, "the mother of all wars."

How could anyone not be appalled by such a declaration? Not shudder at the thought of Israel being attacked? Just thinking of all of you, Nurit, under the threat of missiles with conventional warheads, or, heaven forbid, biological and chemical ones, when we're clearly dealing with a lunatic?

How is it possible to function or even just breathe, when your daughter chose to go to Tel Aviv at such a rotten time?

And why, why, why does this keep happening again and again?!

I tried to call Blair dozens of times, but she didn't answer. There was no response at your place either. Where are you all the time? Is it business as usual over there? What if a missile suddenly lands?

Irit finally picked up. On hearing her voice, I was immediately relieved since I suspected something awful must have happened that only I hadn't heard about yet. I started to cry, and she calmed me down. Irit is an amazing woman. Her two boys are in the army, and yet she spoke calmly, convincing me everything was fine. She also told me she's been in touch with Blair daily. Blair had turned down her offer of moving into their home in the Tzahala neighborhood, but yesterday, the last day before the ultimatum, my stubborn girl gave in to Irit's demands and agreed to seal a room in the apartment. Irit wasted no time, hurrying over with all the necessary equipment—plastic tarps, rolls of tape, scissors, a flashlight, a battery-operated radio, some canned food, dry snacks, and soda cans—and together they sealed the room that used to belong to Jonathan.

I've been trying to grasp the meaning of things from here, but I simply can't.

I thought of calling home, speaking with the kids and with Mike, but suddenly I was overcome with anger. Why doesn't he call me when something like this is going on? She's his daughter too!

But I shouldn't be surprised. I, of all people. Nevertheless, something is holding me back from calling him. That's another thing I'm struggling with. All I can do right now is keep writing, letting out more and more.

Please, Nurit, stay in touch. Tell me how you're getting along by yourself with the children and inform me about the atmosphere on the streets and all the stuff that the news doesn't report. Due to this dizzying turn of events I've broken another one of my rules, and in addition to the television, which has already been returned to my room, I've also asked to get the phone back.

I think this is the right time for me to reconnect with the world. My phone number at the lodge is 1-209-377-486, room 201. If you speak to Blair, please give her the number too. Tell her not to worry about the cost—she can call and hang up, and I'll call her right back.

Hold on, Nurit.

Yours, with love and worry,
Helena

76

It happened on Friday morning, in February 1961. It was raining. Hilde knocked on the door and asked that Naomi come downstairs immediately to help her fix a customer's gown. The dress ripped, she mumbled, when she washed it. She looked so miserable, shaken up, that Ruth urged Naomi to get dressed and go downstairs right away. I still remember Hilde's pale face in those moments, her broken voice and the shock in her eyes. Five minutes later, another knock came at the door.

Three of them walked in. A short, stout, expressionless man in a blue jacket, a crestfallen man with fleshy lips, and an older man with a black briefcase. Irit walked inside with them, pale and ghastly.

I took a few steps back and cried out, "Ruth! Jonah!"

Ruth and Jonah ran over and paused at my side. The three of us looked panicked at Irit, and Jonah howled in a voice I had never heard before, "Gideon! My child, Gideon!!"

Then Irit took one step toward us, tears streaming down her face, and said in a voice not hers, "Not Gideon... Jonathan."

The stout, expressionless man in a khaki uniform introduced himself as Jonathan's commander. When he removed his jacket, I noticed the pilot's wings embroidered on his shirt and the blue Star of David at their center. The glum, fleshy lipped man was a casualty notifier, and the older man with the black briefcase—a military doctor.

I recall those moments as if from within a dream.

A nightmare.

I remember the commander taking Jonah and Ruth's hands in his large palm, an immense tension apparent in his face. He said that Jonathan's death was a great loss for our family as well as the Air Force family. He said everyone in their squadron loved Jonathan very much. He was a brave, charismatic, sharp-minded fellow and a talented pilot.

I remember the doctor asking me for two glasses of water and insisting that Ruth and Jonah swallow tranquilizers.

I remember the notifier holding Ruth's frozen hand, rubbing it between his two hands, and speaking to her in a soft voice that whistled between his fleshy lips.

I remember thinking how lucky it was that my mother was not around and suddenly knew why Hilde had knocked on our door a few minutes earlier.

I remember Irit hugging Jonah and Ruth, her eyes red, saying that Gidi and Esther already knew and that they were on their way home.

I remember my throat was dry, and hundreds of drums beat inside my head as I tried to support Ruth and Jonah. My legs were shaking incessantly.

At some point, the doctor realized he had to take care of me, too, and slipped a tranquilizer in my mouth. My eyes shifted to Ruth. Her mouth was pursed, dark circles around her eyes, but somehow, she was still standing straight.

Not so Jonah. Jonah was not standing at all. He leaked down onto his chair, leaned his elbows on his knees, and held his head between his hands. His scalp was shiny with sweat. I walked over, knelt beside him and embraced his shoulders. I was startled by the uncontrollable shaking of his body.

The door opened. It was Esther, so pale in her green uniform. When I saw her, I felt a mixture of shock and relief. A thought passed through my mind: how dear Jonathan had been to her, how much he loved her. I remembered our trip to the desert and the quiet that had lingered between the two of them. With tears in her eyes, Esther hugged Ruth and Jonah, Irit, and me. There was something soothing in her presence.

Then the door opened again. It was my mother, who must have sensed something, fled from Hilde's apartment, and run upstairs. Her eyes were torn open, her expression mad. Hilde entered immediately after her. Then Gidi walked inside, serious, authoritative, quiet. He held Ruth for a long time, then helped his father to his feet, supporting his bent back with his firm arm, and took him out onto the balcony, which smelled of fresh rain. Later, he spoke to Jonathan's commander, asking that he tell him exactly what had happened and what arrangements had to be made for the military funeral that would be held on Sunday at the Kiryat Shaul Cemetery.

The rumor spread quickly. Through the neighbors I guess, who saw the car outside and the three men entering the building. Nurit arrived. She hugged me, my mother, and Ruth. At Esther's request, she went to deliver the news of Jonathan's death to Alona and urgently send a telegram to Davidi, asking him to come home.

I was frozen. Unable to do a thing.

Then Gidi asked the delegation to leave. "The family would like to be left alone with its grief," he said. He promised to call the doctor if any change for the worse occurred in his parents or in Naomi. After they left, Hilde made a pot of tea and poured it into cups for everyone there.

Then she did something none of us had done yet.

She wept aloud.

When I could no longer take the stifling atmosphere and the crying, I snuck out of the apartment. My legs carried me down Ben-Yehuda, Arlozorov, and Hayarkon Streets to the hill overlooking the sea. When I reached Independence Park I walked by the monument placed in memory of Air Force soldiers Aaron David Sprinzak and Matityahu Sukenik, killed during the 1948 War when they set out to attack Egyptian battleships that had been launching rockets at the Tel Aviv coast. I lingered there for a moment. The monument was shaped like a bird with a broken wing. One wing was made from the wing of an intercepted Israeli plane.

There, at Independence Park, at twilight, I located the bench by the tree. I plopped down on the bench and shouted voicelessly, "Why?"

Suddenly I heard broken sobs that slowly, slowly grew stronger and consolidated into heartbreaking howling. I looked around but saw no one.

Then I realized the crying was my own.

The sea was quiet and black; there was no wind, and the air stood still.

***

On February 20th, we buried Jonathan in the military plot of the Kiryat Shaul Cemetery. There were at least a hundred people there: family, Jonathan's many friends from high school, Scouts, the *Gadna*, and the squadron; dozens of soldiers in khaki and blue. Gidi, Esther, and I arrived at the funeral in our green uniforms; Alona in black. Jonah insisted on coming, although he felt ill the morning of the funeral. Ruth walked silently, painfully, but upright. Hilde did not come. She had volunteered to stay home with Naomi, who was pacing around, her eyes puffy, her hair wild, wringing her hands nervously, and smoking non-stop. Now and then, Hilde succeeded in drawing her into the living room chair. Naomi's fingers gripped the armrests like a drowning person holding onto a lifesaver.

Jonathan's body was in a coffin, wrapped with an Israeli flag, resting on a gurney. Six officers of the same rank as Jonathan lifted the coffin and carried it one their shoulders. When the funeral procession arrived at the plot, and the coffin was carefully placed on two planks over the open grave, Ruth's voice was heard, as if from within a fog.

"My children," she called out. "Where are you, my children?"

Gidi and Esther rushed to her side. Davidi, who arrived only that morning, put his arm around me, and we stood at a distance behind them. Then Ruth turned back and called out again, "Davidi, Helena, where are you? I want all of you beside me!"

This felt oddly soothing. We were all Ruth's children. Davidi and I hurried over, and all of us were now holding each other in an agonized row: Irit, Gidi, Ruth, Esther, Davidi, and I. Jonah was sitting in a wheelchair, the military doctor at his side. He read the *Kaddish* prayer over his son's grave, his voice breaking.

A rustle passed through the crowd: stifled sobbing.

I do not know how I could have made it through this ordeal without Davidi, whose embrace kept me on my feet. After Jonathan's coffin was lowered into the grave, a three-volley salute was shot out. The commander, that stout man with the expressionless face, said a eulogy.

"The sky you loved so much," he said, "is taking you into its arms today. Goodbye, Jonathan. We salute you!"

I watched him through blurry eyes. My hands and feet were completely frozen, my face puffy and red. Esther's military colleague took pictures. A few days later, he gave me one. I can hardly recognize myself in it today.

I was afraid to ask how Jonathan was killed, but I did nevertheless.

I asked Gidi.

Only once.

"It happened during a nightly training session conducted by the Northern Knights Squadron Vautour pilots," he said. "A training accident... vertigo... a maneuver that was too sharp."

When we sat *shiva,* Nurit overheard somebody whispering that Jonathan had taken an unnecessary risk.

Some things are better left unknown.

I did not want to hear anymore. Jonathan was my hero in London after the war and the love of my childhood and youth.

To me he remained a hero in his death as he was in life.

77

She did not wait long. A short while after the one-month anniversary of Jonathan's death, my mother took advantage of a morning when she was left alone and slipped out.

The pharmacist on Ben-Yehuda Street knew her. He would not sell her just any medication. She knew this, so she walked north, turned right on Frishman Street, and continued to Dizengoff. She could not remember where the pharmacy was there exactly but knew for sure that there was one around. She had gone there once with Ruth to get Jonah's heart medication. Now she needed something for her own broken heart.

She held a wrinkled ten lira note in her hand, hoping the amount would suffice. A fracture like hers, she knew, needed lots of medicine. In her skirt pocket was a prescription from the doctor for Jonah's heart medication and Ruth's tranquilizers. She had found it a few days ago on the chest-of-drawers in the hall. She recalled the concern on Ruth's face as she had searched for the missing prescription. When asked, Naomi had said she had no idea where it had disappeared to. She had never lied to Ruth like that before. Now she had no idea how much the pills cost and where the hell that pharmacy was.

She had never gone to the pharmacy on her own in Tel Aviv.

Her legs carried her to the plaza. What a beautiful, round plaza, she thought, with a pretty pond and a fountain at its center. The sky was dark and gray, but it was not raining, and she sat down on a bench for a brief respite. There were mothers with their children. One of them was pushing a white baby pram with thick wooden sides and large tires.

She peeked into the pram. The baby was sleeping.

Once, she had babies too. One of them had been taken away from her, and she had never seen him again.

She had never owned a pram.

She got up and crossed the street. It began to drizzle. Her eyes looked into the distance. There was the pharmacy, right in front of her. She walked inside. The pharmacist was female, no one she knew. She handed her the prescription, and the woman gathered the different pills from the shelves behind the counter, put them into paper bags bearing the name of the pharmacy, and jotted down instructions on the back. When she handed the pharmacist the bill, her hand trembled. To her surprise, the money sufficed, and she even received a few coins as change, which she used to buy a soda at the nearby kiosk.

The way home seemed much shorter. Naomi went up to the third floor and opened the door. To her relief, no one was at home. She walked into her small bedroom, pulled a block of paper and a pen from the drawer, carefully ripped out a page, and wrote down in German everything she had done that morning in chilling detail. She wanted to document it all.

Then she tore out another page and wrote a short goodbye note.

"Jonathan's death shook my soul," she wrote. "And the old wound opened again, the ugly scars gaping, bleeding. Black before my eyes: an abyss at my feet.

I must say goodbye to you, Ruth and Helena, my darlings. I must say goodbye to all of you. I will not live out my life to its natural conclusion. The pain is greater than I can bear."

I have pictured her last living moments hundreds of times. I imagine her biting her lip and spraying a bit of her perfume on each piece of paper, then folding them carefully and slipping them into a simple, white, fragrant envelope. I see her walking to the bathroom, emptying the cup on the sink of its toothbrushes, and filling it with water. Then she walks to her bedroom, places the cup on the dresser, smooths the sheet on her bed, spreads a duvet cover, and lifts the pillow so that it leans against the headboard. That was how we found her. I see her dropping the contents of the two medicine bottles into the cup, then downing the mixture as fast as possible. After that she lies carefully on her back in bed, placing the envelope on her heart.

Then she fell asleep, forever.

I had said before that Mother tried to kill herself twice.

Well, this time, she succeeded.

This time there was no one to save her.

Not even Jonathan.

78

Davidi taught me to love classical music. I loved Beethoven, Mozart, Bach, and Chopin. But one of the pieces that impressed me most was an eighteenth-century group of violin concerti by Antonio Vivaldi.

I first heard "The Four Seasons" at a concert in 1982, when the Israeli Philharmonic played it in celebration of the one-hundredth birthday of its founder, violinist Bronisław Huberman. I was forty-one years old and was visiting Israel with Mike and with Blair, Roy, and Abby, who were eleven, six, and one, respectively. This was two years after Ruth's death. Davidi was invited to the concert as a guest of honor, and Mike, Esther, and I joined him. Four Israeli world-renowned violinists played the piece, conducted by Zubin Mehta. Each season was performed by a different soloist. I sat, quiet and thoughtful, listening to "Winter"—Concerto No. 4 in F Minor.

Winter has always awakened mixed emotions in me. On the one hand, I loved the smell of rain. I loved sweaters and jackets. I loved heavy, fragrant stews. I loved curling up on the sofa with a book and a blanket when it was cold and stormy outside, watching through the window as the rain hit the ground. On the other hand, the sight of naked trees made me melancholy, and haze and grey clouds awoke in me dismay. I was afraid of heavy rainfall, storms, and floods and scared of thunder and lightning, the clamorous intensity of strong winds.

My hand was in Mike's, his fingers rubbing mine. I took pleasure in the music, the playing, his warm hand. All the winters of my life passed through my mind as moving images: London was cold and gray, Atlanta rainy and freezing, and Tel Aviv was neither, as if always expectant of spring. The tune became gradually more passionate. My thoughts wrapped around a single winter that had changed my life.

The winter of 1961.

When the violinist completed the third movement of "Winter," I excused myself and stepped outside. Esther walked out a few minutes later and appeared at my side with two cups of tea from the cafeteria. I didn't have to say a word. She saw the look in my eyes and understood.

But I said something anyway.

I told her that the winter of 1961 was still considered one of the harshest winters the European continent had ever known. It was convenient for me to push the conversation that far away from my personal life. But Esther smiled glumly and got right to the heart of the matter—Naomi, Jonathan.

***

I lived the winter of '61 for many years afterwards.

After Jonathan died, the military delivered his personal effects. There was the gold chain with the Star of David pendant I had bought him. I asked Ruth to let me keep it as a memento, and ever since I have never taken it off. I burned into my memory the smell of his sweat, the touch of his hands, every word we ever said to each other, every look. Deep inside I knew that it was not only I who loved him. He loved me, too.

I never said goodbye to my mother. After she died, I was plagued by a sense of guilt that has never let go. I had never told her I loved her or that I was sorry for the way her life had turned out. I had never told her I was so regretful of the way I had treated her, for feeling ashamed of her, for not being more patient and forgiving. In the last month of her life, she had dwindled beside me, and I had not noticed. I was consumed by my own grief. I have since felt that if I had only acted differently... If I had only held onto her thin, translucent hands, spoken to her, alleviated her fears, she might not have left me like that.

Esther sat across from me on an armchair in the large lobby of the concert hall. She said that Jonathan's death not only led to Naomi's suicide but also to Jonah's death a few years later by heart attack. Despite the pain I felt, I reminded her how strong Ruth had stayed for all of us and that there were many times in my life when I yearned for just a hint of her strength.

Esther's eyes turned red. She said that ever since Jonathan was killed she had trouble balancing out her life, and that for years, until she met Johan, she had been unable to sustain a long-term, steady relationship with a partner. Instead, she had lost herself in photography, turning her camera into an inseparable part of her life, like a third eye.

I told her I never got over Jonathan's sudden, cruel death, either, and that she and Nurit were the only people in the world to whom I had confessed my love for him. I also said that sometimes I was hit by a deep longing for my mother. It would happen out of the blue. For example, when a piece of clothing ripped or unraveled, when I heard a sad tune that reminded me of her, or when my eyes fell on her picture as a young girl, the one Jonah took back in Vienna, before the war, and which I had framed in silver and placed on my desk.

After Mother's death, I began to conceal parts of my past deep within me. My childhood smile was buried along with it. I adopted a different smile, one that exposed a row of pearly white teeth but did not reach my eyes. The tears slowly disappeared too. I escaped to the world of books. The spark in my eyes vanished. Some people thought it improved my writing.

"I've been dreaming of Mother a lot recently," I whispered to Esther. "And in my dreams, she isn't crazy… She doesn't stare into space, and her cheeks aren't wet with tears… And do you know what she does, Esther? In those dreams?"

Esther shook her head and rubbed my hand.

"She tells me stories," I said. "And when she speaks, her eyes sparkle, her cheeks are pink, her pretty lips filled with movement…" I lowered my head and added in a weak voice, that in the years since her death I have been burned by a terrible sense of guilt, as well as an impossible longing for one more hug from her, one more smile, and—most of all—for her forgiveness.

When I looked up again, my lips were trembling. "You want to know the worst part, Esther?"

She said nothing.

"The worst part," I whispered, "is that there is no way I can fix it."

Esther held my hand in her two warm hands and quietly said something it took me almost ten years to process.

She said I ought to write Naomi's story, to understand her, to sketch out her character and describe her voice precisely. "That way," she said, "you can give her new life." Then she added, "Maybe that way, who knows, you might be able to fix things."

***

But in that winter of 1961, I could not write a thing. Only six of the Jonases and Steiners were left. Jonah had Ruth, Gidi had Irit, Davidi had his music and Berlin, and Esther had her camera. I felt like I had nothing. Honorably discharged shortly before Esther, I tried to pick up my pieces, without much success. I clung to Ruth, who offered a shoulder to lean on, an attentive ear, and an open and loving heart. I was not interested at the time in people my age, other than Nurit. I withdrew into myself until Ruth began to worry about my well-being. Another mental illness was more than she could handle.

A month later, I agreed, at Ruth's behest, to have a one-time meeting with my mother's psychiatrist. All throughout the meeting I was unable to speak about anything meaningful, but eventually I dared voice a single question, one that had been tormenting me.

"But why," I cried, "can't I write?!"

The doctor suggested we discuss the matter, but I already had one foot out the door, determined never to return.

79

Salvation came in the form of a thirty-six-year-old man with a lined face and an aquiline nose.

Ever since he learned of Jonathan and Mother's deaths, Will made sure to write to me once a week. In April of that year he came to Israel for a few months to cover the Eichmann trial, which was stirring up the country. The timing, as far as I was concerned, could not have been better.

I was out of the army, completely free, perhaps too free. I was generally unmotivated, and specifically jobless. Will invited me to join him at the trial, and I was lucky enough to receive a special entry pass. I joined him every morning at the courthouse in Jerusalem and had a chance to get a close-up look at the short, bespectacled man, who had been sent by his Nazi commanders to Vienna in 1938, where he developed a method for forced immigration of Jews from Reich territories; the man who, during the war, had become one of the immediate supervisors of the Final Solution, and the one whose fault it was I had never known Opa Michael and Oma Ilse, or my father.

I was there when Gideon Hausner, the state attorney, raised an accusatory finger at Eichmann in his name and in the name of all those who were murdered in the Holocaust. I was there when the writer Ka-Tzetnik fainted on the witness stand. I was there when the accused, in a dark suit and tie, claimed that he could not be held responsible and that the political echelon that sent him to perform the mission was at fault.

And I was shocked.

For several months, more than a hundred testimonies were given by survivors before the glass box, leaving a blistering impression on the Israeli public. The world pronounced the trial an event meant to right an historical wrong—the victims judging their executioners. I was beside myself. It was the first time I perceived the size of the horror. It was the first time I experienced the unbearable thought of what Oma and Opa, Raphael, Vera, Gabriel, my father Mordecai, and Rachel had been through. This stifling thought settled deep inside me and never let go. I listened and internalized hundreds of stories, but my own story was locked behind a hundred locks.

Then Will told me that of his entire family, he and his father were the only ones who had survived, thanks to his father's wise decision to escape Germany in time. He also told me how attached he had been to his maternal grandmother as a child.

I listened carefully, saying nothing. I thought about Ilse and Michael, whom I had never known, and did not think I could tell him about them.

He told me how he had lost his mother, about his early childhood in pre-war Berlin with a talented, melancholic father, and I listened sadly to every word.

I thought about my childhood in the brothel, about being orphaned of a father and sharing my life with a mentally frail mother, and said nothing.

He told me about his father's decision to leave Berlin two months after the Nazis rose to power, about the ship in which they traveled on their way to America, and about his social difficulties as an immigrant born to an immigrant, and I pitied his childhood.

I thought about the day Jonah appeared at the brothel, about the many trains we changed on our way from western Austria to

England, about London, which was full of people who spoke a language I did not know, and about our move to Israel. But even then, I did not understand that just like Will and the dozens of survivors who testified at the trial, I was a survivor of the Holocaust, and that even though I had not been through the concentration and death camps, I, too, had a story to tell.

And most of all, I did not understand what I comprehend now: how much relief there is in the ability to tell.

**

One summer morning, Will suggested we go to Safed to enjoy the cool weather. I prepared a few sandwiches wrapped in napkins with cheese spread and olives and placed them in a basket, wore a blue dress with white polka dots, and grabbed a white cardigan and a headscarf in case we visited a synagogue. When we arrived at the Independence Monument on the top of Citadel Hill, I sat down beneath the monument bearing the names of the fallen soldiers who were killed in the battle of 1948 while conquering the citadel. Will crouched down beside me.

I looked at him, his harsh face, his steely gray eyes, his aquiline nose, and his prematurely graying hair. He had a small red bandana tied around his neck like a cowboy in an American Western. We had met often during the months of the trial, but I had never dared ask him with whom he spent his time when he wasn't with me. He was the experienced thirty-six-year-old, who had already bit into life, and I was the twenty-year-old who was hungry for a taste. I never dared bring him home to Jonah and Ruth, and only Nurit knew I loved Will, and that despite everything I had been through last winter, I would have been relatively happy if our odd friendship had not continued to be so platonic.

The look he gave me was gentle yet broadcast strength. I spoke out.

"Will, the trial will be over soon, and you will leave. And then what's going to happen to me?"

He held my cheek tenderly and turned my face toward him.

"Helena," he said, "you're so beautiful..." I felt his breath on my face. "And sensitive and talented...but your soul is restless, and there are so many thoughts trapped inside of you."

I tried to figure out where this was going.

"You should write," he said then. "That is your calling."

I pushed him away. "Write?" I shouted. "Write?! That's my calling? Is that what you're proposing, Will?"

He said nothing.

"And what about you? Will you just keep coming and going, leaving me behind, confused, embarrassed, in love?"

He looked at me, surprised, and kept quiet. I was startled by my own words. Only two days earlier a journalist from *Ma'ariv* had whispered to me that Will had been married twice, and that he had cast aside both of his wives, heartbroken and childless. Will never told me about it, and I never asked. My face turned red. I cursed my embarrassing tendency to blush that I had inherited from my mother. I had never before confessed my love to him. What had I done? Would he get up and leave? Forever?

I bit my lips and held back pitiful tears. Anything but that.

Then he got up, took my arms gently, and stood me up on my feet.

"It's hard not to fall in love with you, Helena," he said.

I looked at him, confused.

Was this a confession?

"I'm trying to resist, and it isn't easy."

I was astounded, perplexed. I thought about Jonathan. Why did everyone I fell in love with have to stifle their love for me? Why was it always so complicated? I tried to settle my breath.

Then he said it, crystal clear. "It can't work out between us, Helena..."

I gaped.

"We're both on fire, and it's just too hot," he said. "Our bond is something completely different. Something different."

I trembled. I took two steps back. I refused to accept it.

"Helena, listen to me, please..." I thought I heard a plea in his voice. "You're so wounded right now," he said. "You are not available for romance. Let it go."

Let it go? I felt needles in my chest.

"But you can use this pain to write, to create," he continued. "You just don't have enough respect for your own talent."

I felt furious. "Write, Will? Write? My ability to write died along with Jonathan! It vanished when Mother swallowed pills and went to sleep forever and I wasn't there to stop her!"

He shook his head.

"I don't have that gift anymore, Will, don't you see?" I cried, tears beading in the corners of my eyes. "I hear things and see things, but everything is swirling around me. I don't care about anything! I don't know what to write about! I have nothing to say!"

Will walked closer. His hairy chest and his body odor made me feel faint. I fixed my eyes on the red bandana around his neck, but Will held onto my chin, lifted my head, and forced me to confront his eyes again. "Seeing things is not enough, Helena," he said. "You have to know how to examine and discern."

I bit my lip.

"You'll find a story behind every tree, a sentence on every leaf, a word on every flower, if you only let yourself linger for a bit, relax, and really observe."

My eyes filled with tears. "A tree, a leaf, a flower... what are you talking about? What stories will I find there? What is so important to me that I ought to try to write about it?!"

"Don't you see?" he asked.

I bit my lip again to stifle a sob that threatened to emerge. "No," I mumbled. "I don't see anything…"

Will grabbed my arms and shook me lightly. "Where have you been in the past few days, Helena? The past weeks? The past months?"

"I was with you," I stuttered.

"Where were you with me?" he yelled.

"At the courthouse in Jerusalem!" I yelled back. "I've been with you for months, sitting in front of a glass box, watching a man who speaks the language you and I were born into, a man who is responsible for the murder of my grandparents, for the fact that I never had a normal mother or a normal childhood!"

Will tightened his grip on my arms.

"Well, that is your tree, Helena," he said. "You may not know it yet, but you have a story."

***

Will left at the end of summer and returned in early winter to cover the reading of the verdict. Adolf Eichmann was convicted of all fifteen indictment charges.

***

On 1 June 1962, one day after Eichmann was hanged in the Ramla Prison, I began to write my first book, which won me a reputation as a writer, as well as an award for a debut novel.

Love in the Shadow of the Moon was a novel about the love of Uriel and Rachel in Europe of the 1930s, teeming with the chaos of the war. In describing Uriel, I made sure to insert whole sections about his love for Rachel exactly as they were conveyed to me by Naomi in her beautiful storytelling style. I wrote furiously about a great love severed in its prime the night the glass was shattered, after which Uriel was murdered while his lover was away on a secret mission.

I did not know the circumstances of Rachel's death, so I chose to invent them. My heroine was an active participant in the illegal immigration operation, who was captured and tortured in the basement of the Gestapo in Germany and sent to Auschwitz toward the end of the war. Adolf Eichmann was the one to sign the order. The book ended with the execution of the executioner, the cremation of his body, and the scattering of its ashes away from the territorial waters of Israel, the coast of which my protagonists were not lucky enough to explore.

I have never stopped writing since, and it changed my life.

It became my third eye, just like the camera was for Esther.

This all taught me one important lesson. When one is withdrawn from the world, into their own pain and grief, the world outside goes on without you. When things come to a halt in the circle of one's life and in one's soul, nothing goes stagnant out there. I learned that the sky does not fall. It stretches from one horizon to the other as usual, the sun and moon appearing daily at regular intervals.

I should have known that, as one who had survived the war.

Thanks to Will, Ruth, Nurit, Esther, and Davidi, I learned that life is stronger; that it goes on.

I was only twenty years old.

I chose life.

80

24 January 1991
Yosemite Park, California

Dear Davidi,

I had a bad dream last night. I dreamt about gray and black clouds. Jonathan was sailing alone in a small boat that swayed below the clouds like a dinghy in a stormy sea. I awoke at four in the morning, drenched in sweat.

I had a bad feeling. It was morning in Israel. I called Blair.

She has been spending the past few days picking oranges in an orchard near Kfar Saba. Since the laborers from the Arab city of Tira aren't working right now, there is a shortage of hands, and volunteers are needed. Every morning she rides in an open truck with other young people to the orchard, her gas mask hanging off her shoulder, and together they pick oranges and toss them into large bins.

She happened to be home when I called. She said she hadn't gone today but was about to go out with a friend.

I thought I was going to explode. I held back from yelling at her, why would she leave the house when she didn't have to? There are no sealed rooms outside! Blair chuckled when I mentioned the sealed room and said that when a missile lands on a building only God can save the people inside. Besides, she said, the Home Front Command had recently changed its orders, and now the public instruction is to try and reach an underground shelter within two minutes of the alarm, rather than retiring to the sealed room at home. The estimation is that Iraq will not be using unconventional warfare.

I tried to recall the appearance of the shelter in our building on Ben-Yehuda Street. The last time I saw it, the place was a mess, filled with old furniture the neighbors had tossed out. I asked her to try and stay near home, because shelters weren't available just anywhere.

I'm holding onto the not-too-well-founded feeling that our childhood home is relatively safe.

That, and the old oak tree downstairs.

Blair said there was no problem with leaving the home in the daytime. She said the Iraqis only shoot missiles at night, when the coalition's planes have trouble identifying the launchers. And so, in the mornings, the children go to school and the adults go to work, and everyone only comes home around six, when it gets dark outside.

A war's logic.

My throat began to bother me, and all at once it became a blaze.

I listened to her quietly, although inside of me everything was exploding. When she was finished, I told her I loved her and was very proud of her. So was her father, who had also volunteered in Israel during a time of war.

"It was in 1973," I said. "the Yom Kippur War."

When I hung up the phone, you were the first person on my

mind. I needed your hug, your soothing voice. I needed you to tell me what the hell I ought to do now, and if it would be a mistake to call home today, to speak to Mike.

I called that evening. I took into account that Mike might pick up.

But Roy did.

He was so cold to me, Davidi. So cold... I asked him if Mike was home, and he said he wasn't. Our conversation lasted less than two minutes.

Then Nelly came to the phone. I had no energy for more reproaches, but she was wonderful. She must have heard my broken voice, and her kind heart melted like butter. She said she worried about me like a mother. That everyone at home missed me very much. But this time she didn't ask when I was coming back.

The only one who asked was Abby. You should have heard her voice...so sweet and loving. Everything is simpler with her, mostly thanks to Nelly. She serves as a substitute mother to Abby and does everything she can to make this time easier on her. Abby knows I went away for this long to finish writing an important book. According to Nelly, they try not to mention the Gulf War or the missiles when she is around. Abby knows that Blair is there, and nobody wants to give her any further reason to feel anxious. When we spoke, I told Abby I would arrive in late February, in time for her birthday in March, so that we would have enough time to plan a party. The enthusiasm in her voice made roses blossom in my cheeks. Then I asked when Dad was going to be home. She said Dad wasn't feeling well, and that he stayed home today.

It's rare for Mike to feel ill, Davidi. It's even rarer for him to stay home. I wanted to cry. Roy lied to me, and Mike is sick.

After the conversation, I almost began to pack my things so I could head home. I even called to ask about the next flight to Atlanta. But I regretted it instantly. I decided not to go. My mission has not yet been completed, and there is no point in coming home a moment before it is.

Any mother, or perhaps most mothers, would have done everything in their power to get home in this kind of situation.

But I, as you know, am not most mothers.

And I'm still here.

If there's anyone in the world that can still understand me a little, it's you. Under these circumstances, even Nurit would find it difficult.

I miss you. I miss Blair. I miss everybody.

With much love,
Helena

81

2 February 1991
Yosemite Park, California

Dear Nurit,

I tried calling you several times in the past two days. I'm worried your home phone might be broken. I still don't have your number in your new place of work. Please call me. I have to know that you and the kids are all right and keeping sane.

I spoke to Blair today. She told me you've been continually in touch with her and even invited her to move in with you in the Jezreel Valley until things settled down. Thank you, Nurit. I would have been so happy if she had accepted your offer, but of course Blair refuses to leave Tel Aviv. She says every place is dangerous, perhaps except for Jerusalem, which the Iraqis seem to be overlooking because it contains so many holy Islamic sites.

At the end of our conversation, she asked me about Mike. It was the first time she addressed the rift between us. She said that as a little girl she always thought our relationship was one of a kind, the most beautiful bond she'd ever seen, and that nothing was missing from it. I smiled. I thought how lovely her naiveté is. I recalled the mounting silences between me and Mike, the many times his eyes begged me to open the closed chapters of my life to him. I also recalled that one-time slip (I hope it was only one time), and a bitter taste rose from my stomach.

I told Blair that Mike and I have a great love as well as mutual appreciation, but that our relationship isn't perfect. Although the bridge built between us is certainly beautiful and strong and would definitely be included in her list of silver bridges, or, at the very least, the emerald ones, a few foundations are still missing.

Then Blair asked me a question that melted my heart.

She asked if the missing foundations could be inserted after the bridge has already been standing for years.

I said nothing. I didn't have an answer. I sent her a kiss through the phone and quickly ended the conversation.

Yours,
Helena

California

82

My twenties took place in the 1960s. Searching for a direction. Striving for world peace and complete liberty. Love for all the world's creatures. The freedom to be different, think differently, and dress differently. The world belonged to the young. The revolution of drugs, free love, and rock-and-roll.

That phenomenon, which mostly skipped over Israel, did not skip over me. There was a simple explanation for this. I spent more than half of my twenties and the 1960s in America.

There were several reasons for this, some better than others, but one of them took precedence over all others.

Will.

Will didn't touch me until six years after we met. I was twenty-two at the time, and my book *Love in the Shadow of the Moon* had just come out. He asked me to send him the first copy in print. I made sure to pick up the first copy, wrote a dedication, and used the first money I made from publishing the book to buy a plane ticket.

I went to California, to see if it was anything like I had imagine, and to see Will. I simply appeared at his doorstep one morning, with a suitcase containing a few clothes, and the book in my hand. He happened to be home, and by chance he was alone. He opened the door slightly and took a moment to process my presence. Then he widened his eyes, his gaze swallowing me whole, like I was Little Red

Riding Hood and he was the wolf. He grabbed my hand and pulled me into a simple, frugal, messy, and foul-smelling apartment.

I handed him the book and said, "Mail call." He took the book, burst out laughing, and lifted me in his arms, leading me straight to the bedroom, where he dropped me on an unmade bed and tore off my clothes. I did not resist. I had waited six years for this moment to arrive. Now he got two for the price of one: me and my debut novel. The sheets smelled of sex, probably from the previous night. Oddly, that only aroused me more. I noticed some empty beer bottles around the bed. I did not yet know then that Will was an alcoholic.

I breathed heavily. Will was all over me and inside of me, moving with a wildness I had not yet encountered. I closed my eyes, loosened my muscles, and let him do with me as he pleased. I felt as if a vulture with a formidable wingspan was dangling me powerfully in his sharp beak.

After Will came, panting, he rolled over and lay on his back. He reached over toward the bedside table, his fingers searching for cigarettes and a matchbook. He lit two, one for himself, one for me. I watched the way he put the cigarette to his lips. He held it oddly, his forefinger wrapped around it. I held mine the way Mother used to, between two straight fingers. The fingers of his free hand fluttered over my breasts. The fingers of my free hand followed the path of the wrinkles lining his cheeks. I always thought they made him look manly and authoritative. Will watched me with his gray eyes, blowing smoke rings into the air. Suddenly, he put out his cigarette, then took mine and put it out too. With surprising speed, he rolled on top of me, held softly onto my wrists, and pinned them to the bed on the sides of my head. Our eyes met at almost no distance at all, our smoky breaths mingling in the air trapped between us. Then he slipped inside of me again and moved on top of me, making the bed shake, making my body quake, and with it all the desires and yearnings I had contained within me.

I stayed with him for two weeks, until he finished reading my book. His opinion was more important to me than that of an entire army of readers.

And he loved my book.

And he loved me.

***

We spent the following years alternating between Los Angeles and Tel Aviv. We spent lots of time together, but even more time apart. The Sixties' atmosphere of free thought and sexual permissiveness provided both of us with the appropriate backdrop for our lifestyles, and created for me a fertile ground for liberated, uninhibited writing about anything other than those subjects that I had bolted shut. I was swept into a way of life utterly different from the way I was raised. I took part in the revolution of young Americans and simultaneously became a celebrity of sorts in my own city. Tel Aviv of the 1960s was like a beautiful maiden: vivacious but innocent and lacking in experience. A kind of touching naiveté dwelled in its space. The culture of overseas travel was still young, and I, an Israeli and former soldier, who flew to America often even back then, became a kind of local attraction. *Love in the Shadow of the Moon* was translated into English, and my short stories were published in the new literary journal *Achshav—Now*—a platform for young writers. Reviews of my writing appeared in the literary supplements of the daily newspapers, and news of my personal life was prominent in gossip columns. These columns had me in torrid affairs with a theatre actor and a married senior military officer. They waxed hot over my romantic relationship with a Jewish-American writer and journalist who was sixteen years my senior, almost an entire generation. Whenever I read this news about myself, I either laughed or cried. Sometimes I had trouble finding myself in it. I continued to travel to California and tour American cities and towns, mostly on my own, not knowing that the country would soon become my home.

When I went to Los Angeles I mostly stayed at Will's, as long as there was not another specific female presence there. Other times, I stayed at hotels, and for a while even rented an apartment of my own. I matured and ripened. I became a woman. I drank up everything life offered, especially once I realized how helpful this habit was in repressing pain and distracting me from the things I wanted to forget. I made love and danced to rock-and-roll music. In Tel Aviv, I smoked cigarettes and in L.A., marijuana and hash. Sometimes, in moments of elation, I felt as if I was conquering the world, which smiled at me in those years.

Will loved the changes that took place in me. He once said that was how a writer ought to live: in the eye of the storm. We had a savage, survivalist, delightful, yet painful love. We loved and jabbed at each other endlessly. Will had many women in his life, and I even got a chance to meet some of them. I mostly looked the other way, taking heart in my faith that Will did not look at any of them the way he looked at me. But if I dared grumble about the presence of another woman in his life, Will would put his lips to my ear and whisper toxically that I had brought this upon myself.

"You grew up," he said, "and got closer. You made me touch you. You touched me... You ignored the warning signs... You didn't let me keep my distance, Helena. You didn't let me protect you from me..."

83

6 February, 1991
(This letter was thrown out)

Blair,

My beauty, in our last phone call I wanted to ask you who you're seeing, what kind of boys, but it seemed a little silly to ask something like that when missiles are launched every night. I just wanted to tell you to take care of yourself. There are so many dangers out there.

I know, you're a big girl, independent and free-spirited, but nevertheless...

When you were younger, you didn't take an interest in boys. You had a few close female friends but spent most of your free time alone in your room, reading books and writing poems. I loved going into your bedroom and sitting with you, only the two of us, just as I loved hearing your opinion about things. From a young age, you had deep thoughts about life, although at the time they were still dipped in plenty of naiveté and kindness. You loved giving to others and had a big heart and lots of love—to children, the elderly, to all of humanity, and, of course, animals.

Things turned around when you grew up. Puberty hit your

hard, with endless questions and quandaries. When I refused to talk, you insisted that Dad and Nelly give you answers. You began to pay attention to yourself, your appearance, tossed aside the books, the poetry, and the afterschool activities, and looked for excitement outside of the house. When I tried to get closer to you and figure out what you were going through, you pulled away and withdrew, as if behind a wall of briars.

I, Blair, am the last person who can complain about other people's scratches. I have so many.

And yet.

I was afraid you would lose your direction. That like many other people your age, you would fall into drugs and alcohol, those cursed addictions. I know how bad they are, because I've been there. I've seen them kill a man I loved. I know for certain that you've dabbled, even though you denied it.

We took it hard, Dad especially. We had a difficult time understanding how our good, pretty, and smart child could drown her innocence in glasses of booze. Dad fought you like a lion. You were headstrong, protecting your independence, but he was much more stubborn than you. With time, you used your common sense and internalized the dangers. You chose to pull away and to detach yourself from bad company.

I was very proud of your father and the way he managed this battle against you, which was nothing but easy.

I wasn't as strong. I tried to speak to your heart and saw it harden. I wanted to understand where your obstinance came from, what that prickly wall was made of.

Then, in a single moment, it hit me like an epiphany.

I realized you suspected what I had been hiding from you for years.

I don't know how it happened—whether you investigated, or whether somebody told you something.

At that point, I decided it was time to tell. I gathered my courage and went up to your room. My heart was pounding. I was holding a package the size of a shoebox, wrapped in reddish brown paper and tied with two bows of yellow raffia...

84

In early April of '67, I was invited to come to the United States and give a series of lectures on my most recent book, *The Binding of Moses*. Two months earlier, Jonah had a heart attack, and a week later he passed away. I lamented his death bitterly and parted with another significant piece of my life. On the 30-day anniversary of his death I stood at his graveside, reading a poem I wrote to *The Man with the Blue Hat*, who had been like a father to me. Ruth and Esther, as always, were my rock, and Davidi was my ear and shoulder. When I was invited to lecture, Ruth insisted that I go, returning as quickly as possible to my routine.

At one of the lectures, given in a Jewish Community Center in Chicago, an old Jewish man asked about the most recent tension in the Middle East. I was unprepared for this question but realized that, being an Israeli writer, I was perceived as an unofficial representative of my country. The old man was probably referring to the aerial incident in which Israeli Air Force jets intercepted six Syrian fighter jets, some of them over Damascus. I focused my efforts on offering a suitable answer. "This tension is nothing new," I finally said. "It originates from a war over water. Syria has been attempting for some years to divert the natural direction of the water of the Jordan River away from the State of Israel. Israel has been forced to take action to prevent this."

After an exhausting week, I took a break and went to New

Hampshire alone, informing no one of my whereabouts. My mind was preoccupied with thoughts about Will's cool attitude on the phone the night before I came to the United States. I was so focused on my own affairs and so detached, that I was completely unaware of the arrival of high-ranking Egyptian delegations for consultations in Syria, the further incitement of the area by the Soviets, and the fact that while I was touring the White Mountains of New Hampshire and learning that the state's symbols were the purple lilac and the white birch tree, the Egyptian army was plotting to spill its forces onto the yellow sands of the Sinai Peninsula.

I found out all this only after landing in Los Angeles and arriving at the hall where I was slated to give a talk about my book, at a synagogue whose name I cannot recall. Will came to hear my talk. He sat there in the large audience, and even from the stage, as I was speaking, I could feel the restlessness in his body. After I finished talking and answering a couple dozen questions, I finally stepped out into the entry hall, exhausted, to find him waiting for me, even more exhausted than I was.

We stood before each other, two fatigued individuals. I had not seen Will in several months. He was not looking good. He had lost weight, his face even narrower and pointier than usual, and the thin wrinkles I used to love were now venerable cracks through his cheeks, which were sunken, red, and rough like orange peels. The look in his eyes scared me. They were blood-red, piercing me with their sharp steel gaze.

He asked me where I was heading next. I replied that a driver was waiting for me outside to take me to a hotel. This time, I said, I had chosen a hotel farther from the center of town. An older person approached us. He thanked me for the talk, shook my hand and Will's, and told me that when he was young he had spent some years in Israel, even taking part in the breaking open of the road to Jerusalem during the 1948 War. "I truly hope another war doesn't start soon," he said before he left.

I fixed my eyes on Will.

"You don't look well."

He said nothing.

"You aren't feeling well, are you?"

He continued to say nothing.

"Will?!"

He said everything was fine and asked that we only meet up the following day.

I felt hurt. The following day seemed very far away, and when it arrived, Will stayed remote. I should have packed my things and returned to Israel back then, but I ended up choosing to stay in California until the summer, when I finally realized how bad Will's drug and alcohol addiction was.

Things deteriorated from that point on. Will smoked a pipe, cigarettes, and marijuana, and drank unconscionable amounts of alcohol. He woke up late, barely wrote a thing, and went out to pubs and clubs at night, some of them awfully shady. He often treated me crudely, other times ignoring me altogether. He felt up the breasts of women in nightclubs right in front of me. I pondered the difference between the elation I felt during my lecture tour, and the wretchedness that had taken over me now.

Was this the same man I had loved so much?

I felt hurt and angry, confused and perplexed, but also worried and anxious.

After all, this was Will. Will Adler. "The other." He took up such a large space in my heart, and I could not just allow our bond to die. I recalled his stories about his talented and melancholy father, and about how he had ended his life, sick and addicted to drink.

I was mad with worry.

I stayed.

***

In the meantime, the real drama was unfolding back home. In mid-May, in a sudden decision, the Egyptians closed the Straits of Tiran, blocked the Suez Canal, by positioning a few barge bridges alongside it, and poured large land forces onto the Sinai Peninsula. Syria, Iraq, and Jordan were preparing for war, and Israel began an extensive reserve force recruitment. Tens of thousands of high school students were tasked with digging ditches, filling sandbags, distributing pamphlets to civilians, and handing out mail. The Civil Guard was regrouped, and arrangements were made for the supply of vital services in case of emergency. Bomb shelters were cleaned and renovated, and special units were established for the evacuation of wounded and the dead if buildings should collapse due to aerial bombing.

On the morning of Monday, 5 June, the waiting period ended with a surprise attack by the Israeli Air Force on Egyptian Air Force bases, in which the IDF destroyed most of the Egyptian planes while still on the ground. In a phone call to Irit, made on the second day of the war, I learned that Gidi and his troops had been sent to the Jordanian front. In a second phone call, to Ruth, I could practically smell the fear.

Will asked me to pack my things and move into his apartment, and I, despite how hurt and out-of-place I felt, did so the very same day, because I simply could not handle all the stress on my own.

"If anything happens to Gidi," I cried, "it will be the end of our family."

We were unable to pull ourselves away from the news. Will had a direct contact with an American colleague who was staying at the Neot Midbar Hotel in Beersheba, which had become the headquarters of the foreign press. This man said he had seen Winston Churchill's grandson at the hotel bar, speaking to British attaché Rex Harrison Morris. The next day, the grandchild of my childhood hero was quoted in the *Yedioth Ahronoth* newspaper under the headline, "Things Are Bad." The Jewish Agency came out with a heartfelt call to the Jewish people over the world to volunteer for the battle and the never-ending fight for the survival of the State of Israel. The Jewish spirits in America awoke to action. In a single day, thousands of telegrams arrived at the White House and the congress, asking US officials, House members, and senators to help Israel. Israeli consulates were overcome with young Jews and former Israelis who wanted to travel to Israel right away, volunteer in the military and do needed work on kibbutzim.

Concern for the continued existence of Israel affected Will in an unexpected way. In the many hours Will and I spent at home, insane levels of adrenaline flowed through our veins. We slept little and made love to the beat of the news: savage, aching, liberating sex. For a brief period, he quit drinking. He wanted to stay sober. In that sense, it was a wonderful time—the old desire was enkindled between us as war burned across the ocean.

The next course of events exceeded our highest expectations. Within three days of fighting on the Jordanian fronts, IDF forces took over the entire West Bank and East Jerusalem. Gidi took part in the persistent fighting of the paratrooper reserve brigade in the outskirts of the Old City and through its narrow alleys. He was there with his soldiers, at the foot of the Al-Aqsa Mosque, when the brigade commander, Mordechai Motta Gur, cried into the radio those historical words: "The Temple Mount is in our hands!" Gidi was standing so close to Motta that he heard the words coming straight from his mouth. I remember those seven words because Irit called in the middle of the night to tell us. She repeated the words to us several times, igniting a flame in our hearts, our chests bursting with pride.

In the meantime, the fighting went on. On the fourth day, the IDF completed the occupation at the Egyptian front of the Sinai

Peninsula, and on the last two days of fighting, it seized most of the strategic points of the Golan Heights and Mount Hermon from Syria. Six days of war ended with one great Israeli victory.

In the days that followed, I wandered the streets of Los Angeles, proud as a peacock for the victory of my "David" country over several "Goliath" armies, a victory which would soon be commemorated in a series of albums in velvet covers. In a letter I sent to the offices of the *Los Angeles Times*, I wrote that the city of film, which had given birth to *The Longest Day*, *The Caine Mutiny*, and *The Bridge on the River Kwai*, had a lot to learn from this lightning war, for, as we could all see, in this case, reality surpassed the imagination. The local newspapers found me to be an attractive interviewee, almost as young and promising as the country I had come from. In those interviews, I lamented the hundreds of dead and celebrated the joy of resistance, survival, and resurrection.

In each and every interview, I told Gidi's story.

"Gidi is a commander in a paratrooper reserve brigade," I said. "He is my cousin, but we were raised as siblings. Gidi has lost many of his soldiers in the war, and it is so awful that I can hardly bear it. But he was there when history bowed down to reality, making the dream of so many generations come true. He was there when the brigade commander, Motta Gur, announced to the world, "The Temple Mount is in our hands." He was there when the Chief Rabbi of the IDF, Rabbi Goren, arranged a makeshift ceremony outside the Western Wall and blasted the shofar again and again, beside himself with joy. He was there when the rabbi said the prayer of *El Maleh Rachamim* for the souls of the dead. He sang "Hatikvah" with everyone else, and "Jerusalem of Gold," which was written shortly before the war. Then my brave cousin, as the rest of his paratrooper friends, walked over to the Western Wall and touched his fingers and lips to the stones of the wall. They stood there, tired and dusty fighters after a battle, crying real tears...

"Can you imagine what that looks like?" I asked each one of my interviewers, "when paratroopers cry?"

Will and I went to Israel at the end of June and climbed up the Temple Mount with the masses of people, of all ages and social classes, who, just like us, crowded through the narrow alleys of the Old City on the way to the Western Wall plaza, to see, process, and internalize the miracle that had occurred. Two floodlights erected on half-tracks illuminated the Al-Aqsa Mosque and the Dome of the Rock. Will and I pushed our way through to touch our fingers and lips to the large, bare, hewn stones of the wall, out of whose fissures poked wild capers. For a short time, we were immersed in the euphoria that had taken over everyone, as if no cracks had opened between us.

***

But this all changed in the early fall. Will regressed. He smoked and drank, he hurt me and everyone else he cared about, and worst of all, he hurt himself. Despite Davidi, Ruth, and Nurit's pleas for me to leave him and not to waste the finest years of my life on such a painful relationship, I refused to jump ship. I continued to divide my life between Tel Aviv and Los Angeles in the following years, remaining by his side in his time of need. Will went in and out of rehabilitation centers, and I tried my best to always be there when he was released.

Things were very hard when he was "out." My older lover neglected his work as a journalist and sunk into a bitter depression. He published only one short story, entitled "The Bitter Life of an Alcoholic." With me, he had poignant conversations about his life, his minor accomplishments, and, most of all, his great regrets. I tried countless times to save him from himself and failed each time anew.

By the end, we were both extremely exhausted.

I left California in the winter of 1971, the month I turned thirty.

But I only left after making sure Will was sober, on his feet, and in good hands.

Exactly two weeks after I met her.

85

Her name was Monica-Paula Martinez. She was born in Colombia to a teenage boy and girl. Her middle name, Paula, was added by her father when she turned three, to commemorate her young mother, who had just died. She came as a child to California with her father. He did not speak much about her mother, or anything else, for that matter. She had no mementos from her mother other than three wooden figurines of praying nuns that were always on her bedside table and a single photograph from her parents' wedding, which had been held hastily just before she was born. Monica-Paula also had a dim memory of her mother, which had dulled further with the years, as well as having the knowledge of native blood running through her veins, from her maternal grandfather's side.

Monica-Paula's father enlisted into the American military in the 1960s to acquire an American citizenship; that is, not out of ideals or due to a fighting spirit. He had nothing of the sort, neither as a child nor as an adult, and especially after his young wife was killed in a car accident while he drove. Her family blamed him for her death, and he was forced to flee to America and live there for a few years, always fearful, as an illegal immigrant. In August '65, at the age of thirty-one, he joined the Marines and was shipped to Vietnam, one of the older soldiers to be sent over. Before he left, he put fourteen-year-old Monica-Paula in a boarding school in a Catholic convent. He was not a poetic man, and his daughter did not know how he had heard of this custom, but before he left he gave her a yellow ribbon printed with the lyrics to a popular American War tune: "'Round her neck she wore a yellow ribbon, for her soldier who was far, far away." Then, this taciturn man told her that if she ever missed him, she could wear the yellow ribbon around her neck as a sign of solidarity with him and the other fighters at the front.

He was flown to his overseas base and took part in Operation Starlite, the first purely American major land offensive in Vietnam, as well as a few other, smaller operations. After each one, he wrote a letter of few words to his daughter. The entire time, Monica-Paula wore the yellow ribbon, concealed under a nun's white collar, around her neck, and said a prayer for the safety of her father and the other soldiers every night.

In December of 1967, she received the last letter from him. It was a Christmas and New Year's Eve card, in which he announced that he was about to be released and would arrive back in America in February, right before her seventeenth birthday. Monica-Paula was excited and wrote her father a response he never received. She included a New Year's greeting but did not tell him that almost a year earlier, right after her sixteenth birthday, she had decided to leave the boarding school at the convent since she was no longer able to take the strict discipline and daily routine, the countless prayers and the stuffy air in her small room. She did not tell him that she was attending nursing school and had already found work at a small, local hospital, as an auxiliary employee, filling in a few shifts a week. She did not tell him that just a few nights earlier she had helped give a sponge bath to a wounded soldier who had been flown home from Vietnam, and by the time she returned to see him the next morning, his bed was empty.

On the night of 30 January 1968, Monica-Paula's father died in the Tet Offensive. He was killed in the early hours of the operation and did not get a chance to see the South Vietnamese Army, assisted by

American forces, partially push back the combined sudden attack of the Viet Cong and the people's army of north Vietnam. Monica-Paula's last letter to her father was returned to her along with his personal effects.

She was an orphan at age seventeen.

When Monica-Paula was twenty years old, she began working as a nurse at a large hospital in Los Angeles and was placed in the internal medicine ward where Will was hospitalized with an acute liver infection. His short story, "The Bitter Life of an Alcoholic," which had been recently published, made its way into her hands and touched her heart. In her free time, she visited the public library and read all of his writings. She felt that in this way she knew him well. She wanted so badly for him to get better. She circled his bed, bathed him, and placed moist towels on his forehead when he burned with fever. When he was awake, she spoke to him softly and offered her warm, angelic smile.

That had a therapeutic power. Will was on his feet within a month.

By the time he was discharged, he was already in love.

***

Wrapped in our winter jackets, just the two of us, Will told me openly about Monica-Paula as we sat on a bench overlooking the ocean on the Santa Monica Beach. He was sober, calmer and more clearheaded than I had seen him in a long time. He explained what I already knew: that our love was too wild and that we had best go our separate ways before we caused each other any more pain. When he spoke about Monica-Paula, a tenderness I was not familiar with took over his voice and his steel gaze softened. "She's very young," he said, "but impressively mature, with a warm, loving personality and a rare peace of mind."

I cried and cried, and he held me close and rocked me in his arms.

I recalled something Davidi had once told me, after he had separated from his wife Veronique.

"Sometimes," he said, "you have to know when to give up and leave...especially when you love somebody and know they need something you simply can't give them." Veronique wanted children and Davidi refused. He was unswerving opposite the tears of the woman he loved, and because he loved her, he let her go so that she might carry the baby of another man.

Will needed this peace that I could not give him. Perhaps because when I was around him everything within me tossed and turned.

He had found somebody he loved. Somebody who had the peace I did not.

He looked healthy, happy, recovered.

I loved him with all my heart. I knew it was time to let go, to move on.

I asked Will to meet Monica-Paula once before I left. We met at a small restaurant by the ocean. It was raining outside, but pleasant and warm inside. Monica-Paula was pretty and looked younger than twenty. She wore a white, long-sleeved dress that accentuated her dark skin, and had a flower in her braid. She had a round face, big eyes, long dark lashes, a straight nose, a wide mouth, and a gorgeous smile. Despite my feelings toward Will, I liked her exotic look, the way she tilted her head, the way her small hands played with her braid, the pleasant quiet she spread around her, and her warm, velvety voice.

She had the sadness of an orphan.

In fact, all three of us were orphans.

We sat together for three hours, talking. I forgot about how young she was. And without even noticing, I was captivated by my beloved's lover.

Just like Will, I too needed that rare peace she emanated, the kind I had never had.

86

I visited Will and Monica-Paula in California once more during that year. Monica-Paula had begun the process of converting to Judaism, and Will had already put a ring on her finger. The wedding ceremony was modest, and I was one of the only guests. Will wore faded jeans and a white button-down with a striped tie, and Monica-Paula wore a white dress with spaghetti straps that emphasized her thin frame and white leather sandals. Her long, raven-black hair was done in dozens of thin braids, tiny white flowers intertwined in it, and a floral tiara crowned her head.

Will did not look good. In the seven months since I had last seen him, his health had deteriorated again. Monica-Paula had told me in a recent letter that he was very tired and had lost his appetite. That was why she had wanted to expedite the wedding plans. I, she said, was the guest of honor.

I stood there, gazing at the two of them, and my eyes filled with tears.

Will looked feeble and old, although he just turned forty-six. Next to him, Monica-Paula looked like a pretty flower girl, with her thin body, her smooth skin, her flowing hair, and the lightness with which she danced around him, enveloping him with her warm, radiant smile.

At the end of the ceremony they exchanged vows, Will stepped on a glass, and took Monica-Paula in his arms. When his lips touched hers, his eyes sought me out.

I smiled at him, putting my hand on my heart and blowing him a kiss, and he raised his right hand, the one with the wedding ring, to signal that he had seen.

***

It was Monica-Paula who did not allow the special knot between us to unravel. She said it was rare to find your soulmate in this world, and that once you do, you can never let them simply disappear from your life. Will and I accepted her words silently. We both knew the love between us would live forever, even if its shape shifted.

And that what we had was different, strange even.

It was something else.

***

Will and I never discussed his desire to have children, but Monica-Paula and I talked about it many times, especially after she found out she had that disease.

"Primary pulmonary hypertension," Monica-Paula explained. "That is high blood pressure in the arteries leading blood to the lungs and heart. It's unclear why it developed." She saw the shock on my face and added that it was livable, but the part that was hardest for her was the knowledge that a pregnancy could put her life at risk. Nevertheless, she emphasized, it was possible. It would be a high-risk pregnancy and would require close medical observation. But she was willing to take the risk. She was willing to do anything to have a child with Will.

I remember crying on the inside, although on the outside I tried to appear strong. Monica-Paula, the compassionate nurse, the beautiful, vivacious flower child, so young...and a child with Will...

A child with Will…

"The problem is," Monica-Paula interrupted my thoughts, "is that Wilhelm is resisting."

It was the first time I saw her crying. She fixed her green, moist, almond-shaped eyes on me.

"Please," she begged, "speak with him."

***

I asked him to meet me on the bench on Santa Monica Beach, overlooking the ocean, just him and me. I talked to him about having a child, about the new horizons it would open to him, about great love, responsibility, and the circle of life.

Will admitted he did not feel the need to be a father. In different circumstances, he might have accepted it, but not now that her illness had been discovered. He did not want to put Monica-Paula at risk, he said. He was not willing to lose her. But when he saw her fighting spirit, he backed off a little and suggested they adopt a South American child, maybe even from Colombia.

"But she is so stubborn," he said, his eyes sad and tired. "She insists that we have our own child. Her stubbornness is touching."

I looked at him and grew silent. My eyes caressed his pointy profile, his wrinkles, his left eye, which had narrowed into a small slit under his bushy eyebrow, and his aquiline nose. I rubbed the back of his hand and the round, smooth wedding band around his finger.

I told him I was worried about her, too, and that I did not know what the right thing was to do, but I knew that she would not give up.

I felt something strange inside.

I did not want her to give up.

When we got up to leave, I linked my arm with his and we walked together up the path that led from the beach to the paved road above.

87

Monica-Paula did not give up. Her stubbornness just grew stronger. Her dream came true when she finally got pregnant but, nevertheless, her happiness was burdened by weighty concerns. Three months later, Will's condition worsened. He had symptoms of fatigue and loss of appetite, and he lost much of his weight.

In an emotional letter, Monica-Paula informed me that Will was diagnosed with cirrhosis of the liver. The damage, she wrote, was caused years earlier, probably due to excessive alcohol consumption.

I was very worried. About her and about him. I put everything else aside and went to California. I was going there to help but found myself receiving help and mostly moved by Monica-Paula's indomitable spirit, as she belittled her own pregnancy challenges and breathing difficulties to care for Will, trying to evaporate his grumpy mood and fight his growing tendency toward depression.

I stayed in California, eventually renting an apartment. I wrote every day but spent most of my time with Monica-Paula and Will. Will's condition deteriorated as Monica-Paula's belly grew and the fetus in her uterus developed. A month after my arrival, Will was admitted to the hospital, to the same ward where they had met. His liver cells were ruined. Afterward, his liver shrunk, and he contracted jaundice. I visited him at the hospital daily, spending hours sitting by his side. I asked Monica-Paula to minimize her visits due to her condition. I thought the hospital was no place for a pregnant woman, unless she was in the maternity ward. But Monica-Paula was a hospital nurse. She did not listen. She came twice a day—once early in the morning, to open the curtains in Will's room and let some light into his life, and another time in the evening, to make sure he was being treated properly and taking his medication on time. When Monica-Paula came into the room, her smile would melt the iron around his heart, and a light returned to his eyes. Occasionally, momentarily, he even managed to smile. I would look at her with wonder as she removed her sandals, placed her two hands on her belly, and began swaying on the floor of the narrow room between Will's bed and the surrounding empty ones, dancing and humming a song or a prayer to the fetus in her uterus. Then Will would smile languidly, reach over and touch her belly, as if searching for a sign of life in there, his gray, steely eyes turning red and moist with tears, and the two of us would rush to his side and take his large hands in ours, and my heart would be torn.

***

One afternoon, I was alone with him. Soaked in pain and medication, Will slept most of the time, and I was sitting on a small chair beside him, writing in my notebook. His jaundice had gotten worse recently. He suffered edema, bleeding, and nausea.

Suddenly, he called my name. "Helena," he whispered, "my beautiful Helena…"

His eyes were red, his face yellow.

"Will!" I stood up.

He had trouble speaking, and I rubbed his hand to calm him down.

"Please, Will, rest. It's hard for you to speak right now. Do it later, in a little bit…"

But he hushed me with a sharp hand gesture.

He spoke quietly, almost whispering. His body was broken and exhausted. He apologized for having hurt me before and said he had loved me from the day he had met me.

I listened.

Will fell silent and, for several moments, seemed to sink into a hallucination. When he shook himself awake, he looked at me intently and confessed again that his life had been made up of small accomplishments and big regrets. He did not explain what he meant, but, after a minute of silence, he said that his biggest regret would be not being able to hold his child, if he or she were ever born.

I sat there beside his bed in a hospital that overlooked an unattractive view, rubbed his arms, and examined his face lovingly. I knew our day of parting was drawing near. When he sighed, I adjusted the pillow under his head and dabbled his chapped lips with a moist towel. I smoothed his forehead and perused his bushy eyebrows and his vulturine nose, which made him look manly and authoritative even now, and ran the tip of my finger through the wrinkles in his cheeks. From time to time, in moments of wakefulness, his gray steely eyes fixed on me. I looked straight back, my gaze diving into his eyes as they never had before. I saw inside of him, as if he had become transparent to me. The words flowed between us soundlessly. I promised with my eyes to take care of his beloved Monica-Paula. I promised voicelessly to hug his child for him when he or she was born.

If he or she were ever born.

***

Monica-Paula arrived that evening. Her hair was in two low braids behind her ears, and a small flower wreath crowned her head. She breathed heavily, her face pale. She looked at me and took a seat beside Will, touched his cheeks, his lips, and his hand, which was cold. When she closed her eyes, she mumbled a prayer. I was not sure if it was a Jewish prayer, a private one, or perhaps a hymn she had learned in the convent as a girl.

I held her small, cold hand in one of mine, and Will's larger hand in the other. Monica-Paula took his other hand, and the three of us formed a circle.

Monica-Paula linked her fingers with his and kissed them. She whispered to me, between an inhale and an exhale, that this was the day we would be saying goodbye. She had seen it in her dream.

My face paled like a ghost's.

Will's eyes opened suddenly, fixing on her. I think I saw a spark of light in them. Monica-Paula gave him her warm smile, came closer, and kissed his lips softly. Then she told him, still smiling, that she had had a dream.

I felt the blood leaving my body. I was afraid of what she was about to tell him.

But she told him a different part of the dream.

"Tonight, I dreamt that our pregnancy will be carried to term," she said, smiling between her tears. "A full nine months…" As her voice cracked, she continued, "We will have a child from you, Wilhelm, flesh of your flesh, blood of your blood."

Did she say "we" or did I imagine that?

88

14 February 1991
(This letter was thrown out)

Blair,

My beautiful, I remember that when I gave you that package, wrapped in reddish brown paper, you were sitting on the bed in your room, your arms around your knees, your chin resting on top of them.

You asked me what was in the box, and I said that your father and I had something to tell you.

Something important.

I suspect you already knew, although you had never admitted it.

You did not try to make it easier on me, and I understand that completely.

Dad walked in, and the two of us sat across from you, Dad on a chair and I on the edge of the bed.

Then we told you for the first time who your real parents were.

89

That night, we said goodbye to Will.

I'm choosing not to depict the course of that night.

I prefer to spare the details, especially from myself.

Will was buried the next day in the Forest Lawn Memorial Park in Los Angeles, a manicured cemetery that houses the graves of several writers and artists, some of their headstones decorated with reproductions of famous works of art. Throughout the entire funeral, Monica-Paula and I stood, holding hands, among the many mourners, who included old friends, colleagues, and even some of Will's former lovers. Most of them were strangers to Monica-Paula and to myself.

The two of us were the only family he had had.

Somewhat paradoxically, thanks to her, I managed to get over the death of my lover.

Monica-Paula gave me the power to do so through her unique, robust spirit and the weakness of her body. Her dream of carrying her pregnancy to term, despite her severe lung condition, and to give birth to Will's child became our shared dream.

Monica-Paula was admitted to the internal medicine ward two months after the funeral, due to severe shortness of breath. Thanks to her position as a hospital nurse, she received a private room, with an attached bathroom and a pretty view. She spent her third trimester under very close monitoring.

More than once, when I came to see her, I found her connected to an oxygen tank, but when she saw me walking in, she always smiled.

In April '72 her daughter was born in a C-section, at ten past five, at dawn.

90

15 February 1991
(This letter was thrown out)

Blair,

When the nurse told me it was a girl, I was stunned. We always expected Monica-Paula to have a son who would bear Will's name, maybe even look a bit like him…

But the shock faded the moment I saw you.

I was the first to lay eyes on you. Monica-Paula was still under sedation.

You had yellowish olive skin, black hair, and narrow eyes, matchstick legs, skinny arms, tiny fingers, and a button nose.

I couldn't stop the tears. They just came, in droves.

They were tears of happiness.

91

Monica-Paula chose the name.

Blair Martinez Adler.

She arranged a pretty room for Blair in Will's old apartment. She painted the walls a light peach and hung pictures of Winnie-the-Pooh, Tigger, Eeyore, and Piglet. On the floor, she spread a rug in shades of orange and green, and scattered toys in the corners. She sang Blair songs and told her about her father, and about castles, princesses, and bears.

I left them only five months later, after Will's estate was settled, we had found a nanny for Blair—a Mexican girl named Angelica—and after Monica-Paula went back to work part-time. That is, after I made sure they were managing okay. I returned to my Tel Aviv apartment—to writing, to my friends and to my old habits.

But my heart remained there. I worried about Monica-Paula. I was afraid her disease might get worse. I missed the baby, and I missed Will.

Five months later, I received an urgent call from Angelica. She spoke broken English peppered with Spanish. It was hard to understand. The baby was sobbing in the background. I was in California three days later. Monica-Paula was pale and exhausted. She was suffering a quickened pulse and severe shortness of breath. Dark circles surrounded her eyes, and her lips were blue. I admitted her to the hospital that same night. The test results showed a clear narrowing of the blood vessels in her lungs. The blood pressure in her lungs had risen, her heart was having trouble flowing blood through her respiratory system, and the oxygen levels had dropped. After the hospital staff was able to stabilize her, Monica-Paula came home but did not return to work as a nurse. In their apartment, she insisted on caring for Blair herself as much as she could. She worked hard to feed, bathe, and dress the child, and even push the stroller through the nearby park.

When Blair turned one, we threw her a small birthday party. We were only Monica-Paula, two of her nurse friends, Angelica, and me. Blair's room was decorated with pink and white balloons and ribbons; Monica-Paula placed a small floral crown on Blair's head; Angelica made fajitas, churros, guacamole, and fresh tortillas, and I baked a birthday cake in the shape of a butterfly.

Two weeks earlier, Monica-Paula's test results pointed to scarring in her lungs. Her right ventricle had trouble flowing blood to her lungs through her damaged blood vessels, and she suffered from heart failure. The doctors told Monica-Paula she only had a few months to live.

On the evening after the birthday party, Monica-Paula called me into her room. The disease had ravaged her. Her pretty face was so pale that her olive eyes seemed to grow darker. She asked me to sit beside her on the bed, Will's bed, and then slowly opened the drawer of her bedside table, and pulled out some files, bound in a cardboard folder. It was a draft of a will, and it said that she would be leaving all her assets and the assets of her deceased husband to their only daughter, Blair.

She asked me for three things.

The first, simplest request, was to keep for Blair one copy of everything Will ever wrote.

The second, most complicated of the three, was to care for Blair.

92

16 February 1991
(This letter was thrown out)

Blair,

It was so obvious I was going to say yes. It's hard to explain, but I always felt as if you had also come from me, as if you were a shared creation by Will, Monica-Paula, and myself.

Your mother asked, with barely any air left in her lungs, that I care for you. For her and for Will. She wrote it clearly in her will and signed it in front of two witnesses.

She trusted me and loved me. She said she knew that with me you would be in good hands.

Oh, Blair, my child.

If you only knew how tormented I've been ever since. I'm tortured by the thought that I might have pushed her to take that step. That perhaps, if I had stood by Will's side, we could have persuaded her to let go of her notion of getting pregnant, which put her in so much risk. I knew it was dangerous. I had spoken to her doctor, and had heard him explicitly say the words, "life-threatening pregnancy".

But nevertheless.

I supported her decision.

I got carried away with her dream of "us" having a child from Will.

I know your mother's stubbornness was like a flame. I know that if she had given up, you would never have been born.

But I also know, with perfect clarity, that I had no right to intervene.

And that when I voted in favor of the creation of a new life, I participated in the almost certain destruction of another, precious life.

And I feel sick; so, so sick.

93

Monica-Paula's third request was that I give Blair a package from her when the time came.

She pulled out dozens of letters, covered in tight rows of small, pretty, orderly handwriting, she had written to the daughter she knew she would never get to raise. In them, she unfolded her life story from as early as she could remember to the moment of Blair's birth. She recounted the story of her father who never returned from the war, leaving her orphaned, and the tale of her love for Will, intertwining her stories with thoughts, musings, and lines from poems she liked. She also wrote a letter, in which she listed all the books she loved, including everything Will had ever written. She put the letters in envelopes and arranged them by ascending date. Into a separate manila envelope, she slipped the picture of her parents on their wedding day, a picture of her father in uniform, holding a rifle, and about a dozen other photographs of Will and herself, of me with her, and of her with Blair.

After she showed me all of this, she felt weak and out of breath, and sat limply on her bed, leaning back against the pillow to get some air. She was suffering dizziness and nausea. I suggested we connect her to the oxygen and helped her slip the tube into her nose. Her black hair was spread over the pillow, a dark frame for her pale face and blue lips. While trying to fight back tears, I stroked her hand gently.

I asked her to rest, but she insisted on talking.

She had something to tell me.

"You know what the hardest thing is, Helena?" she asked. "What scares me more than anything? I'm scared to think that Blair won't know me. I told her lots of things in the letters, but she won't be able to hear my voice in them or see my face… She'll never know I used to play with my hair when I spoke…"

I looked at her, as if mute.

The next day, I called a friend of Will's who worked at a television studio. He managed to schedule twenty minutes of studio time for her. When the day arrived, I helped her bathe and get dressed. She wore a green dress, a shell necklace, and a white flower in her flowing, black hair. She asked the makeup artist to give her wan cheeks some color and cover the blue hue of her lips with red lipstick.

Monica-Paula sat up in the chair and looked straight into the camera's lens. The first thing she said was that the day Blair was born was the happiest day of her life. Then she spoke to Blair for fifteen minutes, raising her hands into the air, tilting her head, and playing with her hair as she spoke. She smiled, laughed, and cried. Once, she lowered her eyes, let her hair fall on her face, and asked the camera operator to stop recording.

In the last minutes allotted to her, she chose to teach Blair how to make Indian braids, just as she liked to. She got down on her knees, sat up straight, and demonstrated how she braided her long hair into two thick braids with the rapid movement of her fingers.

"First, comb your hair carefully, and make sure there are no knots. Then make a straight part with a comb and divide the hair into two equal parts."

Then she turned her back to the camera, and her voice was only heard in the background.

"Braid each part, starting below the ear."

But when, her back still to the camera, she said, "Half a pinky above the end of the braid, gather the hair with a dark or colorful rubber band," it was possible to hear her voice break in one single moment.

And when she concluded with the words, "You can put beads, pebbles, or even a flower in your hair," you could clearly see her shoulders—now bare after having braided her hair—shaking.

By the time filming ended she was completely spent. She was bedridden for an entire week, intermittently connected to the oxygen tank. At her request, I placed a tape recorder and six hour-long tapes on Will's desk. When she recovered a bit, she moved to the armchair and recorded herself speaking. She told Blair the stories she did not get a chance to write down in her letters and read out loud some things Will had written her. She also read carefully chosen children's stories and sang songs in a voice that grew hoarse and cracked by coughs.

At some point, Monica-Paula refused the many medications she was prescribed. I bought her a decorated cardboard box, inside which she arranged the letters and the tapes in ascending order according to dates. She also included the footage recorded at the studio—which I later converted into VHS—the family photographs, three wooden nun figurines, a faded yellow ribbon, and a jewelry box with a simple, round, thin, golden wedding band in it. She wrapped the box in reddish-brown paper and tied a yellow raffia thread into two merging bows.

Monica-Paula asked me to save the package for Blair.

She asked me to tell her who her parents were.

She asked me to give it to her when she was old enough to understand, process, and cope with the information.

She let me decide when the time was right.

A week later, she had system failure due to a constant lowering of blood flow and oxygen supply.

Two days later she passed away.

Blair inherited Will's apartment, and I, as her legal guardian, was asked to decide where she would live.

As a first step, I decided to keep her in the home where she was born, in the room her mother had made for her, with the faded peach walls, and the pictures of Pooh, Eeyore, Tigger, and Piglet.

I legally adopted her over the summer.

Blair became my daughter.

94

18 February 1991
(This letter was thrown out)

Blair,

Dad went first. He took it upon himself to tell you that you were adopted. He was the one to tell you who your biological parents were.

Fearful and full of admiration, I watched him.

We had argued about it for years. An endless, exhausting argument about when we should tell you the truth. If it were only up to him, you would have known a long time ago—when you were sixteen and got your driver's license, when you were twelve and celebrated your bat mitzvah, or even when Roy was born, when you were only five years old.

Mike always claimed that we had plenty of opportunities to tell you, that it was our duty, and that every year we waited only made things worse.

But I objected vehemently. I insisted it wasn't time yet, first that you were too soft and delicate, then that you were too angry and rebellious, and that only God knew how this kind of news would affect your sensitive soul.

Your father and I had lots of disagreements about this, most of which you must not be aware of.

Mike was very angry with me. He claimed we were doing you an injustice by keeping the truth from you, and that when you did find out you might be furious with us. He said it was only a matter of time before you heard about it from somebody else.

He was right, of course.

But I shut my ears and my heart.

I refused to tell you.

I said it wasn't time yet.

95

18 February 1991
(This letter was thrown out)

Blair,

Why did I do that to you?

The explanation is not simple. It's complicated.

I myself grew up without a father. My mother was mentally ill. Even as a child, I sometimes felt as if I had no mother, as well. I didn't want you to grow up the way I did, in grief. I wanted to save you the pain. I argued that we shouldn't tell you about your biological parents precisely because of this. "Why," I said, "should we take away her beloved mother and father with one fell swoop?" I promised to tell you "when the right time came," when you were older and stronger, and mature enough to understand and accept.

Despite Mike's objections, I stuck to my guns. I closed up. I don't know how he suffered through this or why, in the end he gave in. He didn't want to hurt me anymore, I guess. I was hurt enough.

It was, of course, a big mistake.

Again and again, like some kind of worn mantra, I said I wanted to protect you. And I kept expressing my fear of your response, of how this news would hurt you.

But all this, Blair, was only half the truth.

On the other side was Mike. Dear Mike. All he knew about your biological parents was their names— Wilhelm Adler and Monica-Paula Martinez; that he was a journalist and writer I knew and respected, and she was a nurse. He only knew about my professional relationship with Will, and I swore that nothing else had ever happened between us. He also knew that your mother was very young when she lost her husband, and that I supported her when she became ill and when she had you.

He didn't ask anything more, and I didn't dare reveal the details.

Dad didn't know a thing about my passionate and complicated relationship with Will. He knew nothing of my great love for that man, which began the moment I met him, when I was even younger than you are now, and which continued until the day he died, and, in fact, to this very day. He didn't know I had grown close to Monica-Paula; that she was like a sister to me. He didn't know about my contribution to her death, how my desire to have a child from Will in this world overcame my common sense.

Dad also doesn't know that I'm reminded of them every time I see you.

You look like your mother, Blair, the spitting image of her.

But you also remind me of Will a little, in the cheekbones.

Why did I do that to him? And why did I do it to you? If I had only been honest and brave... if I had only told him the entire truth from the beginning, everything could have been so different now.

Shortly after Dad and I met, the two of us moved into his Atlanta home. He accepted you as my adopted daughter. All he knew was what I told him. He didn't know anyone from my past in California, never read Israeli newspapers or anything said about me in the gossip columns. My family and friends in Israel begrudgingly played along.

Why didn't he ask? I don't know. Dad is a smart, special guy. He always loved me and was sensitive to my turmoil. He knew there were certain elements of my past I chose not to share, but he never thought I had anything to hide when it came to you. Perhaps he convinced himself that it was like this with most adopted children—their past was foggy.

He adopted you just a few months after we got married.

96

18 February 1991
(This letter was thrown out)

Blair,

But all those years, your mother's package, to my mind, was burning in my desk drawer. Before she died, she told me she knew she was leaving it in good hands and that she trusted me to know when the time was right.

I promised to give it to you. I promised to tell you everything— about her, and about him.

These promises were like weights tied to my body.

I was afraid that when the package would be opened, so would a Pandora's box.

The secret grew bigger, becoming an ugly lie twisting between my teeth like a snake.

That's why I put off the moment of revelation for so long.

Until I couldn't take it anymore.

Until everything exploded like a grenade.

97

In late September of 1973, I was invited to give a talk at Temple Emanu-El in New York City. I left Blair with Angelica for a few days and went to the Big Apple.

At the time, New York was becoming a popular destination for Israelis, who arrived from the Tel Aviv airport in jumbo planes. Nurit and her husband at the time, Danny, arrived in one of them. They were joining a tour group for a trip along the East Coast but arrived a few days earlier to meet me. On the first day, we visited the Central Park Zoo, then spent the afternoon wandering around Chinatown and eating an authentic Chinese meal at a restaurant where no one spoke English. Then, we went up to the seventieth floor of Rockefeller Center to get a panoramic view of the city. It turned out we arrived early enough to see Central Park, the Brooklyn Bridge and the Statue of Liberty before they were swallowed in darkness. A tall, skinny, fair-skinned guy whose long hair was loosely tied at the back of his neck pulled a guitar out of a black, tattered case, sat down on the floor, and began to play music by Jimi Hendrix and Bob Dylan. We listened, thrilled, not noticing as night descended over the city, and a myriad of lights illuminated it like a magical carpet of stars. I saw how moved Danny, a guitar player himself, was. The height, the view, the music—it was all so surreal. The idea was born in me in those moments. The next day I rented a car, got a map, and the three of us headed out for the Catskills and Woodstock early in the morning. The narrow roads twisted between the mountains, through miles of trees, their tops already bathing in the deep, glowing red-golden-brown of fall foliage. When we reached Woodstock, we roamed around antique shops and second-hand stalls and ate at a small, shaded restaurant overlooking a creek. But the height of the trip was still ahead of us, a few dozen miles away. After lunch, we drove to the town of Bethel. Four years earlier, the legendary Woodstock Festival had taken place there and gained fame as the biggest, most influential music festival of all time.

We said goodbye in New York on the morning of the third day. Nurit and Danny joined their group of Israelis traveling to Amish Country, Pennsylvania, and I gave a talk at Temple Emanu-El on the corner of 5th Avenue and 65th Street. The next evening, during Rosh Hashanah dinner at the rabbi's home, between blessing the bread and wine and dipping an apple in honey, my mind wandered.

The last few days with Nurit and Danny had done me a world of good, and I allowed myself to smile again, to feel, to let go of some of the pain.

I recalled something Will had once told me: "Seeing things is not enough, Helena. You have to know how to examine and discern. You'll find a story behind every tree, a sentence on every leaf, a word on every flower, if you only let yourself linger for a bit, relax, and really look closely."

I took a deep breath and smiled.

A sudden urge made me decide to prolong my stay in the city by another three days.

***

Some people believe there are things that are meant to be. The hand of fate.

According to that perspective, my decision to stay in New York was no accident.

I began the following day with a visit to the Morgan Library on Madison Avenue. From there, I continued to Central Park. I took a taxi and got off at 5th Avenue and 72nd Street, just next to the statue of Samuel Morse. I chose a path that cut through the width of the park; a pretty, shaded walkway, along which dozens of benches were planted, beneath enormous tree trunks. I paused on the way by a small pond. An older woman and her grandchildren sailed miniature sailboats. Filled with longing, I sat down for a little rest and watched them. The hour had come, I thought, for Ruth to meet Blair. By the time I left the park it was late afternoon, and I recalled another thing Will had once told me. He said if you wanted to see New York as a New Yorker and from its best angle, you had to cross the Brooklyn Bridge over the East River from Brooklyn to Manhattan. I took the subway to the High Street Station in Brooklyn, from which I followed the signs to the bridge and climbed the stairs to the elevated pedestrian walk. I began to walk toward Manhattan with a pounding heart. The buzzing of cars did not bother me. On the contrary, it only augmented the sense of adventure. Ten or twenty minutes later, I saw a gorgeous image of the Manhattan skyline, glowing in the evening sun.

I was wearing a peach-colored wool skirt and a matching cardigan over a white undershirt. A gust of wind ruffled my hair, and I quickly searched my purse for a scarf.

When I looked up again, I saw him.

He was standing by one of the stone towers that support the bridge, staring at me.

His body was firm, his skin tan, his height average, his jaw slightly wide, and his full hair was a chestnut color. He leaned against the enormous stone column, a cigarette between his lips. He handed over the pack of cigarettes wordlessly, and I came closer. He was even more handsome up close. Stronger, tanner, maybe even taller. But what caught my attention more than anything else were his copper, half-moon eyes.

The color was different, but the eyes…

They were Jonathan's eyes.

98

He spoke first. He had a pleasant voice. I think he asked if I was a New Yorker. I smiled. I was befuddled. I did not expect to meet a man with Jonathan's eyes on the bridge. My heart was pounding. I could not let go of the thought that Will was the one who had "sent" me here. I said I was not. He offered his hand. His fingers, I noticed, were bare. He smiled warmly. I liked his smile. I gave him my hand in turn. We shook.

"I'm Mike," he said. "Nice to meet you."

I blushed. "And I'm Helena... nice to meet you too..."

"Oh, Helena... that's not just any name. And you're not just any Helena..." I turned to look at the river flowing beneath the bridge. When I returned my gaze to him, his half-moon eyes were on me. He told me he was born and raised in New York but now lived in Atlanta. When I said nothing, he added he was in town for a conference. "I'm a bridge engineer," he explained, and I widened my eyes, impressed and surprised. He told me that ever since he was a child, bridges had captivated his imagination—wooden or steel beam bridges, arch bridges, suspension bridges, truss bridges with their diagonal, horizontal, and vertical poles, and cantilever bridges— enormous structures born by engineering magic tricks. I watched him, attentive, charmed. I asked him to tell me more. He smiled and said that when he was at school, he studied the process of the building of the Brooklyn Bridge, from preliminary planning in 1870 and until its dedication and opening to traffic in 1883. "The Brooklyn Bridge is a suspension bridge," he said, "supported by enormous steel cables. Its towers are designed in neo-gothic style... There, see the pointed arches in the gates between the tips?" My eyes hung on his copper eyes. I nodded. I was trying not to say anything. I only wanted to listen to his voice. "Hundreds of thousands of people cross this bridge by car every day," he continued. "It's over a mile long, but only few people know the fascinating human story behind its construction..." He spent the next few moments telling me that, just a few weeks after construction of the bridge commenced, its planner, the engineer John Augustus Roebling, died tragically of tetanus. His son, Washington Roebling, took over, and, after he was injured and fell ill, his wife, Emily Warren, guided by him, took the reins. I learned that for thirteen years, six-hundred laborers, engineers, and contractors worked on the bridge, and that twenty-seven of them died in the process. I also learned that upon the bridge's opening to traffic, the American president and the mayor of New York honored it by walking across it, and that on that same day, 1,800 vehicles and tens of thousands of pedestrians crossed it as well. As a final treat, Mike told me that, in an attempt to refute rumors of the bridge's instability, the director of a local circus led a formation of twenty-one elephants across it exactly a year after its dedication.

When he finished talking, I thanked him, and I think I blushed again. I told him I was delighted to be one of the few who now knew this riveting story. As he spoke about the bridge, his eyes caressed my face, and his fingers rubbed the stone tower. I was not yet familiar with his wondrous talent for humanizing the bridges he loved, but I recognized an erotic tone in his attitude toward the bridge. I didn't move. I did not want to leave.

Only then did he ask me what had brought me to New York.

I told him about the talk I gave. I remember he was surprised when I told him I was a writer. "You mean, a writer-writer, the kind who writes books? Real books?" I laughed at his bemusement.

He said he loved my British accent. "I lived in London for a few years as a kid," I said, smiling nervously. We said nothing for a moment, and then I told him I was dividing my time between California and Israel. I distractedly felt for Jonathan's Star of David pendant and drew the collar of my shirt aside. I heard him gasp. He reached for his collar and pulled a similar delicate gold chain with a small Star of David pendant... We were moved, both of us. I told him I never took the chain off my neck, that it was always with me. He gave me his big, strong hand, and I took it, praying for that wretched blush to leave my cheeks, and fast. We started walking together toward Manhattan, looking at the Statue of Liberty, Ellis Island, and the Twin Towers. He did not ask any more questions. Not how old I was, nor if I was married. He behaved as if he already knew everything about me and was not aware of just how much he didn't.

That was Mike. He never asked. And that was me. I never told.

And yet.

One of the first things I did tell him was about Blair, my one-and-a-half-year-old adopted daughter. I didn't say too much, just a few words about a professional relationship I had had with her father and that I had nursed her mother at her deathbed.

But God is my witness, he did not ask, either...

99

24 February 1991
Yosemite Park, California

Dear Nurit,

In the first weeks of my stay, the days moved slowly. Each day resembled the one that preceded it and only differed in what I wrote and where I chose to stroll in the park. But in recent weeks, ever since the Gulf War broke and the television was back in my room, the days have been going by much faster.

Today, Pierre knocked on my door and asked if I'd heard the news— Yesterday, Iraq accepted the Soviet Union's proposal for a cease-fire and the withdrawal of its forces from Kuwait. Although the coalition rejected the cease-fire proposal, it promised not to attack the retreating Iraqi forces, provided they withdrew within twenty-four hours.

Pierre, who knows I have a personal interest in this news, is living this drama with me. We went downstairs to his office together, where we watched CNN. The newest information was that the coalition's forces had begun a massive ground offensive in Iraq. Marcel said it was the end of Saddam Hussein's reign, and that Iraq would soon be defeated. I hugged Pierre and then Marcel and told him, "From your mouth to God's ears." Then I rushed back up to my room.

I tried to call Blair, but there was no answer. You didn't pick up, either. I called Irit and was surprised when Esther answered the phone. She had arrived in Israel a week ago with Johan to photograph the damage caused by Scud Missile attacks on Israel, as well as the streets of Tel Aviv in the late afternoons, almost emptied of people. We hadn't spoken in nearly a year, so you can imagine how excited we were to talk to each other. Esther said she'd gotten together with Blair twice already and was moved to see how mature and pretty she had become. She also promised to send me some pictures, some of Blair, others of our building on Ben-Yehuda Street. She went up to our apartment to have coffee with Blair and found both of them (Blair and the apartment) in reasonable condition.

On another note, I'm glad to inform you that I'm about to finish writing my book. I plan on leaving Yosemite and returning to Atlanta in a week to ten days. It's important to me to get back in time for Abby's ninth birthday. I'll have to read through what I've written, of course, make corrections and edits, proofread, rewrite, and polish, but what I don't get done here, I can finish at home.

Home...

I was often asked in interviews how I know a book is finished. How do I know when to put down the pen?

The answer isn't simple. Sometimes writers plan the end of their book in advance and steer the plot toward it, and other times a story flows itself into a different ending altogether. A book is not finished until the last period is placed.

I've thought long and hard about how to end this book; which bit of information to offer just before the last period. I've decided to end it when Mike and I first met.

This dawned on me when I realized that, for the first time in my life, I was writing a book I had no intention of publishing.

This is not just any autobiography. The whole book is targeted for a small readership. It was written first and foremost for Blair and Mike, then for my other two children. I've had enough of hiding and camouflaging the past from the people dearest to me. If I've ever sinned, it was not done out of any evil or malevolent intentions.

Davidi used to say that people didn't need to be perfect and that what counts is that ultimately there be harmony in a person's soul, between their feelings and actions. He said that I must strive for this harmony my entire life. I strove and strove for so many years, never knowing I was going against the current. In contrast to Frost's *The Road Not Taken*, I think regret is avoidable. I chose to take this long road back into the past to start over. This time, I took the other road, the one not previously taken. A road clear of lies and omissions.

And I took this convoluted journey into the past here—in this incredible park—for close to six months. I dug into the memories with my own fingernails, while healing my soul a bit. I strove with all my might toward the harmony Davidi is always talking about. This time, I hope, I strove in the right direction.

I am hopeful that Mike takes me back, that he takes me in his arms and into his heart. I will place my book in his lap and write an intimate dedication on the inner cover page.

I've done it before.

Once for Mike, and once for another lover.

I'd like to take this opportunity to thank you, Nurit, for your wonderful friendship.

For being able to tell you everything.

Yours with Love,
Helena

100

26 February 1991
Yosemite Park, California

My Blair,

Today I was glued to the television screen in my room for three hours straight. Reports of the fast advance of the coalition forces in the Gulf filled me with so much joy, especially in light of the troublesome impression left by last night's report about the lethal strike of a Scud Missile on an American military base, causing the death of twenty-eight soldiers. When a formal notice was released about the defeat of the Iraqi army, I celebrated by toasting with Pierre and Marcel in the lodge's lobby. Within the general mayhem, my heart raced: no more missiles hitting Israel!

I called you, but you didn't pick up. Then I called Irit. She said that the Home Front Command would soon give orders to remove the plastic sheets from home windows. Everyone will finally be able to put the gas masks in storage. People will return to the streets, breathe again, sleep well at night. Life will get back on track.

Is there any chance you'll come home now?

I'm planning on coming full circle and going home. My book

will be ready soon, and I'll be able to give it to you and Dad, and later, to Roy and Abby, as well.

Of course, I'm excited and shaken from head to toe. Excited to see the kids and Dad, and just to be home. But I'm also very concerned.

For months I've thought only about myself, my life story. On the way, I tried to understand things and forgive, especially myself, but now that I'm about to come home, I'm terribly anxious.

To be honest, my child, I don't know how Dad and Roy will receive me. Nelly, and Abby, of course, will offer a warm welcome, which gives me strength, but Roy is awfully angry with me...

And Dad...

I think back to those moments when we told you everything. You stood frozen and tight-lipped by the desk in your bedroom. You looked so much like your mother. Then you started to cry. Dad tried to hug you, but you pushed him off. You barely looked at me. Then your crying became broken—sniffling, small sobs, halting breaths. I felt your pain and was angry at myself. I recalled my promise to your mother, when she barely had any air left in her lungs, to tell you about her some day and to warmly offer you the letters she'd written to you, the audio tapes she'd recorded, and the studio footage so that you could hear her voice, know her image, see how beautiful she was...

You were sitting tensely on your bed, your knees between your arms, your face cloudy, listening to me in silence. An image, which until that moment had been blurry in my mind, flooded my consciousness all at once. It was an image of myself as a

476 | Tali Asnin-Barel

young girl, listening with a trembling heart to my mother's detailed story about the love of Naomi and Mordecai, sketching the figure of my father in my imagination, and savoring the moving images running before my eyes.

You spent the next few days locked in your room. You read all the letters your mother wrote to you, listened to the audio tapes, and watched the video again and again. The video plainly showed your mother's body language—how she tilted her head, gathered her hair in her hands and shifted it to flow down her right shoulder. How, so quickly, she braided her hair in two thick plaits. You could see that she had the smile of an angel and hear her low, soft voice.

In that video, Blair, her eyes, aimed at the camera, seemed to rest on you. You must have noticed the resemblance between the two of you: average height, skinny build, feminine curves, flowing black hair, olive skin, green almond-shaped eyes. She was a flower child who liked to adorn her hair with a blossom or even a floral wreath.

Then, one day, you emerged from your room with a packed bag and announced you were leaving. Going. Far away. You had pulled all your savings from the bank. You didn't ask us for any help. Nelly may have helped you. I don't know where you got the courage.

You left. And Mike was furious.

But not at you; at me.

Then I broke and left too.

I went far away.

I did it when nobody, not even Nelly, was home. Without saying goodbye. Like a thief sneaking out under the cover of darkness.

It's difficult, my child, to talk about these things face-to-face or even over the phone.

It's easier to write.

In a recent phone call, you said that as a little girl you always thought the relationship between your father and me was "one of the most beautiful." That it seemed like nothing was missing from it. I told you that we do have a great love, but that our relationship isn't perfect.

In this bridge, I said, there are some missing elements.

You asked me a question that melted my heart, and I could not answer.

You asked if we could make up the missing elements after the bridge had already been built and functional for years.

Well, my child, you should ask your father that, not me.

He's the bridge engineer.

I just write books.

With me, anything is possible.

Love,
Mom

101

I have loved three men in my life and was three different women when I was with them. I continued to love Will, just as I continued to love Jonathan my entire life, even as I fell in love with Mike and bound my life with his. My three loves were profound and full of passion. They sculpted my personality and determined the course of my life.

It was Davidi who told me that I must let my heart be independent. That I must let it feel whatever it feels without stifling my emotions. The brain must control actions, but the heart is a different matter altogether. It has endless space for emotions, beyond any limitations of time or space. But it is crucial, he said, that ultimately there be harmony within a person's soul.

Mike had the power to instill me with peace. With him, I was calmer, a little more whole, almost happy, even.

I say "even" due to the many losses in my life.

I say "almost" because I still had another step to take.

I had to get my story out in full to feel complete.

102

1 March 1991
Morning

Nurit,

I tried to call you at the office just now, but your secretary said you had just stepped out. I had to talk to you, to someone, before I go crazy...

A taxi will be here in a few minutes to take me to the airport. I'm using these moments of nerve-racking anticipation to write to you.

We spoke on the phone only two days ago, making a toast, from opposite ends of the world, in honor of the removal of plastic sheets from the windows of your house. I told you that Blair was thinking of coming home.

I've ended my book, but it's not finished yet. I wrote the final chapter late last night.

For a few moments, Nurit, I dared to be happy.

But at six o'clock this morning, as I was preparing to leave for a tour of Mariposa Grove, I turned on the television in my room, as has been my custom in the past few weeks. I wanted to catch another little bit of happiness from the victory celebrations, but the broadcast from the gulf was interrupted by breaking news. The announcer gave a brief report on the collapse of a bridge under construction over the Connecticut River.

It took me about five seconds to get it—it was Mike's bridge.

It's hard to describe what I've been through since. My entire body is quaking, my heart is racing. No one is picking up the phone at home, and one of the secretaries at Mike's office finally answered after two hours of incessant calling. She sounded flustered and hysterical. She had no idea where Mike was and couldn't offer any new information. Pierre isn't here. He and Marcel slept last night outside of the park. Both of them will only be back in the afternoon.

I felt as if I was searching my way in the dark.

I made an urgent call to the lodge receptionist, who booked me a flight ticket to Atlanta and a taxi to take me to the airport. I packed a small bag with the draft of my book and left everything else here: my suitcase, my clothes, my personal belongings, and, in the center of the room, the contents of the wastebasket full of crumpled papers packed with my crumpled thoughts and the things I wanted to say but didn't dare send out.

The taxi will be here in a few minutes. I keep turning the information known about the collapse of the bridge over and over in my head. People were working there all night beneath enormous floodlights. Someone in the local government must have felt eager to expedite the project. The announcer said people were wounded and killed. Her words are pounding in my ears like an avalanche.

But Mike wasn't there… I'm sure of it. He couldn't have been!

Nelly had said that another engineer from Mike's firm had

been appointed supervisor of the site, and that Mike, breaking his regular habit, was visiting the site infrequently, only on rare occasions...

The possibility of him having spent last night there is completely irrational. Not now, just when I'm about to come back...

I want to get home as quickly as possible. Or to Connecticut, if need be. I have to be with him in his time of need. His project, the dead workers... horrific!

These past few nights, before this tragedy occurred, I dreamt of coming home and handing my draft to him. He'd held the drafts of my books in his hands so many times in the past, going over the countless lines and everything in between, reading the small print, even the little notes I made in the margins.

I dreamt I thanked him for the patience he'd shown me all these years, for his acceptance of my underground currents of sadness and my shifting moods. I dreamt I apologized for being so withdrawn, often closing the door to happiness for both of us.

I also dreamt I told him that this book is different than any other I'd ever written, that it came straight from my heart, that this is the book I never thought I would write. He is the first person to get a copy, and there is no one in the world I would rather read it before he does.

The receptionist just called from the front desk. The taxi is here. I'm heading out. On my way outside, I'll drop this letter at the front desk. By the time you get it, I'll be home.

I'm so afraid.

I wish you were here by my side.

Oh, Nurit.

103

1 March 1991
Five p.m.

Dear Helena,

Where are you, darling? I've been looking for you everywhere.

You had an urgent phone call from home. My discreet secretary must not have found you in your room, and before she headed home, she wrote the message she was asked to give you down on a note, folded it, jotted down "For Helena—personal and urgent," and left it on my desk.

Marcel and I only got back to the lodge in the afternoon, and as soon as I saw the message I went looking for you in your room, in the dining hall, even around the park, but you are nowhere.

The receptionist who worked the morning shift has gone into town, and the man who relieved her at noon has no idea where you are.

Your room is just as it was, even the bed is unmade.

Please, darling, contact me when you get back to your room.

I left the note on your desk.

I'll be in the office if you need me.

Yours,
Pierre

104

3/1/91

Helena, my love,

Please come home.

I need you.

Mike

THE BOOK CONTAINS QUOTES, PARTS OF QUOTES, OR PARA-PHRASE ON QUOTES, FROM THE FOLLOWING TEXTS:

* *"The Magic Mountain"* by **Thomas Mann,** 1924 (the motto for the book);

* *"Pine"* by **Leah Goldberg,** from the poet's poems collection "Poems", Volume 2 (1973)

* *"Auguries of Innocence"* by **William Blake,** 1803, from the poet's note-books now known as The Pickering Manuscript;

* *"The Road Not Taken"* by **Robert Frost,** 1916, from the poet's collection Mountain Interval;

* Lines from **Walter Benjamin's diary,** as appear in Frederic V. Grfield's book, *"Prophets Without Honor"*, 1979

Made in the USA
Middletown, DE
14 November 2020